FRAGMENT

**Center Point
Large Print**

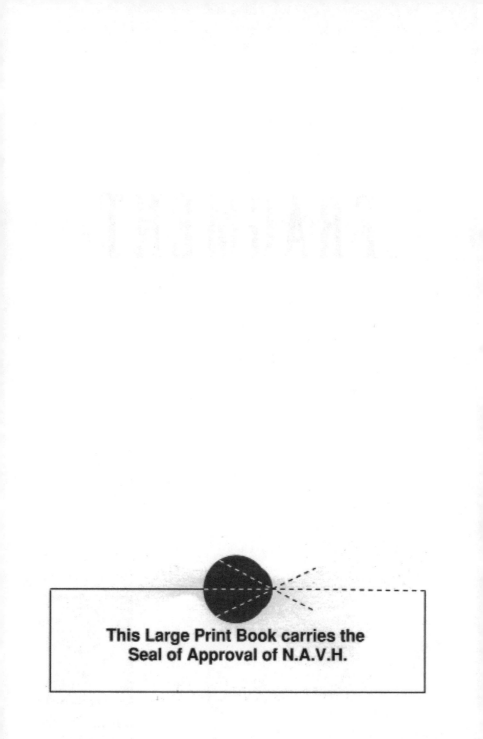

**This Large Print Book carries the
Seal of Approval of N.A.V.H.**

FRAGMENT

WARREN FAHY

CENTER POINT PUBLISHING
THORNDIKE, MAINE

This Center Point Large Print edition is published
in the year 2009 by arrangement with Delacorte Press,
an imprint of The Random House Publishing Group,
a division of Random House, Inc.

This is a work of fiction. Names, characters, places, and
incidents either are the product of the author's imagination
or are used fictitiously. Any resemblance to actual persons,
living or dead, events, or locales is entirely coincidental.
The text of this Large Print edition is unabridged.
In other aspects, this book may vary
from the original edition.
Printed in the United States of America.
Set in 16-point Times New Roman type.

ISBN: 978-1-60285-569-4

Library of Congress Cataloging-in-Publication Data

Fahy, Warren.
  Fragment / Warren Fahy.
    p. cm.
  ISBN 978-1-60285-569-4 (library binding : alk. paper)
  1. Reality television programs--Fiction. 2. Botanists--Fiction. 3. Biologists--Fiction.
    4. Island animals--Fiction. 5. Evolution (Biology)--Fiction. 6. Large type books.
    I. Title.

PS3606.A275F73 2009b
813'.6--dc22

2009018407

CONTENTS

'Anihinihi ke ola.
(Life is in a precarious position.)
—Ancient Hawaiian saying

PROLOGUE

When the American Association for the Advancement of Science met in Anaheim, California, in 1999 to discuss an urgent report on the impact of alien species, the scientists gathered weren't discussing species from another planet—their report referred to species imported to the United States from other parts of *this* planet.

Cornell University ecologist David Pimentel and graduate students Lori Lach, Doug Morrison, and Rodolfo Zuniga estimated the cost to the United States economy from alien species at approximately $123 billion annually—roughly the gross national product of Thailand.

By 2005, a report called the Millennium Ecosystem Assessment revealed that biological invasions had reached epidemic proportions. At least 170 alien species inhabited the Great Lakes, a single species of American jellyfish had wiped out twenty-six species of commercial fish in the Black Sea, and the Baltic Sea now hosted over a hundred alien invaders.

In 1988, freshwater zebra mussels sucked into ballast compartments of a ship in the Black or Caspian Sea were dumped into Lake Sinclair and eventually spread throughout the Great Lakes and the St. Lawrence Seaway. From there, the mussels spread into the American river systems. A female zebra mussel typically lays 30,000 to 400,000 eggs at a time, and by 1991 the hard-shelled little mollusk had spread as far west as the Mississippi River and driven most native species to the edge of extinction. By consuming algae and oxygen and excreting ammonia, this industrious mollusk threatened the entire eastern river ecology of America as it embarked on its biological joyride. It seemed that nothing could stop the zebra mussel.

By the year 2000, however, a cousin from the Caspian Sea, the quagga mussel, was already catching up to the zebra mussel. In only five years the quagga nearly completely replaced the population of zebra mussels in Lake Michigan, clogging irrigation intakes, infesting turtles and ships, and threatening the whole food chain.

In the early 1990s, the western corn rootworm hitched a ride on a jet and landed in war-torn Yugoslavia. While humans were preoccupied with their brief and bloody war, the rootworm launched its own permanent one. A single pregnant female may have unleashed what is now more than a billion-dollar annual loss of crops in Europe.

Of course, alien invaders have wreaked havoc, and driven the course of evolution, throughout the natural history of life on Earth. Five million years ago a land bridge formed between North and South America: it allowed saber-toothed cats to wipe out the flightless nine-foot-tall terror birds that had ruled South America for 20 million years.

Only 12 thousand years ago, humans followed bison across an icy land bridge from Siberia to North America. There, they found a world ruled by saber-toothed cats. A thousand years later, the cats, woolly mammoths, giant sloths, and an entire ecosystem of interdependent fauna had vanished.

When Columbus and other European explorers arrived in the Americas 10,500 years later, they brought with them diseases like smallpox and gonorrhea that virtually wiped out the native human populations of the so-called New World. In return, Native Americans may have gifted the Old World with syphilis. But the ships of explorers brought more than diseases to their destinations. The European black rat and the Norway brown rat came along as well, and were arguably more successful than humans in their conquest of the Americas.

North American crayfish were imported to Europe in the mid-1800s to replace the native species, which had been wiped out by plague. Unfortunately, the plague-resistant North American species was so successful it carried the plague through all the European river systems where it was introduced, wiping out any original crayfish populations that remained.

In the 1930s, Nazi Reich Marshall Hermann Goering decided that the clever American raccoon was an aesthetically pleasing addition to Germany's woodland creatures. Now the American raccoon threatens to eradicate the Rhineland's vineyards and decimates the German wine industry.

Pet owners have introduced their share of unexpected species to their own backyards. Eugene Schiffelin, a Shakespeare enthusiast who thought all birds mentioned by the bard should inhabit the New World, released sixty starlings in Central Park one fine March day in 1890. Because of a single line in *Henry IV*, there are now 200 million starlings in America, all descended from Schiffelin's original thirty pairs.

In 2000, an aquarium owner released two adult Chinese northern snakehead fish into a pond in Maryland. Within two years, one hundred of the voracious carnivores—which grow as long as three feet and have nasty teeth with which they devour fish, amphibians, mammals, and even birds—were discovered in the pond. Officials were concerned because the primitive northern snakehead can walk on its fins and survive three days out of water—and the pond was only seventy-five yards from the Patuxent River. Though the pond was pumped full of poison, snakeheads began showing up in the Potomac, and as far south as Florida by 2004.

The industrious honeybee that we see in our flower gardens was intentionally introduced to

North America by Spanish conquistadors in the 1500s and remains an indispensable partner to agriculture, having wiped out most of the native species that pollinated native plants. Not satisfied with the honey output of the Italian honeybee, bee geneticist Warwick Kerr brought queens of an African bee species to Brazil in 1956. After producing Africanized honeybees, twenty-six hybrid queens accidentally escaped. Since then, their aggressive Africanized progeny have been expanding their range northward at a rate of 375 miles a year, threatening to eradicate all Italian bee colonies in their path.

In 1986, the Varroa "vampire" mite arrived in North America from Southeast Asia. By 2005, forty to sixty percent of North America's beehives were wiped out by the vampire mites, and millions of hives had to be rushed from other continents to save the year's crop.

We are, at all times, in an astonishingly precarious position in relation to the vast web of species around us. All it takes is one new invader—a snake on a piece of driftwood, a seed in a bird dropping, or a pregnant insect in the landing gear of a jet—to throw all the old rules out. The balance that we see around us is a snapshot of a perpetual world war that is, for the most part, acted out too slowly for us to perceive. We prize the fragile ecology of the Hawaiian Islands, and yet 5 million years ago there were no Hawaiian Islands. All of their species evolved from species that were, at one time, *invaders* that upset the balance enough to entrench themselves and flourish, or perished in the effort.

It is on islands, in particular, that these battles of attrition, which usually take place outside the human timescale, come into sharpest focus. On islands, the battles are swift, and the annihilations total, and dominant species with no competition often proliferate to create multiple new species.

Travelers to tropical islands are familiar with the forms they must sign declaring that they will not transport any species to or from their destinations. In the past, however, humans deliberately brought the plants and animals in their biological entourage with them wherever they went—especially to islands.

When Polynesians colonized the Hawaiian Islands, the chickens they brought with them carried avian pox, which swiftly decimated native bird species. Europeans would later introduce cats, pigs, and tree snakes, with what are now predictable results.

In 1826, the H.M.S. *Wellington* accidentally introduced mosquitoes to the island of Maui. The mosquitoes carried avian malaria. Entire populations of native birds, which had no immunity to the disease, were wiped out or driven to higher altitudes. Feral pigs exacerbated the problem by rooting around the forest undergrowth and creating breeding pools of standing water for the mosquitoes. As a result, twenty-nine of the island's sixty-eight native bird species have vanished forever.

As David Pimentel told the scientists attending the AAAS convention after presenting his findings, "It doesn't take many troublemakers to cause tremendous damage."

No one could have imagined that island species could turn the tables on mainland ecologies. No one had even *heard* of Henders Island.

—Elinor Duckworth, Ph.D.,
Foreword, *Almost Destiny*
(excerpted with permission)

1791

AUGUST 21

5:27 P.M.

"Captain, Mister Grafton is attempting to put a man ashore, sir."

"Which man, Mister Eaton?"

Three hundred yards off the island's sheer wall, H.M.S. *Retribution* rolled on a ten-foot swell setting away from the shore. The corvette was hove to, her gray sails billowing in opposite directions to hold her position on the sea as the sailing master kept an eye on a growing bank of cloud to the north.

Watching from the decks in silence, some of the men were praying as a boat approached the cliff. Lit pale orange by the setting sun, the palisade was bisected by a blue-shadowed crevasse that streaked seven hundred feet up its face.

The *Retribution* was a captured French ship previously called the *Atrios*. For the past ten months, her crew had been relentlessly hunting H.M.S. *Bounty*. While the British admiralty did not object to stealing ships from other navies, they had a long memory for any ship that had been stolen from theirs. It had been five years since the mutineers had absconded with the *Bounty*, and still the hunt continued.

Lieutenant Eaton steadied the captain's telescope and twisted the brass drawtube to focus the image: nine men were positioning the rowboat under the crack in the cliff. Eaton noticed that the seaman reaching up toward the fissure wore a scarlet cap. "It looks like Frears, Captain," he reported.

The dark crack started about fifteen feet above the bottom of the swell and zigzagged hundreds of feet across the face of jagged rock like a bolt of lightning. The British sailors had nearly circled the two-mile-wide island before finding this one chink in its armor.

Though the captain insisted that they thoroughly investigate all islands for signs of the *Bounty*'s crew, a more pressing matter concerned the men of the *Retribution* now. After five weeks with no rain, they were praying for freshwater, not signs of mutineers. As they pretended to attend their duties, 317 men stole furtive, hopeful looks at the landing party.

The boat rose and fell in the spray as the nine men staved off the cliff with oars. At the top of one swell the man wearing the red cap grabbed the bottom edge of the fissure: he dangled there as the boat receded.

"He's got a purchase, Captain!"

A tentative cheer went up from the crew.

Eaton saw the men in the boat hurling small barrels up to Frears. "Sir, the men are throwing him some barrecoes to fill!"

"Providence has smiled on us, Captain," said

Mister Dunn, the ruddy chaplain, who had taken passage aboard *Retribution* on his way to Australia. "We were surely meant to find this island! Else, why would the Lord have put it here, so far away from everything?"

"Aye, Mister Dunn. Keep a close counsel with the Lord," replied the captain as he slitted his eyes and watched the boat. "How's our man, Mister Eaton?"

"He's gone in." After an agonizing length of time, Eaton saw the scarlet-capped man finally emerge from the shadow. "Frears's signaling . . . He's found freshwater, Captain! He's throwing down the barrecoe!"

Eaton looked at the captain wearily, then smiled as a cheer broke over the decks.

The captain cracked a smile. "Ready four landing boats for provisioning, Mister Eaton. Let's rig a ladder and fill our barrels."

"It's Providence, Captain," cried the chaplain over the answering cheer of the men. "'Tis the good Lord who led us here!"

Eaton put the spyglass to his eye and saw Frears toss another small barrel from the fissure into the sea. The men in the longboat hauled it alongside.

"He's thrown down another!" Eaton shouted.

The men cheered again. They were now moving about and laughing as barrels were hauled up from the hold.

"The Lord keeps us." The chaplain nodded on the ample cushion of fat under his chin.

The captain smiled in the chaplain's direction, knowing that he'd had the shock of his life these past months observing life aboard a working ship in the King's navy.

With a face as freckled as the Milky Way, Captain Ambrose Spencer Henders resembled a redheaded Nelson, the hero of Trafalgar, to his crew. "An island this size without breakers, birds, or seals," he grumbled. He stared at the faint colors swirled in the island's cliff. Some bands of color seemed to glitter as if with gold in the last light of the setting sun. After sounding all around the island they had found no place to anchor, and that fact alone baffled him. "What do you make of this island, Mister Eaton?"

"Aye, it's strange," Eaton said, lowering the glass—but a glimpse of Frears falling to his knees at the edge of the crevasse made him raise it hastily to his eye. Through the spyglass he found Frears kneeling in the crack and saw him drop what appeared to be the copper funnel he was using to fill the small kegs. The funnel skittered down the rock face into the water.

A red flash appeared at the sailor's back. Red jaws seemed to lunge from the twilight and close over Frears's chest and head from each side, jerking him backwards.

Faint shouts drifted over the waves, echoing off the cliff.

"Captain!"

"Eh, what is it?"

"I'm not sure, sir!"

Eaton tried to steady the scope as the deck rolled. Between waves he saw another man in the long-boat catch hold of the lip of the fissure and scramble up into the shadow of the crack.

"They've sent another man up!"

Another swell blocked his view. A moment later, another rolled under the ship. As the deck rose, Eaton barely caught the image of the second man leaping out of the crevasse into the sea.

"He's jumped out, sir, next to the boat!"

"What in blazes is going on, Mister Eaton?" Captain Henders lifted a midshipman's scope to his eye.

"The men are hauling him into the boat. They're coming back, sir, with some haste!" Eaton lowered the glass, still staring at the fissure, now doubting what he had seen.

"Is Frears safe, then?"

"I don't believe so, Captain," Eaton replied.

"What's the matter?"

The lieutenant shook his head.

Captain Henders watched the men in the boat row in great lunges back to the ship. The man who had jumped into the water was propped up against the transom, seemingly stricken by some fit as his mates struggled to subdue him. "Tell me what you saw, Mister Eaton," he ordered.

"I don't know, sir."

The captain lowered the scope and gave his first officer a hard look.

The men in the boat shouted as they drew near the *Retribution.*

The captain turned to the chaplain. "What say you, Mister Dunn?"

From the crack in the cliff face came a rising and falling howl like a wolf or a whale, and Mister Dunn's ruddy jowls paled as the ungodly voice devolved into what sounded like the *gooing* and spluttering of some giant baby. Then it shrieked a riot of piercing notes like a broken calliope.

The men stared at the cliff in stunned silence.

Mister Grafton shouted from the approaching boat: "Captain Henders!"

"What is it, man?"

"The Devil Hisself!"

The captain looked at his first officer, who was not a man given to superstition.

Eaton nodded grimly. "Aye, Captain."

The voice from the crack splintered as more unearthly voices joined it in a chorus of insanity.

"We should leave this place, Captain," urged Mister Dunn. "'Tis clear no one was meant to find it—else, why would the Lord have put it here, so far away from everything?"

Captain Henders stared distractedly at his chaplain, then said, "Mister Graves, hoist the boat and make sail, due east!" Then he turned to all his officers. "Chart the island. But make no mention of water or what we have found here today. God forbid we give a soul any reason to seek this place."

The hideous gibberish shrieking from the crack in the island continued.

"Aye, Captain!" his officers answered, ashen-faced.

As the men scrambled from the boat, the captain asked, "Mister Grafton, what has become of Mister Frears?"

"He's been et by monsters, sor!"

Captain Henders paled under his freckles. "Master gunner, place a full broadside on that crevice, double shot, round and grape, if you please! As you're ready, sir!"

The master gunner acknowledged him from the waist of the ship. "Aye, sir!"

Retribution fired a parting shot into the crevasse on lances of fire and smoke as she came about, blasting the cliffs like a castle's ramparts.

9:02 P.M.

Captain Ambrose Spencer Henders dipped a kite-feather quill into the porcelain inkwell on his desk and stared down at the blank page of his logbook. The oil lamp swung like a pendulum, moving the shadow of the quill across the paper as he paused, weighing what to write.

PRESENT DAY

AUGUST 22

2:10 P.M.

The *Trident* **cut the** deep water with her single-hulled bow and turned three wakes with her trimaran stern. She resembled a sleek spacecraft leaving three white rocket trails across a blue universe. The storm clouds that had driven her south for three weeks had vanished overnight. The sea reflected a spotless dome of scorching blue sky.

The 182-foot exploration vessel was approaching the center of 36 million square miles of empty ocean that stretched from the equator to Antarctica—a void that globes and maps usually took advantage of to stack the words "South Pacific Ocean."

Chartered for the cable reality show *SeaLife*, the *Trident* comfortably quartered forty passengers. Now an "on-camera" crew of ten who pretended to run the ship, fourteen professionals who really ran the ship, six scientists, and eight production staffers, along with a handsome bull terrier named Copepod, rounded out her manifest.

SeaLife was chronicling the *Trident*'s yearlong around-the-world odyssey, which promised to encounter the most exotic and remote places on Earth. In its first four weekly episodes the cast of fresh young scientists and hip young crew had explored the Galapagos Islands and Easter Island, launching *SeaLife* to number two in the cable ratings. After the last three weeks at sea, however, enduring back-to-back storms, the show was foundering.

The ship's botanist, Nell Duckworth, glared at her reflection in the port window of the *Trident*'s bridge, repositioning her Mets cap. Like all the other scientists chosen for the show, Nell was in her late twenties. She had just turned twenty-nine seven days ago, and had celebrated over the chemical-and-mint-scented bowl of a marine toilet. She had lost weight, since she hadn't been able to keep food down for the last ten days. Her motion sickness had subsided only when the last of the massive storms had passed last night, leaving a cleansed blue sea and sky this morning. So far, bad weather, sunblock, and her trusty Mets cap had protected her fair complexion from any radical new pigmentation events. But she was not checking her reflection for wrinkles, weight loss, or freckles. Instead, all she noticed was the look of despair glaring back at her from the glass.

Nell wore taupe knee-length cargo jeans, a gray T-shirt, and plenty of SPF24 sunblock slathered on her bare arms and face. Her beat-up white Adidas sneakers annoyed the producers since Adidas was not one of the show's sponsors, but she had stubbornly refused to trade them in.

She gazed south through the window, and the crushing disappointment she was trying not to think about descended over her again. Due to weather delays and low ratings, they were bypassing the island that lay just beyond that horizon—bypassing the only reason Nell had tried out for this show in the first place.

For the past few hours, she had been trying not to remind the men on the bridge of the fact that they were closer than all but a handful of people had ever come to the place she had studied and theorized about for over nine years.

Instead of heading one day south and landing, they were heading west to Pitcairn Island, where the descendants of the *Bounty*'s mutineers had apparently been planning a party for them.

Nell gritted her teeth and caught her reflection scowling back at her. She turned and looked out the stern window.

She saw the mini-sub resting under a crane on the ship's center pontoon. Underwater viewing ports were built into the port and starboard pontoons—Nell's favorite lunch spots, where she had seen occasional blue-water fish like tuna, marlin, and sunfish drafting the ship's wake.

The *Trident* boasted a state-of-the-art television production studio and satellite communication station; its own desalinization plant, which produced three thousand gallons of freshwater daily; a working oceanographic lab with research-grade microscopes and a wide spectrum of laboratory instruments; even a movie theater. But it was much ado about nothing, she thought. The show's scientific premise had been nothing but window dressing, as the cynic in her had chided her from the start.

On the poop deck below, she watched the ship's marine biologist, Andy Beasley, trying to teach the weather-beaten crew a lesson in sea life.

2:11 P.M.

Andrew Beasley was a gangly, narrow-shouldered scientist with a mop of blond hair and thick-framed tortoise-shell glasses. His long, birdlike face often displayed an optimistic smile.

Raised by his beloved but alcoholic Aunt Althea in New Orleans, the gentle young scientist had grown up surrounded by aquariums, for he lived over his aunt's seafood restaurant. Any specimens that came under his study were automatically spared the kettle.

He had gone on to live out Althea's dream of becoming a marine biologist, e-mailing her every day from the moment he left home for college to the day he accepted his first research position.

Aunt Althea had passed away three months ago. After surviving Hurricane Katrina, she had succumbed to pancreatic cancer, leaving Andy more alone than he had thought possible after feeling so terribly alone all his life.

One month after her funeral, he had received a letter inviting him to audition for *SeaLife*. Without telling him, Althea had sent his curriculum vitae and a photo to the show's producers after reading an article about the casting call for marine biologists. Andy had visited his aunt's grave to put flowers on it, flown to New York, and auditioned. As if it were Aunt Althea's last wish being granted, he had won one of the highly contested berths aboard the *Trident*.

Andy usually wore bright clashing colors that gave him a slightly clownish appearance. It also made him a natural target for sarcasm. He was as blindly optimistic and as easily crushed as a puppy—a combination that drew out a maternal impulse in Nell that was surprising to her.

Andy fidgeted with the wireless mike pinned to his skinny yellow leather tie. He wore a Lacoste blue-white-orange-yellow-purple-and-green-striped shirt, which resembled Fruit Stripe gum. Paired with the vertically striped shirt, he wore Tommy Hilfiger boardshorts with horizontal blue, green, pink, red, orange, and yellow stripes. To set it all off, he wore green size-11 high-top sneakers.

Andy's teaching props, a number of latex hand puppets of various sea creatures, lay scattered on the white deck before him. Beside him sat a panting, broad-nosed bull terrier with a miniature life vest strapped on his square chest.

Zero Monroe, the lead cameraman, changed the memory stick in his digital video camera. The previous one had blinked FULL in the middle of Andy's lesson, something that had been planned, much to Zero's chagrin, in order to start rattling Andy and get him primed for an eruption.

"Are we ready yet?" Andy asked, flustered but still trying to smile.

Zero raised the camera to his right eye and opened the other eye at Andy. "Yup," he replied. The rangy cameraman used words sparingly, especially when he was unhappy. This job was making him unhappy.

His lean physique, wide aquamarine eyes, and deadpan humor lent Zero a vaguely Buster Keaton–like quality, though he was six-two and broad at the shoulders. He wore a gray Boston Marathon T-shirt that he had earned three times over, and battered blue New Balance RXTerrain running shoes with orange laces and gel-injected soles. His faded brown Orvis cargo pants had fourteen pockets stuffed with memory sticks, lenses, lens filters, lens cleaners, mike filters, and a lot of batteries.

Zero had made his living and reputation photographing wildlife. He had mastered his trade in some of the most inhospitable environments in the world, taking assignments from the infested mangrove swamps of Panama (filming fiddler crabs) to the corrosive alkaline lakes in the Rift Valley of East Africa (filming flamingos). After the last three weeks, Zero was wondering which assignment was worse—this one, or standing in mud that ate through his wading boots while his blood was drained by swarming black flies.

"Let's go, Gus," Zero growled.

A grip clacked a plastic clapper in front of Andy's face, startling him. "*SeaLife*, day fifty-two, camera three, stick two!"

"And . . . ACTION!" Jesse Jones shouted.

Jesse was the obligatory obnoxious member of the on-camera "crew." The real crew wore uniforms and tried to stay off-camera as much as possible. Universally hated by both his shipmates and the viewers at home, Jesse Jones was delighted to play a starring role. Reality shows needed at least one cast member everyone could loathe with full enjoyment, one who caused crisis and conflict, one whom sailors in olden days would have called a "Jonah" and heaved overboard at the first opportunity.

Tanned and muscular, with heavily tattooed upper arms, Jesse wore his hair short, spiked, and bleached white. No one had taken advantage of the show's legion of sponsors quite so much as he had. He was decked out in black thigh-low, ribs-high Bodyform wetsuit trunks, complete with a stitched-in blue codpiece, and over them a muscle

Y-shirt printed with palms and flowers. On his feet were silver Nikes and on his nose rested five-hundred dollar silver-framed Matsuda sunglasses with pale turquoise lenses.

"Where were we, Zero?" Andy said, cranking up a smile.

"Copepods," Zero prompted.

"Oh yes," Andy said. "That's right—Jesse?"

Jesse threw a rubber hand-puppet at Andy, who ducked too late. It bounced off his face.

Everyone laughed as Andy replaced his imitation tortoise-shell glasses and gave a crooked smile to the camera. He slipped his hand into the puppet and wiggled its single google-eye and two long antennae with his fingers. "So Copepod, here, gets his name from this microscopic sea creature."

The banana-snouted dog barked once and resumed panting next to Andy's leg.

"Poor Copey!" Dawn Kipke, the crew's surf-punk siren, crooned. "Why would anyone name a dog after that ugly freaking thing?"

"Yeah, that's uncool, dude," Jesse shouted.

Andy lowered the puppet and frowned at Zero, who zoomed in on his face.

Andy's face turned red and his eyes bulged as he threw the puppet down. "How can I *teach* anything if nobody ever LISTENS TO ME?" he raged.

He stormed off the deck and down the hatchway.

The crew turned to Zero.

"Hey, I'm not in charge, man," Zero said,

walking backwards as he shot. "Ask the guys upstairs!" He panned up to the bridge, where Nell stood looking down at them. She made hand-antlers at them in the window and stuck out her tongue.

2:14 P.M.

"Looks like mutiny, Captain. I think we're going to have to land at the first opportunity."

Captain Sol gave Nell a sly look over his shoulder. A trim white beard framed his tanned face and sea-blue eyes. "Nice try, Nell."

"I'm serious!"

Glyn Fields, the show's biologist, stepped next to Nell to look through the window. "She's right, Captain. I really think the crew's getting ready to storm the Bastille."

Nell had met Glyn during her second year as an assistant professor teaching first-year botany at NYU. Glyn was teaching first-year biology, and his looks had caused quite a stir among the faculty when he arrived. It was Glyn who had persuaded her to try out for *SeaLife*.

Tall, pale, thin, and very British, Glyn had sharp, handsome features, nearly black eyes, and his mother's thick Welsh crown of black hair. The biologist was a tad too vain for Nell's taste, but she may have felt that way simply because he never seemed to notice her (like *that,* anyway). He

37

wore the stereotypical clothing of an English academic: Oxford shirts, corduroys, plain leather shoes, and even blue blazers on occasion. He now wore a blue Oxford shirt, khaki slacks, and Top-Siders without socks—about as casual as he was capable of dressing, even in the tropics. Nell suspected the Englishman would never be caught dead wearing shorts, a T-shirt, or, heaven forbid, sneakers.

She remembered how she had protested to Glyn a year ago that *SeaLife* would create a yearlong detour in her studies. When Glyn had mentioned that the expedition might come across the obscure little island she was always talking about, Nell knew instantly she might never get this chance again. Surprising herself, she tried out for the show and was actually chosen, along with Glyn.

Now, as he saw Nell's hopes dashed, Glyn obviously felt a twinge of guilt. "Maybe a quick landing would be good for morale, Captain."

Second Mate Samir El-Ashwah entered through the starboard hatchway, dressed in the full *Love Boat*–style white uniform inflicted on the *Trident*'s professional staff. A wiry man of Egyptian extraction, Samir's Australian accent surprised at first. "Holy Dooley, the Turbosails are in the groove, eh, Captain? What are we making, just outta curiosity?"

"Fourteen knots, Sam," Captain Sol said.

"That's getting it done, I reckon!"

"I'd say." Captain Sol laughed, scratching the coral atoll of white hair around his bald head.

Nell peered up toward the skylight at the ninety-three foot Turbosail, one of two that towered over the bridge like a cruise ship's smokestacks grafted onto the research vessel. The massive cylindrical shaft passed through the center of the bridge, housed inside a wide column that was smothered in notices and photos. Nell heard motors whirring inside the column as the sail turned above.

Turbosails were pioneered by Jacques Cousteau in the eighties for scientific exploration vessels, including his own *Calypso II*. Ideal for long-range research vessels, the tubular sail used small fans to draw air inside a vertical seam, as wind passing around it produced a much higher leeward surface speed than any traditional sail. Now that the storm had passed, the crew had raised both of the *Trident*'s Turbosails and rotated the seams to catch the nor'easter.

The ship cruised due west at a nice clip, ten degrees south of the Tropic of Capricorn.

"Captain Sol, we'll never get this close again!" Nell said.

"The storm did blow us pretty far south," Glyn said. "And while as a biologist, I have to say Nell's little island is pretty intriguing, the thought of solid ground is even more appealing right now, Captain. It sure would feel good to stretch our legs."

"Why can't we go?" Nell whined.

Sol Meyers frowned. He looked like Santa Claus on vacation in his extra-large orange T-shirt with a white *SeaLife* logo silk-screened on the breast pocket.

"I'm sorry, Nell. We have two days to make up if we're going to make Pitcairn in time for the celebration they're planning for us. We just can't do it."

"A scientific expedition to explore the most remote places on Earth!" Nell quoted the show's opening tagline with naked scorn.

"More like a floating soap opera that ran out of bubbles," Glyn muttered.

"I'm sorry, Nelly," Captain Sol repeated. "But this is Cynthea's charter. She's the producer. I have to go where she wants, barring some emergency."

"I think Cynthea's trying to pair *us* off now," Glyn mused. "Apparently the entire crew has already boffed each other."

Nell laughed and squeezed Glyn's shoulder.

The biologist flinched and rubbed his triceps as if she had bruised him. "You're the most touchy-feely woman I've ever met, Nell," he snipped, fussing with his shirt where she had touched him.

Nell realized they were all getting irritable. "Sorry, Glyn. Maybe I'm part bonobo chimp—they use physical contact to give members of their group a sense of security."

"Well, we British have the opposite reaction." Glyn pouted.

"Hey, I don't mind, Nell," said Carl Warburton. The ship's first mate had a TV actor's tanned handsomeness, black wavy hair frosted gray at the temples, and a late-night deejay's voice to go along with his droll sense of humor—all of which made him irresistible. "Consider me a bonobo," Warburton said, and he scratched his ribs and stuck out his tongue at Nell charmingly.

Captain Sol glanced up at the bridge camera mounted over the forward window. Cynthea Leeds, the show's producer, watched everyone through cameras like this one, which were positioned throughout the ship. Each week's show was cut from footage collected by these cameras, as well as what was captured by the ship's three roving cameramen.

Captain Sol hid his lips with his hand and whispered, "I think Cynthea's trying to set me up with ship's surgeon Jennings."

"She's trying to set *me* up with ship's surgeon Jennings," Warburton said.

Nell did her best Cynthea impression: *"Drama!"*

A loud tone blared suddenly on the bridge, and everyone jumped.

"Captain," Samir said. He checked the instrumentation. "We're picking up an EPIRB, sir!"

"Christ, I thought it was Cynthea," Captain Sol sighed.

"An EPIRB?" Warburton asked. "Out here?"

"Double-check it, Sam," Captain Sol instructed.

41

"What's an EPIRB?" Nell asked.

"An Emergency Position Indicating Radio Beacon." Warburton was moving quickly to Samir's side.

"Got a position?" Captain Sol asked.

"We should after the next satellite sweep . . ." said Samir.

"Here it comes." Warburton glanced over his shoulder at Nell.

"What?" she asked.

"You'll never believe it."

Samir turned to her. Surprise lit his round face and a smile revealed his beautiful teeth. "According to these coordinates, it's coming from your island, mate."

Nell felt her heart pound as they confirmed the signal.

"Hold on—wait—we're losing it," Warburton warned.

Captain Sol stepped around Samir and squinted at the navigation screen. "That's strange . . ."

Warburton nodded.

Nell moved a little closer. "What's strange?"

"You don't fire off an EPIRB unless you mean business," the captain answered. "And if you do, the lithium battery should last forty-eight hours, minimum. This signal's fading."

"There it goes," Samir reported as the next data update wiped it off the screen.

"Sam, you better hail the nearest LUT station.

And check the beacon's NOAA registration, Carl."

Warburton was already scanning the National Oceanic and Atmospheric Administration database. "The beacon's registered. Oh man . . . it's a thirty-foot sailboat!"

"What the hell is it doing out here?" Captain Sol scowled.

Warburton scanned the information on file. "The vessel's name is *Balboa Bilbo*. The owner's name is Thad Pinkowski of Long Beach, California. OK, this is interesting: the registration on the beacon expired three years ago."

"Ha!" Captain Sol grunted. "It's a derelict."

"Maybe the NOAA records are out of date?" Glyn suggested.

"Not likely."

Samir held the satphone to his ear. "LUT reports that we're the nearest vessel, Captain. Since it's too far from an airstrip to get a search plane out here, they're asking us to respond, if able."

"How soon can we reach it, Carl?"

"Around fourteen hundred hours, tomorrow."

"Bring her about, due south. Sam, let the LUT station know we're responding."

"Aye, sir!"

"And try hailing her on VHF."

"On it!"

Captain Sol pushed a button and spoke into the ship's intercom. "All hands, as you can see, we are now making a course adjustment. We will be landing sooner than planned, tomorrow afternoon, on an unexplored island. There will be a more detailed announcement at dinner. As you were!"

Faint cheers rose from the deck outside.

Captain Sol turned to Glyn. "Mutiny averted. That should hold them for a while. Well, Nell. It looks like the wind keeps blowing your way."

The southern horizon swung into view in the wide windows as the *Trident* came about. Captain Sol pointed to the left edge of the navigation monitor, where a small white circle rose on an arc toward the top of the screen.

Warburton smiled. "There it is, Nell."

Nell ran to see the plotting monitor as the men stepped to each side.

"If you want to find an untouched ecosystem, you certainly came to the right place," Glyn conceded.

"It must be twelve hundred miles from the nearest speck of land, I reckon," Samir said.

"Fourteen hundred." Nell's heart pounded so loudly she feared the others could hear it. "Every plant pollinated by insects on this island should be a new species," she explained.

Glyn nodded. "If your theory holds up."

The motors revved as the Turbosail rotated over the bridge.

As Nell's eyes brimmed, the others wondered whether she was looking for more than a new flower on Henders Island.

They all cringed as a voice blasted from a speaker by the camera over the forward window: *"Tell me this is not a joke, please!"*

"This is not a joke, Cynthea," Captain Sol answered.

"You mean we actually got a distress signal?"

"Yes."

"Captain Sol, you're my hero! How bad is it?"

Captain Sol looked wearily at Warburton. "It's probably just a derelict sailboat. But the beacon was activated, so we have to check it out."

"God, that's gold! Nell—tell me you're excited!"

Nell looked up at the speaker over the window, surprised. "Yes, it'll be nice to do a little actual scientific research."

"Tell me more about the island, Glyn!" screeched the electronic voice.

"Well, according to Nell, it was discovered by a British sea captain in 1791. He landed but couldn't find a way to the island's interior. There's no other record of anyone landing, and there are only three recorded sightings of it in the last 220—"

The starboard hatch slammed open and Cynthea Leeds power-walked onto the bridge wearing a fitted black Newport jumpsuit with white racing stripes.

Everyone froze.

"I like that. I like that a lot," Cynthea announced. "Peach, did you get that? Great! Gentlemen—and lady—*congratulations!*"

Cynthea smiled wide, flashing her expensive teeth as she tossed back her bangs in girlish joy. A thin black wireless headset arched over her black hair, which was cut in a razor-sharp pageboy.

Cynthea was a dauntingly well-preserved woman, sexy at fifty. Her mother had insisted on strict ballet training from the age of five—the only thing she considered a kindness on her mother's part. At five feet eleven inches without heels she still had the posture of a ballerina, though her imposing stature was better suited to the high-testosterone arena she had chosen to enter than to ballet.

Like a hermit crab out of its shell, Cynthea looked laughably out of place at sea, or even outside a city. But she couldn't help noticing lately that she was being herded out to pasture in the youth-centric jungle she inhabited.

Cynthea had produced two number-one reality shows for MTV. But the cutthroat environment she lived in would not tolerate a single misstep. After her last network reality show, the misbegotten *Butcher Shop*, had cratered, her only offer was the job every other producer in town had passed on: a round-the-world sea voyage with none of the comforts of home.

Sensing that she had to adapt or go extinct, and in the midst of an acute panic attack, she told her manager to take the offer.

She knew she had won the *SeaLife* gig because

of her talent for spicing up a show's content, which the show's producers were painfully aware could be a problem if the science stuff got dull. Over the last three weeks, however, her efforts to get seasick scientists to mate had been a gruesome debacle.

If this show was killed, she was convinced it would be the end of her career. No husband, no kids, and no career: all of her mother's prophecies checked off. Which would be much easier to bear if Cynthea's mother were dead, but she wasn't—not by a long shot.

Cynthea pressed her hands together in a gesture of thanks to the powers-that-be. "This could not have come at a better time, people! I think we would have killed and eaten each other before we ever got to Pitcairn. Tell me more about this island, Glyn!"

"Well, it's never actually been explored, is the neat thing. According to Nell—"

"When can we land?"

"Tomorrow afternoon," Glyn answered. "If we can find a place to put ashore. And if the captain grants permission to go ashore, of course . . ."

"You mean we can shoot our landing on an unexplored island for the anything-can-happen segment of tomorrow's broadcast at five-fifty? Glyn, you will be my *superhero* if you say *yes!*"

"It's possible, I should think, providing the captain agrees." The Englishman shrugged. "Yes—"

"Glyn, Glyn, Glyn!" Cynthea actually jumped

for joy. "What was it you were saying about a British sea captain?"

"The island was discovered in 1791 by Captain Ambrose Spencer Henders . . ."

Nell was amused to see Glyn's vanity flattered by Cynthea's spotlight.

Glyn looked at Nell. "However, Nell is the one who—"

"That's just *gold,* Glyn! Do me a favor and make the announcement to the crew?" Cynthea interrupted. "At sunset—right after dinner—and really build it up? Oh, pretty, pretty *please?*"

Glyn looked apologetically at Nell. She nodded, relieved to have him do the honors. "Well, all right."

"You know Dawn? The tan, leggy brunette with the tattoo?" Cynthea gestured in the vicinity of her tailbone. "Yes? She was just remarking to me how she thought British scientists were the sexiest men alive." Cynthea leaned forward and crooned in Glyn's ear: "I think she was talking about YOU!"

Glyn's eyes widened as Cynthea turned to Captain Sol. "Captain Sol, can we land?" She jumped up and down like a little girl pleading with her grandfather. "Can we, can we, can we?"

"Yes, we can land, Cynthea. *After* we check out the beacon."

"Thank you, Captain Sol! You know ship's surgeon Jennings is just crazy about you?"

Warburton shook his head.

"Now if we could only find someone for Nell," the producer persisted. "What about it, sweetie? What *is* your type, anyway?"

Nell saw Glyn looking out the window at Dawn, who was performing yoga stretches on the mezzanine deck below. Hard-bodied and sporting buzzed black hair, Dawn wore a midriff-baring mustard mini-T over her imposingly toned core. A purple and yellow sun tattoo peeked over the rear of her black bikini bottoms. "I don't have a 'type,' Cynthea," she said. "And I wouldn't want to be anyone's 'type,' either."

"Always the loner, eh, Nell?" Cynthea said. "You have to know what you're looking for to find him, darling."

Nell looked Cynthea in the eyes. "I'll know him when I see him."

"Well, maybe you'll find a new rosebud or something to name tomorrow, eh? Give us some *drama,* if you do, Nell! Pretty please?"

Cynthea turned and loped out the hatch.

Nell looked back down at the plotting monitor, watching the island as it moved down in tiny steps from the top of the screen. As the sight overwhelmed her, she almost forgot to breathe.

Captain Sol looked at Nell with fatherly affection. He placed a hand on her shoulder. "I'd say it was destiny, Nell, if I believed in that sort of thing."

She looked at him with bright eyes and impulsively squeezed his big, tanned hand.

"Still no response on the emergency frequencies, Captain," Warburton said.

Nell traced a fingertip from their position over the blue plasma screen to the white circle above tiny white letters:

o
Henders Is.

7:05 P.M.

Huddled inside the cramped, equipment-filled brain center of *SeaLife*, tucked within the *Trident*'s starboard pontoon, Cynthea watched three camera feeds of Captain Sol and Glyn making the announcement to the crew after dinner.

"Peach" McCloud sat by Cynthea, manning the editing/uplinking bay. Whatever original audio-visual equipment Peach was born with was buried under his hair and beard and replaced with man-made microphones, headphones, and VR goggles. Cynthea had worked with Peach on live MTV shows in Fort Lauderdale and on the island of Santorini. Her one stipulation when she accepted the job as *SeaLife*'s producer had been that Peach come along as her engineer. Without Peach, the job would have been unthinkable.

Peach had agreed. He always agreed. Anywhere

was his living room if he had a wireless connection. It really didn't matter to Peach if he was on a boat weathering fifty-foot swells or in his Soho apartment. So long as his digital habitat came with him, Peach was happy.

Cynthea spoke urgently through her headset, on a conference call to the *SeaLife* producers in New York. Peach equalized sound levels and switched shots according to the jabbing eraser-end of her pencil as she talked.

"We *need* the segue, Jack. We're getting it right now and can zap it to you in ten minutes. We're landing on an unexplored island in the *Anything-Can-Happen* feed tomorrow, Fred—come on, that's the hook! And it's a *rescue* mission—we're responding to a *distress* signal!"

Cynthea gestured at Peach for confirmation, and Peach flashed ten fingers twice.

"Peach can send it in fifteen minutes," Cynthea lied. "Give us the satellite feed, Fred. Yes, Jack, as you've mentioned several times already, there's no sex. The whole crew screwed each other in the first four weeks. All I've got to work with now are *scientists,* Jack, so come on—cut me some slack! How could I know the crew smuggled Ecstasy on board? Anyway, that's a done deal, Fred, and we're lucky we kept it off the Drudge Report, OK? Are you kidding me? You must be kidding me now. Then Barry should do a show with scientists and try to have sex in it. I fucking dare him to do it, that

51

flaming asshole, especially while they're *puking on each other!* If there were any Ecstasy left I would have slipped it into their green tea by now, Jack! I'm *suggesting* that we go back to the original *angle,* the science thing. Right, *adventure,* Fred, EXACTLY! Thank you! And what comes from adventure but *romance,* Jack—I swear, if this isn't the play that saves this show, you can broadcast my execution. Didn't have to think about that too long, eh, Fred? Well, boys, I'm glad to know the way to your heart. Don't worry, sweetie— tomorrow we're making *television history!*"

Cynthea squeezed Peach's shoulder painfully. "We got it!"

Peach grinned and nodded, dialing in sound levels as Captain Sol addressed the crew. "This is good stuff, boss."

7:05 P.M.

Shooting from port to starboard across the mezzanine deck, Zero framed a pointillist sunset of orange, lavender, and vermilion cirrus clouds.

Candlelit dining tables set for dinner dotted the foredeck as the *Trident* cruised due south. A warm wind played over the tables. The scientists and crew were finishing their dinner of orange roughy, rice pilaf, and green beans almondine. All three cameramen circled the tables as the crew buzzed with curiosity about the upcoming announcement.

Captain Sol finally clanged a glass and, with the South Pacific sunset at their backs, he and Glyn addressed the crew.

"As I'm sure you've all noticed, we are now heading south," the captain began, and he pointed his right arm dramatically over the prow.

Cynthea directed Peach to cut to the bridge-mounted camera that showed the *Trident* heading toward the southern horizon, then to another that showed the prow slicing through the sea, then back to the captain.

"A few hours ago we picked up an emergency beacon from a sailboat in distress."

The crew chattered excitedly.

"We know that the vessel's owner was rescued by the United States Coast Guard off Kaua'i during a storm five years ago. So either this boat has been adrift for five years, or it came aground on the island south of us even before then, or someone else is on board it now. We tried hailing the vessel on emergency frequencies but got no response. Since search-and-rescue aircraft don't carry enough fuel to reach this location from the nearest airfield, we have been asked to respond."

A chorus of "Wow"s rose from the tables.

Glyn cleared his throat. The biologist was visibly nervous now that the cameras and lights turned to him. "The good news," the Englishman announced, "is that the signal seems to have come from one of the world's last unexplored islands."

After twenty-one miserable days at sea, the distress signal itself was cause for celebration. But the opportunity to land on an unexplored island inspired thunderous applause from all.

"The island is only about two miles wide," Glyn said, encouraged. He read from cue cards Nell had prepared for him. "Since it is located below the fortieth parallel, a treacherous zone mariners call the 'Roaring Forties,' shipping lanes have bypassed it for the last two centuries. We are now headed for what could well be the most geographically remote piece of land on the Planet Earth. This empty patch of ocean is the size of the continental United States, and what we know about it is about equivalent to what can be seen of the United States from its interstate highway system. That's how sparsely traversed this part of the world remains to this day. And the seafloor here is less mapped than the surface of Mars!"

Glyn got an appreciative murmur out of the crowd and he charged on.

"There are only a few reports of anyone sighting this island, and only one report of anyone actually landing on it, recorded in 1791 by Ambrose Spencer Henders, Captain of the H.M.S. *Retribution*."

Glyn unfolded a transcript of Captain Henders's log entry. This had been the remarkable glimpse into the unknown that fired Nell's undergraduate imagination nine years earlier. Without stumbling too badly over the archaicisms and nautical abbreviations, he read:

"Wind at WSW at 5 oClock in the AM, with which we hauld due West, and at 7 oClock spotted an Isle 2 miles wide that we could not find on the Chart, which lies at Latitude 46° S., Long 135° W. There is no bottom to catch anchor around this island. We rainged along its shore in search of a suitable landing but high cliffs gird the island completely. Our hopes frustrated and not wanting to spend more time than we had, I had every body to stations to put about, when at half past 4 oClock in the PM a man spotted a Fissure from which water streams down the cliff, staining it dark. Mr. Grafton believed it could be reached by Longboat, and so I emmidiately put down one boat, and the men took some Barrecoes to fill.

"We collected Three Barrecoes of freshwater from a trickling waterfall inside the Fissure. However, we lost one man dear to us in the effort, Stephen Frears—a true man, and strong made, whom we shall all terribly miss, and judged the risk of another man too great.

"Upon the urgings of our Chaplain, and having determined that the island was neither habitable nor accessible by the blackhearts of

HMS Bounty, *we departed with haste and heavy hearts, our heading due West to Wellington, where we all are looking forward to a friendly harbour.*
—Captain Ambrose Spencer Henders, 21st August, 1791"

Glyn folded the worn printout Nell had given him. "That's it—the only reported landing. If we can find a way inland, we will be the first to explore Captain Henders's forgotten isle." Glyn nodded and smiled at Nell.

There was a rowdy round of applause, and Copepod barked.

"So the storms served a good purpose, after all," Captain Sol told them. "Poseidon has put us on a course to help a fellow mariner in distress. And we'll have a chance to visit one of the final frontiers on Earth, where no man has gone before!" Captain Sol raised his fist skyward, a ham at heart.

7:07 P.M.

"God bless Captain Sol," Cynthea muttered in the control room, jabbing her pencil eraser at different screens as everyone cheered and toasted. "We'll have to lay in some music behind Glyn's speech and edit it way down."

"Yeah, that nearly killed us," Peach agreed.

"Find some sea chantey thing, like something

from *Jaws* when Robert Shaw is talking about sharks and battleships. Lay it in behind that speech and it'll be a thing of beauty. Then can it and zap it, Peach. Get it to those bastards in L.A. before the assholes in New York can say no." Cynthea spoke through her headset to her camera crew. "OK, boys, we're done. Eat some dinner. Nice work, darlings!"

7:08 P.M.

Spirits soared following the announcement, and when the annoying lights and cameras finally shut down everyone cheered again, sarcastically.

Nell glanced over at the next table.

Still puffed up from his starring debut, Glyn had seated himself across from Dawn. He seemed terribly interested in what she was saying.

Nell stifled a giggle at the almost inconceivable coupling. Dawn looked like she would eat Glyn alive.

Zero sat down across from Nell at her table and commandeered an unclaimed plate of food. Gouging a bite out of a filet of orange roughy, the lead cameraman looked at her. "So what made a gal like you want to be a botanist?" He broke off a chunk of fish and fed it to Copepod.

Nell sipped her ice water as she mulled over his question. "Well, when my mom was killed by a jellyfish in Indonesia, I decided to study plants."

57

Zero lifted a forkful of fish to his mouth, surprised. "For real?"

"Of course, for real!" said Andy, who was sitting next to Nell protectively, as always, though it was usually she who protected him.

Nell had persuaded Andy to leave his cabin after his earlier tantrum, and he had changed into a more subdued blue plaid flannel shirt open over a yellow T-shirt with a smiley face on the chest. The vintage shirt said, "Have a Nice Day!" with no ironic bullethole in its head or anything out of the ordinary—just a smiley face waiting for the world to deface it.

Nell squeezed Andy's wrist and patted Zero's hand, instantly charming both men with her brief touch.

"My mother was an oceanographer," she explained to Zero. "She died when I was a kid. I never saw her much, except on television. She was abroad most of the time, making nature documentaries in places that were way too dangerous for children."

"You're not the daughter of Janet Planet, are you?"

"Um, yeah."

"'Doctor Janet explores the wild planet!'" he said, mimicking the show's intro perfectly. "Right?" A wide grin spread on the cameraman's face as he remembered the early color TV series, to which he had been addicted as a boy.

Nell nodded. "Yeah. You remember the show?"

"Hell yeah! It brought full-color underwater photography to TV for the first time! It's pretty legendary among my kind. So, why isn't your name Nell Planet?"

Nell laughed. "Our last name didn't play well on television."

"So you're following in your mom's footsteps."

"Except that I chose botany," Nell protested, parrying with her fork. "Plants never eat people."

"Right on." Zero snagged a glass of iced tea from the tray of a passing server and raised a toast to her. "Conquer your fears, right?"

Nell toasted him with her water and frowned at the dark horizon. "Something like that."

AUGUST 23

6:29 A.M.

She sat in the blue glow of the TV screen, holding a strange flower in her hand.

An image of her mother coalesced on the swollen fish-eye lens of the television, dressed in khaki and a pith helmet—Saturday morning cartoon clichés in degraded 1970s color stock, a sick subconscious rerun remarkable for its budgetless sprawl.

Behind her mother swayed a cartoon jungle of leaves, thorns, fur, eyes, pulsing, breathing, all of them melting together in a running liquid of anatomy. The jungle congealed into a giant face, and the face seemed like it had always been there. Her mother kept waving while the mouth in the jungle face opened behind her like a midnight sky. *Just as it always did.*

Nell screamed, soundlessly—the whole dream was profoundly silent, except for the clicking sound of her nails on the glass. Her mother always reached out to her, but she could never touch her through the screen. Suddenly, Nell knew she could break it . . .

Nell swung the flower in her hand at the screen like an ax, and the Monster howled in rage as its voice shrank into the clock radio alarm, beeping beside her.

Nell jerked awake and bashed the beeper off, irritated at its complicity.

She rose on an elbow and squinted at the dim rays streaming through the portholes of her cabin. Her neck and chest felt cool with sweat.

So, she thought, recalling the dream, she'd had a visit from the Monster.

Nell hadn't had this dream for many years. Yet it still crushed her under the same debilitating fear she had felt when she was ten and dreamed it nightly.

Today, on Henders Island, she *would* find a new flower—and she would name it after her mom. And she would finally lay her to rest, in a private ceremony so appropriately far from home.

And with that flower she would finally slay the Monster, too—by giving it a new, and beautiful, face.

12:01 P.M.

A sliver of shimmering light appeared on the horizon, and then the guano-crowned cliff began to rise from the ocean like a snow-capped ridge.

Nell and the others gathered on the mezzanine deck to watch the island as it was raised.

"What a wall!" exclaimed Dante De Santos. The

61

muscular twenty-three-year-old cook's assistant had Maori-style tattoos on his tanned arms, and jet-black hair combed back from a pugnacious face and tiger-opal eyes.

Nell remembered that he was an amateur rock climber who had been itching to pull out his gear and give it some use.

"I could make that ascent, no problem, if we can't find a way to land, man!" he bragged. "Remember to tell the captain for me if we can't get ashore, OK, Nell?"

She smiled. "OK, Dante."

Nell watched the wide wall of Henders Island rise more than twice the height of the Statue of Liberty from the horizon. The monolithic palisade seemed so lonely out here in the middle of nowhere, where so few had ever set eyes upon it. She was reminded, with a pang of uneasiness, how very far away they were from everything.

5:48 P.M.

Revving boat engines echoed off the rock face of a cove as four Zodiacs raced toward a crescent beach.

Two 150-horsepower Evinrude outboards powered the large Zodiac that took the lead with Jesse at the rudder. Jesse's passengers feared for their lives: Nell and Glyn clung to the edge rail as the inflatable jumped the breakers, its dual engines whining as they launched from each crest.

The cliff around the cove rose seven hundred feet straight up, swirled with faded bands of color like pigments in an overturned bucket of paint. Centered in the cliff, a dark crack had spewed broken rock over the beach down to the water. Judging from the fresh red and green color of the rubble, the crevasse had opened fairly recently.

Washed aground on this outpouring of jagged rock, the hull of a thirty-foot sailboat lay on her side like a swollen whale carcass.

"That crack looks new," Glyn shouted.

Nell nodded, grinning. "It may give us a way inland."

The *Trident* rolled on swells in the cove, anchored to one of the few submarine ledges their sonar had picked up around the island. They had nearly circumnavigated the entire island before locating this inlet, which they could have found in a few minutes had they circled in the other direction.

Now they had no time for setup. They had to dive into the boats and go live.

Peach got the camera feeds up as he counted down to the satellite uplink in the control room.

The three cameramen marked Peach's countdown in their headsets aboard the speeding rafts. They carried waterproof videocams and backpack transmitters with a thousand-meter range.

Cynthea looked from the stern of the *Trident* and

fired off orders to her camera crew. "OK, this god-
damn island has a beach after all, and we're in at
5:49, Fred! We're going hot right now! Peach, tell
me you're on top of the uplink!"

"TWO——ONE——ZERO. I'm there, we're
live," Peach said, cuing Zero's feed first.

Cynthea ran down a passageway belowdeck,
toward the control room in the starboard pontoon.
"Glyn! Glyn? Can you hear me, Glyn?"

5:49 P.M.

Glyn wore a wireless earmuff transmitter on his
right ear and carried the *SeaLife* flag at the prow of
the Zodiac. The British biologist sported an orange
SeaLife T-shirt, shorts, and Nikes, the last thing
Nell thought she'd ever see on him. "Yes,
Cynthea," Glyn said. "I hear you!"

Nell could hear Cynthea shouting through Glyn's
earphone: "Plant the flag on the beach!"

Nell grinned with excitement as she gripped the
edge rail of the speeding boat and scanned the
beach. The adrenaline pumping through her veins
made her want to leap out of the boat and fly to the
shore.

5:50 P.M.

Cynthea crashed through the door into the control
room, where three camera shots zoomed toward

the shore in the bank of monitors above Peach's head.

The small Zodiac landed first. Zero and Copepod jumped out into the surf. Copepod barked excitedly and darted up the beach. Zero sidestepped out of the water to cover the other Zodiacs landing.

The rest of the crew watched intently from the decks of the *Trident.*

Andy ran to the ship's rail in striped pajamas. "I can't believe they didn't WAKE ME UP!" he yelled. "They give me the night watch and then they don't wake me up? God damn it, I'm tired of getting SCREWED all the time!"

Andy turned to see a camera recording the moment and noticed some of the uniformed crew laughing nearby. "Screw you!" he screamed.

Cynthea cut back to Glyn planting the *SeaLife* flag in the sand.

"I claim this island for *SeaLife!*" Glyn cried.

Fans cheered in their living rooms and dorm rooms across the globe; Glyn had just become an instant star.

The network chiefs smiled, and for the first time in a month leaned back in relief as they watched their screens.

Millions went *"Ooo!"* as Cynthea caught Dawn flashing a look at Glyn and Nell squinting at Dawn.

Cynthea winked at Peach.

He nodded. "Drama."

"Right! Let's have a look at the boat!" Glyn said.

The landing party scrambled over the avalanche of rock.

Zero and the other cameramen were shooting through Voyager Lite wireless television cameras with transmission backpacks feeding signals to the *Trident*. Peach switched the shots and beamed the signal to satellites that bounced it to relay stations that fed hundreds of cable networks and millions of television screens downstream.

They neared the boat's battered hull that was encrusted with a thick layer of barnacles. As they drew closer they saw its name painted on the transom in faded green letters:

Balboa Bilbo

"That's our girl!" Jesse shouted, banging his hand on the stern.

They circled the boat and saw the upper deck, which was tilted toward them at a thirty-degree angle. The boat had been de-masted and her rig wrenched overboard. She had obviously been at sea a long time before coming aground.

"OK, let's check it out," Glyn said, doing a little impromptu narrating and looking at Zero, who waved him off.

Jesse climbed onto the deck.

Glyn climbed aboard behind Jesse, and Zero followed.

Jesse crawled into the cabin. The glass was missing from its hatches and windows. Much of the cabin's interior seemed to have been stripped: cabinet doors were gone, hinges and all; the glass from the windows seemed to have been pried out. Jesse spotted the beacon in the pilot's seat and picked it up.

"Yep, here's the EPIRB all right. It's still in the 'on' position."

He aimed the antenna of the cylindrical yellow device at Glyn like a gun, laughing.

"What does that mean?" Glyn said, looking at the camera. Zero quickly cut him out of the shot.

Jesse looked around the wreckage-strewn cabin. "Well, *something* had to turn this EPIRB on, Professor."

Copepod barked frantically in the distance.

"Maybe a bird flew through the window and pecked on it or something." Glyn pointed out the window. "The glass is missing, see?"

Jesse looked right at the camera and shook his head. "It'd take three birds working as a team to turn on an EPIRB, dude." He made the cuckoo sign against his head.

"Oh." Glyn nodded. "Right!"

Nell stood on the rocks above the prone body of the sailboat.

Holding the bill of her baseball cap, she searched

the base of the cliff. A purple patch of vegetation caught her eye some distance to the left of the crevasse. Everything else around her seemed to disappear as she focused on the vividly colored growth.

"Hey, where's Copepod?" Dawn shouted.

The cameramen panned. The frantic barking had stopped abruptly. The bull terrier was nowhere to be seen.

Nell jumped across the rocks until she reached the coarse reddish sand of the beach. She jogged up toward the cliff. The afternoon sun lit up the wall of rock and the bright purple plants at its base. Nell saw flecks of gold in the sand. *Fool's gold,* she thought—there must be a lot of iron sulfide in the cliffs.

She was relieved that no cameraman had followed her. The commotion of the landing party receded behind her as adrenaline quickened her steps.

Nell dug her knees into the sand before the patch of purple spears at the base of the cliff, catching her breath.

The stalks looked like a jade plant's, she thought, except the straight shafts had no branches like jade plants, and the color was a vivid lavender. She noticed that the core of each stalk was purplish-blue, while its artichoke-like leaves were tinged green at their fuzzy points. They resembled fat asparagus spears, but she couldn't identify the family they belonged to—let alone their genus or species, as there was no recognizable growth pattern.

She tried to calm her heartbeat as she rifled through the botanical taxonomy in her mind, telling herself that she must be overexcited and overlooking something obvious.

She reached out to the largest of the specimens and pulled a spiked leaf from the plant. It ripped like old felt and melted into juice that stung her fingertips.

She flicked her fingers, startled, and wiped away the blue juice on her white shirt. Opening her Evian bottle she splashed water over her left hand and shirt.

To her astonishment, the plant reacted like an air fern to her touch, folding all its leaflike appendages against its stalk. Then it retracted underground, an action that required internal muscles—mechanisms that plants did not have.

Surprised, she was about to call the others when she saw what looked like a trail of white ants moving along the base of the cliff.

She leaned forward and watched the large, evenly spaced creatures hurl down a groove in the sand, toward a crab carcass. They moved faster than any bug she had ever seen.

5:52 P.M.

"Copey must have gone up into the canyon," Jesse yelled.

"Copey!" Dawn called.

"Maybe that's where the survivors went," Glyn suggested. "I mean, if there are any."

"Someone stripped this vessel, dude," Jesse shouted, shaking his head and banging his fist against the hull. "And somebody turned that beacon on."

Cynthea seized the moment, switching to Glyn's channel. "Go, Glyn, go! We have seven minutes left on the satellite feed!"

"Let's go!" Glyn said.

Cynthea tapped camera two's screen with her pencil.

"Yeah!" Jesse howled, and he raised his fist to lead the charge.

The three cameramen covered the four scientists and five crew members as they climbed the natural ramp of broken rock up into the crevasse.

5:53 P.M.

Nell picked up a sun-bleached Budweiser can that had somehow made it to the shore, and she used it to block the path of the speeding bugs.

One of the creatures fell on its side.

An inch-wide waxy white disk lay motionless on the sand.

She threw the Bud can aside and looked closer. Centipede-like legs emerged from the edge of the white disk. The legs flailed and the bug spun like a Frisbee over the sand in an evasive maneuver.

More of the white bugs arrived, massing in front of her. They were *rolling* on their edges, like unicycle motocrossers, down the groove. Within seconds, dozens had gathered. Suddenly, they tilted in different directions—preparing to attack?

Astonished, Nell stood up and took a few quick steps back. Such animals could not exist, she thought.

She looked around for the others in the landing party; they were gone.

She ran toward the crevasse, yelling, "Stop! Stop! Stop!"

5:54 P.M.

From the control room Cynthea watched the search party as they entered the canyon, whose curving walls were obscured by mists above. The late-afternoon sun etched beams and shadows through the heights of the crack as water streamed and dripped over them.

Struggling over large boulders and climbing natural stairways of smaller rocks, Glyn boosted Dawn over a ledge, admiring the tattoo peeking from the back of her low-slung jeans.

"Hey, look, everybody!" shouted Jesse. "The crack of Dawn!"

Peach switched cameras at Cynthea's pointing pencil. "This is great stuff, boss!"

"We just saved *SeaLife*, Peach," she told him.

71

8:55 P.M. Eastern Daylight Time

On his wafer-thin wall-mounted 55-inch Hitachi screen in his midtown Manhattan office, Jack Nevins watched Glyn give Dawn a two-handed tush-push over a boulder.

"This is great, Fred," Jack said into his cell phone.

Fred Huxley watched his own drop-down TV in the adjacent office, his own cell phone to his ear as he lit up a Cohiba: "This is GOLD, Jack!"

"I think that magnificent bitch just saved our asses, pal."

"I could kiss her!"

"I could fuck her."

"The old gal's got a hell of a survival instinct."

"Next week's numbers are gonna rocket, Baby Fred!"

"Next week's numbers are going to KILL, Brother Jack."

5:57 P.M.

The search party fanned out on a ledge where the crevasse widened. Lush vegetation clung to the walls: a strange purple mat of growth squished underfoot.

The vegetation along the walls arched and wove together to form a cornucopia-like tunnel that stretched up into the twilit distance, speared with beams from the setting sun.

"Nell, you hit the mother lode!" Glyn muttered.

Some of the tall, glistening plants resembled cacti; others, coral. The canopy trembled with fluttering, brightly colored foliage above them. The air smelled sweet and pungent—like flowers and mildew, with a sulfurous hint of cesspool.

Glyn squinted skeptically at the canopy. Sweat trickled into his eyes and the salt burned as he rubbed them. He was still breathing hard from the climb. What should have been leaves, the biologist thought, looked more like ears of multicolored fungus sprouting from the branches overhead. "Wait a minute," he cautioned, winking his left eye repeatedly to clear it.

"Yeah, hold on," Zero said.

The "plants" and "trees" grew in radial shapes like century plants, yuccas, and palms, but with multiple branches. They swayed as if there were a breeze. But the thick air was utterly still.

A buzzing, chittering sound rose like a chorus of baritones humming through police whistles. The green tunnel turned slightly purple. It rippled as if a strong wind was passing over it.

"Hey!" Jesse yelled, making everyone jump. "This plant's MOVING, man!"

Jesse's shout echoed through the stony heights, and the insect noise stopped abruptly. Except for the distant hiss of the surf below, the canyon was silent.

Zero's camera barely caught a blurry shape streaking through the branches overhead.

The insect noise resumed, louder now.

Dawn screamed. Dartlike thorns, attached to a tree by thin cables, had impaled her bare midriff. As the party watched, the tree fired two more thorns like blow darts into her neck.

The translucent cables turned red, drawing in Dawn's blood. With a desperate lunge she broke the cables and shrieked, bleeding from the siphoning tubes as she ran frantically toward the others.

Glyn noticed the branches above reaching down—then something caught the corner of his eye: a wave of dark shapes rushing toward them down the tunnel.

He felt a sharp bite on his calf and yelped. "Crikey!" Glyn looked down at his bone-white legs, exposed for the first time on this trip by the damned L.L. Bean chino shorts he agreed to wear for the landing. He almost couldn't spot the offender against his pale skin. Then he located it by a second sharp pain: a white disk-shaped spider clung to his left calf.

He raised his hand to swat it and hundreds of miniatures rolled off the spider's back. A red gash melted open on his calf as, in the space of two seconds, the yellow edge of his tibia was exposed and more white disks fired into the gaping gash.

Before Glyn could scream, a whistling shriek flew straight at him.

He looked up as an animal the size of a water

buffalo hurtled through the opening of the tunnel.

Zero turned the camera as Glyn yelled, and caught the beast closing its hippo-sized vertical jaws over the biologist's head and chest. With a sharp crunch, the attacker sank translucent teeth into Glyn's ribs and bit off the top of the Englishman's body at the solar plexus. Bright arterial blood from Glyn's beating heart shot thirty feet between the beast's teeth, dousing Zero's shirt and camera lens.

Zero lowered the camera and saw a cyclone of animals shrieking and clicking as they swirled around the rest of Glyn's body.

The others screamed as they were bombarded by flying bugs and more shadows pouring out of the tunnel.

Zero threw the camera toward the onslaught, and a few animals streaking toward him pivoted and chased it instead.

As fast as he could, he slipped from the ledge and zigzagged down the rocks in the crevasse.

5:58 P.M.

Cynthea, Peach, and the world watched in astonishment as all three camera shots panned wildly.

"Crikey!" someone shouted—and there was an awful cracking sound.

A chaos of shrieks overloaded the microphones, and the cameras jerked and spun.

One camera tumbled onto its side. Red and blue liquid spattered its lens.

Another camera fell, and blood-drenched clothing blocked its view.

The audience across the nation heard screams from their suddenly blackened TV screens.

Cynthea cut to the remaining camera just in time to see something fly toward the lens. Then the camera fell and was instantly blackened by swarming silhouettes.

"We just lost the uplink, boss," Peach reported.

One hundred and ten million people across the world had tuned in before the live feed had died.

Cynthea stared at the screens. "Oh. My. *God!*"

8:59 P.M. Eastern Daylight Time

"We're fucked," Jack Nevins said.

"It's been nice, buddy," Fred Huxley said, stamping out his Cohiba.

6:01 P.M.

Nell leaped over the rocks toward the crevasse as Zero came running out. His gray T-shirt was drenched with bright red and blue liquid. He didn't have his camera or his transmission backpack.

Nell called to him but he sprinted past her, lunging down the boulders with a ten-mile stare, heading straight for the water. She followed him instinctively, but halfway down the rocks she swung around and looked back into the mouth of the twilit crack.

What looked like a dog emerged from the shadow of the fissure.

The creature seemed to be sniffing along Zero's trail. When it leaped onto a rock in the sun she saw that its fur was bright red. It was not a dog. It was at least twice the size of a Bengal tiger.

Its head swung toward her.

Nell backed away, turned, stumbled over the rocks around the derelict sailboat.

She spotted the small Zodiac on the beach and raced for it over the rocks.

She saw Zero dive into the sea and start swimming for the *Trident*.

Finally, she hit the hard, wet sand and ran. Without looking back, she reached the Zodiac. She shoved it into the water and flopped in backwards, planting her feet on the transom.

She yanked the pull-start and shot a look up the beach.

Three of the creatures lunged from the rocks to the sand.

Apart from their striped fur, they were nothing like mammals—more like six-legged tigers crossed with jumping spiders. With each kick off their back legs, they leaped fifteen yards over the sand.

Nell yanked the pull-start again, and the motor turned over and coughed to life.

The Zodiac pushed over a breaker, and the three animals recoiled before a crashing wave. Driving spiked arms deep into the wet sand, they pushed themselves backwards in thrusts ten yards long to avoid the hissing water.

Then they reared up and opened their vertical jaws wide, letting out piercing howls like car alarms that bounced and shattered in echoes over the cliffs around them.

Nell stared as the beasts leaped back up the beach and over the rocks toward the crack in the wall.

She stared at the twisted cliff leaning over her in the sky, and froze, breathless. She felt as if she were a child again, paralyzed as her nemesis burst into the light of the day. The face of her monster appeared in the rock, as though it had been waiting in the middle of nowhere for her.

Her head spun and her stomach convulsed. She bent abruptly and vomited overboard, clinging to the tiller with one hand.

Gasping, she splashed her face and rinsed her mouth with saltwater. There was no making peace with it—no way to replace it with a pretty face or flower, she knew. She had to fight it. *She had to fight.* Angry tears streaked her face as she steered the Zodiac toward Zero.

She called to him. The cameraman reached out and she hooked his arm, pulling him into the safety of the boat.

AUGUST 24

12:43 P.M.

The surgical mask muffled Geoffrey Binswanger's amazed laughter. His eyes twinkled with childlike delight.

A lab technician bent the tail of a large horseshoe crab and stuck a needle through an exposed fold directly into the cardiac chamber of the living fossil. The clear liquid that squirted through the needle blushed pale blue as it filled a beaker. The color reminded Geoffrey of "Frost"-flavored Gatorade.

The director of the Associates of Cape Cod Laboratory at Woods Hole, Massachusetts, had invited Geoffrey to see how horseshoe crab blood was extracted each spring and summer. Since the blood was copper-based instead of iron-based, it turned blue instead of red when exposed to oxygen.

Geoffrey had spent several summers as a visiting researcher at Woods Hole Oceanographic Institution, or the "WHOI" (pronounced "hooey" by the locals), but he had never visited the Cape Cod Associates facility. So today he had taken his metallic-lime Q-Pro road bike up Route 28 a couple miles to the lab, which lay tucked inside a forest of white pine, white oak, and beech, to take a look.

Geoffrey wore maroon surgical scrubs over his biking clothes, a sterile hair cap over his dreadlocks, plastic booties over his shoes, and latex gloves. Similarly clad lab technicians removed the writhing arthropods from blue plastic drums, folded their tails forward, and placed them upright in crab-holders on four double-sided lab counters.

"This procedure doesn't hurt, I hope?" Geoffrey said.

"No," said the technician who had been assigned to show him around. "We only draw one-third of their blood, then we drop them back in the ocean. They regenerate it in a few days. Some are destined to be fish bait on the trawlers, though, so it only makes sense that they be routed through us for extraction first. We can tell from scars that a lot of the crabs have donated blood once or twice before."

Geoffrey knew these primitive creatures were not, technically, crabs. They resembled giant Cambrian trilobites lined up in rows over the stainless steel shelves, a bizarre marriage of the primordial and the high tech. But, Geoffrey mused, which was which? This lowly life form was still more sophisticated than the most advanced technology known to man. Indeed, all the equipment and expertise gathered here was devoted to unlocking the secrets and utilizing the capabilities of this one seemingly primitive organism.

"What's the scientific name of this thing?" he asked.

"*Limulus polyphemus*. Which means 'slanting one-eyed giant,' I think."

"Sure, Polyphemus, the monster Odysseus fought on the island of Cyclopes."

"Oh, cool!"

"What's their life span?"

"About twenty years."

"Really? When do they reach sexual maturity?"

"At about age eight or nine, we think."

Geoffrey nodded, making a mental note.

"This whole lab," the technician continued, "was built to extract crab blood and refine it into *Limulus* amebocyte lysate, or LAL—a specialized protein that clots on contact with dangerous endotoxins, like *E. coli*."

Geoffrey looked in a barrel where the crabs were clambering methodically over one another. He already knew most of what he was hearing, but he wanted to give the young lab tech an audience. "Endotoxins are common in the environment, aren't they?"

"Yes," answered the youngster. "They mostly consist of the fragments of certain bacteria floating in the air, and they're only harmful if they enter animal bloodstreams. Tap water, for instance, while safe to drink, would kill most people if they injected it. Even distilled water left in a glass overnight would already be too lethal to inject."

"How do you extract the LAL?"

"We centrifuge the blood to separate out the cells. We burst them open osmotically. Then we extract the protein that contains the clotting agent. It takes about four hundred pounds of cells to get a half ounce of the protein."

"So why do these guys have such a sophisticated defense against bacteria, I wonder?"

"Well, they swim in muck," the technician said.

Geoffrey nodded. "Good point."

"Yeah, they never evolved an immune system, so if they get injured, they'd die pretty fast from infection without a pretty badass chemical defense of some sort." The technician removed the needle from one specimen and lifted it from its cradle, straightening its tail. He placed the living Roomba in a barrel. "Before we had horseshoe crabs we had to use the 'rabbit test' to see if drugs and vaccines contained bacterial impurities." The technician grabbed a fresh donor and handed it to a colleague. "If the rabbit got a fever or died, we knew there were endotoxins present in the sample being tested. But since 1977, LAL from these guys has been used to test medical equipment, syringes, IV solutions, anything that comes in contact with human or animal bloodstreams. If the protein clots, we know there's a problem. This stuff has saved millions of lives."

"Especially rabbits, I guess."

The technician laughed. "Yeah. Especially rabbits."

Geoffrey touched the hard reddish-green carapace of a crab. The shell had the smoothness and density of Tupperware. He laughed nervously as the technician handed him an upside-down crab.

Gingerly, he took the large specimen. Five pincered legs made piano-scale motions on each side of a central mouth on the creature's underside. Geoffrey cupped its back carefully so as not to get nipped.

"Don't worry, these guys are actually pretty harmless. And they're hardy as hell, too. I know a scientist here who says that back in the day he stored some in his refrigerator and forgot about them for two weeks. They were still kicking when he finally remembered to get them out."

Geoffrey watched with childlike delight as the arthropod bent its spiked tail up and revealed the "book" gills layered in sheaves near its tail spine. "Gads, what a beast!"

"When I started working here I thought only aliens from space movies had ten eyes and blue blood." The technician laughed. "This guy's even got a light-sensing eye on his tail."

"Nature's produced a lot of different blood pigments." Geoffrey peered at the maw at the center of the crab, which reminded him of the mouth of an ancient *Anomalocaris*, the arthropod that ruled the seas during the first "Cambrian" explosion of complex life half a billion years ago. He was struck by the color of this creature, which closely resembled the color of the reddish-green trilobite fossils he had collected at Marble Mountain in California as a boy: this crab was a living fossil— literally. "I've seen violet blood and green blood in polychaete worms," he said. "I've even seen yellow-green blood in sea cucumbers. Crabs, lobsters, octopus, squid, even pill-bugs, a relative of these guys here, all have blue copper-based pigment that serves the same function as the red iron-based pigment in our blood."

The technician arched his eyebrows. "You've been humoring me a bit by letting me make my spiel, haven't you, Dr. Binswanger?"

"Oh, call me Geoffrey. No, I've learned a lot I didn't know, actually," Geoffrey assured him. "I've never seen anything like this beastie. Thanks for letting me check it out."

The technician gave him a thumbs-up. "No problem. Did you see *SeaLife* last night?"

Geoffrey squirmed. This was the *fourth* time someone had asked him this today. First, his attractive neighbor, as he left his cottage. Then Sy Greenberg, an Oxford buddy researching the giant axons of squids at the Marine Biological Laboratory, had asked the same thing as they passed on the bike path near the Steamboat Authority. Then the dock manager at WHOI, while he was locking his bike outside the Water Street building where his office was located.

"Um, no," Geoffrey answered. "Why?"

The technician shook his head. "Just wondering if you thought it was for real."

That's what the other three had said. Exactly.

Someone rapped on the window in the hall outside the clean room. On the other side of the glass stood Dr. Lastikka, the lab director who had arranged his tour. Dr. Lastikka made a telephone gesture with his hand to his ear.

"Jeez, it's my lunch hour. Oh well, OK, I'm done." Geoffrey handed the horseshoe crab carefully back to the technician and pantomimed to Dr. Lastikka, *Tell them to hold!*

Dr. Lastikka signaled *OK*.

"Thanks, that was really cool," Geoffrey told the technician.

"Doing your lecture tonight, Dr. Binswanger? Er—Geoffrey?"

"Oh yes."

"I'll be there!"

"I won't be able to recognize you."

"I'll wear the mask."

Geoffrey nodded. "OK!"

This was why Geoffrey loved Woods Hole: everyone was fascinated by science, everyone was smart—and not just his fellow researchers. The general public, in fact, was usually smarter. Woods Hole, he confidently believed, was the most scientifically curious and informed population of any town on Earth. And it was one of the rare places, outside a few college campuses, where scientists were considered cool. Everyone showed up for the nighttime lectures. And then everyone adjourned to various taverns to talk about them.

Geoffrey exited the clean room through two sealed doors. As he tugged off his cap and mask, a lab assistant pointed him to a phone. The front desk patched him through. "This is Geoffrey."

"There you are, *El Geoffe*!"

It was Angel Echevarria, his office mate at WHOI. Angel was studying stomatopods, following in the footsteps of his hero, Ray Manning, the pioneering stomatopod expert. Angel had been out of the office that morning and had left a message saying he was going to be late. Now the researcher was practically jumping out of the phone.

"Geoffrey! Geoffrey! Did you see it?"

"See what? Take it easy, Angel."

"You saw *SeaLife*, right?"

Geoffrey groaned. "I don't watch reality TV shows."

"Yeah, but they're scientists."

"Who go to all the tourist spots, like Easter Island and the Galapagos? Come on, it's lame."

"Oh my God! But you heard about it, right?"

"Yeah . . ."

"So you know half of them got *slaughtered?*"

"What? It's a TV show, Angel. I wouldn't be too sure about that if I were you." Geoffrey stepped out of the cleansuit as he spoke. He nodded as a technician took it from him.

"It's a *reality* show," Angel insisted.

Geoffrey laughed.

"I recorded it. You've got to see it."

"Oh brother."

"Get back here! Bring sandwiches!"

"All right, I'll see you in half an hour." Geoffrey hung up the phone, and looked at the technician.

"Did you see *SeaLife* last night, Dr. Binswanger?" she asked.

1:37 P.M.

Geoffrey entered the office he shared with Angel carrying a few bags of sandwiches from Jimmy's sandwich shop. "Lunch is ser—"

He was shushed by a cluster of colleagues from down the hall who had gathered to watch Angel feed his mantis shrimp.

Watching a stomatopod, or "mantis shrimp," hunt was truly a spectacle not to be missed.

Geoffrey aborted his greeting immediately and set down his helmet and the sandwich bags. In the large saltwater tank, Angel had placed a thick layer of coral gravel and a ceramic vase decorated with an Asian-style depiction of a tiger. The vase rested on its side, its mouth pointed toward the back of the aquarium.

Angel pinched a live blue crab in forceps. "Don gave me one of his blue crabs. Thanks, Don."

"I think I'm already regretting it," moaned Don as he nudged his glasses up the bridge of his nose.

"Whoa!" several exclaimed as Angel's pet emerged.

"*Banzai!*" Angel dropped the unfortunate crustacean into the tank. Morbid fascination compelled everyone to watch.

The ten-inch-long segmented creature moved like some ancient dragon. Its elegant overlapping plates rippled like jade louvers as it curled through the water. A Swiss Army knife's worth of limbs and legs churned underneath. Its stalked eyes twitched in different directions. The colors on its body were dazzlingly vivid, nearly iridescent.

"Here it comes," Don groaned.

The blue crab sculled its legs as it sank through the water, and halfway down it saw the mantis shrimp. It immediately swam for the far side of the vase but the mantis lunged up and its powerful forearms struck, too fast for the human eye. With a startling *pop,* the crab tumbled backwards. The carapace between the crab's eyes was shattered and the crab hung limp in the water.

The mantis shrimp moved in and dragged its quarry back into its vase.

The audience "wowed."

"And that, my friends, is the awesome power of the stomatopod." Angel sounded more like a circus barker than a stomatopod expert. "Its strike has the force of a .22 caliber bullet. It sees millions more colors than human beings with eyes that have independent depth perception, and its reflexes are faster than any creature on Earth. This mysterious miracle of Mother Nature is so different from other arthropods it might as well have come from an alien planet. It may even replace us someday . . . *Bon appetit*, Freddie!"

"Speaking of which, Jimmy's has arrived," Geoffrey said.

"Yay, Jimmy's," said a female lab mate.

"Glad you're here," Angel told Geoffrey. "I've got something to show you."

Everyone took sandwiches. A computer monitor on the lab counter showed a cable newscast with the volume turned down. The *SeaLife* logo flashed behind the newscaster.

"Hey, turn it up!" someone called, as Angel simultaneously cranked up the volume.

"It's only two miles wide, but if what the cable show SeaLife *aired last night is real, some scientists are saying it might be the most important island discovery since Charles Darwin visited the Galapagos nearly two centuries ago. Others are claiming that* SeaLife *is engaging in a crass publicity stunt. Last night the show gave a tantalizing live glimpse of what appeared to be an island pop-*

ulated by horrific and alien life that viciously attacked the show's cast. Network executives have refused to comment. Joining us is eminent scientist Thatcher Redmond for an expert opinion on what really happened."

Everyone in the room groaned as the camera focused on the guest commentator.

"Dr. Redmond, congratulations on the success of your book, The Human Effect, *and your Tetteridge Award which you received just yesterday, and thank you for giving us your insights today,"* gushed the newscaster. *"So, is it for real?"*

"Photosynthesis in action," Angel said. "The man grows in limelight."

"Come on now, Angel," Geoffrey said facetiously. "Dr. Redmond knows all."

Thatcher smiled, showing a row of recently bleached teeth in his ruddy face. He wore his trademark cargo vest and sported his famous red mustache and overgrown sideburns. *"Thank you! Well, Sandy, I only hope that life on the island can withstand discovery by human beings, to be perfectly frank."*

"He's got a point there," muttered one of the female researchers, as she bit into her sandwich.

Thatcher continued. *"So-called intelligent life is the greatest threat to any environment. I don't envy any ecosystem that comes in contact with it. That's the thesis of my book,* The Human Effect, *as a matter of fact, and I'm afraid if this* SeaLife *show isn't a hoax of some sort, I'll soon have to add another tragic chapter to illustrate my point."*

"Oh brother," Geoffrey groaned.

"Gee, I wonder if he wrote a book or something," muttered Angel.

"But do you think it is a hoax? Or the real thing?" persisted the newscaster.

"Well," Thatcher said, *"I wish it were true, of course—as a scientist, that is—but I'm afraid that, as a scientist, I have to say this is probably a hoax, Sandy."*

"Thank you, Dr. Redmond." The newscaster turned as the camera cut away from Thatcher. *"Well, there you have it . . ."*

"No way," Angel insisted. "It's not a hoax!"

The others chattered about the controversy as they carried their lunches back to their offices.

"OK, Geoffrey, you've got to see this. I've got the clip right here."

"OK, OK."

Sitting beside Angel in their cramped office overlooking Great Harbor, Geoffrey watched the chaotic images of the last minutes of *SeaLife* that Angel had recorded.

If someone were trying to stage a schlocky horror film on a very low budget it would probably look something like this, Geoffrey decided. Frankly, it looked like that movie *The Blair Witch Project*, as though the cameramen were deliberately trying to avoid taking a good look at the cheap special effects.

"I can't make out much of anything," Geoffrey said.

"Wait." Angel punched the PAUSE button on the remote and then stepped the image forward. "There!"

He froze the frame as a group of sweeping shadows nearly blackened the screen. Angel pointed a pencil at a shape that looked like a crab leg.

"OK," Geoffrey said. "So?"

"That's a toe-splitter! That's a *stomatopod claw*."

Geoffrey laughed and reached for his sandwich. "That's a Rorschach test, Angel. And you're seeing the species you've been studying for the past five years, because you see it in your dreams, your breakfast cereal, and the stains on the ceiling tiles."

Angel frowned. "Maybe. But I don't think so."

Then Geoffrey noticed something. He stopped eating. As Angel advanced the frames, red drops splattered the camera lens—then a single light blue drop appeared, seconds before the camera went dark.

Angel opened a mini-fridge that had a sign taped to the door: FOOD ONLY. He took out a carton of milk and sniffed it. "So, are you going ahead with the Fire-Breathing Chat tonight?"

Geoffrey turned away from the screen and clicked off the video. "Uh, yep. The Fire-Breathing Chat will go on, despite the intense competition from reality TV shows."

The Fire-Breathing Chat was a tradition Geoffrey had carried on since his Oxford days. It was a forum for heretical ideas, with which he could outrage his colleagues on a semi-regular basis. Afterward they could pummel him with derision to their hearts' content. The public was invited to enjoy the spectacle and to join in.

"Everyone's going to ask you about *SeaLife*, you know."

"Yes, you're probably right."

"You should thank me for preparing you."

"Duly noted."

"Are you really going with the ontogeny-recapitulates-phylogeny thing tonight?"

"Yep. Fasten your seat belt, Angel, it's going to be a bumpy night."

"When are you going to take home one of your groupies, Geoffrey? Everyone already thinks you're a Don Juan, so you might as well cash in on your reputation. The girls are right there waiting after every talk, my man, but you always get into a ridiculous scientific argument with a bunch of geezers, instead."

"Maybe tonight I'll get into a ridiculous scientific argument with one of my groupies. That's the kind of foreplay that would really turn me on."

Angel frowned. "You'll never get laid, my friend."

"You're a pessimist, Angel. And a chauvinist. Don't think about it. I don't."

"But I do. And you don't. Life isn't fair! You need to get laid even more than I do, my friend. There's more to life than biology. And there's more to biology than biology, too."

"You're right, you're so right."

Whatever "Don Juan" reputation Geoffrey had was quite unearned. The scientist lacked the patience for friendly, mindless banter. He remained incorrigibly oblivious to traditional romantic signals. Ideas excited him, but he found the rituals of flirtation degrading and inexplicably obtuse.

He'd had nine sexual partners in his thirty-four years. All were short-lived romances, with long gaps in between. Geoffrey attracted would-be rebels, but when the women inevitably tried to force him into some orthodoxy, he had moved on.

While he worried sometimes that he might be lonely at the end of the day, he refused to trade his sanity for companionship. This was not vanity, or some noble sacrifice in the name of principle. It was simply a fact he had come to acknowledge about himself. As a result, he knew he might well end up alone.

So, love was the one mystery he'd had to approach with faith—faith that he would meet someone, faith against evidence, a necessary irrationality that kept him going, kept him looking toward the next horizon with open-ended hope. Because he had to admit to himself he was lonely . . . and Angel had an irritating way of reminding him of that.

"So what's the ceremonial garb for tonight's riot?" Angel asked.

The Fire-Breathing Chat tradition required the speaker to wear a random piece of clothing of exotic or historical origin—a Portuguese fisherman's hat, an Etruscan helmet, a Moroccan burnoose. Last time Geoffrey had worn a fairly pedestrian toga, and the crowd had loudly expressed their disappointment.

"Tonight . . . a kilt, I think."

"My friend," Angel said, "you're crazy."

"Either that or everyone else is. I haven't figured out which yet. Why does everyone wear the same thing at any given place and time? We all have minds of our own, and yet we're afraid to be unfashionable. It's an example of complete irrationality and fear, Angel."

"Uh, sure. That sounds good."

"Thanks. I thought it sounded pretty good, too . . ."

Geoffrey reversed the video clip. He paused the image as they spoke, pondering the single drop of pale blue liquid at the right edge of the frame.

Someone clever might have added two compelling clues—a stomatopod claw and a splash of blue blood—simply to fool the scientific community and keep a publicity stunt simmering, he mused. But somehow it didn't seem likely that such sophisticated clues would be known to the producers of a trashy reality TV show. Or that they would count on such subtle evidence being picked up by the handful of experts who would notice.

Geoffrey shrugged and put the puzzle away, unsolved.

7:30 P.M.

Enthusiastic applause greeted Geoffrey as he strode onto the stage of Lillie Auditorium.

The hall was packed with a mixture of young students who had fallen under the spell of the dashing evolutionary scientist and elderly skeptical colleagues who were itching for a scientific rumble.

An ageless thirty-four years old, Geoffrey Binswanger was a physically striking man who remained an enigma to his colleagues. His West Indian and German parentage had produced an unlikely mix of islander's features, caramel complexion, and sky-blue eyes. His dreadlocked hair and athletic physique undermined his academic seriousness, in the view of some of his fellow academics. Others, intrigued, wanted to count him in their political corners.

His theories, however, showed an utter lack of allegiance to anything but his own judgment—a result, perhaps, of never thinking of himself as part of a group. For whatever reason, Geoffrey had always needed to see things for himself. He wanted to draw his own conclusions without obligation to anything but what could be demonstrated and replicated under laboratory conditions.

Ever since he was a child, and as long as he could remember, Geoffrey was a scientist. Whenever adults had asked him what he wanted to be when he grew up, he literally did not understand the question. He was conducting formal experiments at the age of four. Instead of asking his parents why some things bounced and some things shattered, he tested them himself, marking his picture books with a single heavy dot next to illustrations of things that survived the test of gravity and a swirly squiggle next to things that did not, which his mother had discovered to her mixed horror and delight.

His parents, who raised him in the upper-class Los Angeles suburb of La Cañada Flintridge, finally conceded that they had a very special child on their hands when they had come home from work at NASA's Jet Propulsion Lab one night to find the babysitter curled up on the couch asleep in front of the television and their six-year-old son sitting on the back patio holding a running garden hose. "Welcome to Triphibian City," he'd said as he presented his engineering feat with an imperious wave of his hand.

Geoffrey had flooded the entire backyard just as millions of toads from the wash of Devil's Gate Dam had spawned. Thousands of the tiny gray amphibians had stormed under the fence through Geoffrey's little tunnel and now inhabited a metropolis of canals and islands presided over by ceramic garden gnomes.

From that point forward, Geoffrey's parents did all they could to occupy their son's curiosity in more constructive ways. They sent him to a camp on Catalina Island, where he was nearly arrested for dissecting a Garibaldi, the pugnacious State Fish of California, although his campmates had already speared as many of the fish as possible, because it was illegal, and had flung them on the rocks.

When they enrolled him in a neurobiology class for gifted children at nearby Caltech, he had never felt more at home. He explored the campus with his genius friends and snuck into the labyrinth of steam tunnels beneath the campus, for which he almost got arrested, yet again.

Geoffrey graduated from Flintridge Prep at the age of fifteen and immediately qualified for Oxford, much to his parents' horror. His mother finally acquiesced, and Geoffrey stayed at Oxford for seven years, earning degrees in biology, biochemistry, and anthropology.

Geoffrey had won a variety of awards through the years since university but he never displayed them in his office, the way so many of his colleagues did. Looking at them made him queasy. He was deeply suspicious of any strings that might be attached to such honors. He accepted them out of politeness, but even then at arm's length.

His latest book had become something of a best-seller for a scientific tome, though to his literary agent's chagrin he resisted opportunities to become what he called a "sound-bite scientist," pontificating on TV about the latest scientific fad and mouthing the majority position with no personal expertise in the plethora of matters journalists asked scientists to expound upon. He cringed when he saw colleagues placed in that position, even though they usually seemed pleased to have appeared on television.

For his part, Geoffrey preferred a forum like this one tonight. The storied Lillie Auditorium at Woods Hole was one of the true churches of science. Through the last century this humble hall had hosted more than forty Nobel laureates.

When the small auditorium was built around the end of the nineteenth century, Woods Hole was already a thriving community of loosely affiliated laboratories with a progressive campuslike culture. Here, men and women had found remarkable equality from the start, the men in their boater hats and white suits and the women in their bodices, bustled cotton dresses, and parasols, hunkering down in the mud together and digging for specimens.

Lillie Auditorium cozily held an audience of about two hundred people, its high ceiling supported by wide Victorian pillars painted a yellowing white like fat tallow candles. Under its wood-slatted chairs one could still find the wire fixtures where men used to store their boaters.

The Friday Night Lectures were the most anticipated of the summer lectures at Woods Hole. They regularly drew top scientists from around the world as featured speakers. The Fire-Breathing Chats, however, traditionally took place on Thursday nights.

Geoffrey's first presentation eight years ago had caused a near-riot—so naturally the directors had reserved some prime Thursday night slots for his visit this year in hopes of a repeat.

Geoffrey had invented the Fire-Breathing Chats so that he and some other young turks at Oxford, after persuading the proprietor of the King's Head Pub to set a room aside every Thursday night, could commit scientific sacrilege on a regular basis. Their enthusiastic audience had soon swollen to standing room only and had proved a thumping good time regardless, in retrospect, of how risible most of the theories advanced had been. But the object was not so much to be right as to challenge conventional wisdom and to engage in scientific reasoning, even if it led to the demolition of the theory being proposed. They had a special prize for that, in fact—the Icarus Award, for the theory that was shot down the fastest.

It was rapid-fire science, theory in action, method in motion, and often in the flaming death of a hypothesis could be seen the embers of a brilliant solution. Pitching a bold idea to the wolves had a thrilling appeal to Geoffrey. When it didn't destroy his theories it improved them, so he had carried the tradition with him wherever he went as a test for his most unscrupulous ideas. He thought of these lectures as "peer preview."

Now he strode across the stage in a Black Watch tartan kilt and held out a hand to calm the applause as he reached the lectern and tapped the microphone. Whoops and wolf whistles rose from his audience, and Geoffrey stepped out from behind the lectern for a bow.

With the kilt, he wore a T-shirt dyed rust-red by the mud of the island of Kaua'i. Green block letters across his chest read, "Conserve Island Habitats." Geoffrey had spent half a dozen summers on the small Hawaiian island, vacationing at his uncle's stilted house tucked in the narrow strip of rain forest between a vine-strangled cliff and Tunnels Beach. He had found no better way to escape civilization than to don a mask, snorkel, and fins. He'd shoot through the ancient lava vents, chasing Moorish Idols, following nonchalant sea turtles, and feeding urchins to the brash *Humuhumunukanukaapuaha'a* fish that took them right out of his hands. He had worn this T-shirt on dozens of his swims through those tunnels, and it was the only common denominator for every Fire-Breathing Chat: he wore it for every talk.

He raised a hand to the easel beside him that announced tonight's topic:

Predator and Prey: The Origin of Sex?

Another round of whistles, applause, and jeers rose.

Geoffrey took refuge behind the lectern and began.

"Good evening, ladies and gentlemen. First—a brief history of the world."

A ripple of amusement crossed the audience as they settled in and the lights dimmed.

Geoffrey clicked a remote, and an artist's rendering of two worlds colliding appeared on the screen behind him.

"After a Mars-sized planet collided with ours and penetrated her surface, spewing a molten plume of ejecta that would congeal into the Moon, Mother Earth remained a cooling ball of lava for a hundred million years."

Geoffrey clicked to a close-up of the full Moon over the ocean.

"It was this fantastic violence that ironically created the hand that rocked the cradle of life. Four billion years ago, as Earth's lunar child circled in low orbit, the first oceans were churned by its wrenching tides. Four hundred million years later, the Earth and Moon would be bombarded by another wave of massive impacts as our fledgling solar system continued to work out the kinks in the clockwork we observe today."

He clicked to a scene of what looked like outer space scattered with clusters of colored spheres.

"During this inconceivably violent age, known as the Archean Eon, the first self-copying molecules coalesced in Earth's oceans. Such molecules are easily re-created in our laboratories using the same inorganic ingredients and forces that bombarded our planet's primordial seas. During the next billion years, the accumulation of replication errors in these molecules created RNA, which not only replicated itself but catalyzed chemical reactions like a primitive metabolism! RNA's replication errors led to the evolution of DNA—a molecule more stable than RNA that could copy itself more accurately and manufacture RNA."

Geoffrey clicked to a computer-generated image of a DNA molecule.

"From this self-copying molecular machine, the earliest life emerged as a simple organization of chemical reactions. The first crude bacteria harnessed methane, sulfur, copper, sunlight, and possibly even thermal energy venting in the dark depths of the ocean to fuel these metabolic processes."

The next slide showed a variety of simple forms that looked like primitive prokaryotic cells.

"The first crude organisms collided and sometimes consumed one another, blending their genetic material. A minute percentage of these blendings bestowed advantages on the resulting hybrids."

Geoffrey clicked through images of waves crashing on shores.

"If you combine extreme tides caused by the nearby Moon, which is still drifting about two inches farther away from the Earth each year, with the constant bombardment of ultraviolet radiation from the sun, then stir and cook the primordial soup for one and a half billion years, you get the most significant innovation in the story of life."

Geoffrey clicked the remote, and the next slide sent giggles through his audience.

"Yes, my friends, it looks like a sperm cell, but it's actually a tailed protozoan called *Euglena viridis*. It is an individual animal, a unique species, a single-celled organism remarkably similar to sperm. The primordial sea had produced the first creatures with the ability to *hunt*, using thrashing tails to chase down other single-celled organisms and consume them. Sometimes these first predators actually exploited the reproductive systems of their prey to facilitate their own reproduction—and sometimes their prey perpetuated itself by hijacking the genes of its attacker.

"In either case, the proposition of tonight's Chat is that these very first hunters and their prey created a new and mutually beneficial relationship that we call *sex*. When certain cells began to specialize in consuming or penetrating other cells for reproduction, others cells specialized in hosting reproduction itself, thus deflecting death and perpetuating both lines of DNA. *Sex is the peace treaty between predator and prey.* The offspring of their union not only combined the properties of both but carried forward each original single-celled organism, now modified as sperm and egg. So there you have the kindling for tonight's Fire-Breathing Chat, ladies and germs. I submit that sex began at the very beginning with single-celled organisms. I propose that the answer to the age-old question, which came first, the chicken or the egg, is the egg . . . and the sperm." Geoffrey stepped aside from the podium and bowed.

Shouts came from the back of the auditorium. Uncomfortable groans rose from the scientists in the front rows, especially from the gray hairs.

Geoffrey clicked to the next slide—a human egg wreathed by wriggling sperm—and he paused to enjoy the slightly nervous titter of recognition that the image always evoked from an audience.

"Egg and sperm may actually be the living echo

of a revolutionary moment that transpired a billion and a half years ago in the ancient seas of Earth. Indeed, I propose that this original love story has repeated itself in an unbroken chain since reproduction began in eukaryotic cells—that is, cells that have membrane-enclosed nuclei inside them. When the first hunter cells grew tails in order to chase down their prey, the hunted cells made peace, if you will, by absorbing the hunter's DNA and facilitating its reproduction, thus ensuring both cells' survival and turning a war into a partnership.

"And since the sharing of genetic material led to a convergent variation in the morphology of their offspring, this innovation accelerated the evolution of superior forms in tandem, continuing to ensure the survival of both kinds of original cell in male and female carriers. And the elaboration of multicellular life issuing from that ever-accelerating partnership would launch both of the original organisms into wildly diverse environments."

The grumblings grew louder in the audience. Geoffrey raised his voice mildly.

"I suggest that this proposition is validated each time sperm penetrates an egg and results in an offspring. All complex life may have developed simply to stage *this* age-old dance of two single-celled species. From octopi to humans to whales to ferns, countless expressions of life on Earth stage this original single-celled rendezvous, just as it occurred in ancient seas, in order to reproduce."

The audience muttered and shuffled as Geoffrey reached his peroration.

"So why are such complex animals beneficial for continuing the partnership of sperm and egg? Because, ladies and gentlemen, unlike sperm and egg, animals can exploit an amazing variety of changing conditions and environments through evolution. We sexually reproducing animals are an astonishingly diversified fleet of sperm-and-egg-carriers that bring the ancient seas with us into ever-new environmental frontiers.

"Of course, such elaborate vehicles were also beneficial to the replication of the original single-celled organisms because they have more fun replicating than single-celled organisms. There's nothing like improved incentives to increase output. But I think we'll leave that topic for another chat."

Geoffrey bowed once again, this time to an enthusiastic ovation, unfazed by the jeers and scowls from the front row.

Now the real fun began. He took the first torpedo from a particularly vexed colleague right in front of him. "Yes, Dr. Stoever?"

"Well, I don't know where to begin, Geoffrey," the baldheaded scientist drawled forlornly. "Sex began with isogamous gametes: two sex cells of the same size fusing together and joining their DNA, which then divided into more cells with a recombination of the two cells' genes. It did *not* begin with ancestors of sperm and egg! I've never heard of such a preposterous theory!"

"That is the general assumption," Geoffrey replied cheerfully. "But everyone concedes that very little is known about the details. I'm sure you're aware of Haeckel's theory, Dr. Stoever?"

"Ontogeny recapitulates phylogeny, of course— everyone is aware of Haeckel's theory, Geoffrey."

There was a smattering of laughter at this and Geoffrey raised his hand to the audience. "Well, just to remind everyone, for a long time scientists observed that during certain phases of development the human embryo looks remarkably like a tadpole, with a tail and gills, and continues to go through other stages that appear to be entirely different animals. What Haeckel proposed is that embryonic development is actually a recapitulation of an animal's evolutionary past."

"Haeckel's theory has been discredited," yelled one scientist from the back row.

"It only applies to the development of embryos, anyway," protested another. "Not to sperm and ova!"

"Ah." Geoffrey nodded. "Why not? Think outside the box, Dr. Mosashvili. And Haeckel is far from being discredited, Dr. Newsom. In fact, this proposition, if it proves correct, might well be his final vindication."

"You can't claim sperm and egg are merely

echoes of the first eukaryotic cells," shouted another irate scientist.

"Why not?" Geoffrey volleyed.

"Because sperm and egg are unlike any other organism. They carry only *half* the chromosomes!"

"Which they combine to produce the next stage of their development," Geoffrey returned, "which, I propose, may be the carrier stage, if you will— which naturally became more and more specialized to reach new environments. The fact that sperm and egg carry only half the chromosomes of their offspring could be a further effect of specialization to symbiotic reproduction, or it could be proof that sex began with separate organisms that combined and doubled the amount of their chromosomes to make sexually differentiated carriers of each original cell. I submit that Haeckel's principle is not only right, but may not have been taken far enough."

"But originating as a predator/prey relationship . . . I don't buy it." Dr. Stoever was scowling.

"Look at bees and flowers," Geoffrey replied. "When insects invaded the land, they devoured plant life. But plants adapted to the invasion. They turned insects into agents of their own reproduction by offering nectar in flowers and seeds in fruit. Examples abound of predator/prey relationships becoming symbiotic relationships, even reproductive relationships. Every one of us is a colony of cooperative organisms, millions of which inhabit our intestinal tract, graze on our epidermises, and devour bacteria scraped by our eyelids off our eyeballs between the columns of our eyelashes. All of these creatures had to have begun as predators but then adapted in cooperation with our bodies so as not to destroy their own homes, and in fact to help their hosts survive and flourish. Without the vast horde of creatures that inhabit us, we would *die*. We could not have evolved without them, nor they without us. Instead of a perpetual war, I believe this treaty of cooperation is the true theme of life, the very essence of a viable ecosystem. Instead of the stalemate of a war, which many believe the natural world reflects, perhaps evolution is always working toward stability, peace treaties, the mutual benefit of alliances. And its central building block is the treaty between the first single-celled predator and its prey: *sex.* That peace treaty had to be struck before the relentless violence of predator and prey inevitably selected both for extinction, which probably happened many times."

"The development of sex in eukaryotic cells is still a mystery," grunted another grizzled scientist. He shook his white-haired head emphatically.

"Maybe the answer to the mystery has been too obvious for us to see, Dr. Kuroshima," Geoffrey replied. "Maybe the explanation has been right under our noses all along, or, at least, under our kilts. Perhaps we've just been too shy to look?"

A wave of grumbles, hoots, and whistles greeted

this flourish, and the eighty-year-old Japanese scientist scoffed benignly, holding a hearing aid to his head with one hand and waving the other at Geoffrey, for whom he had great affection, despite and probably because of the younger man's tendency to stir things up.

One pretty student intern in the audience raised her hand.

"Yes?"

"Dr. Binswanger, can I ask a question on a different topic?"

"Of course. There are no rules except that there are no rules at Fire-Breathing Chats."

The audience seconded this with some enthusiastic applause.

"Your expertise lies in the geo-evolutionary study of island ecosystems," the young woman recited. She'd clearly memorized her program of summer speakers. "Did I get that right?" She laughed nervously, inspiring some sympathetic laughter in the feisty crowd.

"Well, I've touched on pattern analysis in nature, and in biological communication systems in particular," Geoffrey agreed, "but genetic drift and island formation is my current project here at Woods Hole, where I'm overseeing a study of insular endemic life on Madagascar and the Seychelles in a geo-evolutionary context. So, I guess you could say *yes!*"

There was a scattering of academic chuckles,

and Angel Echevarria rolled his eyes; the girl was quite good-looking and Geoffrey had totally blown it, again.

"So . . . Did you see *SeaLife*?" she asked.

This released a unanimous eruption of laughter.

"By the way, you've got great legs," she added.

Geoffrey nodded at the ensuing howls and gave a Rockette kick.

Geoffrey thought about Angel's video of the reality show. The blue blood had continued to bother him. The blurred images of the plants looked strange but not ridiculous—in fact, rather more subtle than he imagined a TV show could manage. But it wasn't enough for him.

He shook his head, stalemated. "Given what is known about isolation events and the duration of micro-ecologies—and given what they can do in Hollywood movies these days—I'm going to have to assume that island's a hoax, like Nessie and Bigfoot."

Boos and cheers divided the room.

"Sorry, folks!"

"But wouldn't you have to see it firsthand to be sure, Dr. Binswanger?" the attractive intern called.

Geoffrey smiled. "Sure. That's the only way I'd feel comfortable commenting on it definitively. But I don't think they'll be asking any experts to take a closer look. It's a perfect place to pull off a scam, if you think about it. It's about as remote a location as you could possibly find. It's not like anyone can just go there and check it out for themselves. That makes me suspicious, and since I'm already skeptical, the combination is deadly, I'm afraid. Yes, uh, you there, with the beard, in the back . . ."

Angel winced, closing his eyes sadly. Geoffrey had no idea that his own dismal ineptitude in pursuing sexual opportunities was the best evidence against his theory that sex cells created more complex animals to perpetuate themselves: if the end product was Geoffrey, Angel thought, total extinction was inevitable.

SEPTEMBER 3

2:30 P.M.

About 1,400 miles south-southeast of Pitcairn Island, the two-mile-wide speck of rock was too inconsequential to be marked on most globes, maps, and charts. That speck was now surrounded by the U.S.S. *Enterprise*, the U.S.S. *Gettysburg*, the U.S.S. *Philippine Sea*, two destroyers, three guided-missile destroyers, a guided-missile frigate, one logistics ship, two Sea Wolf anti-sub attack subs, two submarine tenders, and three replenishment vessels. The Enterprise Joint Task Group had been en route to the Sea of Japan when the President gave orders to blockade the tiny island. In the middle of the biggest expanse of nowhere on Earth, a floating city of over 13,000 men and women had suddenly materialized three days after the final broadcast of *SeaLife*.

Eight days had passed since the U.S. Navy had quarantined the area and a stream of helicopters started bringing back strange and secretive rumors from the island to the surrounding ships. All hands were forbidden any communication with the outside world, under order of a total media blackout, but the ships buzzed with rumors from those who had seen the original *SeaLife* broadcast.

The crew of the *Enterprise* now watched as the last section of StatLab, a modular lab developed by NASA for dropping into disease hot zones, was hoisted off the deck by an MH-53E Sea Dragon helicopter.

The thundering Sea Dragon's heavy rotors *thwapped* as it tilted at the island, dangling the white octagonal tube on a tether as it rose toward its seven-hundred-foot cliff.

To the men and women on the great carrier deck, the section of the mobile lab looked like a rocket stage or a space station module. They had no idea why the lab had been airlifted by NASA to three high-speed hydrofoil transports that traveled from San Diego to get here, or where it was now headed on the island, or why. All they knew was that a potential biohazard had been discovered there.

None of the thousands of men and women of the carrier group could imagine what must be on the other side of the cliffs to justify all of this, and some of them preferred not to know.

2:56 P.M.

Nell removed her Mets cap and absently smoothed back her hair as she leaned forward to look with fierce intensity through the observation bubble.

A broken ring of thick jungle wreathed the bottom of Henders Island's deep, bowl-shaped interior. This section of the experimental lab was designated Section One and had been placed on a scorched patch of earth near the jungle's edge.

A phalanx of saguaro cactus–like tree trunks rose thirty to forty feet at the edge of the jungle. Nell could see their wide green fronds bristling over-head through the northern hemisphere of the window.

She suspected these "trees" were no more plants than the first lavender spears she had touched on the beach thirteen days ago. Warily, she eyed their movements in the wind. Zero had warned her that in the crevasse he had seen trees moving. Actually, he'd sworn they were *attacking*.

When Nell learned NASA was to lead the inves-tigation of the island and that Wayne Cato, her old professor from Caltech, was in charge of the ground team, she had begged him to let her partic-ipate. Without hesitation, Dr. Cato had put her in charge of the on-site observation team aboard the mobile lab.

Hydraulic risers had leveled and aligned two new sections of the lab on the slope behind Section One. Extendable tubes of virus-impervious plastic connected the subway car–sized sections like train vestibules.

Florescent lights lined the quarter-inch-thick steel ceiling. Two-inch-thick polycarbonate win-dows spanned the upper side of the octagonal hull and reached halfway down its perpendicular sides. To prevent the outside atmosphere from leaking into the lab in the event of a breach, "positive" air pressure, slightly higher than the pressure outside, was maintained inside the lab.

The scientists gathered now before the large viewing bubble at the end of Section One. They were preparing to set out the first specimen trap at the edge of the jungle.

They all knew that Nell had been a member of the first landing party. All of them had seen the amazing final episode of *SeaLife* by now, if only on YouTube. They looked at her with some awe, and not a little skepticism. She had shown them her sketches of what she called a "spiger"—the creature that she claimed had chased her on the beach. But what she had seen on the island had not been photographed, which caused doubt. The scientists knew that eleven human beings were said to have been lost by something that had happened on this island, however, and they could see the evidence of that loss in this young woman's obsessive focus.

But apart from the extraordinary flora, they had yet to encounter anything remarkable in their two days setting up the lab. They certainly had not encountered anything dangerous. The few small creatures they had spotted emerging from Henders's jungle had moved too swiftly to be seen clearly or filmed with the limited equipment the half-dozen scientists and dozen technicians had been able to set up at the time.

Six scientists and three lab technicians now watched the lab's robotic arm lower the first specimen trap—a cylindrical chamber of clear acrylic about the size and shape of a hatbox.

"Dinner is served," Otto announced as he operated the arm and maneuvered the trap closer to the jungle's edge.

Otto Inman was a moon-faced, ponytailed NASA exobiologist the Navy had flown in from Kennedy. A turbo-nerd since elementary school, he'd found himself in geek heaven after scoring a job on a NASA research team fresh out of grad school. Although he had also been offered a job at Disney Imagineering in Orlando, it was not even a decision for him. After three years at NASA, Otto still could not imagine being blasé about going to work in the morning.

This, however, was the first time any urgency had been attached to the exobiologist's job. This would be the first field test for many of the toys he'd had a hand in designing, including the lab's Specimen Retrieval and Remote Operated Vehicle Deployment systems, and Otto was thrilled to see his theoretical systems given a trial by fire.

He maneuvered the robotic arm with a motion-capture glove, skillfully positioning the specimen trap on the scorched earth at the forest's edge. The trap was baited with one hot dog, courtesy of the U.S. Navy.

"A hot dog?" asked Andy Beasley.

"Hey, we had to improvise, all right?" Otto replied. "Besides, all life forms love hot dogs."

Nell had made sure to include Andy in the on-site crew. The marine biologist could not have been more delighted, but she worried that he didn't take the danger seriously enough. When she'd told the NASA staff and Andy about the lunging creature on the beach, they'd mostly responded with polite silence and skeptical looks, which only increased her determination to discover what was really happening on Henders Island.

Otto raised the door on the side of the trap. He disengaged the motion-capture to lock the arm in place.

They waited.

Nell barely breathed.

After three seconds, a disk-ant the size of a half-dollar rolled out between two trees. It proceeded slowly on a straight line directly toward the trap. About eighteen inches from the open door, it stopped.

"There's one of your critters, Nell," Otto whispered. "You were right!"

Suddenly, a dozen disk-ants rolled out of the forest behind the scout. As they rolled they tilted in different directions and launched themselves like Frisbees at the hot dog inside the trap.

"Jesus," Otto breathed.

"Close it!" Nell ordered.

When Otto hesitated for a moment, two reddish-brown animals the size of squirrels rocketed from the jungle into the box. They were followed by two flying bugs that zipped through the air and wriggled under the door before it closed and sealed.

"Great work, Otto." Nell patted his back.

"Looks like you bagged a couple island rats, too. Look!" Andy Beasley pointed out the window.

The cylindrical trap was thrashing on the end of the robotic arm.

"Yikes." Otto stopped retracting the arm as the trap shook violently. Its transparent walls were spattered and smeared with swirling blue gore.

"Oh dear," Andy said.

"Blue Slurpee. My favorite," Otto said.

When the trap finally stopped shaking it looked like a blueberry smoothie had been frappéd inside.

"OK, retrieve that and let's dissect whatever's left," Nell told them. "Then we'll set another trap. You better shut the door a little sooner next time, Otto."

"Yeah, guess so." The biologist nodded.

He maneuvered the trap into an airlock, where conveyor belts transported it through a second hatch into the specimen dock, which they had informally dubbed the "trough," an observation chamber that spanned the length of Section One.

This section of StatLab had been designed as an experimental Mars specimen collection station, but it doubled as a mobile medical lab that could be dropped into disease hot zones. The lab was part of a pilot program that focused NASA's unique expertise on Earth-bound applications. Additional funding earmarked for "Dual-Planet Technologies" had provided NASA with the resources that had made the program possible. But no one thought StatLab would ever be called into action, and NASA technicians now crawled nervously over every inch of the lab to ensure that it met all system requirements by at least a twofold safety margin. Nothing freaked out NASA technicians more than planning for unknown contingencies.

Six high-resolution screens hung over the long "trough." Under the top surface of the trough, six video cameras no bigger than breath mints slid along silver threads on X and Y axes, each covering a sixth of the long viewing chamber.

The robotic arm deposited the trap on the conveyor belt, and the airtight hatch closed behind it, sealing with a backwards *hiss*. The conveyer slid the trap to the center of the trough, where the six scientists had gathered.

"Let's hope this soup is chunky," murmured Quentin Brancato, another biologist flown in by NASA. He stuck his hands into two butyl rubber gloves that extended on accordioned Kevlar arms into the observation chamber. He opened the door of the trap manually.

"Careful," Nell warned.

"Don't worry," Quentin replied. "These gloves are pretty tough, Nell."

Several other scientists stood at the controls of a number of smaller traps. Each trap contained a different bait: a piece of hot dog, a spoonful of vegetable succotash, a potted Venus flytrap, a cup of sugar, a pile of salt, a bowl of freshwater, all supplied by the galley of the *Enterprise.* Except for the Venus flytrap, which was a pet Quentin had smuggled onto the flight over. As punishment for breaking the rules, he'd had to sacrifice "Audrey" to science.

Inspired by the idea, Nell had requested that dozens of plant species be shipped in. These included flats of crabgrass, potted pines, wheat, and cactus. All would be exposed to the island around the lab for observation.

Other scientists, spread out along the trough, controlled the cameras, aiming them in the direction of the specimen retrieval trap.

Quentin released the seal mechanism at the top of the cylinder. As he lifted the lid, two flying creatures that looked like whirligigs escaped the hatch.

The pair rose like helicopters, hovering without spinning inside the trough. Their five wings shook off a blue mist. Their abdomens curled beneath them like scorpion tails as they dove straight for the hot-dog-baited trap.

Their heads kept a lookout with a ring of eyes as their legs grabbed the meat and stuffed it into an abdominal maw. Their bodies immediately thickened.

After a stunned moment, the scientist controlling the hot-dog trap remembered to seal the two creatures inside.

"Got 'em!"

"Good work!" Nell breathed.

Quentin inverted the specimen retrieval capsule and dumped the contents onto the illuminated white floor of the trough. Several distinguishable bodies tumbled out in the blue slurry.

He drew a nozzle on a spring-loaded hose from the side of the trough and rinsed the mangled specimens with a jet of water. The blue blood and water sluiced into drains spaced two feet apart in the trough.

Three large disk-ants crawled out of the gore, leaving a trail of blue }}}}}}} behind them as they rolled. Then they flopped on their sides and crawled like pill-bugs, their upper arms flicking off droplets of blood, which spattered around them like ink from a fountain pen. They flipped over and did the same thing on the other side before tipping onto their edges and getting a rolling start, hurling themselves like discuses into the air, at the faces of the mesmerized scientists.

Some caromed off the sides of the trough, their legs retracting into white, diamond-hard tips that visibly gouged and nicked the acrylic. As they banged against the chamber walls they threw off dozens of smaller disk-ants. These rolled down the walls, trailing threads of light blue liquid.

The scientists controlling the cameras zoomed in to watch these juvenile ants wheel toward the baited traps. The rolling bugs hurled themselves onto the sugar and vegetables and even the Venus flytrap. This they devoured from the inside out as its traps triggered one after another.

"Bye, Audrey," Quentin muttered mournfully and Nell patted his shoulder, staring openmouthed beside him.

One large disk-ant rolled to the trap baited with a pile of salt. It turned on its side to feed, but then, before the trap could be sprung, it reared back abruptly on its edge and rolled away, and others in its vicinity scattered.

"Trap the juveniles by themselves, if you can," Nell instructed. "And we need to get tissue samples from the other specimens, Otto, so we can do bacterial cultures and HPLC and Mass Spec GC profiles. We need to dissect these things to see if they have any venom sacs we should know about."

Several scientists sprang their traps at her urging and isolated a few dozen specimens. Reaching their hands into the extendable gloves, they placed the sprung traps into airlocks spaced inside the trough. In the close-up view from the cameras above, they could see the tiny creatures leaping onto their gloves.

"They seem to attack anything that moves," Nell observed.

"Yeah, no matter how big it is," Andy said.

"Don't worry, there's no way they can get through butyl rubber," Quentin said.

"Ever seen *The Andromeda Strain*?"

"Or *Alien*?" Andy said.

"Come on, guys."

The scientists placed their traps in the airlocks, where the outside of the traps were sterilized with a chlorine dioxide bath. They opened the hatches and transferred the traps to individual observation chambers, where the live specimens inside could be released.

The other specimens from the original trap seemed dead, victims of a frenzied carnage. The original hot dog was nowhere to be found.

The two largest animals they had captured were about the size of tailless muskrats or squirrels. Both had eight legs. Though its side was ravaged by its rival, one specimen was clearly more complete. It had bitten off its rival's head and seemed to have died choking on it.

"What . . . is that?" stuttered Quentin.

"Jesus, I've never seen anything like that," one scientist whispered.

"God," Andy giggled.

"OK, let's settle down." Otto was clearly rattled himself. "I'll dissect. Quentin, you operate the camera."

"Gladly." Quentin quickly relinquished the glove box to Otto.

Otto reached in and cleared away the other

animal parts, which included a few half-bitten disk-ants; a half-eaten two-legged thing that looked like a grasshopper fused with a toad; a headless island "rat," as Andy had called it; and, surprisingly, a few chunks of a mouse-sized species.

Each partial specimen was passed down the trough to be rinsed and prepared for preservation. The strangeness of the body parts sent a chill down the assembly line of scientists.

"What are we looking at here?" one said.

"I don't fucking believe this," another muttered, uneasily.

"Let's take this one step at a time," Otto told them. "All right, people, we're about to conduct the first dissection of a Henders specimen."

Otto spread the largest intact animal out on its belly. He washed the blue gore from its velvetlike fur, which turned out to be coffee-ground brown with black and white stripes on its haunches. Strips of iridescent fur radiated over its softball-sized head. The head of the second rat made a bulge in its throat the size of a baseball.

As the last blue liquid was rinsed off, everyone gasped at the impossible specimen.

"OK, let's see what we're dealing with here." Otto's voice cracked. His hands were shaking.

"Steady now," Nell said.

Quentin moved the video camera across the top of the chamber until it was directly over the subject, and then zoomed in, providing an enlarged view on the plasma screens above the trough.

Otto placed his gloved left hand over the specimen's head and blocked throat.

Nell perched on one of the high stools next to Otto and opened her sketchpad. "Just take it easy now," she said calmly. She started to sketch a diagram. "The fur coloration on its haunches looks like an okapi."

"Yeah." Andy nodded, frowning at the captured specimen. "People thought okapis were a hoax when they were first discovered. They thought they were giraffes, zebras, and buffalo stitched together . . ."

"They'd never believe this freaking thing." Quentin gawped at the red-furred chimera.

"The stripes must confuse predators," Nell theorized.

"Come on, this thing *is* a predator," Otto said.

"I think it's probably both—predator and prey," she said. "The front looks fierce and the back says 'I better hide my ass with camouflage while I run the hell out of here.'"

"Hunters that are hunted?"

"That hunt each other," said Andy.

"Check out that tail."

"Are we sure it's dead?"

"Let's find out," Otto said. "Beginning narration of dissection at . . ." He consulted his watch. ". . . three twenty-two p.m. This is the first dissection of a Henders specimen. It is a fur-bearing, eight-legged animal, about thirty-five centimeters long, with okapi-like zebra stripes on its haunches, reddish-brown fur of the texture of really plush velvet or velour on its back, and bright stripes of fur around its face that change color at different angles."

He twisted its round head. They could see iridescent stripes radiating around its toothy mouth.

"Good God," Andy said. "It has crab claws on its *face!*"

"The specimen appears to have four front legs that may function more like arms," Otto continued. "The first pair is connected to its lower jaw and is furless. These seem to be chelate appendages with slender pincers that are white in color . . . very strange. They emerge from a wide lower jaw of an almost frog- or birdlike hinged mouth with long teeth that are packed close together and seem to be rather sharp. The teeth are extremely hard and dark gray. The mouth has dark blue lips drawn back that can apparently close over the teeth."

"What is that, a skullcap?" Nell's pencil flew as she sketched the outlines of the animal. "On top of its head?"

"The subject appears to have a light brown, furless cranial cap of some sort," Otto said.

"Jesus," Quentin said. "Either I'm dreaming or we are making history here, folks."

"You aren't dreaming," Nell told him.

The scientists clapped and whooped, finally releasing their anxiety and exhilaration.

Nell quickly penciled in the snaggle-toothed mouth in the creature's round head, her face frozen with grim concentration. This animal looked like a miniature version of the deadly lunging animals she had seen on the beach, except that its jaws were horizontal instead of vertical like the ones that came from the crevasse.

Henders Rat
Rodentocaris hendersi (*after* Echevarria et al,
*Proceedings of the Woods Hole
Scientific Meetings*, vol. 92:87–93)

"It looks like a deep-sea angler," Andy said.

"Like a cat crossed with a spider." Nell carved its outline deep into the sheet of paper with her pencil.

"Right, like the spigers you mentioned," Quentin said.

"Right." Nell nodded.

"The specimen has a pair of large green-red-and-blue eyes with three optical hemispheres," Otto narrated, and he tested the flexibility of the creature's eyes with a poking index finger. "The eyes are mounted on short stalks that pivot or swivel inside a socket in its head. They also toggle in a socket at the end of the stalks, apparently, having a very ingenious mechanism."

"I sure hope that thing's dead," Andy said.

Otto ignored him and wiggled the forelegs behind the head to see how they bent. "The large legs behind the head are very muscular and have spines at the end. They are fur-bearing, but the heavy spikelike spines are hairless, hard black exoskeleton or horn, and they seem to have a very sharp edge."

"They look like praying mantis arms."

"Yeah, that's how they fold," Otto agreed. "They may be able to act as shears or vises, too."

"Or spears," Nell suggested, shivering as she thought of what the others must have faced inside the crevasse. "The spigers speared the sand in front of them to back away from the water."

Otto continued. "These mantislike subchelate arms are articulated to a bony ring under the skin, from which the neck musculature also extends. The next pair of limbs appears to be true legs. They resemble a quadruped's forelegs . . . with one extra joint . . . and they seem to be attached to a broad central ring of bone that can be felt under the dermis and which forms a medial hump on the dorsal surface of the animal."

"Those are eyes!" Nell exclaimed.

"Huh? Where?" Andy said.

"See, on top of that hump on its back, Otto?"

"Oh," Andy said.

"There are eyes on the medial hump," Otto confirmed, rinsing off more blue blood. "Which are similar to the eyes on the head."

"Do you think it has a second set of optic lobes in its back?" Nell asked. "I mean, look, they're image-forming eyes, not just light-intensity receptors."

"Either there's a brain under there or they have ridiculously long optic nerves," Andy continued.

Otto continued his description. "There are three eyes on the central hump, reminiscent of the eyes on a jumping spider. One eye looks directly behind and one to each side. They each toggle inside a socket. I think you're right, Nell. There could be some kind of ganglion structure under this hump. There's a cranial cap on top of it similar to the one on the head of the animal." As Andy winced, Otto tapped the brown chitinous cap on the hump between the eyes, testing to see if there was any reflex action left in the animal. There wasn't.

Otto picked up a pair of dissection scissors and cut carefully along the mid-line of the cranial cap. He pulled each half apart with forceps. "Yep, it's got a second brain." He looked up at Nell. "This isn't just some enlarged ganglion."

"It's got eyes in the back of its head," Quentin said.

"And a head in the back of its eyes," added Andy.

"See that pair of nerve cords running forward to the head?" Nell pointed at the close-up on the drop-down screen.

"Yeah, and here's another pair that run toward the posterior of the animal. See there?" Quentin pointed. Two white twines of fine string stretched from the brain to the posterior of the animal like jumper cables.

"It may control the locomotion of its hind legs remotely with the second brain," Nell theorized.

"I've never heard of such a thing," Otto disagreed. "Not fucking possible!"

"Maybe it has specialized ganglia for speeding up its attack or evasive reflexes, or to help with digestion like some arthropods do," Andy offered.

"Well, we won't be able to determine that from a dissection." Otto frowned. "We would have to do a detailed neurological study of live specimens. But we'll see if we can follow the nerves later. Moving toward the posterior of the animal we see very powerful, kangaroo-like hind legs, with an extra joint where the tibia would be. These limbs are connected to a wide subcutaneous pelvic girdle that is ring- or tube-shaped like the other rings. The tail—"

"I don't think that's a tail," Quentin said.

"It's a leg," Nell said.

Otto scowled.

"Pull it out from under the body," Nell suggested.

"OK. The tail has a wide base. It is very stiff. It is long and broad, folding more than halfway under the animal to the chest area between the forelegs. The dorsal surface of the tail, which is the bottom when under the animal, is covered with ridged plates and spines in a geometric pattern."

"Traction pads." Nell indicated the bottom of the "tail." "And cleats—like the bottom of a running shoe!"

"Whoa," Quentin exclaimed. "It must rip that tail backwards under it to get air!"

"The taillike appendage appears to be a sort of ninth leg." Otto shook his head in amazement. "This leg might be used to propel the animal higher or faster during leaps."

"It kind of seems like an arthropod that turned into a mammal. Doesn't it?"

"Yeah," Andy said. "I was just thinking that. Spiders are furry crabs, or at least chelicerates."

"This is no arthropod," Otto scoffed. "With a mouth and jaws like that? And this is fur, not tarantula hair!"

"It's bleeding again." Nell pointed.

"The subject is leaking some light blue fluid that may be blood."

"They must have hemocyanin. Copper-based blood, like marine arthropods. See? You can see it turning bluer as the liquid hits the air."

"I'm extracting a blood specimen for analysis." Otto took a hypodermic needle from a dissection kit affixed to the inside wall of the trough.

"Copper-based blood?" Nell looked at Andy.

"Maybe hemoglobin, too," he said. "Some iron-based blood pigments are purple."

"That's *blue*," Quentin said. "Are you color-blind?"

"No, I'm not color-blind!" Andy glared at Quentin.

"Could have fooled me." Quentin was looking at Andy's pink, yellow, and blue Hawaiian shirt.

Nell patted Quentin on the shoulder. "Let's get a look inside this thing."

"I'm now sealing the blood sample," Otto narrated.

"Cut a little tissue sample, too, Otto," Quentin told him. "That'll make it easier to get a nucleic acid sample in case the blood doesn't have any circulating cells."

"Yeah, yeah." Otto expelled the hypo full of blue liquid into a tube and capped it. Then he placed the sample into the specimen cradle, along with a small slice of tissue that he placed in a quarter-sized petri dish. After covering the petri dish, he pushed the cradle into the airlock. "OK, Quentin, let's get a genetic analysis on this thing."

Quentin sprayed the outside of the containers with isopropyl alcohol and then flooded the mini-airlock with yellow-green chlorine dioxide gas. When the gas was vacuumed out he retrieved the specimens through the airlock and handed them to the lab technicians, who immediately prepared blood agar cultures. One started grinding tissue samples in what resembled a test tube–sized blender. Attached to a high-speed tissue homogenizer, this glass chamber prevented the dispersal of any potentially harmful aerosol from the specimen into the air of the lab.

"We could be getting parasite DNA in the sample," Nell told them. "Can you tell the difference?"

"Yep, we can distinguish samples," one of the technicians answered.

Working in biological safety hoods along the other side of Section One, the technicians processed the samples, pipetting the blood and tissue and homogenizing them, adding reagents, mixing, centrifuging, decanting, heating, cooling, and finally pipetting the processed material onto other plates or into specimen tubes.

"My God, this is heaven, Otto," Nell said, admiring the array of machines on the other side of the lab. "Do you know how many weeks it would have taken me to do this work as an undergrad at Caltech?"

"Yeah, this baby's got more toys than a lab geek's wet dream." Quentin smiled proudly.

"I can still remember when I had to pour my own electrophoretic gels for molecular samples. Now it's as easy as putting a piece of bread in a toaster."

"Well, more like making cinnamon toast," a technician remarked drily.

Nell laughed. "We even had to generate our own taq polymerase."

"Give me a break," Andy pleaded.

"I'm with you, Nell," Quentin said. "You youngsters don't appreciate how amazing these instruments are. God, Andy, when are you going to learn some molecular biology, dude? You're more of a dinosaur than I am. PCR didn't even exist when I was in college, but I saw where things were heading, and learned this stuff before I got left behind."

"Well, *somebody* has to keep their feet in the *mud,*" Andy snapped, defensively.

"Bravo," Nell said. "We need both right now, Andy—field naturalists and gene jocks. That machine Steve is using—hi, Steve!—is a Bioanalyzer. It will tell us in a few seconds how pure our RNA extractions are and how much RNA we got in each sample. It's a microscopic electrophoresis unit and gel scanner that examines all the samples on those little chips that look like dominoes. Each one of those dots is equivalent to a whole electrophoretic gel from the old days, when I was in my teens." She pointed. "And when an RNA sample is put into the thermocycler right there, it gets reverse transcribed, making our cDNA library, and in the same tube it does the PCR. That amplifies the cDNA into thousands of copies so we can sequence the genes in this autosequencer right there, or test it in that micro-array machine over there."

"You lost me at Parcheesi," Andy grumbled.

"Dominoes," Quentin teased.

"It's actually pretty simple, Andy," Nell told him. Her eyes glowed with excitement. "All living cells have RNA, which is a message transcribed from the genes in the DNA. So when we run the reactions backwards with an enzyme called reverse transcriptase, we make clones of the DNA—the cDNA—from the RNA! Then, to tell what these critters are related to, we can either run the cDNA on micro-array chips, which is really fast, sequence the DNA, or else isolate, clone, and sequence the actual genes from the cell's DNA, which takes a little longer. You could do any of this yourself after a couple hours of training, Andy."

"I learned the theory in my Bio courses," he said. "I never used all these machines. I didn't think normal people could work these things."

"Who said you're normal?" Quentin taunted.

"Andy," Nell said, preempting his umbrage, "these guys in the lab coats wouldn't know an arthropod from an anthropoid unless you handed them a gene sequence. No offense, guys."

Otto cleared his throat. "Can we get back to the dissection while the gene jocks do their thing?"

"Carve that turkey!" Quentin commanded in agreement.

Nell swiveled on her stool and put her pencil to a fresh page on her sketchpad as Otto turned the animal onto its back and rinsed it again.

"The fur on the ventral surface of the specimen is light tan in color. The specimen appears to have an orifice on the central underbelly, probably for waste excretion, between the central legs. Between the hind legs there appear to be sexual organs . . . both a penislike structure and what may be a vaginal opening."

"Hermaphrodites?" Nell said.

"If so, there goes the arthropod theory," Otto said. "No arthropods are hermaphroditic—"

"Right," Quentin interrupted. "But many phyla of animals have at least a few groups that are hermaphrodites. Worms and snails, for example."

"Barnacles are hermaphrodites," Andy said. "They're arthropods."

"Barnacles are arthropods?" Otto asked.

"Yep."

"Damn. That's weird."

"How do we know how long this ecosystem's been isolated?" Nell intervened. "It's at least theoretically possible that it's had a very long time to evolve. I would say it's probable, given what we are looking at, guys. I mean, come on."

"Is this island radioactive?" Andy asked.

"Nope." Quentin shook his head. "These aren't just mutants."

"Something like this must have diverged a long time ago, then," Otto agreed. "Hell, that's a given. But not from arthropods."

"Well, how the hell else do you explain it, then, Otto?" Quentin was scowling again. "You think this thing came from Mars?"

"I don't know where this thing came from, Quentin!" Otto retorted sharply. "And neither do *you* right now, OK?"

"Let's take a look at the internal organs," Nell interposed gently.

"OK." Otto looked back up at the screen and lowered his shaking scalpel. "I'm starting the incision from the central orifice and cutting back toward the specimen's tail."

"God, I hope it's dead," Andy said.

"Stop saying that!" Otto snapped as he sliced through the thin but tough skin and laid open the animal's belly.

"Hey!" someone shouted.

Everyone jumped and glared at the technician, who was pointing to the bubble window at the end of the lab.

But all they could see was the edge of the forest.

"Sorry! I could swear I just saw something looking at us out there. Big as a man, hanging right on that tree there. Fuck, it must have been a reflection or something. It had lots of arms and it looked like it was spying on us. Sorry. But I *swear!* It was there. Really."

"Christ, Todd!" Quentin groaned. "Lay off the caffeine, OK?"

"I said I was sorry! But, Jesus, I saw it plain as day and never took my eyes off it and then it was just *gone,* man."

Otto sighed and turned back to his work. "OK. Continuing the incision, there is an outer sheath or integument that is translucent grayish white, tinged blue. Making an incision through this sheath . . . it seems to be made of micro-hydrostatic tubes that release clear liquid when severed. Under this are distinct muscle bands running to various points throughout the body . . . they are especially dense at the bases of the appendages. And look at this here . . . we've got branching tracheal tubes extending into all the muscles." He cleared his throat. "And each of them does connect with the integument."

"It's just like the gas exchange system of insects and spiders," Andy intoned.

Otto nodded. "And, yes . . . there is a spiracle on the outer body surface for each trachea. The fur must have covered them."

"Wow, so those trachea deliver the oxygen directly to the muscles from the outside," Andy said. "If they're that extensive it may be what allows such big animals to be so active."

"Look how the spiracles line the sides of the body in neat rows." Quentin pointed at the close-up on the screen over the specimen chamber. "And those rows extend right up along the legs . . ."

"Providing oxygen directly to the muscles." Andy finished his sentence.

Otto cleared his throat again. "And, OK—immediately underneath the layers of muscles and tracheae are two green glands, each with a bladder that is light gray in color—"

"Looks like it has a urethra," Andy said, thankful to see something familiar.

"Yes. These glands appear to empty at the joint at the base of the legs." Otto attached retractors to hold open the incision. He suctioned some pooling, syrupy blood.

"Coxal glands, just like king crabs," Andy sang.

"Spiders have coxal glands, too," Quentin chimed.

"OK," Otto said, irritated. "I'm now cutting anteriad from the central orifice. I'm exposing the rest of a wide, thin bone ring or cylinder that has an aperture in the ventral side. The spiked foreleglike appendages are attached to socketlike shoulders in each side of this bony structure."

"Looks like a segment of a lobster tail."

"But internal?" Otto scoffed. "An *internal* exoskeleton? It doesn't make sense . . ."

"Does anything here make sense?" Nell said.

"We're segmented creatures, too, Otto, just a few steps removed from arthropods. Do *we* make sense?"

"It's a lot of steps." Otto shook his head stubbornly. "How could it molt?"

"Maybe the old shell dissolves or is absorbed internally as the new one hardens," Nell suggested. "Surgeons use dissolving sutures that melt internally. Maybe they have a similar solution."

"A lot of marine crustaceans eat their own shed shells to reuse the minerals," Andy concurred.

"All right, noted," Otto said. But he still didn't sound as if he agreed with them. "Continuing the incision down the belly from the mantislike arms and the forelegs. OK, there's a lot of fluid here! Suctioning that away . . . we see a series of six branching stomachs filled with what appear to be freshly eaten pieces of prey. Each stomach is segmented by a kind of bony grinding mechanism, like a bird's gizzard—"

"Or a crustacean's gastric mill," Andy said.

"—which must masticate the food into finer consistency as it is passed along. Each of these stomachs is connected to a glandular mass—"

"That looks like a crustacean hepatopancreas," said Andy.

"—and each also is connected to its own short intestine," finished Otto.

"If any one of its digestive tracts is damaged it could shut it down and use the other five." Nell had stopped sketching and was staring in fascination at the creature.

"Yeah, it would seem so." Otto nodded, skeptically.

"All of the intestines empty into what appears to be a cloaca," Quentin murmured.

"Crustaceans don't have cloacae," Otto said.

"Yeah," Andy agreed. "Technically."

"And look, the urethra from each kidney empties into the cloaca, too. And what's that mass that looks like angel hair pasta there?" Quentin said.

"It looks like Malpighian tubules like insects and spiders have. Look how they all connect to the same region of the cloaca," said Andy.

"That's impossible, crustaceans don't have Malpighian tubules," said Quentin.

"Exactly," Otto said.

"Both of you have to start thinking outside your comfort zone," Nell said as she filled in a sketch. "These creatures would have had to have diverged from other crustaceans hundreds of millions of years ago, remember."

Otto shook his head and continued. "OK, the cloaca appears to extend through a hole in the bony ring and discharge waste through the anus in the middle of the ventral side of the body. Upon cutting open the cloaca, it appears to contain solid white waste, which we will collect momentarily for analysis."

"It must crap in mid-leap when the tail is

extended back, or else things would get pretty messy." Andy grinned.

"Maybe it uses the muscular contraction of leaping to expel the waste," Quentin said. "Projectile crap."

"Looks like uric acid crystals." Otto probed the material with his scalpel. "Bird poop."

"You mean bird pee," Quentin said.

"Yuck," Andy said.

"Hey, guys! We got our first RNA results," one of the technicians called out.

All turned to the technician. He pointed to a series of peaks in what looked like an EKG readout on a monitor over the molecular toasters.

"Oh shit," Steve muttered as he scanned the graph. "Uh, sorry, folks. Looks like we'll have to run it again. False alarm."

"Why?" Otto asked.

"These results don't make any sense."

"There must be some sort of contamination in the system," the lead technician confirmed.

"Why don't they make sense?" Nell wanted to know.

Steve shrugged apologetically. "Because it's showing three ribosomal RNA peaks."

"What makes you think it's contaminated?" Andy asked the technician.

"Nothing on Earth has three ribosomal peaks, my friend."

"Except for crustaceans," Andy said.

"Whoa—really?"

Andy rolled his eyes. He looked at Nell. "I guess you gene jocks do need a few folks who still know their animals."

"I'll be damned. I didn't know that." Steve looked back at the graph. "Guess we're reading crustaceans, then, guys."

"Bravo, Andy." Nell winked at Andy, and he smiled.

"Looks like we're back to arthropods, Otto," Quentin said.

Otto shook his head, resigned now. "Unless it *is* from Mars."

Quentin shrugged. "Hell, maybe *crustaceans* are from Mars, with three ribosomal peaks and all."

Andy said, "Cut the other direction again, Otto."

"All right. Continuing the incision down the abdomen from the original point of entry now— what seems like more lobes of the hepatopancreas, with multiple blind-ending tubules—"

"Wow, this thing is set up to digest massive amounts of food *very* rapidly," Quentin said.

"This sure looks like a crustacean gut."

"Yes, Andy," Otto said, "*it does.* Continuing toward the hindquarters. Uh—OK . . ."

There was a spasm in the animal's lower belly as Otto drew the scalpel near the rear pelvic ring.

"Back out, Otto," Nell whispered.

Small legs tore at the edges of Otto's incision.

"Something it ate didn't agree with it," Quentin said.

"No," Nell breathed. "It's a mommy!"

"Yeah, and she's live-bearing," Andy warned.

"Back out now," Nell said again, her voice suddenly urgent.

Otto pulled his hands back as a mouse-sized miniature crawled out and snipped a chunk of its mother's flesh with its foreclaws. It fed the bite into its serrated grin. Then it shook its head and shivered off blue blood.

"Don't reach for it, Otto," Nell warned in a whisper. "Just pull out of the gloves."

Another baby thrashed its way out of the womb, crawling out of Otto's incision.

"Those things are fully active," Quentin said.

"Yeah, and we just gave them a cesarean birth!"

"They're protecting the corpse, Otto," Nell said.

"Don't stick your hand too close," Quentin said.

"Pull out, Otto!" Nell said again.

"I'm just trying to scare them so we can see how they move—"

"Back off, man," Andy said.

Otto laughed in excitement. "They're using their back four legs to locomote and raising their arms like a praying mantis! See?"

"They're fast," Quentin said.

Otto grinned at Quentin. "Ever hear of a live-bearing arthropod, Quentin?"

"Actually, some do have marsupial pouches in

which they brood their young," Andy said.

"They won't scare off—they're just getting more aggressive," Nell said. "Pull out!"

"There." Otto pointed as one of the juveniles reared back on its under-curled tail.

A gunshot sound made them all jump back as the juvenile struck Otto's hand in a blur.

"Jesus God damn it!" Otto screamed.

He yanked his hands out of the gloves.

"My God-damned-motherfucking thumb!"

"Close the glove hatches, Quentin." Nell moved fast as the others froze.

"That little shit split my fucking *thumb!* Fuck, fuck, fuck, fuck, *fuuuuck!*"

"OK, narration ended," Andy said.

Quentin gaped at Otto's hand in shock, so Nell reached forward and sealed the glove hatches, banging the button with the side of her fist.

"They're eating their mom," Andy muttered, leaning forward over the trough.

"Quentin!" Nell snapped, giving him a hard shake of the shoulder. "Radio Section Three! Call the *Enterprise.* Tell them we have a medical emergency and need a transport immediately! We won't be able to tell from the blood agar cultures if these things carry hemolytic bacteria for another six hours, at least. So ask them if they have gentamicin, vancomycin, and ceftriaxone. I think we need to treat this as if it were MRSA, until we know for sure what bacteria are in these creatures. *GO!*"

"Oh my God!" Andy shouted at the sight of Otto's thumb—it looked like it had been clipped down the middle by a pair of bolt cutters.

"Andy, give me your tie," Nell said.

"What?"

Nell flipped up Andy's collar, removed his leather tie with her left hand, and looped it over Otto's hand. She slid it up his arm and cinched it tight above his elbow. "Quentin, what did they say?"

"They're sending some guys down here and calling *Enterprise* for a transport!"

"Good work. OK, Otto, let's sit down, honey."

Otto's eyes glazed over. He slumped on a bench, muttering a string of obscenities. Bright red blood pooled on the white floor between his splattered sneakers.

"Andy, get some towels," Nell said. "And the first aid kit. Quentin, sterilize the trough."

Quentin balked. "Why should we sterilize the trough?"

Nell swung around and yelled at him, "DO IT!"

"All right, all right." He pushed a button.

The chamber flooded with a yellow-green cloud of gas.

4:35 P.M.

As the *Trident* bobbed at anchor in the cove, surrounded by the echoing sounds of waves from the

148

sheer rock walls, Cynthea paced the aft deck like a caged animal.

She could not take being this close to the story of the century without being able to document it. If she didn't do something about it soon, she would go mad.

The others weren't exactly overjoyed about being quarantined, or imprisoned, on the *Trident*, either.

The Navy was kind enough to bring them supplies, including current magazines and DVDs, but they were strictly prohibited from going ashore.

Approximately two hours after the last episode of *SeaLife* had aired, the U.S. government had officially ordered them not to move from, land on, or transmit any communication from Henders Island.

Her show was officially and irrevocably canceled. Cynthea seethed at their assumption of authority, which out here had no basis other than the big guns they used to back it up. She had to hand it to the Navy, though. They had certainly outdone any network executive in the power-play department.

Zero stretched out on a deck lounge, soaking up some rays on his long, lean runner's body, his eyelids closed.

Cynthea stalked around him as she spoke, wondering occasionally if he was even listening to her.

"You have GOT to get on that island, Zero! An

hour of footage is worth more than enough to retire on for both of us. Are you listening to me, asshole?"

Zero popped an eye open at her. "Yup."

"Well?"

"No way am I going back there," Zero said. He closed his eye.

"I can get on that island." Dante, the ship's assistant cook, had been loitering on the outskirts of their conversation.

Born in Palo Alto, California, Dante had learned to climb in the High Sierras, conquering El Capitan solo at the age of nineteen. On one team climb, when he was sixteen, he had been struck twice by lightning while sleeping suspended 1,200 feet up between a cliff and the granite pinnacle of Lost Arrow in a rainstorm. The wet lines he was suspended on had partially grounded the lightning strike, but he had still spent three weeks in a hospital bed before he could walk again.

Dante pointed at the crevasse. "I could climb right up that crack, where no one could ever see me."

Zero opened and closed one eye. "You don't know what you're talking about, kid."

"I saw the footage! What attacked you came from *below,* on the ground. I could climb right up the cliff inside that crack, all the way to the top."

Zero sat up. "That's an eight-hundred-foot ascent. Are you nuts, kid?"

"What do you say?" Dante said to Cynthea. "Want me to do it?"

Zero glared at the producer and the light flickered and went out in her eyes. "No. No, that sounds too dangerous." She gritted her teeth and glared back at Zero. "But there must be some way. Zero, come on, baby! If you figure out a safer way, I guarantee I'll make you the happiest man on Earth. The deal I could make for us . . ."

Zero leaned back and closed his eyes again. "I'm listening."

"I can take a camera with me," Dante said.

Cynthea turned toward him, grinning. "That's—"

"Cynthea," Zero growled.

"—too darn dangerous, Dante. Thanks for offering, though, sweetheart! You're my hero today!"

Cynthea turned to stare longingly at the giant cracked wall of the island surrounding them in the cove. "God damn it! What am I going to do?" She glanced at Zero, who was apparently sleeping again. "Shit! And Nell wouldn't even take my camcorder with her, that freaking little scientist snob!"

Zero chuckled.

"So what's it going to take, Zero? Come on! Get me some footage of this island!"

"I'm still listening." Zero flopped over to lie on his stomach as Dante stalked off, steaming.

Cynthea glared again at the crack in the island.

For millions of years, the battered wall of Henders Island had defeated tsunamis, ice floes, and all passersby. Defeating her would not be so easy.

8:33 P.M.

A chopper carried Otto to the *Enterprise*, where medics set, stitched, and splinted his thumb. He was heavily sedated, dosed with antibiotics and anti-viral drugs, and put under twenty-four-hour observation in a quarantined sick bay, much to his despair.

The first specimens and tissue samples from Henders Island had arrived with him, carefully packed and sent along on the same Sea Dragon helicopter. They were then taken to the *Philippine Sea* for CAT scans, X-rays, biochemical profiles, and gene sequencing. From these results, the ship-based science teams could start making—or attempting to make—physiological and taxonomic identifications of the island's species.

Since no live specimens were to be allowed off the island, Nell supervised the preservation of dead specimens and the isolation and study of live ones as teams worked throughout the first day and night. Keeping everyone moving without becoming careless turned out to be a doubly exhausting duty, but now that the investigation had finally begun, Nell drove herself well past twenty hours without sleep.

Night was falling when she took her first breather. She broke away to look through the long window at the darkening slopes outside the lab.

As her mind drifted, the hillside seemed to writhe and glisten in the moonlight.

She rubbed her tired eyes and looked closer.

Tendrils arched up out of the ground in radial clusters, like ferns. The ends of the tendrils fanned out into pads, visibly growing and stretching. Wisps of steam rose wherever the frondlike branches pressed down on the field.

"It's like they're grazing."

Nell jumped, startled, and turned to see Andy at her shoulder.

"Sorry," he told her. "Quentin thinks those things eat the stuff that grows on the slopes."

"Only at night? And the bugs graze the fields by day . . ." Nell smiled and rubbed her forehead, marveling at the depth of the mysteries on this island.

"It changes color at night, Nell. Quentin shined a flashlight on it and it's purple now! After a few minutes under the light it started to turn yellow and then green again."

"It must be some kind of lichen." She shook her head. "We've got a lot to learn."

"Check this out!" The technician boosted the feed from the outboard microphones, which had finally been hooked up to the inboard speaker system.

Wails arched like a quintet of alto-saxophones over the jungle's hum, echoing over the giant amphitheater of the island. The eerie sounds were remarkably like whale calls punctuated with rhythmic inflections and trilling scales of vowels as they reverberated and intertwined.

Andy whistled in amazement and laughed. "Thanks for letting me come along, Nell!"

"No thanks required, Andy. We need you."

Andy beamed. "I don't think anyone's said that to me, like, *ever,* other than my aunt."

Impulsively, Nell kissed his cheek, causing him to blush in surprise. "You're harder on yourself than anyone, Andrew Beasley. You shouldn't be."

"I wish you were my girlfriend, Nell," Andy blurted.

Now it was Nell who was blushing. "Thanks, sweetie." She tousled his hair. "But I'm nobody's girlfriend." She looked at him with a grateful but decisive nod. "I don't know if I'll ever be. Formally pairing off is such a strange tradition anyway. I don't really understand it, to tell the truth."

"You deserve a great guy, Nell. Though I'm not sure he deserves you."

She laughed.

"Hey, man! You wouldn't believe these things!" Quentin shouted from the other end of the lab. He was pointing to a trap full of flying insects. "They glow in the dark!"

"Look outside!" someone yelled.

As night deepened, swarms of green sparks had appeared in the profound darkness. Swirling along the edge of the jungle, they linked together in spiraling chains that resembled nucleotides twisting over the fields.

"Maybe they're mating," Quentin said. "Copulating in flight like dragonflies."

"They look like those strings of Christmas lights at Tavern on the Green."

"Macro-DNA," Nell whispered.

She sighed, laughing. She had been up for twenty-six hours troubleshooting the lab's first day of operations, and she hadn't slept much for a week. "I'm going to catch a few hours in Section Two."

"I think you better," Andy told her. "But they said it's not quite powered up yet."

"Right—but it's quiet." She nodded wearily, moving toward the hatch. Her whole body suddenly felt heavy with fatigue.

"They said the ROVs will be working tomorrow. Then we can finally get a look inside that jungle."

"Yep. That'll make Otto happy, when he gets back," she said over her shoulder. "Make sure the latest specimens, data zips, and dissection logs are packed and ready for transport to *Enterprise* for the morning pickup. That's at five. I'm planning to be unconscious. Please walk past me quietly, OK?"

"Right." Andy nodded. "Good night, Nell."

"Right." She saluted him, and opened the sealed hatch to the vestibule that led to Section Two. She entered and swung the hatch behind her, hearing the reassuring suction of the seal.

She yawned as she walked up the flight of aluminum stairs inside the plastic tube between sections. The green LEDs of microbe sensors glittered like a field of emerald stars on the wall of the tube. *No breach,* Nell thought.

She unsealed the far hatch and stepped into the deserted Section Two.

For the past three days the scientists had occasionally grabbed a nook in this section to catch some sleep as NASA technicians set up the rest of the lab.

She had heard there were bunk beds in the newly arrived Section Three, but it was swarming with technicians now. They were no doubt busy getting the electrical and computer systems up and running.

The air in Section Two smelled of new plastic, packing materials, and the ozone of electronics. Junk littered the floor: coils of cable and hastily opened boxes, torn plastic bags, broken Styrofoam molds, cable twists, box openers, and other detritus awaiting disposal. Right now any flat surface beckoned, so she climbed atop one of the long specimen chambers, similar to the trough in Section One, which was the only surface free of lab junk.

Lying on her back, using a plastic bag stuffed with packing peanuts for a pillow and a big plastic bag for a sleeping bag, Nell gazed at the starry sky through the window curving overhead. A few fire-flylike bugs streaked by like meteors. For a fleeting moment she thought she saw a face looking down at her with multi-colored eyes before sleep carried her away insistently.

SEPTEMBER 4

Midnight

Thatcher Redmond found the button on his armrest and *pinged* the stewardess.

He smiled craggily when the young Asian woman appeared. "May I have a few bags of peanuts? Not the warm nuts, but the *bags?*" he asked her.

"Surely. Let me get some for you, sir."

Although she was pretty, Thatcher turned away in irritation. This whole last-minute trip to Phoenix had filled him with a grating sense of panic. And now, with his mission accomplished, just when he thought he could finally put it all behind him, they had been sitting on the tarmac for six unbearable hours as some Keystone Kops series of fuckups kept them stranded at the airport. He didn't like the idea of being recognized. And guessing at the reason for the delay was toying with his sanity.

His hair flowed down in distinctive muttonchops that curved up to join a thick mustache. This red W of facial hair was Thatcher Redmond's tonsorial signature. As a celebrity professor and a public intellectual, his image was his autograph, as his agent often repeated. As a result, he could not change his look any more than he could change his name. Sometimes, lately, he had caught himself feeling a twinge of envy for his peers, who still possessed all the little freedoms of their anonymity, such as shaving their facial hair. Sometimes, but not very often . . .

At least he had been able to upgrade to business class on the return flight. On the flight to Phoenix earlier this afternoon, he'd been wedged between two large identical twins, who snored. They had bought window and aisle seats intentionally. Before they had fallen asleep the twins had told him they were embarking on a southwestern vacation that was to culminate in Las Vegas, Nevada, and it had irritated him to know that.

Thatcher was an accomplished gambler. Despite the fact that he was currently $327,000 in debt, the result of an improbable series of setbacks, he was convinced that he had a mathematical aptitude that verged on genius. Thatcher could almost see probabilities like a slot-machine display in his mind.

Whether or not this intuition was right more than fifty percent of the time, it had paid off enough times to seem like it was, and it had brought just enough windfalls to make betting on his intuition a secret way of life. Only recently had it become a full-blown crisis, just when his divorce from his third wife was reaching the *ugly stage.*

And in the middle of all of that, out of the blue, his teaching assistant from three years earlier had threatened him with a paternity suit. The harpy was actually claiming to have had his son, who was apparently now two-and-a-half years old, and she wanted to discuss marriage or a "suitable settlement" with him to provide for their love-child.

It was not a threat so much as blackmail, served warm and lovingly. In her phone call to him, Sedona had explained that she had seen him on television since his book's astonishing rise to best-sellerdom and his subsequent ascension as the media's favorite intellectual. In a single breath, she had complimented him on his success and attached his financial obligation to her progeny like a tick on his back.

For years, Thatcher had managed to keep his gambling strictly private and separate from his career as a professor of zoology at the Massachusetts Institute of Technology. He had gone for broke on his latest gamble, however, and had shattered all his own rules. It was a professional wager that was quite public, unlike his others, and though it had been the safest bet he had ever placed, it had paid off bigger than any other.

At the age of fifty-nine, Thatcher Redmond's career had hit the jackpot with the recent publication of his book *The Human Factor*, which had won two prestigious awards, including, just twelve days ago, the coveted Tetteridge Award for Popular Science Writing.

With any luck, he would bag another trophy, the

prestigious half-a-million-dollar MacArthur Genius grant, which would be announced in a few weeks. Though nominations were supposed to be confidential, he knew that his name had been dropped into the hat.

There might even be a Pulitzer in the works after that, if the MacArthur grant materialized. Thatcher was on a roll.

After years of publishing dry, unsensational papers on genetic correlations between fruit flies and related fauna, works that would never be read by anyone other than a dozen colleagues and a few hundred of his put-upon students, Thatcher had gambled that nothing would pay more richly than playing the part all *non-scientists* wanted scientists to play. Sincerity, or even knowledge, need not even enter into it.

Indeed, Thatcher suspected even the most sincere scientists who had been playing this game longer than he had done so with at least a little cynical self-interest, considering how rich was the prize and how easily it was obtained.

The sea of grant money, honorariums, awards, book deals, and royalties—not to mention popularity, fame, and career opportunities—was deep, warm, and inviting for the scientist willing to provide his expert opinion, especially to the government or media, and thus lend scientific backing to the cause du jour. The water was fine, and it welcomed the sincere and the insincere, the idealist and the opportunist alike. Thatcher's only regret was that he hadn't dived in sooner.

Since his late bloom of fame, the zoologist had found himself eagerly sought out for commentary on an astonishing range of issues and causes, and he had been enjoying the ride thoroughly. As long as he echoed the most fashionable trends in science, there was no end to the requests for appearances and sound bites.

Thatcher knew that at this moment in human history it was fashionable to decry the impact of human beings on the environment, and so he had set out to write a book that would cash in on the current trend by going so far out on that trajectory that everyone else on the catwalk would look frumpy and outmoded. And his strategy had succeeded—*brilliantly.*

Knowing he was exploiting a niche many of his colleagues had already colonized ahead of him, Thatcher had decided to invade at the top of the food chain. Bypassing academia, he'd gone straight for the minds of the non-scientific public. It didn't take a biology degree to discover where the mother's milk of his profession came from. His run might not last long, but it didn't have to. He would get in, grab what he wanted, and get out in time to retire very comfortably in Costa Rica. He already knew the house he wanted to buy. It helped that he did not care if in the process he damaged academia or even the cause of environmentalism. In fact, after years of toiling fruitlessly in the vineyard with little or no recognition or appreciation, he got a positive thrill out of calculating that probability.

His book was bringing in the kind of royalties and speaking fees he needed to fend off his bookies and his latest spouse. Against all odds, Thatcher Redmond had proven fit enough to survive, after all.

And then this Sedona business came along, and fucked *everything.*

The Airbus A321 finally taxied down the runway and throttled up, surging down the tarmac. A delirious cheer filled the plane and a wave of relief surged in his chest as it lifted off the runway.

He replayed the day's events in his mind one more time. Seven hours ago he had sat in the back of a taxi heading for the uppercrust Camelback Mountain section of Phoenix. The exaggerated rock formations outside the window had reminded him of *The Flintstones.* Even though she was living in a mansion on a mesa in the wealthiest suburb of the city, owing to her well-to-do family and friends, the harpy had made him go there to hit him up for a child he had never wanted or even knew he had.

"Wait here, Thatcher," Sedona had said to him, he recalled now.

"Here" happened to be an airy, sun-drenched family room decorated with expensive dolphin art in the mansion she was house-sitting for a friend.

It had a high, open-beam ceiling and a sliding glass door looking out over the pool. The door stood open a crack to a dry Phoenix breeze.

Sedona warned that Junior had a tendency to jump in the pool outside if nobody stopped him.

The redheaded brat ran around screaming and crashing into things the entire time.

She had told him the little monster never remembered to use his sea-serpent life preserver, that he always ran straight for the pool and jumped right in.

But that sliding glass door was open a crack . . .

"I'm waiting for the cat to come in. Don't worry, the baby can't fit through that," Sedona had told Thatcher. "He's not strong enough yet to push the door open by himself and get out."

Then she left to answer the front door, some sort of delivery . . .

Was it a setup? There were practically neon signs around it. He'd looked around for a hidden camera as the probabilities whirred like slots wheels in his mind.

He rubbed the edge of his rubber shoe now as he leaned back in the comfortable airline seat. After the miserable outbound trip, he had opted for a later flight in exchange for an upgrade to Business Class. His prize had been a six-hour wait, but almost an entire section all to himself.

As his cab waited for him fifteen minutes later, he had spoken to Sedona on the front doorstep, reassuring her that he would help her. He promised her that he would be in contact with her soon. He even kissed her on the cheek as the smoke-gray cat had run out the front door and curled around his leg, nearly tripping him as he walked to his taxi.

When the cab passed an ambulance a couple miles away, speeding in the opposite direction, his heart had pounded.

With the siren blaring and the lights flashing on top, it looked like a million-dollar slot machine paying off, Thatcher had thought.

"Hey, aren't you Thatcher Redmond?" came a loud voice.

He turned, startled, to the man across the aisle. "Yes."

"Well! I read your book, mate!" The sunburned Australian shook his hand vigorously. "You really figure human beings are going to wipe everything off the planet, eh?"

My dear rube, Thatcher mused, *you just increased that very probability in my mind.* "It's a distinct possibility." Thatcher smiled graciously.

"I don't know." The man shook his head. "I travel a lot, and I look out this window and I can hardly tell we're even here, eh?"

"Can you see a deadly virus inside a human being?"

"Well, no, now that you mention it."

"Free will is a virus. All that is necessary to create destruction is to set it loose and power it with reason. You can bet on it every time."

"Well, I'm sorry to hear that. Not too good. Ah, well . . ."

"Don't worry. The shit probably won't hit the fan for a couple of centuries. We're safe." Thatcher winked obscenely at the man and grinned.

"Ah, that's good for us, then! Too bad for our kids, though, I reckon. Oh, sorry to bother. I can see you have things on your mind."

"Not at all," Thatcher said, relieved to end the conversation.

"Here are your peanuts, sir."

Thatcher flinched as the flight attendant at his elbow surprised him.

"Thank you!" he snapped, irritated that he had been identified by a witness on this plane and trying to calculate the damage.

Thatcher clicked off the overhead light and looked into the black window as he leaned his chair back. He tried to focus on the appearance he was scheduled to make tomorrow night on CNN to discuss the subject of Henders Island, again. But his thoughts drifted as he watched his reflection in the darkened pane. *It won't matter,* he thought. *Of course I visited her. No one can prove a thing.*

He snatched a glass of champagne from the tray of a passing steward.

Finally allowing himself to relax, he toasted himself. And felt the same welling thrill in his stomach that he felt whenever he struck the jackpot.

SEPTEMBER 5

5:10 P.M.

The entire bubble window at the end of Section One was now covered with green, yellow, and purple splotches of growth.

Emanating from the jungle, similar vegetation had already spread over one-fourth of the section's side windows as well.

But outside the rest of the windows could still be seen flats of common plants and potted trees that Nell had requested be flown in and set down on the sloping field, each accompanied by an ROV to record their fate.

Quentin congratulated Andy as they looked into the trough at the live Henders rat. It was the first living adult rat they had been able to trap for observation.

"What do those eye movements remind you of?" Quentin brought the camera overhead as close as possible without spooking the animal.

Andy nodded. "Yeah, wow!"

"What?" Nell asked. The grinning face of the creature chilled her. Its cockeyed eyeballs seemed to be staring right at her no matter where she moved.

"Most animals on the island seem to have eyes like mantis shrimp," Quentin told her.

"So?"

"So mantis shrimp have compound eyes, with three optical hemispheres."

"*Trinocular* depth perception."

"We have binocular depth perception," Andy said.

"Yes, I know, Andy," Nell said.

"These things can see the same object *three* times with *each* eye. So they perceive three dimensions better with one eye than we do with two."

Quentin pointed up at the eye of the creature magnified on the monitor, making a side-to-side gesture with his index finger. "See how each eye is slowly scanning now?"

"One of them sideways and one of them up and down? Wow!" Andy laughed in awe.

"They're 'painting' polarization and color data like a friggin' Mars Rover, only a lot faster," Quentin said. "Oh yeah, that rat can see us all right, right through the glare of this acrylic."

"Their eyes also have saccadic motion," Andy said, looking at Nell. "That's what lets us read without the small eye movements blurring our vision."

"And they see five times the number of colors we see—at least," Quentin said.

"They do?" Nell looked at Andy grimly.

"Humans have three classes of color receptors: green, blue, and red. These things may have up to ten classes of color receptors!"

"There goes the Christmas tree." Quentin pointed out the window as the gnawed remnant of a Norfolk pine, one of their test specimens, collapsed amid a swarm of fluttering bugs.

The hatch at the far end of the lab beeped a loud alarm as it opened, and Chief NASA Technician Jedediah Briggs stepped through and closed the hatch behind him.

"This section of the lab is caked with crap three feet deep on the outside," Briggs informed them. He was a tall, athletic man with a Kirk Douglas chin protruding over his helmetless blue cleansuit. Everyone had pretty much grown to dread him. "And we just started to detect a slow drop in pressure. So it's time to evacuate Section One, boys and girls!"

"Hey, Otto, how many ROVs do we have left?" Nell asked.

"We have sixty-eight left of the ninety-four stored under StatLab-One."

"Can you control them from any of the lab's sections?"

Otto thought for a second. "Yes!"

"OK, let's relocate our base of operations to Section Four," Nell said, glancing at Briggs. "And, in the meantime, we'll use sections Two and Three as long as possible. How's that, Briggs?"

"That works for me." Briggs nodded. "Now, if you would all get your asses out of here as fast as possible, that would be, well, mandatory!" he shouted.

Everyone scrambled to gather up laptops and as many specimens as possible as they exited the hatch and climbed the stairs to Section Two.

"Sterilize the trough, Otto," Nell said sternly. "You know we can't keep a specimen that size safely."

Otto frowned. "OK, OK."

8:10 P.M.

On board the *Trident*, dinner was served: canned potatoes, mandarin salad, and a batch of deep-fried mantis shrimp the chef had trapped right off the starboard bow last night.

Zero chewed a succulent morsel of the crustacean as he studied the brilliantly starred sky, lying on a lounge on the mezzanine deck, the empty plate of food resting on his crotch.

"You know you want to," a voice coaxed.

"I don't know what you're talking about, Cynthea." He sighed, and stretched back in the lounge chair.

"You can't pass up an opportunity like this."

"Maybe," Zero said.

"I've offered you half of the money, damn it. What else could you possibly want?"

Zero grinned. "Keep talking, darlin'."

Dante smirked at the loafing Zero and stalked off to go below.

9:31 P.M.

The moon floodlit the cove outside the porthole of his room while he organized his gear.

Dante chose to use a minimal rack, rigging his Black Diamond climbing harness and gear slings with nuts, cams, carabiners, and a number of grigris. Then he tied together six sixty-meter pitches of Edelweiss dynamic rope for the solo climb.

He checked the Voyager Lite camera and transmission backpack he had stolen from *SeaLife*'s stowage compartment. The battery meters read nearly full, and the Night Vision switch brought up the expected greenish display. He located the transmit button, easily reached on the backpack.

He stowed the backpack, rope, and climbing gear in a five-foot-long waterproof duffel bag. Then he hoisted a body-surfing raft he had brought along so he could sneak the equipment ashore below the Navy's radar.

The full moon hung directly overhead as he slipped into the sea from the stern, beside the large Zodiac, placing the bag of gear on the raft. Once in the brisk water, he slipped on a pair of swim fins. Then he paddled quietly to shore with the tide, conserving his leg muscles.

9:32 P.M.

Nell gazed out the window of Section Four, studying the glistening nocturnal grazers as they sprouted in the moonlit field. What kind of symbiont could alternate its chemistry to feed on so many different sources of nutrients? she wondered.

She rubbed her forehead as she turned the problem over in her mind.

Andy studied Nell. "What are you thinking?"

"It's not lichen."

"OK. So what is it, then?"

"I'm not sure . . . The top growth rate of lichen is about one or two centimeters a year. The stuff on these fields grows faster than bamboo. Its geometric growth pattern reminds me of Ediacara fossils, some really primitive organizations of single-celled life. Whatever it is, it seems to be the base of the food chain here."

"If it's not lichen, what is it?"

"Let's call it clover. The clover photosynthesizes by day and eats rock by night—and these grazers come out at night to eat the clover. Maybe the grazers prefer the minerals the clover consumes at night, or don't like chlorophyll . . . We know that some green algae in birdbaths turns red to protect itself from too much light or salinity—but it takes days to make that color change . . ."

"Hmm . . ."

"But we know lichen is a symbiont formed from algae and fungus." She opened her eyes and looked at Andy, but her focus was distant and inward. "In lichen, the algae provides oxygen and organic molecules like sugars and ATP through photosynthesis. The fungus helps dissolve rock and provides nutrients for the algae to synthesize organic molecules." She focused on Andy. "You with me?"

"Sure!"

"OK, so now—what makes this clover turn purple? The only thing I can think of is purple bacteria." She looked out the window as though she could suddenly see through a fog. "This may be a symbiont of cyanobacteria and proteobacteria, which uses sulfur as an energy source—and turns purple! There's a lot of iron sulfide, fool's gold, on the island. I noticed it on the beach . . . So if this is some kind of cyano-proteobacteria symbiont, then the purple phase of this stuff would produce hydrogen sulfide gas—and stink like rotten eggs, like Zero mentioned! But during the day, when photosynthesizing, it would produce *oxygen* . . . while the sulfur-reducing bacteria might retreat underground . . ."

She leaned forward, intently watching one of the nearest fernlike creatures pressing down a translucent frond on the field. White smoke curled around the pads at the end.

"Of course!" She looked at Andy with wide eyes as three thoughts slammed together in her sleep-deprived mind. "If those 'grazers' only come out at night, they may be so ancient that they have to avoid oxygen! They may *need* the hydrogen sulfide gas to protect themselves and re-create the primordial atmosphere that they evolved in. See?"

"Go on, go on!"

"And if these grazers eat this stuff when it's purple, they could be ingesting purple bacteria like *Thiobacillus* to convert the hydrogen sulfide in the plants into *sulfuric acid*—which they may be using to scour the clover off the rocks!"

"Nell," Andy gasped. "You're amazing. I don't have the slightest idea what you just said, but it's amazing! I told everyone down in Section Two you thought it was lichen, so they're all calling it lichen now. Sorry."

She laughed wearily. "That's OK, Andy. It's hard to believe this is even our planet. I'm glad we're here, though. If I couldn't do something after . . . I think I might have gone crazy on that ship."

"Yeah. I think they call it survivor's guilt."

"No." Anger instantly erased the humor from her face. "If survivors do something about it, there's no reason to feel guilty, Andy. Unless they don't."

"It's up to the living to avenge the dead, eh? Isn't that how the saying goes?"

She stared at the darkening jungle below, thinking of her eleven shipmates that were now gone. "Something like that," she answered softly.

"But can you take revenge on animals, Nell? After all, we were the ones who intruded on them. Animals can't help what they do. They didn't have a choice. I know what happened to your mom, Nell, but—"

Her eyes scalded him.

"OK." He nodded, and backed off. "I'm sorry."

She looked back out the window, focusing on the glistening creatures emerging across the purple slopes of the island.

Glowing swarms of bugs came out of the tangled vegetation now and swirled across the fields in clusters as they grazed.

9:45 P.M.

Dante tugged off the swim fins. He dragged the raft up the beach toward the rocks. Ditching his fins on a high rock and stashing the raft sideways between two boulders, he dragged the duffel bag of climbing gear up the beach and over the rock outpouring to the edge of the crevasse.

He opened the bag, stepped into his harness, attached the pre-strung loops of gear, and slipped on a new pair of his favorite Five Ten climbing shoes. Then he zippered the bag, slung it over his back, and bouldered up into the crack.

About seventy feet in, Dante spotted an ascent route on the left face. He glanced warily into the rock-strewn canyon ahead, weighing his options. He poured some chalk on his hands from a small bag strapped around his waist. Then he felt the cliff-face, carefully examining the surface.

The rock was abundantly pitted with pockets and cracks for nuts and cams. He decided he could climb this face clean, without using the rock hammer or the pitons, and he felt a surge of confidence. It would be a perfect solo climb.

Dante visualized the first line of holds in the moonlight, then he donned his gear and tested his balance. Carrying the heavy gear disturbed his center of gravity—and the camera on his chest would prevent him from hugging the rock. He decided to strap the camera on the backpack instead—it made the center of gravity worse, but at least it was not in his way.

He looked up. A hundred-foot vertical face rose above him to a perfect ramp, a diagonal crack that stretched almost to the top of the 230-meter face. The tricky part would be an overhang on the last thirty feet.

He hoped to climb two-thirds of the way to the summit, find a ledge, and sleep until dawn. Then he would contact Cynthea and film his remaining ascent, transmitting the first live images of Henders Island to the world.

So much for Zero.

Stacking six connected rope coils on a flat rock at the base of the cliff, he tied the end of the rope to a cam, and hooked the cam to his chest harness. He felt the adrenaline pump inside him as he jumped up and grabbed the first hold, pulling the end of the rope with him.

Suddenly, a sound like a Mack truck air horn blasted him from behind, nearly stopping his heart in the deep silence of the night.

He leaped upward instinctively, "smearing" his feet in a mad scramble over the rocky surface.

"What the fuck!" he shouted, clinging to the rock and twisting to look below him. What he saw resembled a giant spider the size of a Chevy Suburban, covered with stripes of glowing fur, crashing into the rock wall below Dante's feet.

A black spike reached up from the spider. It gouged the cliff beside his right leg, clawing a groove down the hard rock face. Dante sprang six vertical feet in a single terrified lunge, to grab the next set of holds with his chalked hands.

Amped with adrenaline, he chimneyed backwards off a wrinkle and climbed the next fifty feet faster than he'd ever scaled a rock in his life. Pausing for breath at a ledge, he leaned out to look down the face. Three large shapes prowled like phosphorescent tigers below. "Please tell me you can't climb," he whispered, panting.

He reached both hands into the chalk bag, dusted them together, and resumed the climb, casting an occasional nervous glance downward at the shrinking forms below. The ramp was another fifty feet above him.

His hand fell on a strange smooth texture, and he momentarily recoiled from what looked like a serving-tray-sized, boomerang-headed cockroach. But it was motionless, and he quickly realized it was just a fossil. He saw others around him, dark and glossy on the moon-washed rock face.

When he reached the ramp he set another cam rigged with a gri-gri, for protection, then he crawled forward to the corner and looked down into the crevasse.

Farther up the crack he saw the cornucopia-like tunnel of jungle growth, its glowing outline etched by the swirling sparks of a million flying bugs. He decided to stay out of its line of sight as much as possible to avoid being detected by anything.

Around the corner, he chimneyed backwards to a bucket of stone that emerged from the cliff like a sharp-edged bowsprit of rock. He set another cam there and marked his elevation—about two hundred feet up. He faced a waving vertical climb of about seventy feet, in the open, until another ramp of rock would take him to the crux.

He chalked his hands again and started up.

The moonlight glint of another fossil caught his eye, so he climbed toward it to have a look.

It leaped off the rock and snapped its jaws at his face—devouring a glowing bug that whizzed past his ear.

Startled, hands slipping and scrabbling, Dante lost his grip.

He fell.

The cam he had set expanded in the crack as his weight tightened the gri-gri. He swung beneath the stone bucket—he had fallen about thirty feet, but the protection held.

Now, shuddering, he got a good look at the creature skittering down the cliff face, moving like a huge beetle welded to a flying fish.

Dante pulled himself up the rope to the hold point and dangled there, watching as more of these living fossils darted around him, snapping up the flying insects that were now buzzing past him.

10:08 P.M.

"Quentin, save the rest of the ROVs for daylight, OK?" Nell said. "Let's concentrate on lighting and time-lapsing the field specimens till morning."

Quentin triggered the outboard lights for the cameras that would continue shooting a frame of the plant specimens exposed outside every thirty seconds through the night.

"God!" she said as she ran replays of the time-lapses from the last forty-five minutes. She looked out the window and saw that some of the specimens had already been stripped, uprooted, and replaced with something else.

"Hey, what's that?" a NASA technician asked.

A strange hum buzzed in the air.

The entire lab seemed to vibrate and then rock gently back and forth.

"Probably a tremor," Quentin said. "The military said they noticed low-level seismic activity in the island a few days ago."

"Hang on, folks," Andy warned.

Nell grabbed the edge of the lab counter and looked out the window, at the trees quivering at the jungle's edge.

10:09 P.M.

Dante felt the rumble before he heard it. At first he thought the entire cliff was falling, but then he realized it was only the slab he was clinging to—separating from the cliff with a slow crumble. He lunged sideways, finger-locking a crack with his left hand and swinging up to catch a dead-point with his right, simultaneously edging a hold with his left foot. It was the most incredible dyno he had ever made—but he didn't care, because he was terrified.

Flakes of rock rained down around him, and he realized the last protection he had set was fifty feet below—he needed to get to that ramp above, *fast.*

The cliff-gliders grew bolder. They lightly grazed his shoulders, back, and heels as he climbed, flittering around him in greater numbers like flying crabs swarming over the cliff face. "Hang on, bro," he said to himself nervously.

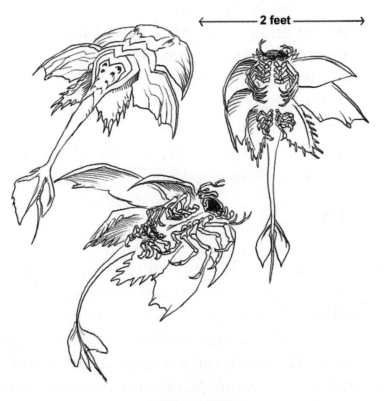

Cliff-gliders
Megatriops hemapteryx
(*after* Joel, *Revision of the Notostraca of the World*)

10:09 P.M.

The humming stopped.

Andy sighed. "Now I know what an earthquake feels like."

"OK, it's over," Nell said, hopefully.

Briggs came through the hatch from Section

Three. There was a serious look on the chief NASA technician's face.

"Hey, Briggs. Is there any way I can run down to Section One and get my Mets cap? I think I left it down there." She smirked at him.

"That's very funny, Nell. That would be a 'no.' So, now we have *earthquakes?*"

"Not too bad, so far."

"Yeah, sure." Briggs glared at her. "Bring on the mudslides and hurricanes!"

10:11 P.M.

Dante began to suffer from forearm pump as the fingerwork bulged his arms and weakened his grip. He tried shifting more of the weight to his feet, and finally, painfully, he reached the crack and wedged himself in. He shook out his arms in the womb of rock and then set some protection, overcamming it into a hole above him, and hooking it in with a locking 'biner.

He was not confident about bivouacking on the rock face—sleeping here did not seem like such a great idea, after all. Crawling deeper into the crack, he discovered a vertical crevice that shafted into the roof like a ladder, straight to the overhang at the top. He felt a surge of hope. If this was as clean as it looked, he could reach the top in fifteen minutes.

He decided it was time to transmit, using the

camera's night vision mode. He turned on the *SeaLife* walkie-talkie and called in.

10:26 P.M.

Every three and a half minutes Peach nibbled a peanut M&M as he played the twenty-sixth level of Halo 5—when suddenly he caught a signal icon blinking in a corner of his monitor.

He clicked the icon as though he were blasting another alien, and the raw feed of Dante's camera suddenly filled the screen, muddy and crackling: *"I'm here on Henders Island, about a hundred meters from the top of the cliff. Do you guys hear me? I hope your walkie-talkies are on, man . . ."*

Peach looked around for his walkie-talkie but couldn't find it.

10:26 P.M.

Cynthea was sleeping in her cabin when the beeper of her walkie-talkie went off on her night table. She sprang up as she heard Dante's voice.

She dashed in her navy blue pajamas toward the Control Room with the walkie-talkie to her ear. "Dante! You shouldn't be doing this!" she scolded as she ran.

"Hey, it's done, Cynthea. I told you I could climb this thing. Here I am!"

"Oh my God!" she groaned.

As soon as she reached the Control Room and saw the live feed, frustratingly dark and erratic as it was, she grabbed the shipboard satphone and speed-dialed.

"This is Cynthea Leeds, may I speak to Barry? Just wake him up, honey. Trust me, OK? DO IT!" She looked at Peach, frowning, and put her hand over the receiver: "Can you bring down the contrast and brighten the image or something, Peach? We gotta get more than that." She took her hand off the receiver. "Barry, I've got a rock climber with a camera thirty feet from the top of Henders Island, ready to go live. Wake up, Barry. Wake up! We've got to go LIVE now! This is the broadcast of the century! We can get it through the news blackout from Henders Island! Damn it, that's our hook! Barry?"

Peach could hear Barry breathing through the phone's ear speaker.

"Do you know what time it is on the East Coast right now, Cynthea? It's one-thirty in the morning!"

"That's what makes it legendary television, Barry!" Cynthea shook her head, glancing at Peach. "Do it! You'll have the exclusive rights to a MILLION RERUNS! This is like the first MOON LANDING, BARRY!" She put a hand over the receiver. "Tell Dante to hold off from getting to the top—Barry's getting his fat ass out of bed and is going down to the office, but Dante has to stay put for ten minutes." She put the satphone to her ear. "OK, Barry, sweetie. Thank you, my darling!"

10:27 P.M.

"OK, I hope this night vision is coming through—I have the camera strapped to my chest now and you're looking at the cliff above me," Dante said. "I'm climbing a seam. You may be able to see some gliders just outside the crack. I'm protected from them in here, but they've been getting a little close for comfort—one of them seems to have taken a nip out of my elbow. But mostly they seem to eat these big fireflies that were coming after me . . ."

Dante climbed fifty feet before setting some pro. He estimated that he was now a hundred feet from the top.

Peach's voice suddenly crackled through the walkie-talkie. *"Can you stop about thirty feet from the top and wait for a green light, Dante?"*

"No problem. Don't make me wait too long, though, the last bit's an overhang, dude."

"OK, cool. Keep videoing, we're getting all this. You shouldn't have done it, you know," Cynthea scolded. *"But you're going to be a superstar, baby!"*

"Woo-hoo!" Dante grinned as he steadily climbed up the crack, ducking occasionally to avoid a swooping glider.

10:39 P.M.

"Are you getting this, Barry?"

"We're getting it, we're getting it. It's exciting stuff."

"Are we live?" There was a pause and Cynthea glared at the phone. "Barry?"

"It's great stuff, Cynthea, but I don't know . . . I'm having dinner with Congressman Murray tomorrow night from the FCC Oversight Committee to hash out the merger details—"

"Why, you cocksucking motherfucking backstabbing son of a bitch," Cynthea snarled.

"Now, Cynthea, we can maybe get better airtime and a real special out of it later without getting in trouble with the FCC or violating the goddamned Patriot Act or God knows what else the lawyer is nodding his head at me about right now, all right?"

"Don't let me down, Barry!" Cynthea threatened.

10:40 P.M.

Dante dangled from a pair of cams that he had chocked into the roof of the overhang, thirty feet below the cliff's summit. As he looked across the chasm, the opposite cliff face seemed to draw nearer, then recede. "It's kind of gnarly up here, man. We're having another earthquake, I think. I hope you're getting this, man!"

"Try to hold it steady." Peach's voice came over the walkie-talkie taped to Dante's upper arm.

"You try!" Dante snarled.

Dante set two nuts in small cracks above his head and equalized the tension on the tie-ins. Cliff-gliders leaped past him, devouring the flying, glowing bugs attracted to his dangling body.

He swung forward and caught the edge of the overhang, locking off with one arm and reaching up with the other to place a final cam.

He was ten yards of rock away from the top. "Tell me when, guys. And make it *fast,* OK?"

10:42 P.M.

"Come on, Barry! You've got a live feed from Henders Island all ready to go, damn it!"

Peach heard Barry reply through her phone's receiver: "I don't want another slaughter on TV!"

In the background they could hear Dante's narration as he pointed the camera across the crevasse. *"A few feet to go here on the crux—What the hell?"*

The other wall was only about twenty feet away. The dark trilobite-like creatures seemed to be congregating into a mass directly across from Dante.

"That doesn't look good," Peach told Cynthea.

"I don't like the look of these things, man," came Dante's voice. *"Ow! They're comin' at me from all directions now—I can't hang around*

187

here longer, man. I'm going for it."

"OK, we're cutting in live in five seconds," Barry said. "So get ready, Cynthea, damn you, you fucking bitch!"

"I could *marry* you, Barry!"

"OK," Dante grunted. *"I am almost to the top of Henders Island . . ."*

"We've got a live shot coming from Henders Island as one of the crew of *SeaLife*, without our permission or authorization, is about to reach the top of the island's cliff, and broadcast the first images of the island's interior," Cynthea narrated. "What do you see, Dante?"

"Damn it—those things have teeth, I think. Uh, fuck, I'm just getting up the last bit here, hang on." The camera swept across pale rock illuminated by night vision as they heard his grunts and hard breathing.

"Keep talking, sweetie, keep talking!" Cynthea coaxed. "Don't swear, though, honey!"

10:44 P.M.

Dante reached a grasping hand up over the lip and hauled himself to the top of the cliff. His muscles trembled with exhaustion, and he lay still on his back for a moment, breathing and giving thanks. He had made it.

He raised himself to his feet.

"Oh shit!"

One of the giant tigers flashing orange-and-pink stripes sat in front of him. The thing was the size of a tractor.

As Dante spun and dove back into the crevasse, he saw a luminous figure, on the opposite side of the crevasse, jump in the air and spread out four arms in an X.

"Oh *shiiiiit!*" Dante heard it screech, in a warbled imitation of his own voice.

10:44 P.M.

"We're cutting this off, Cynthea!" yelled Barry.

"Are you *crazy?*" she screamed.

10:44 P.M.

The rope yanked on his harness as it belayed inside the gri-gri and tightened the cam driven into the ledge.

He dangled and spun, head downward, on the rope. A cloud of bugs circled him, chased by leaping gliders.

He righted himself and climbed the rope, drawing his body up under the ledge.

Above him, the tiger-spider suddenly loomed over the edge, blocking the moonlight. He saw it reach two long black spikes down into the crack and hook his rope. It pulled Dante up like a fish caught on a dropline.

As its jaws peeled open, revealing dark appendages, he smelled the sour stench of its breath and felt a splatter of stinging drool on his face. The rope lunged upward as the beast yanked it with two arms, and its head stretched down over the rocky edge on an elastic neck. He felt its hot breath and his heart pounded as the creature screamed a sound he never imagined could come from a living thing.

Dante heard the taunting voice of the other animal, from somewhere above on the cliff: "Oh *shiiiiiit!*" it echoed.

He knew that with one more pull of the rope he would be inside the monster's mouth. Dante chose to die another way.

"Bye, guys," he said, and he unclipped.

The creature screamed like a hoarse siren, its voice receding away from him as he fell.

10:45 P.M.

The last thing they saw on-screen was the camera eye tumbling through the chasm as the scream of the beast faded—the transmission fizzled on impact with the ground.

"Cynthea, Christ! What are you doing to me?" Barry yelled.

"Oh God," Cynthea screeched. "When did you cut it?"

"Not soon e-fucking-nough!"

Captain Sol used surgeon's forceps to place a small brass cannon on the gun deck of the *Golden Hind*.

"Good." Zero nodded.

"Does it look straight?"

"Yeah," Zero said.

"Good." Samir nodded.

Captain Sol lifted his thimble-sized shot glass. "Here's to it, eh?" He toasted Zero with a sip of añejo tequila.

Zero toasted him back.

Watching Captain Sol build his model was just about the only entertainment available on the *Trident* lately.

The ship-to-ship phone bleated suddenly and Samir rose from his chair and picked it up. He listened for about ten seconds. "Uh, wow, I think you need to speak to the captain," he said, handing the phone to Captain Sol. Zero looked on curiously.

The captain smirked, putting the phone to his ear as Samir shrugged.

"Captain Sol, this is Lieutenant Scott of the U.S.S. Enterprise *informing you that a communication signal has been detected coming from the vicinity of your vessel. In fact, we believe it came from your vessel. Broadcasting is unauthorized and contrary to the orders you have been given from the U.S. Navy. We must demand you prepare for immediate boarding."*

"Cynthea!" Captain Sol growled.

"Please copy that again?" said the voice on the radio.

"Thanks, *Enterprise*, I agree, whatever you are detecting is unauthorized. Let me check my ship now to find out what's going on, over."

"Uh, we will help you, Trident. *Is that understood?"*

They heard motors and saw three high-speed gray inflatables speeding into the cove, toward them.

"Yes, *Enterprise*! That is understood." Gritting his teeth, Captain Sol turned off the radio. "Damn it, Cynthea, what now?"

SEPTEMBER 7

7:32 P.M.

TONIGHT'S FIRE-BREATHING CHAT:
WHY WE DIE
by Dr. Geoffrey R. Binswanger

Once again, Lillie Auditorium was packed to the rafters on a crisp autumnal Thursday night.

The lights dimmed and Geoffrey strode out onto the stage wearing yellow sneakers, jeans, his Kaua'i T-shirt, and a lime-green velvet Nehru jacket with red piping.

"Good evening, ladies and gentlemen. Why does a Galapagos tortoise live a hundred and fifty years, a mayfly a single day, and a human being rarely past the age of eighty? Is it simply because our parts wear out at different rates? Or is there a reason, or even some evolutionary advantage, for the very shortness of life? And if there is some positive biological purpose, does this mean the clock can be reset, presuming evolution has used some mechanism to 'set' the timer of life in the first place?"

Geoffrey clicked the remote. A close-up of an egg timer on a 1950s-style kitchen counter appeared behind him, to a smattering of nervous chuckles.

"The question I want to pose and offer a possible answer to tonight is: *Could the speed with which death arrives have a survival advantage?* On its face, it seems like a ridiculous notion, but I believe there might be a very simple explanation for the variation in animal life spans: Animals may actually grow old and die only to *prevent* them from breeding with their own offspring."

Geoffrey clicked to a picture of Cousin Itt from *The Addams Family.* A few laughs bubbled up from the audience.

"Of course, we have had strict taboos against incest since time immemorial. Indeed, parent/child breeding causes particularly disastrous damage to the genetic integrity of almost all life on Earth, causing sterility in both plants and animals in only a few generations. Prior to human taboos, nature may have enforced its own taboo by imposing life spans to prevent that genetic catastrophe from occurring."

Geoffrey clicked again. A scene of microscopic cells on a blue field appeared.

"In the ancient seas of Earth where DNA first formed and single-celled life helped replicate it for over a billion years, there was no need to limit life span. Bacteria and most cells did not even reproduce sexually, and if they did, the chances of encountering one of their own progeny were practically nil. Scientists have speculated that certain forms of bacteria may actually be immortal. In the year 2000, researchers at West Chester University found bacteria that had remained alive for two hundred and fifty million years, locked inside salt crystals buried deep underground."

Geoffrey clicked to a picture of a terrarium over-crowded with hamsters.

"But animals with access to much smaller breeding groups have a problem. The more off-spring they have with each pregnancy, the more serious the threat to the gene pool they become, unless DNA protects itself by implanting a time bomb in such animals set to go off before cross-generational breeding can occur."

The next slide showed a close-up of a pier piling stacked with mussels.

"To see if such a correlation might hold true, I began comparing animal life spans to their repro-ductive behavior. Mussels may live up to a hun-dred years. They live in colonies and simultaneously mingle billions of sex cells into the seawater to reproduce. With the tide flowing in one direction during their synchronized spawning and the sheer multitude of participants, the chance of incestuous reproduction is virtually nonex-istent. No discernible life span is present. Giant clams, which reproduce much the same way, can live five hundred years. Tubeworms thriving near thermal vents at the bottom of the sea and many corals that reproduce this way are believed to live for centuries."

Geoffrey clicked to another close-up image.

"Barnacles, on the other hand, also live in colonies but have life spans of only one or two years. Why? Barnacles reproduce in a very different way. Male barnacles extend penises nine times the length of their bodies, longer than any penis relative to body size in the animal kingdom, in order to copulate with other barnacles."

Amusement fluttered across the audience. Geoffrey laughed.

"Size may matter, but not that much. Barnacles necessarily have a very small group of breeding partners. The risk of cross-generational breeding is high enough to require them to die before a second generation is ready to breed. Death occurs at about twice their breeding age."

Geoffrey clicked to another image: the vast trunk of a California sequoia fringed by ferns.

"Conifers, the first trees to use pollen to reproduce, did so before the help of insects. Like coral reefs, they had to spew vast clouds of sex cells into currents of air flowing over forests, making it nearly impossible for cross-generational breeding to occur. We know of bristlecone pines nearly five thousand years old, and giant sequoias, cedars, and the New Zealand kauri pine are some of the longest-living organisms on Earth. In 2008, researchers discovered a thriving spruce tree nearly *ten thousand* years old."

The next slide showed what looked like a giant

scowling rat. Its naked tail was coiled around the branch it was climbing. Miniatures clung to its underside and back.

"Opossums, the only North American marsupial, are solitary, don't migrate, and stay in the same neighborhood throughout their lives. They have up to thirteen young in a litter, which reach sexual maturity after only one year. If there was ever a case that could make cross-generational breeding possible, this is it. But since opossums don't just play possum but actually die at only one to two years of age, no cross-generational breeding can occur."

The next close-up image set the audience squirming in disgust.

"The humble earthworm, on the other hand, exists in vast numbers, makes no social connections, and constantly shuffles the deck of its breeding partners. Its life span is about a decade."

The slide of a tiny furry mammal elicited cooing noises from the auditorium.

"Voles, which eat earthworms, are tiny mammals that live in communal burrows and reproduce rapidly; they live only two to six months before shuffling off their cute and fuzzy little mortal coils. Considering the frequency of their mating and the early age they reach sexual maturity, that's just in the nick of time."

A wave of revulsion rippled through the room as

the next slide showed the caramel bead of an insect head that was seemingly being squeezed out of a large waxy bag of flesh.

"Queen termites," Geoffrey said, "are monogamous. Together with the king termite, they generate tens of millions of offspring over the course of their lives. About the same size as the vole that lives only one hundred days, queen termites may live one hundred *years*."

The next slide was an image of Bugs Bunny, which got a laugh.

"Cottontail rabbits are legendary breeders that live in small warrens, all marks against them, if this principle is correct. They live twelve to fifteen months on average, and thirty-five percent of them die in the first month. Interestingly, rabbits in captivity can live eight to twelve years. And if they are spayed or neutered, up to twice that, since their risk of cancer is greatly reduced by the procedure."

A slide showed a whale's fluke dripping a beaded curtain as it arced over the sea.

"Blue whales have ninety-year life spans. They travel in pods of relatively small number, like rabbits; but unlike rabbits, they congregate in vast numbers to breed. This shuffling of the deck during mating season reduces the odds of cross-generational breeding to near-zero. Bowhead whales may live more than two hundred years. We have found living individuals with stone arrowheads, which have not been used since the 1800s, still lodged in their flesh."

Geoffrey proceeded to click through a gallery of animals.

"One of the most prolific congregators is the normally solitary whale shark. They can't even breed until they are thirty years old, and they do so in large groups off the coasts of Mexico, Australia, the Seychelles, and East Africa as they follow their seasonal breeding tour like a social calendar of endless mixers. Whale sharks live more than a hundred and fifty years.

"Spiny lobsters also congregate, marching in great single-file conga lines across the ocean floor to breeding zones every year. They may reach ages of fifty years or more if they don't wind up on a dinner plate first.

"Sea turtles, which live eighty years and sometimes more than a hundred and fifty years, travel thousands of miles to congregate and shuffle the genetic deck. The giant tortoises on the Galapagos and Seychelles live in vast colonies year-round and are famously long-lived.

"Squirrels, however, don't congregate or migrate—and predictably live only one to two years, or twice the age they reach sexual maturity. In captivity they may live up to fifteen years. So, obviously, biological life span is balanced against life span in their natural habitat. No need to limit life span biologically if predators are already doing it. So long as all the knobs are set to prevent cross-generational breeding, the genetic line remains healthy."

Geoffrey clicked from a close-up of a chubby squirrel to a portrait of a croaking frog.

"Bullfrogs live up to sixteen years in the wild, ten years on average—five times longer than squirrels. But why wouldn't they have even longer life spans, given this equation, since they have access to large numbers of breeding partners, as do mussels, pine trees, and tortoises? After all, each female bullfrog lays up to twenty thousand eggs at a single spawning, and they live in vast numbers within proximity to one another. They make no social bonds. The chances of them mating with off-spring seem similar to those of other animals that live in vast colonies.

"Bullfrogs fall victim to predators more frequently than whales or giant tortoises do, of course, and must replace themselves faster to survive as a species. But the answer, I believe, lies in the fact that bullfrog habitats don't necessarily provide access to large breeding pools. Bullfrogs frequently get isolated in ponds as water levels recede. In the worst-case scenario, with one male and female bullfrog sharing one pond, the female may produce twenty thousand chances for cross-generational breeding if the parents live long enough. So why don't bullfrogs have short life spans? Because their offspring swim as polliwogs for an amazing *five years* before becoming frogs and reaching sexual maturity. Thus, they are five when they mate, as their parents die at ten, twice the age of sexual maturity."

Geoffrey clicked to an image of a stork couple in a great nest atop the chimney of a Swiss chateau, the Alps shining in the background.

"Monogamous birds like white storks, bald eagles, and Canadian geese live up to three decades. The monogamous ostrich lives fifty to seventy-five years, with pairs observed breeding together for forty years. Many subspecies of wild turkey, by contrast, do not congregate or migrate and are not monogamous. They live only two to three years in the wild. The Asian house mouse, which breeds promiscuously within a small social group, lives one year; the monogamous deer mouse, native to the United States, lives seven years. But what happens if all the rules are violated?"

The image on the screen was now a sitting cheetah, its fur ruffled by wind as a storm cloud darkened the sky behind it.

"The cheetah lives about ten years in the wild. Female cheetahs reach maturity at two years, males at one year. This is unusual, since females of most animals generally reach sexual maturity first, a staggering that helps prevent cross-sibling breeding in animals that have multiple offspring simultaneously. Yet, strangely, male cheetahs don't get the chance to breed until their third year, as they stay with their mothers far longer than females. This, by the way, is a phenomenon also observed among certain species of graduate student." He smiled as his audience roared with laughter. "This means cheetah offspring have two years to breed with their own mother."

A resounding "Yuck" came from the audience.

"This appears to contradict the principle altogether. And perhaps with disastrous results. The cheetah, one of the oldest species of cat, enjoyed large breeding groups during its four million years of evolution. But now that its habitat has been fragmented and breeding partners greatly diminished, cheetahs are inbreeding at an alarming rate, threatening the entire species as offspring become susceptible to disease and infertility. It is thought that at some point in the past cheetahs faced a very near extinction event, so that all existing cheetahs have descended from as few as one breeding pair. If so, the same cheetah behavior that may have saved the species then may threaten it now."

Geoffrey clicked to a new slide.

"African elephants live in small groups. They do not congregate to breed, but they can live up to sixty years. How can this be? First of all, seventy percent do not survive to reach thirty, and half die by the age of fifteen. And, though female elephants become fertile at twenty, and males reach maturity at about age fourteen when they either leave the herd or are forced out by the females, male elephants remarkably do not breed until their *thirties,* when they have finally attained the size and skill to compete with other successfully breeding males. Thus, elephant social behavior avoids the possibility of cross-generational breeding through what I have dubbed the 'late-bloomer' effect. As with hippos, whales, and bullfrogs, delaying the breeding age increases life span while not violating the principle that *life span equals no more than twice breeding age.*"

A slide of bundled-up revelers giving thumbs-up in Times Square appeared.

"Throughout human evolution, the life span of our ancestors never averaged much more than thirty years. Human groups rarely exceeded two hundred individuals during the millions of years of our evolution, and were often much smaller. Such a very small gene pool invites genetic compromise. Human males reach sexual maturity at about the age of fifteen, females reach maturity between the ages of eight and fourteen. This leaves a seven-year window of opportunity for parent/offspring mating and seemingly violates the rule.

"To this day, however, the human pituitary gland starts shutting down about age thirty-five. Add to this that males reach the peak of their sexual potency and physical strength at about the age of seventeen, and you now have a competition between young, strong, horny males and older, tired guys who would probably rather just play golf.

"Surely, this math is no accident. The sexual peak and the drop-off correspond exactly, even in humans. I submit that it is not because we die that we have to replace ourselves—*it is because we replace ourselves that we have to die*—and we have to do it on a tight schedule to avoid generational overlap. Indeed, it wasn't until the last two hundred years that world life expectancy increased from about twenty-five to sixty-five for men and seventy for women. It turns out that in captivity we humans, too, live much longer."

As a wave of laughter rippled, Geoffrey made a motion and the lights came up.

"So the remarkably predictive correlation of life span to cross-generational breeding opportunity suggests a genetic mechanism and purpose, if you will, for the length of lives. Scientists have already discovered 'clocks' that are built into the human organism. Women have a finite number of eggs. After forty, erectile malfunctions become as frequent among males as the television ads promising them a cure. Human cells, we now know, have a genetically imposed limit on how many times they can divide, and this limit has already been removed in laboratory conditions, producing virtually immortal cell lines.

"So, there is evidence that life span has been

superimposed, therefore, on the human organism." Geoffrey clasped the edges of the rostrum. "I propose tonight that such limits are not arbitrary, but, indeed, have the very specific purpose of maintaining an organism's genetic integrity over time by preventing the possibility of cross-generational reproduction."

There was a growing commotion in the audience.

"What are the consequences of such a proposal? They are profound and astounding. There may be a genetic knob that we can tweak to reset the timer of human life. And if so, the extension of human life will present a challenge to many of our cherished social conventions."

Geoffrey pointed to a hand vigorously raised in the third row.

"But don't barnacle larvae get carried off by ocean currents, eliminating the chances for cross-generational mating?"

"Eliminating? I'm not so sure. Barnacles are weird crustaceans. They swim, and I'm not sure how much they drift, especially when attached to flotsam in the middle of the ocean, before colonizing new shorelines. Darwin studied barnacles for decades, and I can see why anyone who studied barnacles that long would ponder the theory of evolution."

"What about overpopulation? Thatcher Redmond has argued that human life-extension is the worst idea he has ever heard, if that's where you're headed next."

Laughs chased groans in the auditorium.

"Well, some, indeed, argue that longer life spans will lead to overpopulation," Geoffrey conceded. "Thatcher Redmond, who has been very vocal in the media of late, is quick to point out that human population has doubled in the last fifty years, to over six billion. But to put that number in perspective, consider: Given five square feet, standing side by side, all six billion living human beings would fit inside the state of Rhode Island, with room for 200 million more. I often urge people considering this idea to look out the window when they take airplane trips and consider this idea against what they actually see. Compare the vast stretches of unpopulated land and sea to those places that are inhabited by human beings. Personally, I don't think it's time to panic yet."

"But Redmond also points out in his book that the spatial ratio of a virus to its host body is far smaller and yet can still prove deadly to the whole organism," shouted a voice from the crowd.

"That may be true, Dr. Thomas," Geoffrey answered. "However, I do not agree with the premise of Thatcher Redmond's overpopulation arguments. Human beings are creative as well as consumptive. I understand that Redmond claims our creativity is what likens us to a virus's facile mutation, its ability to adapt and exploit with hyper-accelerated iterations. But I would argue that unlike viruses, we humans can *choose* whether to destroy or preserve our own environment. It's an advantage that, far from likening us to viruses, differentiates us from all other forms of life on Earth. If we may be the planet's greatest enemy, then we may be its savior as well, for the same reason."

There was a smattering of applause, and a few growls of dissent from the front row.

Geoffrey noticed a man enter the auditorium through a side door behind the audience.

The newcomer's buzzed hair, charcoal suit, and blank expression gave the impression of someone who had come here tonight for business, not pleasure. The stranger sat down, after apparently offering some rolled-up paper money to a young man on the aisle of the back row for his seat.

Geoffrey continued, still looking thoughtfully at the late arrival. "But let's challenge your basic assumption for a moment, Dr. Thomas: the notion that human population size would *increase* because of the extension of our life span. We know that the rate of population growth is stabilizing and should level off by mid-century if current trends continue, so the question of unlimited growth of population might already be moot. But every half-century or so, human beings *must* be replaced by an entirely new cast of characters. The considerable social pressure exerted to encourage procreation within a small window of opportunity will be greatly eased with the extension of life spans."

Geoffrey clicked back to the image of the egg timer, to a scattered round of chuckles.

"Just think about it! If people do not have to beat the deadlines of their biological clocks to procreate in time for their parents to see their grandchildren, family values would be radically redefined. The current shortness in life span creates pressure to replace ourselves in a hurry, or there would be no future for the human race—and we need a future, like no other creature on Earth, because we can *conceive* of the future.

"There would be other benefits, too, of course. Women could hit the snooze button on their biological clocks and focus on other pursuits until the day, if ever, they decided to have children. The birth rate would actually fall dramatically if people could have children on their own terms instead of nature's and at their own pace instead of biology's. Of course, they would need to get nose and ear jobs occasionally, since cartilage never stops growing. But perhaps people would care more about the future that their actions today might cause if we all lived longer. After all, the debt we leave to our children now, we would be leaving to ourselves, as well."

The audience shuddered at this.

"All priorities and values would be reordered accordingly," Geoffrey continued. "As human values have always readily adapted to new threats, opportunities, and conditions, they will adapt, again, to this new reality of longevity. The 'family values' of today bear no resemblance to the family values of yesterday. Dowries? Arranged marriages? Virginity? Please! The family values of the future will be as different from ours as ours are from those of the past.

"Of course, traditionalists who prize today's values, believing our fleeting context to be divinely inspired rather than a mere expedience of nature, will recoil instinctively at any spectacular advance in human life span. The moral implications are profound. Therefore I believe that a new understanding of the origin of life span is especially crucial now that we are on the verge of this turning point in human history. If we discover that our limited life span is not ordained or even necessary, but merely the expedience of genes that needed protection from cross-generational recombination, we can discard any moral weight or divine significance to our given life span and accept our ability to extend it."

Geoffrey clicked off the video projector. "Thank you, ladies and gentlemen. And now, of course, you are invited to bombard me with rhetorical Inter-Continental Ballistic Missiles."

Hands rose like missile launchers all along the

front row. Geoffrey glanced again at the stone-faced man who sat in the back row.

"I must say, I'm very skeptical, Geoffrey," one colleague remarked from the front seats.

"Good," Geoffrey said. "I was hoping you would say that, Dr. Stoever!"

This got a laugh from some of the regulars.

"It would take a lot of research across a wide variety of organisms to see if your principle holds up," Stoever retorted. "And I'd certainly be curious to know how many cases you checked before going with your hypothesis here tonight."

"Quite a few," Geoffrey replied. "I haven't found a single solid exception to the rule."

Angel Echevarria raised his hand. "What about lemmings? Perhaps population control is a factor in life span, eh? Did you think of *that?*"

"As a matter of fact, Angel," Geoffrey said, grinning, "lemmings aren't really committing suicide when they leap into the sea. They are attempting to migrate to richer feeding grounds. Lemmings only live about two years, even though females are ready to breed at *two weeks*."

"That blows your theory right out of the water, then," Angel retorted.

"Nope. Turns out lemmings, unlike mice, voles, or rabbits, are solitary animals that don't live in close proximity to their own offspring. So the fact that they breed so young and frequently actually *decreases* the odds of parent-child breeding. If anyone would like to offer any other organisms that might violate this principle, I welcome all challenges!"

"Now we know the real reason for these chats of yours, Geoffrey," fired Dr. Fukuyama. "Free research assistants."

"You're on to me." Geoffrey grinned as a laugh rose from the audience. He pointed at another raised hand.

"So what do you think of the latest broadcast from Henders Island, Dr. Binswanger?"

It had to happen sooner or later, Geoffrey told himself. "Well, my lab partner pointed out the new YouTube video to me. Very dramatic. But could you actually *see* anything? The camera was moving around and was pointed at the ground, and it was dark. It's not something I would call *proof.* Seems more like a viral video marketing campaign. Sorry to disappoint you!"

As controversy erupted in the audience, Geoffrey saw the man in the charcoal suit rise from his seat and abruptly leave the auditorium—which only made his appearance there that evening even more bizarre.

SEPTEMBER 10

5:10 A.M.

Nell sat in the dark living room before the swollen blue eye of the TV.

A vague noise banged like thunder in the distance as she stared at the monster watching her through the glass.

Its two large eyes, twitching on stalks, locked onto hers. Each of their three pupils lined up vertically and it saw her six times simultaneously.

Nell suddenly realized she was awake, and her eyes were open!

She was not dreaming this . . .

A 1,200-pound spiger sat on the window over her bunk bed in Section Three.

The rush of adrenaline seized her chest. She couldn't even scream as she recognized one of the things that had chased her on the beach.

She watched, petrified, as the creature cocked its head and raised its arms, preparing to strike.

A sound like a cannon shot boomed against the thick polycarbonate window as the creature slammed its arms down, sending a shock wave through the whole lab.

Dizzy from the concussion, Nell reached down.

She yanked off one of her Adidas sneakers, having fallen asleep without removing them.

The beast glared through the window, its eyes toggling slowly from side to side. Its dark icicle teeth gnashed in its grinding vertical jaws, and its fur pulsed red, orange, and pink patterns, suggesting motion like a neon dragon, though it held perfectly still.

In a flash of anger, Nell shouted and hurled her shoe right at the creature's face.

Instantly, its head recoiled and its eyes disappeared under a sharp chevron of brow ridges.

It reextended its neck. Its head tilted curiously at her as its eyestalks reemerged. The filigree of stripes on the spiger's face rippled colors as a pair of panting nostrils on its chest stenciled colons of steam on the window.

Before Nell could break herself away from its gaze, it raised its arms again to each side of its head and smashed them down against the window, again and again, in a relentless assault on the quivering polycarbonate sheet.

Stunned by the sonic blasts, she barely noticed a swarm of flying creatures that had appeared, hovering over the beast.

They dive-bombed its back, causing it to twist its head upward at them and roar. Suddenly, in swift succession, three badger-sized animals slammed into its side.

The spiger shrieked like a train whistle as the

"badgers" dug into its twisting torso. Then it catapulted backwards off its tail, gouging scratches in the window as it bit one of the smaller animals in half and shook off its other assailants in midair.

Spiger
Pantherocaris rex
(*after* Binswanger-Duckworth and Echevarria,
Expeditionary Reports of the Trident Expedition,
vol 2: 1–180)

The window was empty—just blue sky. For an interminable moment after the animals fell from view, Nell stared at the sky. Three blue blood spatters dripped down the window, which had somehow withstood the assault.

Her ears were ringing but she could faintly hear Andy and Quentin open the hatch to the sleeping quarters, yelling.

"What was that?"

"Are you all right, Nell?"

"It sounded like gunshots!"

"You didn't see it?" she asked.

"No."

"What was it?" Quentin said.

She propped herself up on her elbows and swung her legs down over the edge of the bunk. Her hearing was still weak and tinny—her ears and head throbbed. "A nightmare."

"Are you all right?"

She laughed nervously. "I'm glad NASA built this thing," she said loudly over the continuing din in her ears.

She slid down and hugged Andy, and hid her face on his shoulder for a quick, controlled sob, and Andy obliged, squaring his narrow shoulders and looking back at Quentin, protectively.

The NASA biologist was studying the deep gouges in the surface of the window. "Whatever it was, I hope it doesn't come back. It must have spotted you through the roof like a lemon meringue pie at a lunch counter, Nell."

"God damn it, Quentin," Andy scolded.

"Sorry."

9:01 A.M.

"Captain, the *Enterprise* is hailing us," said Samir El-Ashwah on the bridge of the *Trident*.

"Put it on speaker. Yes, *Enterprise*?" Captain Sol delicately glued a window frame onto the back of the Spanish galleon model he had set up on his chart table.

"Captain, this is Lieutenant Commander Eason of the *Enterprise*. We have a request from the highest levels for a professional cameraman to do some work on the island. Conditions will be safe, he'll be in some sort of NASA vehicle. Do you have anyone who might fit the bill?"

"What highest level, *Enterprise*, just out of curiosity?"

"Uh, that would be POTUS, the President of the United States, sir."

Captain Sol widened his eyes at Samir and Warburton. "I think we may be able to accommodate you, *Enterprise*." He pulled off his reading glasses. "Let me get back to you in the next ten minutes."

"Ten minutes will work, Captain. Thank you!"

"Oh crap," Captain Sol said, with a sidelong look at Samir. He reached for the ship's intercom. "Cynthea and Zero, please report to the bridge."

"I gotta see this," Warburton said.

Minutes later, Cynthea crashed through the door. Zero sauntered in after her.

"The Navy asked for a cameraman to go ashore," the captain told them. "Apparently, the President of the United States himself has authorized it. Are you interested, Zero?"

"Zero!" Cynthea cheered.

216

Zero narrowed his eyes at Cynthea.

"Oh no!" Cynthea exclaimed. "Just watch, Captain, now he's going to say no. He's been saying no all week!"

"Eh, Cynthea? Are you involved with this?" The captain frowned.

"What are the details?" said Zero.

"I don't know. You'll be in something NASA built, they said." Captain Sol looked at Cynthea grumpily.

But Zero smiled at her. "Does your last offer still stand?"

"Of course . . ." She blushed.

Zero's grin widened. "OK, baby."

Cynthea avoided Captain Sol's scrutinizing eye as she raced past him to give Zero a huge hug.

11:46 A.M.

The mongoose sat so still it might have been a stuffed specimen in a diorama. Only its nostrils moved as it sniffed the air.

It found no familiar scents, but caught nauseating whiffs of sulfur in the air. Strange stimuli baffled its instincts, and its ringed tail, whiskers, and ears twitched in unison.

The animal was fitted with a black nylon harness. Mounted on top was a Crittercam, a device invented by Greg Marshall for the National Geographic Society. At the end of a curving black tube, a pencil-wide camera lens peered over the mammal's supple shoulders.

The tiny camera beamed a real-time image from a Starburst candy–sized titanium-cased transmitter on the animal's back. Its signal was good for a maximum range of about five hundred meters.

The grizzled and faintly striped fur of the mammal shimmered in the diffused light as it crept up over a tree branch that seemed to be coated in scales like a reptile.

The mongoose kept lifting its head on its long, flexible neck, temporarily blocking the tiny camera's view. Flinching at every unfamiliar noise, it surveyed its surroundings.

The mongoose's reputation for astonishing athletic ability is well earned, though the popular belief that it is immune to the poison of the cobra—its archenemy as depicted in Kipling's famous children's story—shortchanges its prowess. In fact, the mongoose relies solely on its lightning-fast reflexes to prevail over the world's deadliest snake. Likewise, the supposed close contest between the mongoose and the cobra, perpetuated by Kipling's tale, was a myth. It wasn't really a contest at all.

The average mongoose approaches a cobra with almost playful zeal. Their confrontation is a pitiful thing to behold. The mammal toys with the venerated reptile, easily dodging its strikes with eye-blurring leaps, taunting it with its jerking ringed tail as it times its fatal assault. So precise is its coordination on that final strike that the mongoose counts on biting the cobra's head *behind* the hood to deliver the coup de grâce. Mongooses have even been known to pin their victims down, rip out their fangs, and taunt their toothless quarry, like a cat would a mouse, before condescending to feed on their still-coiling prey.

Deadly snakes, of course, are not the only victims of the fearless mammal. Birds, rodents, reptiles, and fruit all find their way to its stomach. Its keen sense of smell can even locate scorpions underground, a mongoose delicacy.

It froze now. Its senses were on fire with foreign cues, its instincts confused by conflicting danger signs. Spooked by the motion of the unfamiliar foliage, the mongoose leaped from the branch to land on the feather-strewn ground.

A buzzing rushed toward it. The mammal sniffed the air, switching its tail, eyes darting from side to side as it attempted to locate the source. It jumped, spinning onto its back in the air like a high-diver performing a double twist.

A whining bug zipped toward its head; the mongoose caught it with both front paws as it landed on its hind feet.

The feisty bug bit the mongoose's nose with surprising violence, and the mongoose hissed, wrestling it ferociously and kicking up feathers on the forest floor.

The insect's power baffled the mongoose. Its pinching knife-edged legs managed to cut off two of the mongoose's toes as the mammal bit the bug nearly in half through a crunchy exoskeleton.

Even as the mongoose chewed its carapace, the bug fought, leaking blue blood over the mammal's chin. The strange, tangy taste reminded the mongoose of pill bugs, and it spat the bug out as it scanned the trees.

A flying swarm swooped down through the branches. The mongoose leaped, barely avoiding an animal its own size that had narrowly misjudged its trajectory.

When the mongoose hit the ground, it ran.

It slalomed around tree trunks and under logs to lose its pursuers.

In the parting mist of a ravine, a cobralike shape reared up, and the mongoose sprang sideways.

It switched its tail, going into attack mode as a familiar sight finally engaged its scrambled instincts.

When the mongoose lunged at the snake-shape, something streaked in from its right.

It tried a midair twist, but a pulse of agony jackknifed it forward as something snipped off its tail.

The snarling mammal hit the ground and spun to

face its attacker, its back raised and the bleeding stub of its tail twitching. It faced its opponent—a Henders rat.

The bulbous eyes of the rat swept back and forth on diagonal stalks. Long, crowded crystalline fangs filled its wide mouth and colors pulsed in stripes around its jaws. White crab claws on its lower jaw fed the still-curling tail of the mongoose into its mouth, bite by bite as though into a sink disposal. It trained both eyes on the trembling mongoose and spat out the tip of its tail. Then it closed its lips over its mouthful of fangs and blew a piercing whistle from two nostrils on top of its round head.

The mongoose hissed, stepping back as the high-frequency noise pierced its eardrums. In shock from pain, the mongoose froze, its senses over-loaded. It tried to focus on its opponent, whose face rippled with dazzling stripes of color.

The velvet-furred rat held its thick tail curled under its body, tucked between its four legs. A sharp cleat hooked down on the tip of its tail like a scorpion's stinger, gripping the ground.

The rat's second brain toggled the eyes on its back, ready to direct the creature's leaps with the hind legs and the "tail," which could launch the animal twenty feet. It rose up on its four legs and extended long knife-edged arms at the mongoose, as though sensing it with antennae, the claws on its lower jaw extending in anticipation.

The mongoose preempted its strike and lunged at it, catching the back of the rat's neck in its teeth.

The mongoose bit down and gave a vicious jerk of its head to snap the rat's neck—but there were no bones in its neck to snap. It gave a few more furious shakes as the rat blew another whistling screech. The mongoose bit down again and again before it released the mortally wounded rat and sensed the wave of animals approaching. Panicked, it spun and leaped away, tipped off balance without its tail.

Another Henders rat sailed through the air, tackling the mammal with its knife-edged arms.

It clamped the mongoose's hind legs with its own and twisted it to the ground. The mongoose's supple back rippled and curled like a whip as it writhed in a death grip with its attacker, kicking up more dust and feathers.

But the invertebrate was more flexible. The claws on either side of the rat's wide jaws grabbed the mongoose's belly and its teeth bit deep.

Attracted by the snarling fracas, a riot of other creatures arrived. They plunged into the shrieking ball of carnage on the forest floor.

The Crittercam's lens was suddenly sprayed blue and red.

The transmission went dead.

The mongoose had survived two minutes and nineteen seconds.

11:49 A.M.

Moans of disappointment filled all three still-operating sections of StatLab as the monitors went dark.

Presidential envoy Hamilton Pound stared in frustration out the windows of Section Four, which was farthest from the jungle and highest up the slope of green fields that rose to the island's high rim.

Pound thought the inside of StatLab resembled the interior of a large Gulfstream jet jammed with workstations, monitors, and specimen-viewing chambers, each attended by grim-faced scientists and technicians. All seemed very depressed by what they had just witnessed.

"Damn," Dr. Cato said. The slender scientist had neatly trimmed white hair and wore a peach-colored Caltech polo shirt. The usually keen, youthful sparkle in his gray eyes was absent now. The fate of the mongoose had filled him with dread. "OK—scratch mongoose off the list, Nell."

Nell nodded and shot him an ominous look.

For his part, Hamilton Pound was confused by what he had just seen. And a little dizzy, too. He wore a rumpled, sweat-stained Brooks Brothers shirt with rolled-up sleeves and a loosened blue-and-red Hermès tie around his unbuttoned collar. His receding hair was slicked back with sweat. He was suffering from a bout of dysentery as his system battled a microbial invasion, and he swigged thirstily from a bottle of Mylanta.

As Special Assistant to the President, Ham Pound had been dispatched on this fact-finding mission by POTUS himself. It was his first opportunity for a solo performance, and at thirty-two he knew it was an impressive milestone in what had already been referred to in the *Washington Post* as a "meteoric diplomatic career." Unfortunately, his own illness, the weather, and canceled flights due to equipment failures had cost him three days en route.

And it was just his luck that yesterday two Sea Wolf attack subs had detected and confronted a Chinese sub only fifty nautical miles north of Henders Island. The incident had precipitated a dangerous diplomatic standoff, and the President wasn't happy about it. The Chinese had backed down, for now. But the ball was firmly in Pound's hands, and he had to score.

"So much for Crittercams," Nell sighed, patting Dr. Cato's shoulder.

Dr. Cato looked troubled. This phase of the investigation, wherein common invasive species would be tested against Henders species, had been designated "Operation Mongoose." The Navy brass needed to have a name for this task, apparently, even though the whole operation was top secret. Cato was the one who suggested "Operation Mongoose," since mongooses were notorious island conquerors. Now that an actual mongoose had met such a swift and terrible fate, however, he wasn't so comfortable with the name.

Nell reached for the newly arrived diplomat's hand. "Welcome to our home away from home, Mr. Pound. Sorry, but we were a little busy when you came in, as you can see."

"Nice to be here." Pound nodded, only half-facetiously, as he replaced the cap on his Mylanta and shook Nell's hand. "Call me Ham."

Both Nell and Dr. Cato balked at the suggestion.

"Nell is one of only two survivors of the original landing, Mr. Pound," Dr. Cato explained, "and a brilliant former student of mine. She's proven to be one of our most valuable on-site project leaders. I don't think she's slept a minute since the first section of the lab touched down nine days ago. Have you, Nell?"

"Nice to meet you," Pound said, annoyed by the academic niceties.

"Have a look at these," Nell said.

The woman was all business, Pound decided. *Good.*

She presented a brightly lit viewing chamber. Inside was what looked like a collection of buttons.

"Those are disk-ants, as Nell here, who discovered them, calls them," Dr. Cato explained, looking over Pound's shoulder.

Nell zoomed in with an overhead camera to show a top view of one of the disks on a monitor over the specimen chamber. The one she focused on was waxy-white with a bruisy blue in the center. The "faceup" side of the disk-ant looked like a pie sliced into five pieces. At the center, a shark-toothed mouth grinned across the seams of two slices. On either side of it were dark eyes anyone could take for buttonholes.

Facedown ants were embossed with three spiraling horns radiating from the center on their upper sides.

"You have to give them a real name, Nell," Dr. Cato said.

"Later. We discovered these ants must not have a queen, Mr. Pound. But like normal ants, they're pack hunters and scavengers." Nell looked at the presidential envoy to make sure he was following. "All the creatures on Henders Island have blue copper-based blood, like crabs and squids do. But they also appear to have energy-boosting adaptations. Their mortality rate is extremely high, but their birthrate is *so* extremely high that it seems to make up for it."

Nell increased the magnification. She moused an arrow cursor on the screen to indicate the curving edge of a disk-ant. "Those are eyes on the edge, see?"

She looked at Pound, who coughed and nodded.

"Twenty stereoscopic eyes between their twenty arms," she continued. "The arms retract telescopically. We think their optic nerves have on-and-off switches activated by an inner-ear-like position detector so they can see ahead, behind, or above them as they roll, as if through a zoetrope."

"A zoetrope?" Pound glanced at his Chronoswiss Pathos wristwatch, but he couldn't remember what time zone he was in and all the dials seemed to blur together.

"You know, one of those old rotating novelties," Dr. Cato said. "If you look at a series of photos through slits as it spins, the photos look like one moving image."

"Oh right." Pound removed his glasses and rubbed the steamed-up lenses again. "Keep going."

"The sophistication of the nervous system is just staggering for an animal of this size," Dr. Cato explained.

"The size of their ring-shaped brain in proportion to body mass is twice the relative size of a jumping spider's brain," Nell added.

"And jumping spiders have the largest brain in proportion to body mass of any known animal," Dr. Cato said. "When these ants are not rolling, they can walk on either flat side and carry food on top. When rolling, they can carry food on both sides, feeding themselves and their offspring at the same time."

Pound replaced his glasses. "OK. So?"

Nell panned the camera to a facedown specimen.

"On the 'tails' side, you see three Fibonacci spirals radiating from the center toward the edge. One of these spiraling tubes is the birth canal. It feeds vitellin, a kind of primitive yolk, to the unborn juveniles. The other tube is a waste canal. And the third spiral," Nell zoomed in farther, "is actually a row of babies hitching a ride, lined up like puka shells on a necklace. So each ant you can see is really a colony. The babies go into action when their mothers molt, helping to devour and remove the old exoskeleton. We haven't figured out their sex organs yet—but they appear to be hermaphrodites that mate once and give birth *constantly* for the rest of their lives, using a stored packet of sperm from their mate. They can probably self-fertilize, too, like barnacles." She looked drily at Pound for a reaction, and found none. "They give birth to ready-to-go miniatures that infest them until they're large enough to leave home or eat their parent—unless Mom or Dad eats them first. As they grow larger they give birth to larger offspring, which tend to graze on the smaller offspring, striking a tenuous balance—until food becomes scarce. Then, in a heartbeat, it becomes every disk-ant for itself."

Henders Disk-Ant
Rotaformica hendersi
(*after* Steele and Benton, *Proceedings of the
Zoological Society of Washington*, vol. 36: 12–27)

She increased the magnification again, to 100X. On one of the "baby" disk-ants was a similar spiral of miniatures hitching a ride on its back.

"The ant's offspring give birth, too, down to the size of mites." She looked at Pound. "And they are constantly infiltrated by other passengers from different disk-ants, which line up according to size automatically."

"Each individual you see," Dr. Cato added, "is a colony of thousands, which help one another molt and recycle the components of chitin to the next scale down."

"And help attack prey and the armies of parasites that protect their prey." Nell knocked on the thick window.

At the sound, the disk-ants lying on their sides snapped up on their edges. Their centipede-like legs telescoped out and rolled them forward toward the noise of Nell's rapping knuckles. Some of them launched like Chinese throwing disks. Retracting their legs, they banked off the window, leaving pinpoint nicks in the acrylic. Pound could see many other such nicks on the window. One of the ants stuck: a flood of tiny ants flowed down from the doomed ant's back and spread out on the window as others stayed behind and instantly began devouring their host.

"Jesus," Pound muttered. They reminded him of the crabs he had acquired while engaging in a particularly ill-advised spring break activity in Fort Lauderdale during his Dartmouth days.

Nell was glad to see him appropriately alarmed. "You should see what they do to army ants. We caught these specimens by extending a hot dog into the jungle on a robotic arm. In ten seconds you couldn't see the hot dog. Ten seconds later, it was gone. The hot dog practically melted as the nano-ants unloaded from their parents and attacked."

Nell looked right into Pound's eyes, touching his arm. "They are omnivorous, Mr. Pound. They graze on the green stuff growing on the island's slopes and the jungle's canopy, as well. You came just in time to see another of our tests."

Pound tried to look impressed, but he just wasn't. He needed to see the big picture, the full tour. The President had little patience for minutiae, and these creepy disk-ant things were the definition of it. "Don't give me the labor pains," POTUS was fond of saying, "just show me the *baby!*"

"Why can't we go down to the lower section of the lab and get a look inside the jungle?" Pound said irritably. "I'm here to get a video record of this place to the President three days ago."

"There's plenty to see right here, Mr. Pound," Dr. Cato reminded him.

Pound lowered his voice, glancing at the other scientists working around them. "Doctor, I don't think you appreciate how much pressure this investigation is under. We need to find out whether this island is a serious biohazard. We can't maintain a media blackout forever while you're studying bugs, with all due respect. The rest of the world is getting . . . antsy." He glanced at the disk-ants lying dormant again on their sides inside the specimen chamber, and scowled. "And frankly, this is *not* what the United States needs from a P.R. point of view right now." He glared at Dr. Cato, whispering, "Nobody's happy about us monopolizing this situation!"

"I never said we should keep other countries out!" Dr. Cato sputtered indignantly.

Pound spoke with urgent softness to both of them now: "The President has decided that we need to preserve a military option, which quickly becomes impossible with other countries involved. We've already included British scientists, since the Brits have a tenuous claim on this island, but any more than that and no matter how dangerous the life forms here turn out to be, the problem will be uncontainable. We need to know what's going on *in there.* I don't understand why we can't go down to the other end of the lab and get a good look inside that jungle for the President."

The other scientists in earshot zinged some dirty looks at Pound.

"I'm afraid that we're having a few technical difficulties in Section One, Mr. Pound," Nell told him. "Why don't you have a look at this instead . . ."

12:02 P.M.

The visor of NASA technician Jedediah Briggs's helmet was already fogged up as he entered the vestibule connecting Section Two to Section One.

As he descended the aluminum stairway to inspect the damage to Section One, he heard shrieking whistles around him. A rhythmic pounding reverberated through the lab below. He peered out of his hazy visor at the sensors studding the plastic tube.

About the size of smoke detectors, the sensors lining the vestibule sniffed out any microbial life that might breach the outer lining. They monitored the hermetically sealed space between the outer and inner layers using LAL extracted from the blood of horseshoe crabs, which had been injected into each unit.

A small glass tube in the sensors was supposed to turn yellow in the presence of microbes. NASA had already used similar devices to ensure that interplanetary probes were microbe-free during construction.

As Briggs crept down the aluminum stairway toward the hatch of Section One he noticed that all the green LEDs on the sensors had turned red—and the test tubules had turned bright yellow.

Thankful for the blue cleansuit he had been cursing a moment before, Briggs reached the bottom of the stairs and peered through the hatch window into Section One.

Halos of sunlight streamed into the lab from ring-shaped clusters of holes punched through its roof.

The shafts of light illuminated the creatures crawling, flitting, skittering, and leaping throughout the lab.

The center between one of the rings of holes in the roof fell out and larger animals immediately poured through.

The swarms of creatures gathering below seemed to notice him peering through the window at them and they all moved with unnatural speed straight toward him, creating a cyclone of paper and flying debris.

A rain of wasps and drill-worms splattered like

bugs on a windshield as Briggs jerked back from the window. A sudden, piercing alarm sounded.

He turned and ran up the aluminum stairway.

All around him the lining of the vestibule was twinkling now with purple LEDs. He remembered as he ran that the inner layer was laced with fiber optics that detected structural damage to the vestibule. The whole tube turned purple-red as the inner lining was breached around him.

Briggs cursed the baggy cleansuit as he vaulted up the creaking aluminum stairs.

12:03 P.M.

"Technical difficulties?" Pound snapped. "NASA spent 180 million dollars on this lab, Dr. Cato. I thought it was designed for this!"

"Designed for *this?*" Nell stifled a laugh, looking at Dr. Cato ruefully.

"Some adaptations have been made," Dr. Cato answered patiently. "Even while the lab was being shipped, and ever since it got here. It's quite miraculous what they've been able to do. But StatLab was primarily designed as a modular mobile lab that could be dropped into remote disease hot-zones, Mr. Pound. It wasn't designed to be under siege by anything larger than a virus."

Nell guided Pound along with a firm hand on his waist.

"We should be getting word shortly on the status

234

of Section One. In the meantime, let's take a look at some things that we've already found, OK?"

12:04 P.M.

The afterburners of an F-14 Tomcat roared as it was catapulted from the deck of the U.S.S. *Enterprise.*

When the bone-rattling tumult had passed, a Navy officer resumed shouting at Zero over a revving V-22 Sea Osprey, which stood behind her on the gray plane of the flight deck.

"You're the only one who's been in there and survived," the officer yelled.

Zero looked around at the busy men and women on top of the gigantic aircraft carrier. "What makes you think I would go *back* in there?" he shouted back.

"Cynthea said you wanted to get off the *Trident*," she yelled. "You'll be quarantined on the island until this is over. The President needs a cameraman there—if you want it, the job is yours!"

Zero looked around wryly in the direction of the *Trident.* "I'll be damned," he muttered. He pointed at a monster RV. "In that thing?"

Sitting on the deck with a thick cable attached to its roof was the most macho off-road vehicle Zero had ever seen. Aside from the word "NASA" stenciled in red on its side, impressive by itself, the rover had two monster knobby tires in front and halftracks behind. It had four bubble windows like those on a deep-sea sub, three in front and another at the rear. Protruding from the front of the vehicle was a wedge-shaped grille like the cowcatcher on a 19th-century locomotive. Two heavy robotic arms were folded to either side of the front bubble, like the arms of a praying mantis.

"The XATV-9," the Navy officer shouted over the Osprey's engines, pointing behind her. "NASA's experimental Mars rover! Shipped in by special order of the President himself. You couldn't be safer in your mother's arms, sir! What do you say?"

The lensman in Zero answered. "OK," he shouted, cursing himself at the same time.

"You need to get in *now,* sir!"

Two flight deck crewmen rushed Zero forward. They sealed the airtight hatch behind him as he climbed into a sunken shotgun seat before the three bubble windows. A control panel out of *Buck Rogers* glittered between Zero and the driver, who was a clean-cut man in a navy blue jumpsuit. He gave Zero a confident thumbs-up and then pointed at a nice Steadicam on a folding robotic arm mounted to the roof above the shotgun seat.

"Strap yourself in quick," the driver advised. "You ain't never had a ride like this."

Zero clicked the seat harness and grabbed the handles of the Steadicam, which swung down weightlessly from the ceiling. He put the wide viewfinder to his left eye just as the Osprey yanked them off the deck.

"Woo-Hoooo!" the driver yelled.

They swung out over the ocean. Zero gulped as he aimed the camera out the window.

12:05 P.M.

Nell led the presidential envoy past workstations where scientists monitored remote cameras.

One screen showed disk-ants rolling down trails; another glimpsed nasty-looking creatures seemingly attacking the camera.

Each monitor Pound looked at seemed to go dead on cue. The scientists observing them groaned as if they had come to expect it.

Pound turned to Dr. Cato. "I really must insis—"

"You may want to video this," Nell said, patting Pound's arm. "For the President."

Persuaded by Nell's persistence, Pound awkwardly placed a glossy white plastic headband camera over his head and extended the arm of its viewfinder, wondering where his promised cameraman was. He centered the third-eye-like lens on his forehead, then tapped the side, illuminating a green operating light under the viewfinder's miniature screen.

Three large, vicious-looking yellow-and-black insects shot through a clear tube into the viewing theater.

"Japanese giant hornets," Dr. Cato said, appreciatively.

237

"A hunting pack of thirty can slaughter an entire hive of thirty thousand honeybees in less than five hours," Nell said.

"Their larvae feed them an energy-boosting amino acid that enables them to fly twenty-five miles per hour for sixty miles," Dr. Cato added.

"Whoa," Pound said.

"Watch closely, Mr. Pound." Dr. Cato pointed at the chamber to make sure the envoy didn't miss it. "A single Japanese giant hornet can kill forty bees a minute. They chop them to pieces with their mandibles. Scouts spray a pheromone to mark their prey. Then they attack as a pack."

"Their stingers pump venom so powerful it dissolves human flesh," Nell said. "They kill about forty people a year in Japan."

"We've been upping the stakes lately." Dr. Cato chuckled.

"Christ! I've never even heard of them." Pound's eyes were glued to the specimen chamber.

Nell glanced at Dr. Cato. "OK, Steve, let in the Henders wasps."

High-speed cameras whirred as their motors revved up and locked on two five-inch-long Henders "wasps" that emerged from a tube and hovered vertically on five transparent wings.

Their dragonfly-like abdomens swung forward as they tackled the Japanese hornets in midair.

With their ten double-jointed jackknifelike legs, the Henders wasps ruthlessly sliced the hornets into pieces that fell to the ground still moving.

As the ring of eyes on their "heads" kept watch, the wasps landed on five legs. They dipped their tails to devour the sliced bits with five-jawed maws.

Henders Wasp
Pentapterus tomobranchiophorus
(and Japanese Giant Hornets, *Vespa mandarinia*)
(*after* Wirth et al, *Annals of the La Jolla Natural History Museum*, vol. 47: 1–112)

"Yuck," the presidential envoy said. "They eat with their *butts?*"

"They have two brains, Mr. Pound," Dr. Cato said grimly.

"Like many of the creatures we've studied here," Nell said.

Pound looked confused.

"Is this how *every* experiment has gone so far, Nell?" Dr. Cato asked quietly.

Nell nodded, sharing a worried look with him.

Pound fiddled with a knob on his headcam.

"Henders species," Nell continued, "have not only matched every common species we've tested, Mr. Pound—they've completely annihilated them."

The envoy shrugged. "Sounds like we're talking about a bunch of bugs. Why can't we just spray a little DDT and be done with it?"

"We're talking about a lot more than bugs, Mr. Pound," Nell sighed.

"There are creatures here bigger than tigers, according to Nell," Dr. Cato said.

"Spigers, I call them, Mr. Pound," she said. "Eight-legged creatures at least three times the size of tigers."

"Ham," Pound said, feeling lightheaded. "Call me Ham, please. Why can't we see some of those? Spigers? That's what I really need to see!"

12:05 P.M.

The *Trident*'s sequestered crew played checkers and sat around the decks, utterly bored. Nineteen days of looking at a beach they could not set foot on was mixing an explosive cocktail of anger, fear, and insanity.

At night, they could see the spy satellites watching them, slowly crossing each other's paths in a precise and perpetual changing of the guard overhead, like the guards at Buckingham Palace.

Cynthea, Captain Sol, and First Mate Warburton stood on the prow of the *Trident*. They watched the roaring Osprey pass over the inlet in which they were anchored.

"There he goes," Warburton exclaimed. "Lucky bastard!"

Captain Sol shook his head. "I don't envy him."

Cynthea peered through her opera glasses at the helicopter carrying the rover until it had disappeared behind the island's cliff. "Come on, Zero!" she urged, squeezing a crimson-nailed fist. "If you come through for me, you are my lord and master for all eternity, baby!"

Captain Sol and Warburton exchanged wide-eyed looks.

12:06 P.M.

"Watch this, Mr. Pound," insisted Dr. Cato.

"Otto is going to send in one of our last remote-operated vehicles," Nell explained.

Dr. Cato tapped Otto's shoulder and startled him as he sat at one of the workstations in Section Four. "Where are we going now, young man?"

Otto pulled up his VR goggles and grinned up at Pound. The biologist's left thumb was encased in an aluminum splint. It had not stopped him from operating the ROVs he'd helped design. He was feeling no pain, thanks to the kick-ass Novocain pads the Navy doctor had given him for his thumb. "Welcome to the jungle, guys." Otto put the VR goggles back on. "We're about to penetrate the outer edge with a small robotic vehicle and take a little peek inside. This usually only lasts a few seconds, so don't blink!"

"All right." Pound glanced reprovingly at Cato and Nell. "Now we're getting somewhere!"

"We've already deployed about eighty ROVs," Nell said, patiently. "We only have about a dozen left. We've made it pretty far across the fields, all the way to the rim of the island. But we're using all the rest now to try to get into the jungle, where most of the action seems to be."

The ROV was the coolest Christmas present a seven-year-old kid could ever imagine finding under the tree. Several outboard cameras captured images as it emerged from a rack under Section One. The remote-controlled vehicle turned left on the slope toward the jungle.

With the soft zither of servomotors the robotic vehicle rolled over purple patches of Henders "clover" and left brown tracks behind it in a rearview cam that showed in the bottom half of the screen.

Otto steered it toward the edge of the jungle and slowed down.

"Hang on," he said, and throttled the ROV into an opening between the trees. On the monitor above, the ROV's camera weaved swiftly around the trunks of trees that looked like palms crossed with cactus. Some were covered with reptilian scales, thorns, what might have been eyes—even snapping mouths.

Slaloming around the tree trunks, the ROV came to a tunnel-like corridor lined by dense trees whose trunks were curved like ribs or giant tusks and whose interlacing canopies of mistletoe-like clover were pierced by sunbeams. The ROV raced under the dangling clusters, chains, and spirals of colored berries on translucent tendrils that rose and fell like jellyfish tentacles along the corridor.

A streaming horde of insects and animals buzzed and roared past the speeding ROV, rushing toward it in the lower screen from the rear-cam. Otto zigzagged down the curving tunnel as a rush of creatures seemed to miss it at every turn. He hung a right turn at breakneck speed as the corridor forked. They could make out nothing but a whirl of blurring shapes hurtling around the ROV as it raced down the jungle tunnel.

Something large darted out from the side.

The rover's camera dove into the dirt. A bird

feather was all they could identify, pressed against the lens.

"Yee-haw!" Otto pulled off his VR goggles. "We see lots of bird feathers," he explained to Pound, who stared at the screen with a blank expression.

"I want you to give me some of your best ROV footage inside the jungle, Dr. Cato, to show to the President," he said.

"Well, that was it, right there!" Otto announced triumphantly.

"That's as far as you've gotten?" Pound asked.

"That's the record, man!" Otto gave Nell a low-five. "You can see why those bastards have eyes in the back of their heads, Nell! We rigged a rearview cam that I could see in the bottom half of the goggles that time. There is no way I'd have gotten that far without it. But man, that is a LOT of stuff to process—they *need* two brains!"

Dr. Cato pointed at another monitor, noticing Pound's eyes glazing. "Look at this remote we were able to set up next to a disk-ant trail, Mr. Pound. This one's lasted three days. Right, Otto?"

"Ri—"

The camera went dead.

"—ght." Otto looked at Pound and shrugged.

"I still don't understand why we can't just go down to Section One and take a look inside the jungle there!" Pound complained. "What's the point of having all this million-dollar equipment if we can't even use it when we need to?"

12:06 P.M.

Briggs slammed Section Two's lower hatch behind him. It sealed with a squeaking *hiss* as he sagged against it to catch his breath.

He ripped off his helmet, and the bulbous blue cleansuit deflated. He straightened up as he addressed the eleven jumpy scientists in Section Two, who were staring at him, bug-eyed, from their workstations. "Duct tape is not an option!" the NASA technician announced. "Listen up!" Briggs barked as he extricated himself from the cumbersome suit. "Section One is now officially *off limits!*"

He kicked off the last leg of the cleansuit and surveyed the scientists with an almost contemptuous air. "And drill-worms *fly*. Yeah, just for everyone's information, OK? And those damn worms are getting through the inner lining of the vestibule down there."

Briggs casually rapped his knuckles on the hatch window behind him. Everyone flinched as drill-worms viciously attacked the other side.

The animals' trio of spiked, folding legs resembled glossy black landing gear on a 1950s sci-fi rocket ship. Their sucked-lozenge heads had three ring-shaped eyes and a flexible neck. They hovered and twisted with precision in midair, using black wings that popped like flower petals from a three-paneled bud under their necks.

They bent their yellow drill-bit abdomens to the window. Their grappling-hooked forefeet scrabbled over its slippery surface.

Briggs looked over his shoulder and jumped as he saw the alien creatures so close at hand.

"OK." He turned back to the other scientists. "Drill-worms have now penetrated the vestibule! But that's not what breached Section One's hull. Something else did that. Hello, is there a doctor in the house? Because we lowly NASA technicians are a little out of our league here, OK? I can't guarantee our safety if you can't tell me what's going on!"

"Hey, we're just here to collect data," said Andy, sarcastically.

Andy wore a bright tie-dyed T-shirt streaked red, yellow, and green. He looked like he hadn't slept in a year. "All those prima donnas on the *Enterprise* are supposed to figure it out for us. Or so we've been told."

"In so many words," Quentin grunted. "There's a couple up in Section Four right now getting a tour, if you want to complain, Briggs." He aimed a finger at a plasma screen showing a rooftop view. "Hey, check it out: Henders lichen is spreading over us right *now.*"

Red and yellow scales bloomed over the roof in Quentin's monitor. The lichenlike growth visibly spread in polygons that changed color and shape, seeming to feed voraciously on the layers of white paint, gray primer, and steel. Each hexagonal tile was bisected by a half-hex "fin" angled to catch the sun. Sunlight turned these sail-fins green as they fluttered in the wind. A permanent cloud of angry bugs swarmed where the jungle was relentlessly swallowing Section One, like antibodies reacting to a wound.

"This crud turns red on iron, yellow on acrylic, and white on paint, man." Quentin shook his head in admiration and pulled off a bite of a Zagnut bar. "I think it's actually eating the lab," he mumbled.

"Some bacteria eat metal, gold, even CDs," Andy said. "Bacteria probably ate the limestone in giant caves—in addition to your teeth, Quentin."

Quentin shrugged. "It's photosynthesizing, too." He clicked two keys and zoomed in as he tore off another chew. "See those scales—the ones catching the sun are tinged green. Henders lichen eats whatever it can get, man," he said with his mouth full the entire time.

Andy frowned. "The maximum growth rate of lichens is about one to two centimeters per year."

"This stuff's growing a million times faster than that," Quentin mumbled.

"Not a million times," Andy objected.

"OK, I was, like, exaggerating?"

"The point is, it *isn't* lichen, Quentin! It's some kind of freaking superplant, like Japanese dodder or something. Everybody keeps calling it lichen."

"Well, *you're* the one who called it lichen!"

247

Briggs put his hands on his hips and watched them in amazement.

"Yeah, I *know,* but I was *wrong,* OK?" Andy snarled. "It's pissing Nell off that everyone keeps calling it that!"

"OK, so what's she calling it, then?" Quentin ripped away another bite of candy with his teeth.

"Clover."

"Oh yeah, like it's clover?" Quentin sputtered, laughing.

"Excuse me, boys!" Briggs yelled. "It's not the moss or lichen or clover or whatever the FUCK you want to call it that's worrying me right now." He pointed a finger at the roof. "You see those vines?" He stabbed a finger at Quentin. "Scientists aren't supposed to exaggerate! And quit eating that thing!" Briggs grabbed the last half of Quentin's Zagnut bar out of his hand and hurled it across the lab.

Quentin shrugged with a *chill-dude* look at Briggs as the NASA technician zoomed the camera in on one of the plantlike organisms on the roof. It looked like translucent fern fronds sprouting from a glass vase.

"Yeah, they just started popping up on the roof the last few hours," Andy said.

"*Mmm,* can't be vines, though," Quentin said.

The translucent stalks of the stretching fronds were coated with sticky green transparent eggs. A Henders wasp landed on one of the vines and ate a few of the eggs with its posterial maw. Then it flew toward the camera, triggering the *whizz* of the autofocus as it switched to macro mode. The bug deposited an egg stuck to its leg onto the lens and flew away. The egg immediately sprouted five tiny translucent "fronds."

"Wow! There's their life cycle, folks."

"They eat the clover," Andy said, recognizing the species. "These things usually come out at night. Looks like they use the bugs to spread their eggs."

Briggs pointed at the screen. "Look at that!"

The fern-shaped fronds of a larger "plant" unrolled. Their five finger-pads smoked as they pressed down on the roof directly over them.

Briggs pointed: five spots of white paint bubbled in a ring on the steel ceiling. The spots matched the pattern of pads on the fronds.

"*That's* what's eating through the hull in Section One." Briggs was looking at Quentin. "OK, genius?"

"Whoa. The lichenovores must use acid to dissolve the lichen off the rocks, man. Bitchin'!"

"*Lichenovores?*" Andy said.

"OK, how about *clovores,* then?"

"Better. Hey, wait a minute! Nell said those things might manufacture sulfuric acid!"

Briggs shook his head. "What? OK, that's it!" he snapped, closing his eyes. "Attention, EVERYBODY!" he shouted. "It's time to pack up your hard drives and your Nerf balls and your iPods and

Abba Zabba bars and Incredible Hulk action figures and whatever else you brought along, because we are *ee-vack-you-ating.* Got it? That means *you,* cowboy!"

"Hey, why are you singling me out!" Andy protested.

"Because you're handy," Briggs shot back. "Now MOVE YOUR ASS!"

"Because I'm *ANDY?*"

"Come on, Andy, damn it," Quentin urged.

"Is that what he said?"

"Don't be so sensitive."

"But is that what he just *said?*"

"What else would he say, after one look at you?" Quentin laughed.

12:07 P.M.

"We've tried drones," Nell said, "but they can't see through the canopy. We tried remote-controlled chopper-cams, but they just attract swarms."

"We tried Crittercams," Otto said. "You saw how well that worked."

"Even with the brief glimpses inside the jungle that we've had, Mr. Pound, we've been able to distinguish as many as eighty-seven distinct species," Dr. Cato said, "some of them quite large. Of the specimens we have been able to capture, many have eyes similar to those of a mantis shrimp. That means they see colors we can't imagine, and their ability to track fast-moving prey is equally super—"

They heard the *chop-chop* of a Sea Osprey's dual rotors reverberating through the walls very nearby.

Pound swung around nervously to peer through the window.

The NASA XATV-9 rover touched down on the slope with a jolt to its shock absorbers, rattling the lab.

"I'm sorry, Dr. Cato." Pound smiled, and heaved a sigh of relief. "I'm going to have to pull rank on you. We're going in. You're welcome to come along, of course, as well as any of your team. I'm sure the President would appreciate all of your input."

The tether detached from the roof of the rover as it backed up the hill on monster tires and halftracks to link up with the extending docking-tube of the lab.

Nell grabbed Pound's arm. "You can't go in there!"

Pound pulled his arm away, gently. "I'm afraid we have to, Doctor."

"This place slaughtered thirteen people and a dog in less than a minute."

He smiled. "If that wasn't a hoax for a TV show."

"Don't you get what those *bugs,* as you call them, can do?" Nell said.

But Pound had already turned and was heading for the hatch.

She followed him. "This is an entirely alien ecosystem, at least a *dozen* new classes of animals. Just one of these species could probably knock the legs right out from under any common ecosystem, Pound. You have no idea how dangerous these species are!"

"That's precisely why we need to find out what we're dealing with here."

"Sure, but this island's been sitting here for half a billion years! What's the rush?"

Pound turned to her, a patronizing arch in his eyebrow. "Thanks to *SeaLife*, everyone on Earth knows where this island is, Nell. And if these *bugs* are half as dangerous as you think, they could be used in biological warfare." He smiled with chill condescension. "I'm sorry, but it's my job to think about those things." He turned and continued walking toward the docking hatch. "So you don't have to!" he threw over his shoulder.

Nell watched him, incredulous. "Wait! Ham, seriously—*don't do it!*"

The docking vestibule slowly extended to the hatch of the rover.

"Tune in on channel one, we'll beam the camera feed back to you," Pound called as a technician pulled the hatch open.

At the same moment, Andy entered through the hatch at the other end of Section Four and immediately waved his arms. "Hey, wait! Let me go!"

"If he's going, I'm *definitely* going." Quentin

pushed in behind Andy. "I know this island's topography better than anyone!"

"OK, you're both in," Pound decided. "Dr. Cato, want to come along? And really get a look at this island? You're welcome!"

Dr. Cato glanced at Nell and was alarmed at the horrified look on her face. "I don't think so, Mr. Pound. I think I'll just catch a ride back to the *Enterprise*."

"Wanna come along, Nell?" Andy said. "I'm sure we could use a botanist."

Nell gripped his hand as he passed her. "You shouldn't go, Andy!"

"I never get to go," Andy groaned. "Besides, we'll be safe in that thing. NASA built it."

A sense of foreboding overwhelmed her, and she clung to his hand.

"It's too upsetting, I understand, Nell. You stay here," he said. "But this time I'm *not* getting left behind!" He pulled away.

"All aboard who are going aboard!" Pound shouted, and he thrust the hatch open.

Andy followed the others who entered the docking tube.

They closed the hatch just as Andy reached it.

"Hey!" he yelped.

The hatch opened.

"Just kidding," Quentin told him. "Get in."

"That isn't funny!"

"Yes, it is." Quentin laughed.

As Andy crawled into the docking tube a lab technician secured the hatch behind him.

Briggs opened the hatch from the section below and entered Section Four, his face grimmer than usual.

He noticed Nell at the far end of the lab. She looked grief-stricken, for some reason.

Briggs then noticed a skinny scientist next to him who was examining a drill-worm in a specimen chamber. "You brought drill-worms in here?" he growled.

"You mean *Rotopodiensis taylori*?"

Briggs looked at the young scientist's name badge: *Todd Taylor.*

"Uh, no. I mean the things that drill through rubber, silicone, and maybe even acrylic, like your little terrarium there." He clicked the wall of the specimen chamber with a fingernail, and the drill-worms inside immediately leaped at the noise, startling young Taylor.

"Listen up!" Briggs yelled as he walked down the aisle toward Nell. "We have to evacuate StatLab! Section One's already compromised and Section Two is a lost cause."

"We can't go yet," Nell protested.

Briggs faced her. "Why not?"

She pointed out the window as the rover charged down the slope.

"Great," grumbled Briggs. "Just what we needed . . ."

Otto switched to channel one and brought up Zero's video feed on the screen as the rover barreled straight toward the jungle.

"Check it out," Otto yelled. "We got front row seats to Henders Island!"

12:11 P.M.

Zero had both his video cameras trained through the bubble window of the XATV-9. The rover crew leaned forward instinctively, grabbing handholds.

"I don't think we should just blast in like this," Andy shouted.

The driver paid no attention. If anything, he seemed to accelerate.

The XATV-9's cowcatcher grate bashed into the forest. It wedged open the trees at its edge, throwing the five men forward against their shoulder harnesses as the towering sections of the cactuslike trees snapped apart and thudded over the roof, spraying blue fluids.

"No worries. That's ten-inch-thick acrylic," the driver assured them. "These windows are designed for submarines."

"That's good, 'cause we're about to punch through into the first corridor," Quentin muttered as trees continued to fly apart around them.

"Slow down!" Andy yelled.

The rover muscled forward, its massive tires and rear halftracks digging in and thrusting them through the dense undergrowth. They heard branches snap and thud against the sides and roof. Sagging clusters of berries dropped from the trees and splattered turquoise, yellow, and magenta juice across the bubble windows as the rover finally started to slow down.

Knocking aside the last few branches, the rover finally broke into an open corridor inside the jungle and came to a stop.

"How's this?" asked the driver.

Quentin grinned. "Perfect."

The tunnel lined by trees extended in a long arc toward them and curved out of sight in the other direction. The rover had pierced an elbow of a winding corridor.

A tornado of creatures chased one another through the tunnel from right to left, curving around a banked corner in front of them and launching down the corridor to their left before swerving out of sight around a forked bend.

As the torrent of animals whipped past the rover's windows, some snatched berries or eggs off tendrils that hung down from the dense canopy. Others became ensnared in the tendrils, which reacted like tentacles, jerking their victims up into the treetops.

"Want to listen in?"

"Yeah!" Quentin said.

The driver pressed a button on the dash that turned on the outboard microphones.

Over the speakers came a deafening drone of insects. The sound was punctuated by hoarse shrieks, anguished screams, and bloodcurdling howls that sounded like a haunted house ride.

"Jesus H. Christ," the driver muttered. He turned and looked at the others.

"Hey!" Andy pointed up the corridor to the right.

A wave of badger-sized animals pounced with astonishing speed after a pack of fleeing Henders rats.

The rats jumped thirty feet through the air down the corridor and landed right in front of the rover. Changing direction, they stayed one step ahead of the badgers, who hammered into the bank of earth right behind them.

One of the yellow-striped badgers tripped on a fallen branch. It was attacked by rats that doubled back, swiftly followed by a wave of disk-ants and wasps coming up from the rear. A deadly gang-fight instantly ensued.

As the badger struggled to shake off its attackers, a dog-sized animal with a head like a grouper and a crown of eyes plunged out of the trees directly across the corridor from the rover and devoured them all with bone-crunching jaws. The retreating grouper shook its head and threw off a few rats, which skittered over the ground and were immediately buried by a swarm of what looked like mouse-sized barracudas with twenty rippling legs, and a platoon of disk-ants hurled into the fray.

The fractal explosion of violence left the human beings inside the rover speechless.

Bugs smashed into the right hemisphere of the front window, building up a coating of pulpy blue slime that other creatures tried to eat quickly before being attacked.

It was a perpetual street riot, Zero thought, as he tried to suck it all into his lens, his heart pounding. He could die after this—if he survived it—and ascend to photographer Valhalla.

12:13 P.M.

The scientists watching the video feed from the safety of StatLab fell silent.

Nell's awe overcame her fear as she contemplated the alien world unfolding on the high-def monitor. The rhythms of carnage and regeneration were so obscenely accelerated it was like watching a war inside a maternity room.

We don't belong here, she thought. *Nothing from our world belongs here.*

12:14 P.M.

Pound looked pale. "Just what are we looking at, gentlemen? Please cut the damn sound!"

"Sure thing," the driver agreed.

The others stared with open mouths at the hurricane of death and birth swirling outside.

"Uh, yes, OK, this is completely alien animal life," Quentin said. "I mean, it has DNA, RNA, basic cellular components, it uses ATP as an energy currency just like other organisms on the planet, all right? But these animals resemble nothing science has ever seen. Instead of a vertebrate design, we're talking about a segmented endoskeleton that looks like a vestigial exoskeleton. The bugs here have exoskeletons like most of the insects on the planet, but their body plans have a radial symmetry that is totally alien. The plants are not only photosynthetic but heterotrophic—*carnivorous,* actually—and they all have copper-based blood."

"They can't be plants if they have blood, Quentin," Andy protested. "Some of the larger forms appear to be photosynthetic organisms that are firmly rooted in the soil, but they're not really plants."

Quentin pointed. "Even these things that look like big palm trees, Mr. Pound, have copper-based blood. I don't know how they pump it up so high, but I think they must have hearts—really *big* hearts. If so, then we'll definitely know they're not plants."

"We think they might actually be related to the disk-ants and the other bugs," Andy said.

"Did you say 'alien'?" Pound's head was swimming. "You mean this stuff came from another planet?"

"No, it's alien but it came from this planet," Andy said.

"How can that be?"

Quentin had a fixed grin on his face as he gazed up and down the corridor outside the window. "We think Henders Island is all that's left of the supercontinent this stuff crawled out on more than half a billion years ago." He shot a quick glance at Pound. "It's been evolving separately ever since."

"Holy shit, *everything's* dropping eggs and babies," the driver exclaimed. "Look at 'em crawling on the glass there!"

A disk-ant rolled across the curve of the window, dropping miniatures that rolled away from it to gorge on splattered blue blood.

"Every Henders organism we've studied can breed at birth," Quentin said.

The driver nodded his head, impressed. "Born ready," he said.

"Some are born pregnant," Andy said. "They mate in the womb."

"Now, that ain't right." The driver looked back at Andy angrily.

Jumping like supercharged frogs or grasshoppers, a wave of guinea pig–sized animals with coffee-brown pelts and leaf-green stripes on their haunches swept down the corridor.

"More Henders rats?" Pound asked as they flew past.

"I don't think so. They're something else. Here come some rats."

"Those are rats?" Pound smirked. "They don't look anything like rats!"

"They're not rats. They're not even vertebrates," Andy told him. "They're more like mongoose crossed with praying mantises. We just call them rats. They use those spike arms like kung fu masters and spear animals so fast you can't even see it happen."

"Look how they move, man!" Quentin said, breaking into a giggle. "When they jump they launch themselves through the air off their *tails!* Check it out! Nell, you were right!" he shouted at Zero's camera.

12:18 P.M.

"Yeah, baby!" Otto cheered, staring at the screen.

Briggs looked at the image, slack-jawed.

"Don't stay too long, guys," Nell whispered. "Can we get radio contact, Otto?"

12:19 P.M.

Andy and Quentin looked at each other with wide congratulatory grins on their faces.

They all flinched as a badger-sized creature landed on top of the right-side bubble window with a rat in its jaws.

The driver grabbed the gearshift. "What the hell is that?"

"Rats get pretty big, I guess," Quentin said.

"Or it may be a different species," Andy said. "Its coloring is different."

"Maybe the coloring changes as they get older . . ."

The coconut-sized head of the animal, which looked like an overgrown Henders rat, peered at them from the end of its telescoping neck.

It had the Bruegel nightmare face of a deep-sea fish, with large eyes on stems and lips that seemed to open in a smile around rows of dark fangs. Iridescent stripes of fur on its face pulsed waves of color away from its mouth.

Its spiked front arms tapped the window as its eyes panned in quick motions. Quentin, Andy, Pound, Zero, and the driver all thought the three "pupils" in each eye were staring directly at them—and in fact the compound eyes actually were focused on each of them simultaneously, though the pupils were an optical illusion. Its body moved around, continuously adjusting its position on the window, but its head remained almost stationary on its flexible neck as it looked through the window at them.

"We know mantis shrimp have at least eight classes of color receptors," Quentin said worshipfully. "Humans only have three!"

"Christ," Pound said. "Shrimps see better than *us?*"

"Not shrimp, really," Andy said. "Somebody just called them shrimp when they were discovered, but they're a totally different family."

"This guy here could be related to mantis shrimp—we think."

The overgrown Henders rat scrambled across the upper hemisphere of the window suddenly. Then it stopped over Andy, both eyes pointing down and converging on him.

"Mantids have a special eye movement for tracking prey," Quentin said. "Each eye can move independently seventy degrees in a microsecond while staying in focus."

"Why is it staring at me?" Andy said.

"I think it likes you." Quentin chuckled.

"It likes your shirt," the driver said.

Andy rubbed his tie-dyed Jamaican T-shirt with three big diagonal stripes of saturated green, red, and yellow—the Rasta tricolors. He remembered that someone at a recent party had told him with absolute certainty that it was bad mojo for him to wear this shirt.

"We should keep moving," Zero said.

As the creature repositioned the rasplike bottom of its wide tail to balance on the curve of the window, three juveniles popped out of an orifice in its side and sprang away in different directions. Two of the juveniles were instantly tackled in midair by wasps; they fell, taking the deadly fight to the ground. Zero followed one of them with his camera. To his surprise, it actually won the battle: it devoured the wasp fifteen seconds out of the womb.

"Whoa!" Quentin laughed as he drummed the back of the driver's chair. "Did you guys see that?"

Each had seen something else. "Yeah!"

A big wasp splatted on the window and the Henders badger extended its head and grabbed it with the two blue crab–like claws on its lower jaw, stuffing it into its gnashing teeth. Then it smacked its lips in an unsettling Mick Jagger sort of way.

"Those jaw-claws are hard as your molars, but they molt, like the cranium-plates all over the jungle floor, which we thought were cockroaches at first."

"Un-fucking-real," the driver muttered.

"If this thing has a strike like a mantis shrimp . . ."

"Oh shit," Quentin said. "Remember what that juvenile rat did to Otto?"

"And that thing that went after Nell—"

"What?" Pound demanded.

"Mantis shrimp have been known to bust out of aquariums made with double-paned safety glass," Andy told him. "Their front claw strike has the force of a small-caliber bullet."

"I don't like the sound of that," the driver said.

"We should move," Zero said.

The driver shifted into first gear with his foot on the brake. The rover lurched forward.

The badger lost its footing on the slick window

and tried to jump off as three Henders rats latched onto its back.

A shimmering creature descended on a spring-like tail. It engulfed the badger and its attackers in furry, cuttlefish-like arms, then sprang back up into the canopy.

"*Whoa, whoa!* Did you see it?" Quentin yelled.

"A 'shrimpanzee'!" Andy shouted.

"Huh?" Pound dabbed his forehead with his soaked handkerchief.

"We don't know much about that one yet. It's only been seen a few times, very briefly."

"All right, just keep talking." Pound shook his head, putting a hand on Zero's shoulder. "You're getting all this, right?"

The cameraman looked up at him with one eye as he videoed through the other: "Yup."

"Good." Pound nodded.

"Some of the animals we first thought were different species could be the same species at different stages."

"But what's cool is that they might still repro-duce miniatures of whatever stage they've reached and might not start reproducing sexually until the final stage, like Chinese liver fluke worms."

Pound coughed and swallowed. "Fuck. OK—go on!"

"So it's possible that any one of them may be able to build an entire ecosystem of inter-connected creatures around itself."

"Which may explain how this ecosystem protected itself from global extinction events. It's just a theory."

In a motion stretching across all three windows, six animals devoured each other, one after another, in a balletic food chain that ended when a leaf slapped the last one and rolled it up like a cartoon tongue. The plant's fruit or eggs ripened red like salmon roe on a branch above, which drew swarms of wasps, mice, and rats that raided the fresh food supply, some getting caught in other extending tongues while others carried off sticky eggs attached to their legs.

"My God." Pound gripped the back of Zero's chair, sweating profusely now. "Is it . . . springtime?"

"Well, we're near the subtropics," Andy said. "So the seasons are all pretty much the same."

"We found no seasonal detritus layers in the one core sample we managed to collect from the forest floor," Quentin said.

"It took nine robot-armed ROVs to bring it back from only six feet inside the jungle."

"It was a core-dart dropped by a helicopter."

"OK, OK." Pound squeezed his eyes shut. "So why is this place like the Texas chainsaw massacre? What the hell is going on? And please speak English to me."

"Here's what we think: the copper-based blood pigment in these animals is superefficient,"

Quentin told him. "It exhibits a Bohr and Root effect more dramatic than that of any organism I've studied."

"Huh?"

Andy stepped in. "Bohr and Root effects are what keep marathon runners like Zero here going."

"Under stress," Quentin explained, "blood chemistry changes to deliver more oxygen to muscles so you can run faster, longer."

"And?" the bewildered presidential envoy demanded.

"The copper blood in these things delivers more oxygen in a single heartbeat than any pigment I've ever tested, from bumblebees to cheetahs," Quentin said.

"Terrific," Pound muttered. "I still don't get it."

"Everything here kicks major ass," Zero translated.

"Yeah," Quentin said. "These animals move farther faster than bugs, lizards, birds, or mammals. Some probably even have amino acid superchargers."

"Hey! That's a bird!" Pound was relieved to finally see something he recognized. He pointed at a white seabird that fluttered down through the canopy. "Right?"

From a branch over the rover's middle window a thorn fired, trailing a translucent tendril.

The harpoon struck the bird. It instantly fell,

limp, swinging toward the window. Two more thorns launched from other branches. They pierced the fluttering frigate, and it dangled in front of them suspended by three harpoon strings that turned red as they siphoned off the bird's blood.

More thorns fired as wasps and drill-worms swarmed, producing a flurry of spiraling feathers.

"Yes," Quentin said. "That was a bird."

"Oh dear," Andy sighed, watching its last few feathers seesaw to the forest floor.

"Did you get that?" Pound asked Zero.

Videoing with his right eye, the cameraman opened his left eye wide at Pound.

"All right." Pound nodded. "Could you turn the air-conditioning up in here?"

"Sure thing, boss." The driver flicked a switch.

The right bubble window looked like a trucker's windshield after the eighth plague of Egypt. Rats and larger animals leaped onto the surface to gobble up the splattered bugs, and everything attacked anything that stayed too long. This wasn't predator versus prey; it was *everything* versus *everything*.

A two-legged creature the size of a turkey landed on the front window and promptly knocked its anvillike nose against its surface like a jack-hammer.

"What the hell is that?" Pound had gone pale.

Andy peered at the featherless biped. "That's definitely a new one."

"I think it sees its reflection," Quentin said.

"It sees a *rival,* Quentin," Andy corrected.

"Yeah, a big one on a convex mirror. These things don't back down, man!"

Zero raised the camera from his eye. "Um—can we go now, guys?"

The driver lifted his foot from the brakes just as a white-and-yellow jellyfish-like thing splattered on the middle bubble, clawing it with spiderlike arms and a rodent-toothed maw.

As the rover jolted forward, the creature was torn off, leaving a meringue ring behind.

The driver hit the throttle: a hail of thuds drummed against the starboard hull as they crossed the corridor.

The five men clung to the safety straps as the rover bulldozed deeper into the jungle. Parting trees splattered it with juices and eggs as they broke apart, and though their fanlike fronds brushed off some of the debris, when the rover finally emerged from the forest onto a green slope its roof was snarled with foliage and yellow clover was spreading over its fenders.

"OK," Quentin said. "That slope across this meadow goes up to the desert area in the center of the island. It's the lake on the other side of the core that we really want to take a look at!"

They plowed down the green meadow, relieved to be in open country.

To their left they could see a spill-basin where

water seemed to have flowed in from a narrow crack in the outer wall. A white rind of crystals surrounded the oval pool at the end of the narrow stream, resembling a sperm cell that had impregnated the crack in the island cliff.

Zero pointed to the south, panning his camera. "What's that?"

"It looks like saltwater," the driver answered.

A dead zone of white salt crystals, barren of life, surrounded the pool at the end of the stream. As the rover moved down the slope they caught a glimpse of daylight and ocean through the fissure in the cliff from which the pool must have been fed.

"Seawater must get in at high tide or during storms," Zero said.

"That crack looks pretty recent," Andy pointed out.

"Based on the salt buildup on the rocks, that pool must be at least a few decades old," Quentin corrected.

"I meant recent by *geological* standards."

"Everything's recent by geological standards."

The rover climbed the other side of the meadow. The landscape dried out as they passed from the clover to the barren core of weather-carved rock formations at the island's center.

The driver searched for a passable route through the core to give them a shortcut across the island.

12:33 P.M.

The rumble of the rover vibrated the rock and sand, waking the hives.

The low-frequency vibrations triggered pheromone signals inside the purple honeycombed towers that lined the flat bottom of the ravine.

The pheromones stimulated hundreds of drones.

Budlike panels under the drones' heads popped open. Three translucent wings expanded like blue flowers.

The fanged lamprey-mouths flexed on their abdomens, ready to latch onto passing prey to suck its blood and feed their colonies.

The towering hives were the nurseries of drill-worms. These half-worms were their juvenile form. When they matured, the vampire drones would double in size by growing a new segment shaped like a drill bit with three legs and a second brain and mouth. Then they would leave the hive to hunt in the jungle, drilling through the hard sheaths of the trees.

A mature drill-worm bitten in half could regenerate its other half. Either segment could mate and give birth to polyplike eggs—eggs that multiplied into new hives that budded vampire drones.

The XATV-9 throttled forward across the canyon's flat bottom, which cut directly across the island's arid core.

The men observed a gallery of urchinlike cacti,

yuccalike trees, and bloated purple towers lining the canyon walls to either side of the rover. The towers reminded Zero of termite mounds or pillar coral.

The driver turned on the outboard mikes again and as the rover passed the men inside heard the sibilant buzz of the purple hives coming to life. Blue swarms emerged, attacking the rover's windows then retreating to their hives.

The silent men gazed through the rover's windows down the lush green slope on the far side of the island's core. The lake in the distance lay still and dark inside the outer ring of the jungle.

"There it is." Quentin pointed over the driver's shoulder as they roared down to the green plain at sixty miles an hour, headed straight for the lake.

12:35 P.M.

The rover braked abruptly and stopped at the water's edge.

A hundred yards to their left rose the outer ring of the jungle, rimming the far side of the lake.

Only thirty feet to their right, an isolated cluster of three tall trees rose on the shore. Two of the three trunks split into three branches, each of which bore crowns of long fronds covered with green clover. Like a broken umbrella, the tallest tree pointed five splaying fronds up into the air. Chains of red berries dangled under the fronds of all three trees, twitching and coiling as they caught bugs lured by the fruit.

"We should not stop," said Zero.

"We're safe, don't worry," said the driver.

Radio static burst from the speakers, and they heard Briggs's voice: *We're evacuating StatLab. Repeat, we are evacuating StatLab! Return— base—*

Then they could hear Nell's voice over the breaking signal. *We're los—transmission signal. The com—array—choked—tation—over?*

"Oh great," Quentin groaned.

"The clover must be eating StatLab's dish." Andy turned pale.

Pound frowned. "Are we in danger here, if we can't go back to the lab?"

The driver shook his head. "We'll just radio *Enterprise.* She'll send a transport. They'll hook on and take us home."

"How can they take this thing back to a ship?" Zero asked. "Who knows what's stuck to it now?"

"They'll take us to the *Philippine Sea*," the driver said.

"They'll sterilize and quarantine it there," Quentin said.

"Don't worry," the driver said. "They'll hose this thing down with chlorine dioxide, formaldehyde— hell, the Navy'll probably scuttle the whole damn ship when this is over, just to be on the safe side. They're plenty paranoid."

Pound grabbed the radio mike. "StatLab, proceed with evacuation. We'll catch our own ride home."

They heard Briggs's voice over the radio: *"Can't—Over?"*

Pound shouted into the radio. "We'll get our own ride home, StatLab. Copy?"

12:44 P.M.

Nell and the technicians stared over Otto's shoulder as the video feed broke up.

"Damn, we lost them!"

"Keep trying," Nell urged.

"Their com array must be damaged." Otto checked the camera overlooking one of StatLab's microwave dishes. "It's definitely not on our end."

"OK," Briggs said. "That's it! I want all hard drives packed and ready to go when the Sea Dragon gets here, people. All euthanized specimens need to be sealed in sterilized specimen cases. No live specimens are to leave the island under *absolutely* any circumstances. *No* pets! And *no* souvenirs!"

12:45 P.M.

The men inside the rover heard nothing but a blizzard of white noise on the radio.

"Yeah, their com array's definitely down," Quentin said.

Andy nodded. "Lichenovores must have gotten to it."

"Clovores, you mean."

"Oh right."

"How'd you guys like to get a look inside the lake?" asked the driver, who still seemed reassuringly gung ho, despite being cut off from the lab.

Quentin glanced at Andy, arching his eyebrows. "You can actually do that?"

"Sure can!" the driver said.

"Bitchin'!"

"We should call the *Enterprise* now," Zero said.

"Right after this, we will," Pound agreed. "Let's make sure to tape this for the President, OK?"

Bugs were starting to swarm around the rover as an ROV deployed from the end of one of the robot arms, maneuvering down into the lake on a thin, Day-Glo orange tether.

The driver used what looked like Xbox controls to steer it and flick on its headlight, illuminating the black water. The crew watched the ROV's camera view on a screen above the forward window.

The small vehicle buzzed down into the depths.

"How deep can it go?" Andy was giddy.

"About three hundred feet," the driver said.

"Awesome." Quentin grinned at Andy.

A huge animal, like an overgrown fairy shrimp, appeared on the screen, paddling in the inky darkness, and suddenly a wondrous world of

Cambrianesque creatures materialized on the screen around it.

Segmented creatures of fantastic designs crossed the camera's view like apparitions: spiked saucers, horned boomerangs, finned champagne glasses, a Christmas tree with kicking legs.

"Omigod," Quentin breathed. "Stephen Jay Gould, eat your HEART OUT, baby!"

"It's the Burgess Shale come to life." Andy sounded shell-shocked.

"We were right!" Quentin said.

"Wow, OK, guys, keep talking. Are you getting all this?" Pound asked Zero.

Zero looked up from his videocam. "We should move. We shouldn't stay—"

Even as he spoke, he was cut off by a huge *BOOM!*

The rover lurched, and then they heard another *BOOM!*

The rover pitched forward and a third of the front window plunged into the water.

"What the hell just happened?" Pound yelled.

"Oh shit," the driver said.

"We can still drive, right?" Pound said.

"That wasn't supposed to happen," the driver said.

"We can still drive, though . . . right?" Zero asked.

The halftracks bore into the wet bank of the lake

as they backtracked, but the front axles of the blown tires gripped the steep bank like anchors and the vehicle sank lower as it dug in. Then they suddenly stopped functioning. Red lights flashed on the control panel.

The driver looked at them. "Uh . . . that would be a negative."

"We've got halftracks, for Christ's sake—why can't we just power out of here, man?" Zero asked.

"This is a prototype—it was designed to terminate functionality in the event of any malfunction that might cause damage to equipment worth millions of dollars."

"Inflatable rubber tires?" Andy screeched. "I thought this thing was a Mars rover!"

The driver shook his head. "It's experimental. And those tires are ten-inch-thick steel radials, for Christ's sake! I don't understand how both of them could blow like this."

Quentin looked out the side window and saw the shredded rubber above water. "Oh shit, it's smoking!"

Zero videoed out the right window. "Same on this side."

"We may have run over some clovores."

"What?"

"Animals that eat clover and probably use sulfuric acid to dissolve it," Quentin told Pound. "The acid inside them may have eaten away our tires, I guess."

"Shit!" the envoy snapped. "Why didn't you tell us?"

"You were the one in such a huge frickin' hurry!" Quentin shouted.

Andy jabbed a finger at the driver. "He said we can radio for a transport!"

"Radio the ship for a transport now," Zero said.

The driver nodded and flicked on the radio. "Kirk to *Enterprise*, Kirk to *Enterprise*."

He glanced up at the others, who were glaring at him. "It's my NAME, OK?" He clicked the radio again. "This is XATV-9, do you read, *Enterprise*?"

White noise.

"Do you read, *Enterprise*? This is XATV-9 . . . Kirk to *Enterprise*?"

Kirk looked up at the rest of them, shrugged.

"Keep trying!" Pound urged.

"But don't say 'Kirk to Enterprise,' " Andy said.

Zero put the camera in his lap, popped out the memory stick, slid it into his pocket, snapped the flap, and hung his head down over his lap. Laughter gently rocked his body. "Why did I trust you idiots?" he moaned.

"Don't worry," Kirk told them. "We can just sit tight. Sooner or later they'll send a transport."

A shrieking alarm sounded; blue lights flashed at the rear of the rover.

"Now what?" Andy yelped.

Kirk looked puzzled. "The smoke alarm!"

He squeezed between them and rushed to the rear of the rover to disable the blaring siren. Looking up at the ceiling, he shook his head grimly.

"What?" Pound demanded. He squeegeed the sweat off his forehead with the side of his hand, like a windshield wiper.

"Hey, that's funny," Kirk said.

"What's funny?" Zero said. "I need a laugh."

Kirk pointed at the roof. "Something seems to be burning through the hull here . . ."

"Ha ha."

"What's the hull made of?" Quentin asked.

"Superhardened plastic, so there's no way any impact could—"

"Oh shit." Quentin looked at Andy.

"You guys better take a look at this." Zero pointed at the ROV monitor.

Large shadowy creatures stirred on the screen just beyond the range of the ROV's headlights.

"Jeez, we were right!" Quentin crowed.

"Right about what?" Pound's voice cracked.

"Giant mantis shrimp—that eye must be attached to an animal as big as a saltwater crocodile!"

The ROV appeared to shine its spotlight on the football-sized compound eye of a slumbering leviathan.

"Call off the ROV now!" Zero said.

Kirk killed the light. He reversed the winch on the ROV's cable, zipping it up at top speed.

Andy and Quentin cringed as the camera pulled away from the creature. Pound sagged in relief.

"Good man," Zero said softly.

Through the partially submerged window of the rover they had an above-and-below view of the black lake as a chevron of ripples headed toward them across its surface.

More ridges appeared on the water, moving parallel to the first.

12:51 P.M.

The scientists and technicians quickly donned blue cleansuits as they prepared to evacuate StatLab.

Nell watched through the window as the first wave of scientists boarded the first two Sea Dragon helicopters. All carried sleek titanium hard-drive containers and stacks of aluminum specimen cases onto the loading ramps, which slowly rose like drawbridges as the helos took off.

"Damn it, Briggs," she said, "these suits are a waste of time. Any microbes here must have evolved to attack a totally different biology from ours. Zero and I breathed the air on this island and nothing happened to us!"

Briggs rolled his eyes. "Interesting theory, Nell. Better start suiting up!"

She looked over Otto's shoulder at the static-filled screen. "You go ahead, Briggs. Come on, Otto! Keep trying to make contact with them!"

Briggs frowned as Otto typed rapidly, the aluminum splint on his thumb clicking the computer keys.

12:52 P.M.

"Can't you reel that thing in any faster?" Pound complained. The arrows of ripples on the lake's surface all pointed straight at the mired rover.

"Stop reeling it in," Zero said.

"OK. I'm cutting it loose!" Kirk said.

"Good thinking!" Zero agreed.

Kirk flicked a button and a cable-shear on the end of the robot arm chopped the tether. The monitor went black.

"I've got a satellite phone," Pound suggested.

Kirk shook his head. "Good luck using a sat-phone inside this thing. You need to be out in the open."

"Do you think we can step outside for a minute?" the presidential envoy asked.

"Are you kidding?" Zero laughed.

"We don't have cleansuits on this rig," Kirk said.

"Zero's been out there and lived," Pound reminded them, stubbornly. His face was slick with sweat.

"Germs aren't the problem."

Two giant animals with iridescent green-and-red plates rippling down their bodies exploded from the water in front of the windows. They flew up into the air in a jet of white spray that drenched the rover.

When the "mega-mantises" landed on the roof they jolted the rover forward, nosing it deeper into the black lake.

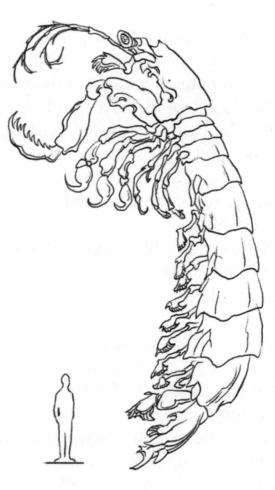

Mega-Mantis
Magnisquilla manningi
(*after* Echevarria et al, *Proceedings of the Woods Hole Scientific Meetings*, vol. 92: 61)

The five men heard the creatures' legs scrambling mightily overhead as one of them fell off to the left side, hitting the mud and surging backward into the lake.

An explosive *BANG* stunned their ears. The cabin's roof cracked with tendrils of sunlight as a shock wave shattered the overhead fluorescent light fixtures.

"That was a claw strike," Quentin shouted, holding his head.

"We gotta get out of here!" Andy yelled.

"That thing'll open this up like a walnut!"

Kirk climbed out of the cockpit and squeezed past the others to the rear of the rover.

He yanked open a cabinet door on the wall. Inside were four sinister long-barreled guns attached to backpacks with tubes and straps.

"We should be able to hold a circle long enough to get off a call, I think," he told them, passing one of the weapons to Quentin.

"Flamethrowers?" Quentin said, impressed, as he passed one along to Andy, who quickly handed it off to Pound.

Kirk nodded, handing him another. "Strap the fuel tank on your back. Tighten it with the belly strap."

"That's what I'm talkin' about!" Quentin said.

"Careful now," Kirk said.

"Zero, will you join us?" Pound asked the cameraman. "We could use a little advice if something comes at us. You're the only one who's been out there."

Zero saw the mega-mantis's arms ratcheting for another strike on the domed window behind Pound. "Get down!" He ducked to the floor, putting his hands over the back of his head and ears.

The shock wave knocked all of the other men over. It also spread three fine cracks through the forward bubble window.

"Give me one of those, God damn it!" Zero snarled.

"Plus one of these!" Pound's ears rang as he thrust a very NASA-looking plastic headband at Zero. "It's a head-cam—hands free!"

Zero stared at Pound as if he'd suddenly burst into song.

"Tap the side to send video back to the lab on Channel One," Pound told the cameraman. "We're out of range now, but it will reach them if you can get within a mile of the lab. It holds twenty-five hours on each memory stick. That's a viewfinder on that arm there."

"Will it give me brain cancer?"

"Of course not!" Pound scoffed.

Zero couldn't resist placing it around his head and swinging the viewfinder into place. He squinted into the small transparent screen that hung about two inches in front of his left eye. "OK."

Another bone-rattling blast seemed to crack the roof. A shard of knife-edged plastic grazed Andy's arm. He screamed as the mega-mantis on the roof tightened tendons like trebuchets inside its massive forelimbs to let loose another strike across the middle window.

The five men reeled at the shock wave. Kirk staggered to the hatch, unsealed it, and kicked it open.

The arm of a mega-mantis reached down over the hatchway, followed by a giant multicolored compound eye.

"Hit it!" Kirk screamed.

He and Zero shot thirty-foot streams of fire out the hatch, frying the eyeball that was the size of a Weber barbecue grill.

Through the forward window they could see the wounded mega-mantis lurch from the roof back into the lake, pushing the rover even deeper into the muddy bank. The middle window was now half-covered with water that churned as other creatures surfaced from the deep to tear into the injured giant.

Kirk and Zero cut the flames, and all five men jumped out onto the green shore of the boiling lake.

They smelled the treacle stench of death and sulfur in the air, and the humidity slapped a sheen of sweat on their skin immediately. The creatures wrestling in the water clacked and squeaked as they shredded the fallen mega-mantis in a feeding frenzy, turning the surface pale blue.

A shrill insect noise from the distant jungle choked the air.

The men ran in a group from the water's edge and quickly formed a circle around Pound.

Andy was the only one without a flamethrower.

Pound fussed nervously with his satellite phone, his flamethrower slung over his shoulder by the strap.

The buttons on the phone looked like a chaos of symbols as Pound tried to sort out what he had to push and in what order. Blood trickled from one of his ears. The shellshock of the mantis strikes had fogged his brain, along with lack of sleep and a voracious fever.

The others blasted the flamethrowers to defend their circle, as more swarms emerged from the crowns of the trio of nearby trees.

Quentin dropped his flamethrower. "Cover me!" he yelled to Andy.

"Huh?"

Without replying, Quentin ran to the tallest tree on the edge of the lake and extended a stethoscope to its trunk. The roiling water turned milky blue beside him as the battle under the surface spread.

"What's he doing, giving it a checkup?" Kirk yelled, stunned.

"Yeah . . . yeah . . . yeah! This thing has *hearts,*" Quentin shouted. "It's an *animal!* I knew it had to have a vascular distribution system—"

The tree suddenly retracted into the ground. It clamped its fronds down over Quentin like an umbrella closing.

The ground quaked violently under their feet, causing Pound to punch the wrong last digit on the satphone. "God damn it!" he screeched. The rocking earth pitched him backwards. As he hit the ground, the butt of the flamethrower broke his fall and he accidentally fired a stream out its muzzle behind him—which torched the rover's still-open hatchway.

Frothing waves splashed the lake shore near the trees, where they could still hear Quentin screaming under the tightly closed fronds.

"Quentin!" Andy shouted frantically, running toward the tree.

"Andy! Don't!" Zero yelled.

Fronds of the other two trees leaned forward over Andy and a shimmering creature that seemed to be a larger version of a shrimpanzee descended on a bungeelike tail and snatched Andy, who screamed as it yanked him off the ground, all in a second.

The earthquake finally settled and stopped.

A wave of creatures came out of the wall of jungle a hundred yards away, and headed straight for the men.

Zero turned and ran.

Pound and Kirk ran, too.

1:00 P.M.

Zero looked behind him and fired his flamethrower at a swarm of flying bugs diving down at him. "Goddamned flying piranhas," he muttered, fending them off. As he ran ahead of the others, who followed him, gasping in panic, Zero remembered the NASA camera. He tapped the button over his right temple and flipped the band over to see behind him. He swiveled the arm of the viewfinder forward—he had a rearview mirror.

With one eye on the viewfinder, he ran for his life, more or less following the tracks of the rover up the hillside as he faked left and right like a running back on the longest sudden death touchdown run of all time.

1:01 P.M.

Otto picked up the video feed from Zero. "I got something!"

On the monitor they could see Zero's pursuers and the two other men running desperately behind him.

"Oh NO!" Nell crumpled into a chair behind Otto, staring at the screen.

1:02 P.M.

Zero sprinted uphill along the tracks of the rover, toward the island's core.

Wasps dive-bombed around him as he constantly zigzagged like Red Grange. As creatures leaped through the air at him, he dodged or slowed or sped up to avoid them.

Kirk and Pound ran behind him up the hillside. Pound was winded and staggering when five wasps hit him simultaneously. He screamed.

As their abdominal maws pierced his neck, back, and arms, the wasps injected capsules of embryos. These hatched instantly and bored their way through his flesh.

Pound dropped the flamethrower and fell writhing in agony to the ground. The twisting larvae devoured nerve after nerve. The explosions of pain sent his body into deep shock. His glasses fell off, and the world became a blur. He tried to yell for help but could not. Two drill-worms landed on his forehead, and he screamed involuntarily as they bored their abdomens through his eyelids.

1:02 P.M.

In the headcam's viewfinder, Zero saw a cloud of bugs cover Pound as the President's envoy flailed on the slope behind him. It seemed to Zero that Pound screamed for a long time.

Kirk pumped his feet over the squishy field of green vegetation, running behind Zero, who was headed for the canyon they had originally traversed in the safety of the rover. Halfway up the clover fields, Zero continued to gain ground, but suddenly Kirk doubled over, exhausted. His head was swimming and sweat stung his eyes, as he struggled to catch his breath. The sole of his right shoe seemed to be melting.

Kirk pivoted and blasted his flamethrower blindly at the train of creatures racing up the slope behind him. Undaunted by the tongue of flame, they swirled around him in tight circles and, singed and smoking, struck into him with ravenous spikes and jaws.

Kirk screamed and spun around, staggering as he tried to pull a rat off his chest with his left hand and fire the flamethrower wildly with his right. Two Henders rats, hurtling up the slope in twenty-foot lunges under the stream of fire, clamped on to his legs. He heard two loud *pops* as their claw-strikes severed the muscles in his calves. He shrieked in pain and fell forward, his legs useless.

As a swarm of small animals overran him, he rolled onto his back and blasted his flamethrower up the slope, desperate to fry as many of Zero's pursuers as possible.

But it was Kirk's flesh that helped Zero more. It bought the cameraman a few precious seconds as the hungry horde behind him slowed, then doubled back to help devour the fallen driver.

1:02 P.M.

Nell watched the monitor as Kirk screamed on the slope behind Zero.

She sat frozen in the chair, watching as it happened again—her nightmare coming to life on a television screen.

Otto sobbed and turned away from the monitor, retching.

"God damn it, come on, Zero!" Nell yelled, tears streaking her face as she stared at the screen. "Come on, *get out of there!*"

1:03 P.M.

Watching through the viewfinder, Zero blasted the flamethrower in irregular short bursts behind him, hearing Kirk's dying scream.

He ran fast but erratically, continuously changing direction and speed to confuse the trajectories of the long-jumping predators, which continually sailed past him, missing by inches. He never stopped for more than a second.

He reached the top of the slope and the flat ravine they had driven through only a half hour earlier. It felt like a lifetime ago.

Finally on level ground, he sprinted over the rover's tracks into the canyon.

Then, for only a heartbeat he relaxed his pace, breathing raggedly as the animals pursuing him dropped out of sight below the rise behind him. The air was fresher here and there was some relief from the heat and humidity generated by the clover. He watched the viewfinder as he jogged, relaxing his pace and sucking air into his chest. About thirty yards back, his pursuers crested the rise and poured into the canyon.

He sprinted again, zigzagging and firing the flamethrower in bursts behind him.

Three rats closed the distance in two leaps and two seconds. Zero fired a steady flame over his shoulder and fried them into flying meatballs. The sautéed rats hit the ground rolling and screaming, drawing off some of his pursuers.

He ran straight for about twenty yards, drawing a column of predators, which lunged as he turned abruptly left.

He saw a leaping rat in the viewfinder and slowed his step, catching it like a football player over his shoulder with both hands. In the same motion he jammed its head into the maw of a cactus-barnacle-like thing sprouting out of the canyon wall beside him. The "cactus" bit the rat's head off. Zero dropped its headless body and kept running.

Blow-dart urchins shot across the canyon on tendrils forcing him to leap, duck, and hurdle, always trying to keep his forward motion unpredictable. It was a constant struggle against the instinct to run as fast and hard as he could.

The purple bug-hives they had passed earlier lined the corridor before him.

The vampire drones began popping out of the hives. Zero ran straight at them, firing the flamethrower in front of him until it ran out of fuel.

He unstrapped the tank and flung it away, and the devouring bug clouds descended on it instantly.

Zero reached the edge of the mesa. Below was the salty pool they had passed earlier.

Skidding down the slope on the greasy ground-cover, he saw that it had turned purple as the mid-afternoon sun cast it in shadow. A strong stench of rotten eggs wafted up the hillside. He almost stepped on a sprouting clovore, and slipped, landing painfully on his butt. He scrambled back onto his feet without losing a beat and continued pounding downhill.

In the viewfinder he saw the wasps, vampire drones, and rats that had made it through the gauntlet of vampire bees. They were emerging from the canyon, on his trail.

Then, charging around the slope of the island's core, he saw two large red beasts.

Two marauding spigers had picked up his scent and were lunging down the slope to cut him off.

1:05 P.M.

Otto sobbed. "Come on, man!" he pleaded.

Nell wept with fear and frustration as she watched the red spigers soar through the air toward the viewscreen.

An alarm sounded.

At the other end of the lab, Todd Taylor jumped from his chair and peered through the hatch window of Section Four. "Guys, I think something breached the vestibule down here!"

1:06 P.M.

Zero was fading. His head was spinning, and his eyes burned with sweat. Running in zigzags was exhausting, and there had been no opportunity to pace himself. He let gravity pull him forward now and gave up trying to vary his course—with all his remaining strength, he pumped his legs hard and headed straight for the pool.

A fresh wave of seawater spilled into the pool from the fissure in the island's outer wall—maybe an aftereffect of the quake, Zero thought vaguely as he ran, gasping for breath.

In the viewfinder, he saw the spigers soaring through the air behind him, and he dove into the pool.

As he splashed into the salty water, the creatures pursuing him stopped cold, veered away, or pulled back like common bees.

One rat with too much momentum hit the pool beside Zero. It squealed frantically as it tried to paddle its eight legs, which soon slowed as it sank beneath the water.

Zero crouched in the water, his feet touching bottom and his head barely gasping above the surface, before he noticed that nothing was attacking him.

None of the creatures were even *flying* over the pool. It was as though some kind of force field was repelling them.

The spigers had driven their spiked arms into the ground, stopping on a dime. Now they sprang back from the water's edge, examining him crossly.

1:07 P.M.

Nell stared at the screen in awe. "Saltwater?" she breathed in astonishment.

"What?" Briggs said, looking up at the screen.

"They don't like saltwater!" She turned to Briggs in elation, slapping his big biceps.

"How can you tell it's saltwater?"

"How can *they* tell is the question," Nell challenged, looking intently at the images on the screen. "Come on, Zero, figure it out!" she yelled.

1:07 P.M.

Zero laughed deliriously and splashed more water over his Long Beach Marathon T-shirt, wheezing as he struggled to catch his breath. He whacked big splashes at the wall of waiting, hovering creatures, which immediately pulled back.

The bugs that he downed flailed wildly on the pool's surface, exuding a chemical slick. On the bottom of the pool he could see the carcasses of animals that had recently drowned.

After catching his wind, and before his muscles started to seize up, Zero submerged himself one more time and rose from the pool, sopping wet.

Then he leaped out of the water and made his final run up the far sunlit bank.

The air was fresher and the field green in the sunlight as he headed toward the blackened tracks of the XATV-9, which could still be seen on the field leading from a hole blasted into the forest edge.

He drove his body forward as the animals rushed around the edge of the pool.

He used up his lead to reach the jungle opening ten feet ahead of the frontrunners.

He plunged into the thick jungle, following the rover's tracks.

Nightmarish shrieks and howls filled the fetid air as Zero wove around and over the tangled growth, ducking and dodging stinging darts from the trees.

He nearly ran into the trunk of a tree covered with vertical sharklike jaws spiraling up its surface. At the last moment, he dodged around it; two pursuing Henders rats struck the trunk and disappeared into snapping mouths.

He tried to stay focused and not allow himself to fall into any rhythm.

The rubber soles of his running shoes were losing their treads, dissolving off his feet. He kept moving. Somehow, as sweat evaporated from his body, it seemed like a bubble had formed around him, repelling the creatures with an invisible wall. He dodged across the shooting galleries of jungle corridors unscathed. He had no time to wonder why or how this was happening.

In the dense jungle between the corridors he veered randomly while trying to stay near the plowed tracks of the rover, until he came to an unexpected dip and lost his footing on slick mud. "Oh shit!" he muttered as he slid down a giant lavender leaf, avoiding the hooks on its surface as the leaf folded closed behind him in sections.

"Oh shit!" someone said in the trees ahead.

Zero felt a spurt of adrenaline and lunged instinctively toward the human voice.

"Oh shit, oh shit!" the voice said, and Zero realized it was his own voice. He looked up and saw a shrimpanzee hurtling out of the canopy toward him. "Oh shit, oh shit!" it said, spreading six legs wide above him.

Zero rolled under a fallen tree and then leaped up, running and dodging a fusillade of disk-ants shooting through the air like discuses toward his legs. He pole-vaulted on a yuccalike stalk that split open and tried to curl down over his hands before he let go and somersaulted under a clover-covered dead trunk that absorbed a hail of darts fired from nearby trees—except for two, which stabbed Zero's right calf through his pants.

He ripped out the darts immediately but he could feel the leg going numb as he pulled himself to his feet and pushed on.

He had lost the rover tracks and despaired, fearing he was lost. His hands and arms were scratched and bleeding, his whole body dripping with sweat. His right leg was dragging, but he swung it forward with his right hand, crashing through the undergrowth. He ducked and snaked awkwardly around branches and trunks. The air grew hot and more putrid. At last, he spotted the sunlit opening above where, an eternity ago, the rover had penetrated the jungle.

With a gasp, he emerged onto the slope. To his right, he saw StatLab staggered like a derailed train up the hillside.

His lungs burned, his throat wheezed, his head pounded and his eyes stung as he limped up the hill. The muscles of his right calf were seizing, barely functional. The soles were peeling from his shoes and leaking blue gel.

Heaving himself forward, he banged on the encrusted bottom of Section One.

1:15 P.M.

Scientists and technicians inside Section Four continued to pull on their cleansuits to exit the lab.

Todd Taylor, suited up except for his helmet, looked nervously at a hairy woodpecker-like creature that had landed on the hatch window over-looking Section Three. The pseudo-bird smashed its pick-ax head against the window rhythmically. "What the hell is it doing that for?" Todd shouted, waving his arms to scare it away, which only seemed to make it strike faster.

In the video feed on the monitor, Nell sat frozen, watching the edge of the jungle recede behind Zero. Then she could see the lower sections of StatLab through his camera! She turned quickly to the window and saw Zero staggering up the hill.

"It's Zero! Let him in!"

"He's outside the seal!" Todd yelled. "We can't—"

"Bullshit!" Nell snarled and ran to the upper docking hatch.

With a crash, the "woodpecker" smashed the window inches over Todd's head, and Henders wasps and drill-worms poured in, followed by Henders mice and rats, all moving so swiftly that they ricocheted off the ceiling and walls.

Two rats squeezed down the neck of Todd's cleansuit; he screamed as they thrashed inside the belly, ripping into his gut. His cries drew other predators, which circled back to converge on him, and several squeezed into his mouth before he could close it.

Zero limped to the closed upper hatch. Nell waved him off, motioning him toward the Sea Dragon helicopter that was landing on the slope above.

Zero turned and clambered up the slope on his hands and feet like a wounded ape.

The scientists in Section Four, seeing the invading horde now vomiting through the shattered hatch window, panicked. They stampeded toward the upper hatch. The animals attacked, taking chunk after chunk from the exposed necks and faces of those at the back of the pack and homing in on those who screamed.

Nell punched the code into the keypad and bashed the "PURGE" button with her fist. The hatch's bolts exploded and the door shot off like a bullet into the side of the hill.

Suitless in the Henders air, Nell yanked on Briggs's elbow, and he kicked off the one pant-leg of his half-donned cleansuit.

"Come on!" she urged the hesitant scientists behind her, and she and Briggs jumped from the hatch and ran up the scorched field.

Zero was first onto the Dragon's loading ramp, and he turned to help Nell on board. Then he collapsed, groaning, against her side. She propped him up as Briggs, Otto, and a handful of scientists and technicians jumped onto the ramp.

The rest lumbered in the awkward cleansuits as animals poured from the hatch of StatLab at their backs: the long segmented lab had become a pipeline straight out of the jungle.

Wearing a helmet offered them no protection:

teeth and claws easily slashed the flimsy clean-suits. The tears admitted hordes of Henders beasts that turned the suits into gruesome feedbags within seconds.

Even those closest to the Sea Dragon fell, screaming, as it lifted off.

Nell saw a huge red spiger leap up the hill in two bounds and launch itself at the helo, but the wind from the rotors battered it down and the beast barely missed hooking the edge of the ramp with its spiked arms.

"Jeezus!" One of the helicopter crewmen hissed, the cool expression shocked from his face as he glanced out the window at the carnage. "Guess we need a new lab . . ."

Zero hung on Nell's shoulders, and she hugged him tight against her.

"We may need a new planet," she said.

8:51 P.M.

Andy woke up in the dark and saw a glowing Henders wasp inches from his face.

He jumped back.

The movement startled other bugs all around him, also trapped in jars and bottles, which illuminated a strange chamber with cans, bottles, and other garbage piled against the walls.

A human skull in a niche wore a U.S. Air Force pilot's hat.

The room, Andy realized, was an old airplane fuselage.

Suddenly there were snorts and scratches at a round door cut into the wall across from him. Fear immobilized him—all he could move were his eyes. He knew he was going to die and only hoped it would be quick.

The door in the wall opened inward and Copepod ran into the room.

The bull terrier licked Andy's astonished face.

Andy stared as the creature he had only glimpsed earlier appeared behind the dog like an apparition in the room.

He hugged Copey in horror, but the burly dog barked and wriggled away, then ran right at the creature.

SEPTEMBER 15

12:06 P.M.

The Muddy Charles Pub, overlooking the river that bore its name, buzzed with MIT professors and students consuming pizza and beer.

Among those gathered to hear the much-anticipated *SeaLife* announcement was noted zoologist Thatcher Redmond, who nibbled his trademark roasted pumpkin seeds and sipped a plastic cup of Widmer Brothers hefeweizen.

Though he professed to be a strict vegetarian, Thatcher cheated in private. He disguised his paunch under the camouflage of his Banana Republic cargo vest, which he wore over a pale denim shirt with each sleeve folded twice.

Today, as usual, students thronged Thatcher's table, and this time his colleague Frank Stapleton had decided to join them to watch the breaking news about Henders Island.

Frank Stapleton was an academic bear with black-framed glasses and frazzled gray hair. An old-school man, he made an enjoyably stodgy sparring partner to Thatcher's crowd-pleasing sensationalism: students loved to hear their public exchanges just for the entertainment value.

This time, however, something else had stolen their attention.

"Wait, wait! Here it is," shouted the student wielding the remote control.

A mutual *shushing* quelled the pub chatter as everyone trained eyes and ears on the large television screen mounted over the bar.

The CNN anchorwoman finally reached the story that had been teased all day:

"After the apparently disastrous final episode of the reality show SeaLife, *a network spokesman has now admitted that the much-discussed cliffhangers were in fact hoaxes created for no other purpose but to generate ratings."*

Groans and curses filled the pub.

"Issuing an apology and an announcement that the show is going into an indefinite 'retooling' break, the show's producers released the following clip."

A video clip ran showing the *SeaLife* cast smiling and waving from the stern of the *Trident* and sailing off into the sunset.

"*That's* the hoax!" someone shouted, triggering another avalanche of *shushes*. The newscaster continued:

"However, relatives have been unable to contact their loved ones on the show since the last episode aired twenty-three days ago. Two crewmember families will make a public statement on Live Current *later tonight. And while official complaints against the United States and Great Britain by other members of the U.N. Security Council were formally filed today, Defense Department officials are continuing to deny a firestorm of Internet rumors of a naval blockade around Henders Island and a media blackout. Our own requests for satellite images of the area, whose coordinates have been closely followed by millions of viewers on the show's website, have been denied. According to all satellite services, the Pentagon purchased exclusive rights to all satellite photos of Henders Island within hours of the final airing of* SeaLife.*"*

The anchorwoman blithely moved on, over a chorus of angry groans, to a story about a man who murdered his entire family and then committed suicide.

"Why don't they just kill themselves first?" Stapleton grumbled.

"Courage, I think," Thatcher replied. "It takes far less courage to commit suicide when you've done something so bad everybody will want to kill you anyway."

"That's about the sickest goddamned thing I've ever heard," Stapleton snapped, looking at Thatcher. "Thanks for clearing that up."

Thatcher shrugged.

A student in a black King Kong T-shirt chimed in. "*SeaLife* beat out *sex* for the most looked-up word on the Internet last week. How sick is *that?*"

"That's it? After three weeks of waiting we're supposed to believe it was just a huge scam for ratings?" Thatcher Redmond's attractive blond research assistant, Sharon, glowered at the television screen.

"Face it," the T-shirted student snorted, "it was a brilliant piece of marketing, Sharon. They sucked *you* in."

"It's not a hoax," Sharon insisted. "What they just showed was CGI, and not even good CGI."

"That wasn't CGI," someone said.

"It was an old clip!" another shouted from across the pub.

"They doctored an old clip with CGI," another said.

"What the hell is CGI?" Stapleton grumbled.

"Computer Graphic Imaging!" everyone in earshot shouted.

"We could probably prove that's CGI in less than an hour," Sharon insisted. "The other governments of the world can definitely tell. So why are they trying to get away with it?"

"Coca-Cola and Nike sales?" offered the guy in the black T-shirt.

Thatcher Redmond grinned and drummed his fingers on the table. He enjoyed any form of chaos. He was immediately attracted to anything that roiled the thin film of "order" that human beings tried so vainly to impose over reality. "I almost wish it weren't a hoax."

Frank Stapleton looked up. "You can't be serious, Thatcher."

"Wouldn't it be delightfully ironic, Professor Stapleton, if in our rush to shine light in every corner to dispel our primal fear of the dark, we opened up a Pandora's box that finally wiped us off the planet?"

"Yes, it would be ironic, but I don't see what would be so damned delightful about it."

"At least something might have a chance to survive on this planet, Professor Stapleton, if humans were eradicated. I realize, of course, that this whole thing is almost assuredly a fraud of some sort. The chances that anything remotely as dangerous as our species could be found on so small and isolated an island are slim to none. But if such a thing actually did happen, I believe it might be cause for celebration."

Sharon stared at her mentor with the mixture of angst and awe characteristic of all his research assistants. "Why, Dr. Redmond?"

Stapleton shuddered. "Please, for the love of God, don't encourage him."

"Intelligent life is an environmental cancer, Sharon," Thatcher replied. "By rearranging nature, the human race has created new viruses, diseases, drug-resistant bacteria. We are alone responsible for all manner of mayhem that could never have occurred in nature. After centuries of domesticating plants and animals, genetic engineering is now directly *corrupting* the code of life. We're crossing wires of evolutionary circuitry billions of years in the making and precipitating a genetic breakdown that could soon rage through our environment like a molecular plague."

"Very dramatic, Thatcher." Stapleton regarded him with curiosity. "But if you believe that, how do you get up in the morning? For that matter, how do your students?"

"We have spliced the genes of jellyfish into mice to make them glow green in the dark," Thatcher replied dryly. "We have manipulated *Hox* genes to give houseflies a hundred legs and millipedes six. We have inserted the genes of insects into plants and the genes of plants into animals. There is practically nothing on Earth that mankind does not use and nothing that he will not 'improve' if given the chance. And whatever is left, we carelessly discard. Pollution and global warming are merely precursors to the environmental apocalypse to come. Before the century is out, if we have not destroyed ourselves first, or even if we have, we humans will probably have pounded the final nail into Mother

Earth's coffin. If we were just wiping ourselves out it would be of little concern: we merely got what we deserved, like many other obnoxious species before us. But at the hands of the rational ape, life on Earth and in her seas is likely to suffer a mass extinction as nano-engineered genetic viruses cascade through keystone species and collapse whole ecosystems, one after another. All multicellular organisms will disappear as single-celled organisms are forced back to the drawing board to reinvent what mankind has fatally sabotaged. If that's what you call *dramatic,* Professor Stapleton, I agree. And if that's what you call *me* for pointing it out, then so be it. Intelligent life is the ultimate biohazard. Any worthy opponent would be a welcome discovery, for the planet."

A smattering of grim applause broke out at Thatcher's oration.

"Look, I'm as much an environmentalist as the next guy," Stapleton argued, "unless the next guy's *you,* I guess, but don't you think that's a smidgen on the absolutely hopeless side?"

Thatcher eyed the green plastic container from which Stapleton spooned his lunch. "What in heaven's name are you *eating,* Professor?"

Stapleton swallowed a mouthful and dabbed his lips with a napkin. "Calves' brains and scrambled eggs. I tried it on leave in Paris when I was in the Army. My wife makes it for me sometimes." He scooped up another bite.

"I see."

"I'm on the Prisby Diet."

Thatcher shook his head. "A quack diet."

"Hey, I've lost twelve pounds. You should try it." Stapleton took a sporkful and chewed it defiantly.

"And so now you are eating cow brains."

"Actually, baby cow brains. With mango chutney," Stapleton corrected, his mouth full.

"Surely you've heard of *mad cow disease,* Doctor?"

Stapleton swallowed. "OK, let's say you're right, Thatcher. In twenty years, the average gestation time of CJD, you and I will both be in an old folks' home anyway. At least I'll be the one laughing." He winked and dug for another bite.

There were gasps of disgust and snickers around the table.

"Professor Stapleton," Thatcher sighed, "you are a living object lesson of my book's thesis. In what natural scenario would the brains of a domesticated, hormone-injected, Franken-fed, genetically engineered calf become a part of the diet that your Homo sapiens body evolved over the last five million years to consume?"

"Thatcher," Stapleton shook his head, "the great thing about human intelligence is that we don't *have* to do things in one way or another. Human beings might *not* do these things that you predict. Don't you account for that possibility?"

Thatcher stared off into space as a memory of his smiling son running to the sliding glass door, toward the pool, flashed in his mind. He remembered the pressure on his foot as he'd nudged the door open . . . "It *will* happen because it *can* happen, Professor. It is merely a matter of time. Probability fulfills itself just as a Japanese pachinko game always fills up with a bell curve of ball bearings. If there were only one or a few of us, human virtue might play a role. But there are billions of us. The cumulative effect of our allegedly 'free' will over a period of time is indistinguishable from instinct or predestination. Since sentient beings *can* do anything, they *will* do anything, no matter how stupid or destructive, over time. You still haven't read my book, have you, Professor Stapleton? I'm afraid my optimistic conclusion is that only a preemptive extinction event that eliminates intelligent life can save an environment once it is infected."

"There are plenty of cultures that have managed to live in harmony with their environment for thousands of years, Thatcher," Stapleton retorted. "What about North American Indians. Or Polynesians?"

"The Polynesians imported bird viruses that decimated native populations wherever they went, and Native Americans coincidentally arrived just before all the greater fauna of North America vanished. But I must point out that one of the most pristine environments humans inhabit is Papua New Guinea, famous for its head hunters, who may well have contributed directly to the preservation of *their* environment."

"Jiminy Cricket, how do you feel about *us,* then, Thatcher?" Stapleton demanded.

Thatcher smiled. "As Jonathan Swift said, 'All my love is toward individuals, but principally I hate and detest that animal called man.'"

There was an uneasy ripple of laughter around the table.

"Charming. You give environmentalists a bad name, my friend."

"Well, I'm sorry, Dr. Stapleton. But environmentalists are people, too." Thatcher winked at the gallery.

"Oh, I see! No points for effort, eh?"

"It won't make any difference."

"Dear Lord, you are such a Cassandra."

"One thing most people seem to forget about Cassandra is that as unpalatable as her dire predictions were, she was always *right*."

"She wasn't happy about it, though."

"I'm happy all the way to the bank, my friend." Thatcher chuckled, and the students in the gallery applauded their rally.

"I don't think it's funny!" Sharon protested. "You're talking about the end of life on Earth as we know it."

"It's all right." Thatcher raised a calming hand.

"You're quite right, Frank. Eat your brains. It *is* inevitable."

Thatcher shrugged and smiled, and everyone laughed except for Sharon. She could not understand how her mentor maintained his graceful sense of humor about the bleakest of truths. "Unless, of course, Henders Island is *not* a hoax," Thatcher added serenely, winking at Sharon. He rose and raised his plastic cup of wheat beer. "To Henders Island!"

To this, everyone toasted, and the Muddy Charles churned once more with eddying scientific debates.

Thatcher noticed a large man wearing sunglasses and a black suit who had sat alone throughout lunch nursing a single Coke. A thin white cord trailed down from an earpiece and disappeared under his lapel. As he studied the man, the stranger got up from his table. He walked straight toward Thatcher.

Thatcher's pulse vaulted as the man approached, seemingly in slow motion. *Here it is,* he realized, remembering the thing he had kept nonverbal in his head until now. Ten days ago, his "son," as it turned out, had become a statistic, after all—and not even a devastated Sedona had blamed him for it. He knew there was a chance the authorities were investigating him because of the boy's sudden death—that they suspected him, even—and were keeping it quiet to lull him into a false sense of security. He knew, too, that they had no proof. He had placed a napkin between his shoe and the sliding glass door frame, and he had thrown the napkin away at the airport. The child's drowning could not be traced back to him.

Nevertheless, as the man took his glasses off and reached a hand out to him, panic seized Thatcher. He found himself rising instinctively and surrendering both of his wrists.

The man smiled and shook his head. "No, Dr. Redmond!" he laughed. "I'm not here to arrest you."

"Oh? What, then?"

The man leaned near and whispered in his ear.

"Ah!" Thatcher smiled at the others, who watched in curiosity. "I'm being requested by the President, it seems."

The Secret Service agent gave him a sharp look.

Thatcher put a finger to his lips apologetically. "Sorry, good man. I'm afraid I'll have to bid you all adieu. *Au revoir*!"

With a bow and a flourish, Thatcher excused himself from the staring faces around the table.

"Wouldn't you know it?" Stapleton wagged his head, marveling at Thatcher's run of luck.

12:43 P.M.

Returning from a quick swim at Stony Beach, Geoffrey pedaled his bike down Bigelow Street.

When he turned onto Spencer Baird Road, he glanced over his shoulder. A man with a crewcut, a white polo shirt, and navy blue shorts was following him. The big man sat awkwardly on his bike, but he pedaled hard, gaining on Geoffrey.

He looked like the guy in the suit who had stood up and left at the end of his last Chat. Instinctively, Geoffrey pedaled faster.

The big man seemed to match Geoffrey's speed, pedal for pedal, as both headed down Spencer Baird Road. Geoffrey took a hard turn down Albatross Street and swerved to avoid an SUV coming off the boat ramp. He flew past the Aquarium of the National Marine Fisheries and took a fast turn onto Water Street.

As he blew past Crane Monument the road narrowed and cars lined the curbs. He risked going down the center of the street, weaving around the clogged traffic and earning some honks. He heard more horns behind him and realized that his pursuer was heading down the middle of the street, too!

As he looked up the road, the light for the drawbridge turned red. It would be raised at any moment. Pedestrians and cyclists gathered as the harbormaster walked the yellow swinging gate closed on the Sound side of the street at the far end of the bridge.

He threaded his bike through the crowd and reached the bridge as the harbormaster began to swing the gate closed on the Eel Pond side. Geoffrey decided to go for it. He tore over the bridge and slipped around the shouting harbormaster as his bike shot through the narrow gap between the two gates—only to hear the big man, huffing and puffing, only a few feet behind him! *Jeeze lou-fuckin'-weeze,* Geoffrey thought, standing up on his pedals to pump them as hard as he could.

When he reached the WHOI building that contained his lab, he rode straight up to the entrance and jumped off his bike, letting it skid to rest at the foot of the steps.

He unsnapped the strap of his helmet and yanked it off, ready to swing it at his pursuer, who hit the hand brakes of his bike and stuck out a pale leg to stop his bike in a fishtailing slide.

"What the hell is your problem!" Geoffrey yelled, just as Angel Echevarria came out the door.

"Geoffrey, yo, what's going on, man?" Angel asked, looking at the stranger, whose polo shirt was drenched with sweat. The man clutched his diaphragm as he struggled for breath.

"Ask this turkey. He's been following me all the way from Stony Beach!"

"I'm sorry, Dr. Binswanger," the man wheezed. "The President has requested . . ." He took a couple breaths. "Your presence . . . on a matter of . . . national security. May I . . . have a moment, sir?"

"You have got to be kidding me," Geoffrey said, laughing.

"No shit?" Angel said, ready to believe it.

4:18 P.M.

Geoffrey had been driven home in a blue SUV with tinted windows to pick up a hastily packed duffel bag. Then he was taken straight to Hanscom Air Force Base. There, a C-2A Greyhound stood waiting on the tarmac.

As he climbed aboard the cargo delivery plane, four crewmen motioned him to the back.

He set his bag on some crates as he made his way to the passenger section. There were only two window seats, which faced the tail next to small portholes behind the wings. The only other passenger occupied the portside seat to his right, a bearded man digging a hand into one of the seventeen pockets on his Banana Republic cargo vest. Geoffrey instantly recognized the man, who looked up and studied Geoffrey with expressionless eyes.

Geoffrey extended his hand. "Thatcher Redmond, right?"

"Yes . . ." Thatcher squinted in the shadowy cabin. "Dr. Binswanger, I believe?"

Geoffrey shook the older scientist's hand and took his seat. "Call me Geoffrey."

"They told me you were the other passenger we

317

were waiting for. I'm afraid I haven't heard of you before."

Geoffrey knew Thatcher was lying. They had met at a conference six months ago, even shared a table at the banquet. They had both immediately caught the scent of their natural enemy in the scientific jungle, however, and marked it for future reference. This was going to be a long plane ride, Geoffrey thought. He forced a smile. "Pretty crazy, isn't it?"

"I have to say I always believed it was a hoax." Thatcher tossed a few peanuts in his mouth.

Geoffrey looked out the small window as the plane taxied down the airstrip. "I did, too."

4:23 P.M.

Almost as soon as they were airborne, Thatcher launched his first volley.

"So here we sit in a military plane speeding toward a newly discovered pocket of untouched life, like antibodies rushing to destroy an infection. It's obvious, wouldn't you say, Doctor, that humans are the real threat to this planet, not some precarious ecosystem on some island in the middle of nowhere. We may have stumbled across the last place on Earth that was actually safe from our meddling . . ."

"Surely we can preserve as well as destroy, Thatcher," Geoffrey said.

Thatcher shook his head. "The curse of intelligent life is that it must destroy, eventually, Doctor."

"Oh yes, you believe free will is equivalent to determinism. Isn't that right, Thatcher? And don't call me *Doctor*."

"Oh dear, you're not so religious as to believe in free will, I hope! Or to confuse such a belief with science!"

"Depending on the definition, free will need not be a religious notion."

"Free will is madness, nothing more. Reason and religion make it dangerous."

"Not necessarily. Reason can make free will sane, though sanity is not automatic, I will agree."

"You seem to put a lot of stock in human nobility, Doctor. Considering what we have done to this planet, I find that to be a rather surprising attitude for a man of science."

Geoffrey knew that no matter what position he took, Thatcher was going to take a more fashionably radical position just to stay out in front. He sensed that Thatcher was now trying to place him in some undesirable political camp, so Geoffrey stopped responding altogether.

Geoffrey knew this species of scientist well: Thatcher's battleground was the court of public opinion; Geoffrey's was the laboratory. Either could be fatal to the other, and the scientific arena did not always favor the fittest. When battle lines were drawn between the establishment and the truth, even in the halls of science, the truth did not always win, at least in the short term. And that short term could last generations. Raymond Dart's revolutionary discovery of the missing link in human evolution had languished in a box in South Africa for forty years while the entire scientific establishment dismissed him and worshipped at the altar of Piltdown Man, a phony fossil made of spare ape parts and an Englishwoman's skull stained with furniture polish. At that time, it had been politically correct to believe that the missing link would be found in Europe, and that bias had been sufficient to override other evidence to the contrary for four decades. It was scientists just like Thatcher who caused this sort of mischief, Geoffrey knew—and he was smart enough to give them a wide berth.

Geoffrey leaned back and continued to look out the window, which did not stop Thatcher from continuing to restate his case for a good hour more. Geoffrey could not decide whether he was amused or alarmed by the man's mind-numbing persistence.

Geoffrey had concluded months ago that the MIT star's "Redmond Principle" was quackery of the first order. After the most cursory perusal of Thatcher's best-selling book, it was apparent to Geoffrey that it was the kind of parlor trick that scientists employed to exploit popular opinion and gain attention: make a wild claim that capitalized on current fears, ascribe it a "conservatively low probability" in order to make it appear plausible, and then *ram it home!* Whether Redmond really took seriously the slipshod science in his book, or its melodramatic clichés, Geoffrey was not sure— but Geoffrey was impressed by the shrewd social science the older man had displayed. While Thatcher's hysterical predictions of impending doom could not possibly be proven or disproven in even a decade's time, if ever, they could not fail to cash in on the present zeitgeist—something Geoffrey's work had rarely ever accomplished.

Thatcher, for his part, certainly recalled Geoffrey from the conference in Stuttgart the previous year. He had marked the young man immediately as one of those self-styled "maverick" scientists Thatcher despised—those who traded on good looks and an affected iconoclasm to dazzle their pretty female students into the sack. Youth had a certain automatic fashionability that Thatcher deeply resented, and the fact that Geoffrey was African-American made the younger man strategically difficult to attack—which Thatcher also resented. Above all, he despised the air of integrity that charming rogues like Geoffrey exuded. They were so proud of their uncompromised vision when, in all probability, their vision had never been exposed to any challenge in the first place. Things had not been so easy for Thatcher.

While he supposed there were some scientists from the younger generation who were passionate and sincere crusaders, Redmond had bought a ticket on the gravy train strictly to pig out. Idealism was a business to him. Science was nothing more than a means to an end. He had never been a political animal, cleaving neither left nor right on the political spectrum. But he was capable of going in either direction if it gave him an advantage. Ironically, he had gone left in order to become a capitalist; he had become an environmentalist for his own personal enrichment. He planned on strip-mining the environmental cause purely for his own profit. And he was honest about it, at least to himself—which was more than he could say for most of his colleagues.

Geoffrey's silence was making him uncomfortable. "So what do you say, Dr. Binswanger? You haven't stated your position."

"Um, sorry, Thatcher." Geoffrey excused himself with a dip of his head as he unlatched his shoulder harness and went forward to talk to the crew.

SEPTEMBER 16

4:14 P.M.

Geoffrey and Thatcher skipped like a stone across the globe, landing twice before taking a Lear jet to Pearl Harbor, where they boarded a different C-2A Greyhound and found themselves in the same place they had started, sitting in the window seats behind the plane's wings.

"Imagine a world where there is no intelligent life—where there is no mankind," Thatcher droned on to a numb Geoffrey. "Imagine, Doctor, how nature would advance only in exact proportion to the resources available and retreat with perfect modesty as those resources became scarce. There was a stretch of time that lasted for millions of years before the arrival of so-called 'rational' apes, when the rain forest covered continents, and countless species of more humble apes flourished. Life intelligent enough to enjoy interacting with nature, but not intelligent enough to challenge it, to harness it, or to attempt to control it: the golden age of primates. Surely this step, just before Reason, was the most sublime reached by life on Earth, wouldn't you agree, Doctor? The 'rational animal' is the most grandiose oxymoron in existence: a ventriloquist's dummy that mimics and mocks nature with its mysticism and science."

Geoffrey had been enduring Thatcher's droning Jeremiad for the better part of six hours now on this last, unbearably long leg of their trip. He had been spared only by a fitful nap two hours earlier, and even then he had dreamed an infinite loop of the scientist's dreary doomsaying.

It was bad enough having the Redmond Principle wielded at him, but if Geoffrey had to suffer one more oblique reference to Thatcher's Tetteridge Award, or the big fat check that would accompany the Genius Grant he was suspiciously so certain of receiving, or the Pulitzer Prize he was laying odds on winning, or another celebrity he'd had lunch with, Geoffrey would probably need to use the barf bag affixed to the back of the seat in front of him.

Geoffrey heard something clunk loudly on the roof of the plane. "Excuse me, Thatcher." Grateful for the distraction, he climbed out of his seat and walked forward.

When he got to the cockpit he saw a gleaming KC-135 Stratotanker detach its fuel probe and pull away from the Greyhound in a graceful display of aerial acrobatics.

The Greyhound pilot gave a thumbs-up to the Stratotanker. *"Muchas gracias, muchacho!"* The pilot glanced back at Geoffrey. "Sky bridge!" he explained. "This is one of two C-2As the Navy fitted for aerial refueling. They're the only aircraft that can reach this place and land on an aircraft carrier."

"So that's how this thing can fly so far in one leg?" Geoffrey asked.

"Correct. We had to set up the sky bridge as soon as the carrier group was in place."

Geoffrey grinned, marveling at the circuit that had been put into place to reach the incredibly remote location.

"Speaking of, I think that's your island right there!" The copilot pointed.

Far below, Geoffrey saw dozens of huge naval vessels ringing a brown-cliffed island on the distant horizon. As they drew nearer, Geoffrey thought the island resembled a wide Bundt cake, slightly glazed with white guano around its rim.

The pilot hailed the *Enterprise*'s control tower.

"You better get back to your seat and strap in, Dr. Binswanger. If you've never landed on a carrier deck, when the tailhook catches us you'll be glad you're facing backwards."

"OK." Geoffrey hurried back to his seat. "We're about to land," he told Thatcher.

Thatcher was irritated at the interruption. He tossed a few sunflower seeds into his mouth from a vest pocket. "As I was saying, if this isn't a hoax, perhaps it's Mother Earth's perverse way of eradicating us—a little curiosity out here waiting to kill the cat." Thatcher chuckled.

"Mm-hmm," Geoffrey said.

"Intelligence, wouldn't you agree, Dr. Binswanger, is the snake in the Garden of Eden? The fatal virus planet Earth was unlucky enough to contract? Or is that too heavy for you?"

Geoffrey shook his head and looked out the window. Seeing a few of the gray leviathans of the *Enterprise* Joint Task Group, the seriousness of the situation they were about to enter finally struck him.

Thatcher continued, seemingly intoxicated by his own baritone voice. "Unfortunately, I doubt Henders Island will live up to the hype. Island ecologies are wimpy. No offense, Doctor."

Geoffrey wondered what Thatcher was driving at now, but then he remembered he was wearing his T-shirt from Kaua'i that said "CONSERVE ISLAND HABITATS" in faded green letters on the mud-red fabric. He shook his head. "None taken, Thatcher. Island ecologies *are* wimpy. That's why we can learn so much from them. They're the canaries in the coal mine. Which is why I doubt we'll see anything to write home about here. Canaries rarely eat cats."

Thatcher raised his bushy eyebrows. "Ah, but don't you admit a certain morbid hope? I mean, what if this *were* something world-changing? After all, giant dodder from the island of Japan is spreading across North America. You know, the stuff that looks like yellow Silly String? If you're not aware of the study, a three-inch cutting produced a growth the length of three football fields in just two months during an experiment conducted in Texas in 2002. When you attack it, it germinates. If you chop it up, every part grows into a complete plant. And the most amusing thing about giant dodder," Thatcher leaned toward Geoffrey confidentially, "is that it *kills* any plant it infects, whether it be the lowly weed or the mighty oak." Thatcher giggled with genuine joy.

"I'm familiar with dodder, Thatcher, but I'm not sure we'll find anything quite so dramatic here." Geoffrey pointed out the window. "Especially if *that's* the island we're talking about."

The airplane had rapidly lost altitude. Now, it made a low pass around the island's cliff as they approached the carrier. Geoffrey noticed the trimaran yacht anchored in a cove cut into the western wall of the island.

"Hey, that's the ship from the show! I guess that much wasn't faked. They really did come all the way out here."

"We'll be landing on *Enterprise* and a Sea Dragon will Charlie you to Henders Army Base," the pilot called back to them. "There's a top-level meeting at seventeen hundred hours."

Geoffrey adjusted his watch to the time-zone uncertainly. "That's less than an hour from now. Right?"

"Right," the copilot said.

"Can't we stretch and get something to eat first?"

Thatcher wadded up the plastic wrapper of his sun-flower seeds and stuffed it in pocket number twelve.

"Attendance mandatory, sir," the pilot replied. "The President called the meeting!"

After a sharp involuntary intake of breath, Thatcher smiled. "I never imagined I would be summoned by the President. Did you, Dr. Binswanger?"

Geoffrey looked out the window as the carrier deck rose beneath them. He braced for impact. "No."

"Hold on, guys!" the pilot shouted.

Thatcher gasped. "Dear Lord!"

4:49 P.M.

Still buzzing from the adrenaline high of the tail-hook landing on the nearly five-acre flight deck of the *Enterprise*, Geoffrey clung to a handle inside the cockpit of the thundering helicopter as it made a dizzying ascent over the island's sheer putty-brown palisade. Both Geoffrey and Thatcher wore blue hazmat suits, their helmets in their laps.

Scanning the cliff's overhanging face, Geoffrey noted the metamorphic banding and buckled red layers of rock, deeply corrugated by eons of erosion. They appeared even more weathered than the ancient shores of the Seychelles that had been iso-lated 65 million years ago at the edge of the age of dinosaurs. As the helicopter cleared the rim, a green bowl opened under them. At its bottom, a broken ring of jungle spread outward like a dark wave from a bald central mesa of weathered rock.

"Looks like a creosote plant," Geoffrey observed.

Thatcher nodded.

"How so, Doctor?" asked one of the helicopter crewmen.

"Some individual creosote plants are probably the oldest multicellular living things on Earth," Geoffrey answered. "From the air you can see large rings of vegetation across the floor of the Mojave Desert in California. Fossilized root systems show that the rings are from a single plant growing outward for ten thousand years."

"No kidding!" the young pilot exclaimed, impressed.

Whether it was the geology, the deeply sculpted weathering of the topography, or the strange growth pattern of the vegetation—or all of these cues taken together—Geoffrey's instincts and training told him that this remote island was considerably older than he had first assumed.

Below, they glimpsed the four sections of StatLab at the outer edge of the jungle. The NASA lab's first two sections appeared to be dissolving under a wave of multicolored growth, and the other two sections were strangled and encrusted with vegetation. The jungle seemed to be literally consuming the lab and a plume of swarming bugs poured out of the end of the last section.

"That's the old lab," the crewman told them. "We had to abandon it last week."

"Last week?" Geoffrey asked. The ruin looked like it must have been there for decades.

Farther up the slope they saw the Army's base of operations on the island, a mobile theater command center. NASA had clearly had its chance and failed.

"That's the Trigon," said the pilot. "That's where we're going."

The new facility was made up of three olive drab sections joined together in a triangle.

"That baby's blast-resistant, has virus-proof windows and magnetic-pulse-protected power and communications systems," bragged the pilot. "It's a mobile theater base designed to survive germ warfare as well as high velocity direct fire, direct hits by mortar bombs, and a near-miss from a twenty-five-hundred-pound bomb. You'll be safe as a baby in a cradle there, guys!"

The new base had been established on a level tier carved into the green slope about four hundred yards away from NASA's crumbling lab. Twelve Humvees and three bulldozers sat in neat rows near the Trigon on the freshly graded terrace.

The Trigon was encircled by a moat lined with butyl rubber and filled with seawater hauled in by helicopter, the pilot informed them. Every thirty seconds powerful fountains sprayed a white wall into the air around the base.

Twenty-two 300,000-liter demountable water storage tanks rested on shelves graded higher up the slope, sprouting PVC pipes that fed moats and sprinklers around the base. Geoffrey recognized the tanks from his visit to Haiti after Hurricane Ella—the giant tanks could be transported to disaster areas anywhere in the world within twenty-four hours—by land, sea, or air—to provide safe water supplies.

As they approached the base, Geoffrey wondered why there were so many tanks. Why did they need so much water? He watched a helicopter filling one from a distended hose, like a robotic Pegasus relieving itself.

"Time to get those helmets on. We're about to drop you two off. After you hear the click just twist them clockwise till you hear another click."

The Sea Dragon descended over a landing zone, and the rear hatch opened, admitting a gale of hot wind and the urgent pulse of the helicopter rotors.

Geoffrey and Thatcher braced themselves for the ramp to touch down, but instead it hovered about five feet off the scorched and salted ground.

"We're not allowed to land!" the pilot shouted. "Jump! Then run down the path to the building. You'll be all right."

"Er—OK." Geoffrey poised himself for the jump.

But Thatcher balked. "You must be joking, young man."

"Jump NOW, sir!"

As the ramp dipped, they both jumped and Thatcher took a tumble. "Fuck!"

Geoffrey hit the ground on his two feet, his knees flexing with the impact.

The helicopter rose and the downwash of its rotors pounded their backs.

Geoffrey helped Thatcher scramble to his feet and they both ran down a wet path of glistening rock salt bordered by fountains that sprayed a tunnel of cold water over them.

"I've had friendlier welcomes," Thatcher groused, panting.

The fountains subsided for a moment and for the first time Geoffrey looked out across the island they now stood on. "What are they? Triffids?" He remembered the old science fiction movie in which experimental plants invaded the earth. The desperate humans discovered that saltwater killed the vegetation only moments before it had strangled the entire planet.

"What, pray tell, are 'triffids,' Doctor?" Thatcher wheezed as they ran.

"Never mind," Geoffrey answered, and a thrill swelled inside him—what on Earth had they found here?

Chlorine dioxide gas was replaced with filtered air, and the hexagonal entry hatch inside the Trigon's germ-warfare-proof air dock swung open.

Standing before them was a slender redheaded woman in a T-shirt, jeans, and Adidas sneakers. "You can take the helmets and suits off now," she instructed in a crisp voice.

Geoffrey pulled off the helmet and his ears popped as they adjusted to the higher air pressure inside the base.

Geoffrey cocked his head; she was not only attractive, but seemed very familiar. "Do I know you? Oh, *SeaLife*—of course. You were on the show! Sorry."

She forgave him with a nod and a friendly smile. "They wouldn't let me go home, so I persuaded them to let me hang around and help. In real life I'm a botanist, though not as esteemed as the ones they've shipped in."

He extended his hand. "Geoffrey."

"Geoffrey . . . ?" She took his hand.

"Binswanger."

She frowned. *"Hmm."*

Geoffrey smiled. "Problem?"

"I could never marry you." She smiled.

"Oh really?"

"My name's Nell Duckworth. The only reason I

ever wanted to get married was to change my last name."

"Ah."

"Sorry."

"Uh-huh."

"You could always hyphenate it," Thatcher interposed drily, clearly unhappy at having his presence disregarded.

"That's funny, Thatcher. You with your great name. By the way, Nell, this is *Thatcher Redmond.*" Geoffrey presented Thatcher with a regal flourish.

"Pleasure," Thatcher said with a curt dip of his head, but he avoided eye contact with Nell and moved on toward a cluster of others gathered farther down the corridor.

She shook her head. "Another Nobel Prize winner, no doubt."

"Tetteridge, as a matter of fact," Geoffrey said. "Nobel Prize winners are *much* nicer. You could always just keep your own name, you know." He winked.

She reached out to poke him in the ribs but hesitated. Geoffrey sensed that her moment of levity had passed, and her eyes drifted as some sadness caught up to her.

Geoffrey smiled, curious. "What's going on, Nell?"

"I was hoping you were going to tell me."

He detected a surprising fear under the irony. "Seriously?"

She sighed. "A lot of people have died here. And they were my friends." She looked at him.

Geoffrey was alarmed, and also intrigued by the intelligence he saw working in her eyes. "I see."

Thatcher returned, walking briskly up to them. He gave Nell an up-and-down look and then addressed Geoffrey. "I believe we're being summoned, Doctor."

"Don't call me *Doctor,* Thatcher," Geoffrey sighed, and smiled encouragingly at Nell. "Come on." He gently jabbed her in the ribs with a finger. "Let's crash this party."

5:21 P.M.

The conference room, which doubled as an observation bay when the table was pushed against the wall, occupied most of the north side of the Trigon.

The tilted window of laminated glass overlooked the lime-green slopes that rose to the straight edge of the island's rim against the blazing blue sky.

Seated around the conference table were a scattering of military brass and about twenty American and British scientists, some quite well known, some Geoffrey did not recognize. He spotted Sir Nigel Holscombe, a favorite of his, who had hosted many a classic BBC nature documentary series.

A satellite-uplinked teleconference screen dominated the western end of the room. In the Oval

Office, the President sat behind his massive desk with his advisors seated nearby, among them the secretaries of Defense and State.

"I hope we're coming through all right," the President began. "I apologize for the delay."

Geoffrey glanced at Nell with wide eyes.

But Nell's focus was on the screen, her expression intent.

Dr. Cato answered, "Yes sir, Mr. President, we hear you fine."

"Good. As everyone here knows by now, I trust, the tragic incident on *SeaLife* was unfortunately not a hoax. The cover story was invented to buy us time to make an important decision. I wanted to share what we have now learned with the most distinguished scientific minds we could assemble before having to make that fateful decision. Dr. Cato, please bring us all up to speed on the situation as it now stands."

Thatcher munched on a peanut from a bag he had stashed in pocket number eight. He observed Dr. Cato with contempt. Suffering from an apparent bout of professional jealousy, Cato had roundly snubbed Thatcher at the Bioethics Convention in Rio last winter, and Thatcher, for one, had not forgotten it.

"Thank you, Mr. President. I'm Wayne Cato, chairman of Caltech's Biology Division and project leader of the *Enterprise* research team. To give us all some crucial background, Doug

336

Livingstone, our on-site geologist, will explain how we think Henders Island got here in the first place. Doug?"

The tall geologist with a wing of salt-and-pepper hair over his craggy face rose and introduced himself in an upper-class British accent. "This graphic put together by the geologic team on the *Enterprise* illustrates what we have been able to reconstruct about the origins of Henders Island."

An animation of the Earth appeared on a presentation screen behind him.

"Seven hundred and fifty million years ago, a supercontinent known as Rodinia split into three pieces. One hundred and fifty million years later, these pieces smashed back together. They formed a second supercontinent we call Pannotia."

On the screen, the Earth rotated as a sprawling supercontinent cracked into three continents and slammed together.

"Another hundred and fifty million years passed. Then, just as the Cambrian explosion of life introduced an astonishing variety of multicellular species on Earth, Pannotia tore into four vast segments. These pieces would become Siberia, northern Europe, North America, and the supercontinent geologists call Gondwana, which included Antarctica, South America, Africa, India, and China."

Livingstone waited as the animation caught up.

"Tens of millions of years passed as the new continents converged to form Laurasia, which slammed into Gondwana two hundred seventy-five million years ago and formed the super-continent known as Pangaea, where dinosaurs emerged. Pangaea started breaking apart a hundred and eighty million years ago into the seven continents familiar to us today, which is why dinosaur fossils can now be found on every modern continent."

The geologist flicked through some stock images of the violent coasts of Cornwall and Alaska.

"Over the eons, landmasses continued to split and collide, dragging mountain ranges under the sea and shoving ocean beds up to create the Andes, Rockies, and Himalayas. Fragments of land continued to break off continents. Some drifted thousands of miles. We know that Alaska, for example, is a train wreck of giant chunks cast off from China and other parts of the world."

Livingstone clicked to the next animation, which appeared to be a tighter detail of the previous globe.

"We now believe that there was a fifth fragment of Pannotia. Probably about the size of New Zealand, this fragment somehow managed to dodge the geological pie-fight for half a billion years, riding up and down the Pacific rim while being relentlessly ground down between tectonic plates. All that remains above water of this fragment today is Henders Island, which seems to have been upthrusting just faster than erosion can melt it under the sea."

Livingstone clicked to an image of a geological cross-section of the island. It looked like a jagged pillar or a tapering candle rising from the sea floor.

"We put together this profile from sonar mapping data collected by Navy subs during the past few weeks. Rock samples from the cliffs indicate that this island is a continental microplate with a craton or basement core composed of prelife Archean-aged rock. Excavations for this command center and rock samples collected during a mountaineering expedition indicate the overlying younger rocks to be freshwater stream and lake deposits that contain fossils of completely unknown organisms with no parallel in the rest of the world's fossil record.

"So, Mr. President, this small island's humble appearance disguises an epic legacy. The fluke of its natural history has helped hide it from the eyes of science. Its remoteness has kept it out of the path of human beings. From the air, it looks like the typical caldera of a volcanic island. Its imposing cliffs have fended off tsunamis from meteor impacts, as well as the few travelers who may have come across it, for millions of years. Recent seismic activity, however, indicates that the island's substrate is weakening. This accounts for giant fissures in the island's escarpments that have allowed access to the island's interior for the first time."

The lanky scientist pointed toward the window.

"The vegetation covering the majority of the island seems to be a bacterial symbiont that absorbs a variety of minerals and photosynthesizes. Combined with other organisms that use acid to scour the vegetation off the rock, this is probably what carved out the island's bowl-shaped topography, disguising it as a volcanic island in satellite images."

Livingstone glanced at Geoffrey and the other scientists seated around the table. "When the supercontinent Pannotia existed, the ocean was nearly fresh. Many believe this played a role in the rise of complex life during the Cambrian explosion. Complex life might also have evolved in the vast freshwater inland seas of Pannotia before migrating down rivers into the open seas. This island seems to have carried life on a separate journey from that evolutionary explosion all the way to the present day."

"Don't give me the labor pains, just show me the baby, Dr. Livingstone," the President said, to some laughter around the table. The President's advisors did not laugh.

Livingstone cleared his throat. "To put it in perspective, Mr. President, Australia was isolated seventy million years ago, and look how weird kangaroos and platypuses are. Life on Henders

Island has been isolated almost *ten* times that long. For all practical purposes, it might as well be an alien planet."

Geoffrey felt almost physically dizzy. Thatcher, he saw, was looking at Dr. Livingstone with an expression of awe that bordered on delight.

The Secretary of Defense spoke for the first time. "So I guess that means we can rule out biowarfare programs—this isn't the Island of Doctor Moreau?"

There was a general release of laughter.

Dr. Cato nodded. "Right. And it's not from outer space, or a so-called lost world frozen in time, or a land of radioactive mutants. Scientists in Romania recently discovered a cave sealed off for five million years. The cave contained an entire ecosystem of thirty-three new species. The base of their food chain is a fungus growing in an underground lake in total darkness. Thermal vents at the bottom of the sea have revealed ecosystems previously unimagined that might reach back to the first single-celled organisms. The ecosystem on this island has been evolving much longer than any other land-based ecosystem on Earth." He gestured toward Nell. "Dr. Nell Duckworth, one of our project leaders, will now summarize what we know about life on Henders Island. Dr. Duckworth?"

Nell rose and Geoffrey looked at Nell in surprise, after the humility of her introduction, to discover her authority here.

Nell's expression was quite serious, grim, even, to the point of bleakness.

"Normally, island ecosystems are fragile and vulnerable to 'weed species'—alien flora and fauna that destroy native species." She advanced through some images. "Mosquitoes, mongoose, gypsy moths—even house cats have decimated island ecosystems."

She clicked the wireless mouse and brought up a blue screen that read PLANT TESTS. She clicked again: six potted plants appeared in split-screen on the large monitor. "Here is some time-lapse footage of some of Earth's most formidable plants—like kudzu, leafy spurge, giant dodder—after being exposed on Henders Island."

In speeded-up motion the specimens on the screen were strangled, dismembered, dissolved, and devoured by Henders vines, clover, clovores, bugs, and animals. The pixilated massacres resembled stop-motion scenes from the original *King Kong* movie. Specimen after specimen shown in the windows on the screen was raided, razed, and replaced with sprouting Henders varieties.

Grumbling rose from the audience.

Nell raised her voice, keeping it authoritative and firm. "None of the over sixty plant species we tested lasted more than twenty-four hours. Most perished in less than two hours."

Geoffrey noticed that many of the scientists at the table looked as shocked as he felt, and many of the military officers had clenched their jaws defiantly. The President and his advisors, he noted, seemed to have seen this incredible footage before.

Nell clicked the mouse. A title appeared: ANIMAL TESTS. A split screen showed a series of animals filmed in slow motion as they battled Henders counterparts.

"After matching common Earth animals with Henders species in artificial laboratory conditions, we found the same result. Rattlesnakes, pythons, scorpions, jumping spiders, tarantula hawks, cats, army ants, cockroaches . . . None of these lasted more than a few hours. Most lasted only a few *minutes*."

The officers, civilians, and scientists alike were agitated and indignant to see the familiar monsters hunted down and slaughtered so easily. Even if they were deadly and troublesome species, they were *our* deadly species, and a certain loyalty was offended by the sight of their swift destruction. The Henders species seemed to move at a different speed, always attacked first, and responded to any resistance or counterattack with a frightening escalation of violence.

Thatcher glanced at Geoffrey and then looked back at the screen. A smile widened under his red mustache.

"Jesus H. Christ!" said one of the Navy brass across from Geoffrey. "Sorry, Mr. President. I hadn't seen this until now."

"That's all right, Admiral Shin." The President nodded. "That's why you're here. I'm seeing some of this for the first time myself. I empathize with your sentiment."

"Laboratory conditions are not ideal tests," Nell continued. "Henders species are even more lethal in the wild. As we found when we released some common specimens equipped with cameras."

Footage of the ensuing carnage played behind her.

"Mr. President," interposed Brigadier General Travers, who sat across the table from Geoffrey. "This is potentially more deadly than any military threat we have ever encountered, sir."

Thatcher forgot to chew his last peanut as he stared at the screen: he swallowed it whole as a Henders rat bit off the head of a pit viper.

Geoffrey kept looking from the screen to Nell and back. He could not believe what he was seeing—but it seemed impossible to him that this could be faked or that this woman would be participating in some deception.

He blurted out, "Is this how every species on the island—I mean, there must be *something* that is *nonaggressive* in this ecosystem! I'm sorry, Mr. President—Geoffrey Binswanger of Woods Hole."

Nell answered Geoffrey's question directly and calmly. "Henders Island's entire ecology consists of weed species, Dr. Binswanger. Earth's most lethal flora and fauna are no match for any of the Henders species we have tested. If any of them were to spread to the mainland, they would soon wipe out everything in their biological niche. And each species here can occupy a wide variety of niches throughout its life cycle."

High-speed and slow-motion clips on the screen showed a pine tree, a praying mantis, a flat of wheat, Africanized bees, crab grass, and a mongoose—all ravaged and scavenged by Henders opponents.

"Every insect is outmatched. Every common plant is shredded. Every predator from our world is slaughtered and consumed, bones and all," Nell told the hushed room. "There are animals that reside in the island's lake that are bigger than T-Rexes, and there are land predators twice the size of African buffalos. There are mite-sized creatures equally lethal. We haven't even been able to find nematodes in the soil—in their place we found tiny armored worms that eat detritus and aerate the soil. These armored worms devour nematodes for breakfast. We have found no species from the external biosphere here at all except for a few fungi, molds, and bacteria that appear to have adapted to subsoil environments." Nell was silent a moment. Then she added: "Nothing from our world can survive here."

"Now, come on!" protested Sir Nigel Holscombe. "You've got to be joking!"

"Sadly, no," replied Dr. Cato. "Extrapolating from the data we've collected using the most conservative computer model projections, if this biology mixed with ours, human trade would distribute Henders species to all five continents within a decade. Every living thing the human race takes for granted, from cows to apple trees to dogs and the fleas on their backs, would go extinct within a few decades."

"We would be the oddballs, living on islands with kangaroos, kiwis, and giant tortoises, Sir Nigel, praying that species from the mainland never reached us," said Nell.

Exclamations of shock, awe, and disbelief exploded around the table.

Geoffrey leaned forward, fascinated by what he'd seen and heard. "So why hasn't it happened yet?"

"Yes, and are we safe on this island?" Sir Nigel chimed in. The old scientist looked deeply rattled and excited, simultaneously.

"Fourteen hundred miles of ocean surrounds Henders Island in every direction," Dr. Cato replied. "I'm told that a cameraman is the one who discovered that saltwater is toxic to Henders biochemistry. Like insects and birds, these species invaded the land by switching from excreting ammonia—which is very soluble in water but toxic if stored in the body—to excreting uric acid. As a result of their terrestrial compromise, Henders creatures lost their ability to hypoosmoregulate—to keep their blood less salty than seawater. Since they can't get rid of excess sodium, calcium, or magnesium, exposure to salt-water causes a magnesium buildup in their blood like a fatal dose of anesthesia."

"Many Henders species spray pheromones when they sense salt to signal danger," Nell told them. "This is what is known as a Schreck reaction. It has been observed in rainbow trout that release an olfactory marker when one is attacked, triggering the whole school to scatter."

"A pheromone repellent," Dr. Cato continued, "saved the cameraman when he jumped in a salt-water pool and was coated by it. Saltwater is a reliable secondary repellent to Henders animals, hence the perimeter of fountains we have set up around the base. So, Sir Nigel, to answer your question, we are quite safe here, and our vehicles are now equipped with tanks of seawater as well." Dr. Cato gave his friend a reassuring nod.

Geoffrey shook his head, still unable to reconcile this with everything he knew about sustainable ecosystems.

"Dr. Cato." The President's face was grim. "What is your bottom line?"

Dr. Cato glanced darkly at Nell before answering. "Sir, the bottom line is this: if the oceans had not continued to get saltier since Henders Island was isolated about six hundred million years ago, life on Earth would probably be *extremely different* today."

"So far we've been very, very lucky," Nell said.

All turned to look at the President.

"Well, we obviously can't cover the world in salt," he said.

"No, sir," Nell agreed.

Thatcher Redmond looked around at his colleagues. "Mr. President, are we actually contemplating the *destruction* of this ecosystem? If that is what you've asked us here to condone, sir, I simply cannot think of a more horrific legacy for America. Or for the human race!"

Geoffrey found himself agreeing with Thatcher. "This ecology might yield benefits we cannot even begin to imagine, Mr. President."

"It is a matter we have considered, Dr. Binswanger," the President said. "Unfortunately, I must weigh potential benefits against potential hazards, which in this case appear to be extremely serious. Don't you agree?"

Geoffrey frowned.

Thatcher bristled. "If the Navy were to keep guard around this island, how could anyone transport live specimens off it? How do we know these computer models are correct? We have not had nearly enough time to make such scientific conclusions with any certainty, with all due respect to Dr. Cato and his team!"

The President nodded. "Thank you, Dr. Redmond. I'd like us all to hear what the Secretary of Defense has to say about the capabilities of the United States against this threat."

The secretary, a spry silver-haired man wizened by warfare, looked irritated as the camera panned from the man behind the big desk to him.

"Well, we can't simply strand and support such a large investment of assets in the middle of nowhere indefinitely," he stated. "There are other threats in the world and a limited budget to deal with all of them. And no matter what we do, there are innumerable ways specimens could be smuggled off the island. High altitude airdrops and balloon-released specimen carriers would be exceptionally difficult to detect. Corruption of those entrusted to keep guard, even accidental transference . . ." He shook his head grimly. "The variables are too many. And even one incident, judging from what we have just heard here today, would be sufficient to compromise global security. No one could ever put the genie back in the bottle."

"Dr. Cato," the President asked, "what do your computer models project might happen if even a few of these species reached the outside world?"

Dr. Cato nodded at Nell and she clicked a handheld mouse that put a new graphic on the screen.

Next to a silhouette of each Henders organism was a computer-generated globe over which spread a series of graphic wildfires from different points of origin: Portland, Los Angeles, Panama, Sydney, Nagoya, Hong Kong, Kiev, Morocco,

Durban, Salerno, Marseilles, Portsmouth, New York Harbor. The spreading crimson waves left a blackened Earth that represented total extinction of native species. A date ticked in the lower right corner showing the estimated year that each species tested would cause global collapse: 2037, 2039, 2042, 2051.

Nell gestured at the terrifying countdown. "Computer models generated by the *Enterprise* team have predicted that any *one* of these species could be enough to topple our ecosystem like a house of cards."

"God help us," muttered one of the Navy brass. Someone else cursed softly.

"Mr. President," Nell said, "to the native life on Henders Island, the rest of the world is a banquet table. Not even our parasites, microbes, or viruses have been able to invade this island. Most Henders species can alter the pH levels of their blood chemistry almost instantaneously in response to infection. They have existed, on a continuum, much longer than any animals in our biosphere. They have survived atmospheric changes, ice ages, global warmings, and extinction events that replaced the dominant species on the rest of the planet half a dozen times over. If any of these animals made it off the island . . ." Geoffrey saw the intensity in her eyes as she addressed the President on the conference screen, "virtually no other ecosystem on Earth could survive it."

"Fuck me!" exclaimed Sir Nigel. "Apologies, Mr. President."

"It is extremely doubtful that we could survive it, either, Nigel," said Dr. Livingstone.

Geoffrey raised a hand. "I still can't believe there aren't *any* species that don't pose a threat here. I just got here, so I may be speaking out of turn, but, surely, something must be benign on this island and can be preserved in controlled conditions for future study! I have to agree with Dr. Redmond: computer models and algorithmic projections seem like a pretty flimsy standard of evidence when you're condemning an entire ecosystem."

"I'm interested in preserving any life that we can here, Dr. Binswanger, and that's one of the reasons you are here," the President told him. "Ladies and gentlemen, unfortunately, we have precious little time. Mr. Secretary, I'd like you to fill everyone in on recent developments."

The Secretary of State did not look comfortable with the President's request. He cleared his throat after a stern nod from the Commander-in-Chief. "We have already had to rebuff Chinese and Russian warships from this area, and both of these confrontations have been . . . *hairy,* I think is the word I'm officially allowed to use."

The scientists present registered disgust at the military brinksmanship.

The military brass looked grim.

"The British are claiming this island as their territory since it is named after a captain in the Royal Navy who discovered it 220 years ago—we have respected that position and so have included eminent British scientists in the investigation team. However, this quarantine we have imposed is hatching conspiracy theories. It is also fomenting a worldwide diplomatic backlash against the United States and Britain. International relations are rapidly reaching an unsustainable level of destabilization." The Secretary looked at the President. "We must decide if we should sterilize the site with a tactical nuclear weapon. And we must decide *now.* The human race may never have another window of opportunity."

An eruption of furious exclamations burst from the scientists.

"Dr. Duckworth," the President said, ignoring the interruptions.

Nell was startled at the acknowledgment. "Yes, sir?"

"You were the first person to witness these species. You are also one of only two who survived that first encounter. You have experienced firsthand the destruction the life forms on this island are capable of. What is your recommendation?"

"Nuke the island," she answered without hesitation, astonishing herself with her bluntness. Her cheeks colored faintly, but her gaze met that of the man on the screen steadily and without flinching.

The scientists around the table gasped. Geoffrey

was stunned that a colleague would take such a position; most of the military appeared gratified by Nell's bald statement.

"And how do we know nuking it won't blow pollen or regenerative cells from its organisms into the stratosphere?" Geoffrey demanded, standing. "How do these organisms reproduce? We could be spreading the threat across the entire biosphere!" He crossed angry glances with Nell as he sat back down.

"Mr. President," interrupted the Secretary of Defense, "we had a chance to destroy smallpox forever, and we know now that the Russians didn't do it and we didn't either, just in case the disease might be used as a weapon. Now we chase rumors that terrorists may well have gotten their hands on it. I do not like the idea of what terrorists might do with a few samples of life like *this!*"

"How do these animals reproduce, Dr. Cato?" the President wanted to know. "Is there any danger that a nuclear weapon could spread these organisms beyond this island?"

Dr. Cato shook his head. "There is nothing to suggest anything here procreates by means of pollen. That's one of the reasons it has remained biologically isolated. All the animals on the island appear to be hermaphrodites that mate once for life and reproduce indefinitely. Even the plantlike life produces eggs that stick to mobile organisms for only a few seconds before falling off. That's why birds have never transported species off the island."

"Is there any species that is benign, as Dr. Binswanger suggests?"

"All of these creatures have been swimming in the same shrinking pond, so to speak, Mr. President," Dr. Livingstone replied. "I'm afraid that to make it here they've had to become tougher than any common Earth species—far tougher, in fact."

Geoffrey suddenly noticed a light outside the window, flashing about halfway up the north slope.

"Ladies and gentlemen," the President said, "I'm afraid I cannot, in good conscience, allow even the American government to have the opportunity to weaponize life from this island. The results could be catastrophic."

Thatcher rose now, his face flushed with anger. "Mr. President! If we destroy this ecosystem we will be committing the greatest crime in the history of the planet. And we will only be foreshadowing what we are well on the way to doing to our own world, as well. Nothing could illustrate the thesis of my book more vividly than such a wanton and total annihilation of a completely unique branch of life purely for our own selfish benefit!"

The man in Washington did not flinch. "It may surprise you to know that I accept your verdict, Dr. Redmond. And I won't stop you from yelling it from the mountaintops, either. Unfortunately, the question is *which* crime to commit, not whether to commit one. I do hope I have your sympathy, if not your agreement, on that. Because I sincerely wish to have it."

"I'm not sure I can give it to you, sir," Thatcher retorted, glaring at Cato. "I think this atrocity will only prove humans far more dangerous than anything on this island. I'm sure Dr. Binswanger agrees with me!"

Geoffrey heard Thatcher with irritation, but he said nothing. The flashes on the ridge, he thought, were not an accidental trick of light: they appeared to be a regular and repeating signal. But from whom?

"Nevertheless, Dr. Redmond," the President said, "my responsibility and allegiance must be to the human race and the life forms that sustain it. I'm afraid I must give the order to sterilize Henders Island, within forty-eight hours. This should allow twenty-four hours for final specimen collection and documentation of the island and twenty-four hours to evacuate and achieve a safe distance from the blast. I will not impose a gag order on any of you after this matter is resolved. I will not silence academic debate, even though I realize that I will probably be eternally condemned for this decision, especially by the scientific community. The notion that a President should put a limit on the appetite of science, which by its very nature must be limitless, is against everything I believe in. But to put a limit on nature itself is an even more grievous and permanent act of destruction. That is the burden I have to bear alone. I caution you all now, however, that you should understand how seriously this course of action will be carried out."

Geoffrey nudged Nell urgently, pointing to the flashing light on the far slope. Nell could not imagine why he was distracting her at a moment like this but she turned, angrily, toward the ridge to which he pointed.

"Any attempt to smuggle life off Henders Island will be met with deadly force, with no questions asked," the President pronounced. "In the interest of science, however, we must collect as many euthanized specimens as possible in the time that we have left. Dr. Binswanger, I fervently hope that you and your colleagues can find a benign species that can preserve a living legacy of this world for future generations. But any live specimens must be put under the heaviest guard. They can be transported for off-site observation only after approval by Dr. Cato, the joint chiefs, and myself. And such specimens, if they are found and verified, may only be transported to the U.S.S. *Philippine Sea* for quarantine. Is that understood, Dr. Binswanger?"

Nell mouthed the Morse code as she read the flashing light on the distant ridge. *S . . . O . . .*

"I'm sorry, Mr. President," Geoffrey said, rising. "There seems to be a signal, sir, on the north ridge of the island!"

"It's an S.O.S.!" Nell confirmed, rising beside him.

The room broke into commotion as everyone turned toward the window. The light blinked on a step of what looked like a stairway of rock reaching out of the dripping jungle, halfway up the northern slope.

"Well! Thank God. Let's get a rescue party over there pronto, people," the President ordered.

"Yes, sir," Dr. Cato said. He turned to Nell, but she was staring at the flashing light, her face pale with desperation.

"You have twenty-four hours, people," the President said. "I hope that we will all use them well, and that God may forgive us for what we are now called upon to do. Godspeed!"

The screen went black. Then everyone rose and rushed from the room.

5:59 P.M.

Geoffrey followed Nell. She seemed to be ignoring him now as she strode behind the others through the clogged corridors to the hatch.

"Wait, Nell! Where are you going?"

"Out there."

Several other scientists had started zipping into

hazmat suits. She reached for the hatch control console on the wall.

"Hey, aren't you going to suit up?"

"No feedbag for me, thanks. Anyway, the only reason to wear them was to protect the island from our germs, and that's a moot point now. I see the military stopped wearing them a while ago."

"Yeah," one Army staffer said. "Some of the scientists like to wear them."

Sir Nigel Holscombe, who had started zipping in with his camera crew, overheard them. "Balls!" he said. "If she's not wearing one, I'm not wearing one!"

A wave of zippers unzipping followed as the others stepped out of their suits.

Thatcher and several others crushed into the air hatch. Geoffrey was pressed up against Nell's back as more squeezed in behind him.

"Still there?" she asked as the hatch was closed.

Her icy tone made him wince. "Everything I know about successful ecosystems suggests that they evolve toward cooperation and away from predation," he said to her stiffened back.

"You can't be a vegetarian if there aren't any plants."

Thatcher overheard them from the back of the airlock, having squeezed in at the last second.

"But the growth on the fields," Geoffrey said. "Something must eat that?"

"Everything eats that, and it eats everything. Everything eats everything here."

"That's impossible!"

"On Henders Island, Dr. Binswanger, I'm afraid you have to think outside the box," Nell said crisply, as the outer hatch unsealed and opened. "Either that or you better stay in the box and hope like hell nothing gets in."

She strode out onto the path outside without turning back to see if he was following.

6:01 P.M.

Army personnel were mobilizing within the base perimeter. They were assembling a search-and-rescue convoy to investigate the distress signal, which still flashed steadily on the island's northern slope.

The challenge lay in bringing a ground vehicle to the survivor. Two helicopter teams searched the craggy jungled slope, but so far had been unable to spot the source of the signal. And besides, helicopters were forbidden to land, drop anyone down, or pick anyone up. Dangling from a rope over Henders Island had proven to be a fatal mistake.

Under the saltwater drizzle of the fountains, scientists and soldiers hurriedly prepared for a last blitz of specimen collecting. They loaded saltwater tanks and cannons, aluminum specimen traps, and as much video and scientific equipment as they could cram into the remaining Humvees. They ran hunched over, shielding the gear and their eyes from the rain of seawater, as they quickly fueled and loaded the train of vehicles.

The High Mobility Multipurpose Wheeled Vehicles, or Humvees for short, had been fitted with "Mattracks," individual tank treads for each wheel that made them sit a few feet higher off the ground than they would have with tires. An engineer had designed Mattracks after his eleven-year-old son Matt drew a picture of a truck equipped with tank-treads on each wheel. Young Matt's idea had turned out to be quite ingenious. The tracks could be retrofitted to any vehicle, and the treads chewed through rough, flooded, and steep terrain with equal ease. The U.S. military had gleefully bolted them onto nearly every kind of field vehicle in their fleet. Only Mattrack-fitted Humvees had been airlifted to Henders Island after the disaster with the XATV-9's tires, which had led to the deaths of two scientists, a diplomat, and their driver.

The three Humvees assigned to investigate the distress signal were ready to roll at the head of the line. Behind them, Sir Nigel Holscombe and his camera crews frantically loaded their two Hummers.

Nell climbed into the backseat of the first Hummer, and Thatcher followed her. Thatcher smelled a triumphant sequel to his book, and the prospect of that payoff charged his soul with a form of courage: nothing could stop him from tagging along on this expedition.

Geoffrey opened the door on the right side of the Hummer and climbed in next to Nell. "Mind if I join you? Oh, hello, Thatcher."

"Still hoping for a benign species?" the botanist asked.

Geoffrey smiled. "Nell, it just seems impossible to me that something from this island can't be preserved."

"I felt the same way, Geoffrey. I don't anymore," she said. "More than a dozen people I knew have been killed on this island. If you expect me to apologize for wanting it nuked, forget it."

The driver barked responses into the radio. He wore green camouflaged Army fatigues, body armor, and a helmet. Nell saw him kiss a gold crucifix that hung around his neck and tuck it under his armored vest.

Then she recognized the man sitting in the shotgun seat, holding a camcorder. The cameraman also wore body armor and Nell noticed the NASA headband camera on the photographer's head with the viewfinder retracted over his ear.

She tapped him on the shoulder.

"Hey, Nell!" Zero Monroe shouted, and he turned toward her with a big grin.

"Back for more?"

"You, too, darlin'?"

Nell squeezed his arm. "You OK?"

"Yeah. They patched me up. The poison wore off. I can even move my leg again." He laughed.

"Does Cynthea know you're here?"

"No, not this time—when I heard this was going down I came straight from the *Enterprise* sick bay."

"Somebody's *out there,*" she said softly.

"I know." He nodded. "I keep wondering if someone survived that first day . . . But that's impossible." He shook his head, grimacing, remembering the sound of the shrieks inside the crevasse.

Someone tapped on the window next to Zero. Zero opened the door.

"Got room for one more?" Dr. Cato asked.

"Sure, but you'll have to sit in the middle. I need the window," Zero said, jumping out.

The white-haired scientist climbed in and greeted Nell in the backseat. She frowned.

"It may not be safe, Dr. Cato. Are you sure you want to come along?"

"Well . . ." Dr. Cato sighed. "It looks like the last chance I'll get to see this island up close." He seemed a bit distracted. "I'd never forgive myself if I didn't take the opportunity, Nell." Then he turned and met her gaze. "Besides, somebody should look after you and make sure you don't do anything too dangerous out there, my dear."

Zero climbed in and slammed the Hummer door.

"OK, listen up!" the driver yelled to get their attention. "I am Sergeant Cane! You scientists have been embedded on this mission, but it is *my* mission, and I do *not* like the idea. So you all need to know that I make the rules here, and my rule is FINAL. Is that understood?"

"Yes," Geoffrey said. "That's cool!"

Cane glared at each of the others. "Does everyone *else* understand?"

"Yes, sir." Dr. Cato nodded.

"You got it," Nell said.

"Very well, Sergeant," Thatcher sighed.

"Yup" came from Zero.

"Good!" the sergeant said. "So here's rule number one: do not open any windows. We don't even want *one* of those wasps gettin' in here. Because they will MESS YOU UP. Is that understood?"

"Yes!" everyone said, except for Thatcher.

"Rule number two: do not go near the jungle. Do I hear an 'OK, Sergeant Cane'?"

"OK, Sergeant Cane," they all said.

"Does this thing have rubber tracks?" Zero asked.

"Kevlar and steel." Cane hit the gas and the rescue convoy left the safety of the base.

The signal, which appeared to be reflected sunlight, continued to flash intermittently from the highest visible ledge of the rock stairway. As the sun sank behind the western rim, the shadow it cast across the island spread toward the sunlit ledge. They knew the signal would be doused all too soon.

Thatcher gazed out the window at the swarms of insects flying into and out of the roof of the jungle below, and the strange animals that streaked over the open ground.

"Hey, Helo One and Two," Cane said into the radio. "Have you guys spotted anyone? Blue One over." Cane pointed at the two helicopters circling the north ridge.

"Still negative, Blue One, infrared vision shows warm-blooded creatures all over the ledges. We can't pick out anything human down there."

"Thanks, guys. The cavalry's coming."

The three Hummers rumbled toward the north slope in single file up a curving grade of strata that made a natural road.

"That was quite a power play back there," Thatcher sniffed. "The President as God! But I can't say that I'm surprised."

"It seems that either way we're playing God, Thatcher." Geoffrey gazed out in wonderment at the green slopes rising to the edge of the bowl. The buckled strata ringing the island gave it the appearance of an enormous ruined coliseum. The broken rows seemed to have been carved for giants.

"Maybe God's playing God here," Dr. Cato mused, sadly scanning the landscape around them.

"Geoffrey's right," Nell said. "If we don't do

this, we'll be unleashing Armageddon. It would just be a matter of time."

Thatcher looked avidly out the window at the jungle below. A pack of four enormous spigers loped over the clover fields with their back legs pumping like locomotives as they tried to head off two Army Hummers along a lower road near the jungle. The lead Hummer opened machine-gun fire and felled one of the beasts. The others immediately turned on their wounded comrade and ripped into its flesh. "That just might be the best thing that ever happened to this planet," the zoologist murmured.

Geoffrey groaned and Dr. Cato shook his head.

"Excuse me?" Nell said, glaring at Thatcher.

"Armageddon might just save the world from humanity." Thatcher turned to face her with a paternal smile. "Of course, I'm only joking, Dr. Duckworth. But if what we've heard so far is true, no intelligent life could ever evolve in this environment. It's no wonder this ecosystem has lasted so long, evolving on an unbroken continuum since the Cambrian explosion itself. We may have discovered the perfect ecosystem!"

His eyes twinkled, but Nell looked away in disgust.

Zero turned from the window where he was shooting and gave Thatcher a deadly look. "I think you need a little quality time with the local wildlife, Professor."

6:16 P.M.

The Humvee climbed the natural road all the way up to the northeast edge of the island. As the vehicle crested the rise at the cliff edge, Sergeant Cane pointed out the right window.

"Check out these critters, Dr. Redmond!"

Thatcher leaned over Nell to see.

Sprawled and tangled on the sheer cliff of the island's rim, dry tendrils swirled to form what looked like nests, occupied by hundreds of birds' eggs and hatchlings. Geoffrey saw chicks suckling at appendages that rose from the tangled mass— bulbous pods shaped disturbingly like birds' heads. "What the . . . ?"

"Hatcheries," Dr. Cato told him, peering out the window in awe.

Thatcher grunted as he nearly flopped across Nell's lap to peer out. "Really?"

"Could you explain that?" Geoffrey said.

"Some seabirds migrate here to breed," Dr. Cato replied.

"The plants eat the parents, and the nestlings hatch and imprint on their new mommies. Later they return here all fattened up as adults to nest, lay their eggs, and get eaten. The circle of life." Nell smiled darkly at Geoffrey, who looked back at the hatcheries, speechless.

"We've even discovered a subspecies of frigates that has adapted its juvenile beak to fit the nipples on these things," Dr. Cato told them. "So apparently these creatures have been good bird mommies for a very long time."

"My God," Geoffrey whispered, his heart racing at the implications. "A predator-prey relationship in which the *prey* is evolving to improve the predators' chances? I think I'm going to be sick. These things have hijacked the frigate's natural selection. They're fricking *breeding* their own food!"

"Just like we do," Thatcher drawled. "Haven't you seen a chicken? The difference is that this has carefully evolved in tandem with its prey to preserve just what it needs to survive and not expand beyond its resources. You could devote a lifetime to studying any one of this island's organisms."

"A short lifetime," Zero muttered.

Sergeant Cane chuckled sourly as they passed the squawking nesting grounds rimming the high cliff.

Zero videoed intently, cursing when a stream of cloudy juice sprayed the window, obscuring his shot.

Sergeant Cane laughed. "The vines around the nests squirt concentrated salt-juice at your eyes. They can zap wasps right out of the air at twenty feet."

Geoffrey noticed an adolescent bird flung out of a nest. Each time the bird tried to climb back in, a spring-loaded plant stalk flung it back out.

Thatcher was ecstatic. "Fantastic!" he crooned,

leaning fully across Nell now as he looked at the bird breeders.

"OK, enough," Nell said, shooing Thatcher back into his seat.

The ramp of exposed strata sloped down from the island's edge as it continued around the island. Cane pushed the throttle, and the train of three Humvees accelerated down the natural ramp.

Geoffrey gripped the back of Zero's seat and watched Nell, who stared at the shadow of the island's rim as it reached the ridge and doused the flashing light.

Eventually they reached a flat lower stratum. They continued around the bowl to the north, leaving brown tracks in the clover that gradually turned green again behind them.

The shelves of the high slopes were melted soft by erosion like the terraced hills of the Peruvian Andes, pelted with green, gold, and purple clover.

Ahead, patches of jungle topped the succession of rock ledges that erupted from the slope.

"See that highest ledge there?" Cane said, pointing through the windshield.

"Yep, that's where I made it out to be," Zero said.

"Good, no jungle on that ledge." Cane spoke into the radio: "Blue Two and Three, we're going to start on the highest shelf. Suggest you guys search the next two down for the survivor. Over?"

"This is Blue Two. We copy you, Blue One."

"This is Blue Three. Sounds good."

"Looks like we got a swarm, guys," the first voice said.

"Copy that, thanks." Cane twisted the handle of a crudely retrofitted valve on the ceiling of the cab as a swarm of wasps attacked the caravan of Humvees.

They could hear the squeak and hiss of faucets spurting to life.

Sprinkler-heads telescoped on the roofs of the Hummers, and a fine umbrella of water sprayed over each vehicle.

Sergeant Cane chuckled. "Bastards don't like saltwater."

Zero turned his head and gave a deadpan look at Nell.

"I see that we've already adapted to this environment," Thatcher drawled, "and dominated it with our technological defenses."

Cane chuckled. "It's like the Marines say, 'improvise, adapt, overcome.' The Army just does it better."

"Exactly," Thatcher sneered.

Cane turned off the Hummer's sprinklers after the swarm retreated. Blue One dug in its four Mattracks, powering up the steep incline beside the giant stairs.

The other Humvees followed close behind, each one peeling off at its assigned ledge. Blue One rumbled onward, rising fifty more feet to the highest ledge, a curving tier of rock jutting out of the slope.

They turned onto the flat lip of rock. On the left side swayed the palmlike crowns of trees rising from the lower tier. On the right side stood a sheer, three-story rock wall, which the ledge hugged, curving around a bend and out of sight ahead. Above this thirty-foot escarpment, the green fields rose unbroken to the island's rim.

A fallen tree blocked them from driving farther onto the ledge.

Cane tried to drive over the log, but it was five feet thick, too much even for Mattracks to climb over: it looked more like the neck of Godzilla than the trunk of a tree.

"That's the outer cuticle of a giant arthropod," Dr. Cato pointed out. "The trees are actually related to the island's flying bugs."

"Good God," Thatcher chuckled.

"Looks like a rockslide brought it down." Geoffrey pointed at the fresh chunk missing from the cliff above. "So this island's pretty unstable?"

"Yeah. There's been a lot of seismic activity," Nell replied.

Cane eased off the throttle and they heard something so incongruous they didn't register it at first: a dog was barking.

"What the hell?" Cane muttered.

A bull terrier sprinted out on the ledge from around the cliff, yapping wildly. Then it darted back around the corner and disappeared.

"Copey!" Nell cried.

"I don't believe it!" Zero said as he steadied his hand on his camera.

Copepod sprinted out from around the cliff once again, barking furiously, then ran back around the bend out of sight.

Nell grabbed Cane's shoulder. "He's trying to get us to follow him. Let's go!"

Cane throttled forward against the trunk one more time, then stopped. He shook his head. "We can't get over this tree in the Hummer. And no way are we getting out of this vehicle, not with that jungle so close."

"*Somebody* signaled us and needs help, Sergeant! If Copey survived here, so can we! There's somebody there!"

"No way. I'm not going out there."

"Zero." Nell turned to the cameraman. "You survived out there. Can we just run down quick and have a look around the corner? And then run back?"

Zero frowned. "Do we have any weapons?"

"Super Soakers," Cane said. There was a moment of stunned silence. "Seriously. Full of saltwater. And if you leave the Hummer you have to put sterile booties on. In those packets. And before you get back in the Hummer take them off and throw them away." The sergeant looked at Nell and shook his head. "But I don't like it. That jungle's too close." He pointed off the side of the ledge, where the trees waved in the wind.

371

"It's just a few treetops," Thatcher said.

"Super Soakers?" Nell said. "Give me your gun, Cane."

Cane locked eyes with her, hesitating.

"OK." He finally nodded, and gave her his M9 Beretta handgun. "It won't do much good out there," he cautioned as he slid off the safety.

"Nell!" Dr. Cato turned around in the front seat and glared at her disapprovingly. "You can't go outside!"

Nell smiled sadly at him as she clicked on the safety and tucked the gun into her waistband. "I'm sorry, Teach. I have to."

The elderly scientist shook his head. "It's too dangerous!"

"Someone's survived here," she said.

Cato reached out a hand, squeezed her arm.

"I don't want anyone else to die on this island," she said fiercely.

He sighed, knowing better than to try and order her. "Neither do I!" he pleaded.

"I'll be careful," she promised him.

Dr. Cato closed his eyes.

Geoffrey was already opening a foil packet of sterile footwear. "Wow. Rubbers."

"Safe socks." Nell winked as she pulled on a plastic booty over her Adidas tennis shoe. "Coming along, Dr. Binswanger?"

He nodded. "I'm still looking for a benign species," he reminded her.

Nell touched his knee and looked into his eyes. "Just don't look too long, OK? What about you, Thatcher?"

"I'll watch from the car," the zoologist replied.

"Douse yourselves with saltwater," Zero instructed, spraying himself with one of the Super Soakers.

"Hey, not in here!" Cane growled.

"Sorry," Nell said, pumping spray over Geoffrey. "In here! It may not help much but it should trigger a bug to spray repellent if it lands on us."

"The water already has bug repellent in it," Cane told them. "It's taken from the moat around the base."

"That's good," Zero said. "You can dry-clean the upholstery later, Sergeant. Do my back, Nell."

"Any advice on how to move out there?" Nell asked, spraying Zero down as Geoffrey soaked her with the spray gun.

Thatcher cringed, sniffing the noxious musk mixed with the smell of seawater.

"Don't run in a straight line," Zero answered. "Zigzag. And never stop, not even for a second."

"Zigzag?" Cane shook his head, bewildered. "You scientists are all fucking nuts. Good luck, man. I got absolutely no responsibility over this."

"Yes, good luck," Thatcher said.

Cato squeezed her hand. "Be careful, young lady!"

Zero gave Nell and Geoffrey a hard look. "Ready?"

Soaking wet and armed with their saltwater rifles, Nell, Zero, and Geoffrey climbed out the door of the Hummer and over the reptilian tree trunk.

Geoffrey instantly smelled sulfur and a sweet, cadaverous reek wafting out of the vegetation below the cliff. The air was damp. The growth covering the ground was surprisingly flimsy and tore apart under his feet. The intensity of the insect noise coming from the jungle below the ledge shocked him—it was a thick sonic mat of whistles, buzzing, shrieks, and clicking.

Zero tapped on the NASA headcam over his temple as they jumped from the log onto the ledge.

Copepod dashed away, barking as he once again vanished around the curving wall.

"Keep moving," Zero whispered.

The three men in the Humvee watched the three run full speed after Copepod. The dog darted out of sight, then reappeared as the ledge curved back into view farther ahead—then Copey disappeared into a crack in the cliff.

Watching from the Hummer, the sergeant muttered, "Don't go in there . . . come on, don't go . . . oh no."

Before the gash in the cliff wall, Zero, Nell, and Geoffrey stopped in astonishment.

6:22 P.M.

Ten feet inside the shadowy crack stood a skinny figure in a bright tie-dyed T-shirt. He had a black eye and his broken glasses had been crudely repaired. His blond mop of hair was dirty and tangled. "Get away! STAY BACK!" he yelled.

Stunned, Nell gaped at him with disbelief. "Oh my God!"

Zero laughed. "Hey, how the hell—"

"STAY BACK! THEY'RE COMING!" At Andy Beasley's heel, Copepod hunkered down and growled. Andy pointed at the edge.

Zero pivoted immediately, pumping the water-rifle; but the nozzle was clogged with salt crystals. It put out a pitiful squirt.

The jungle noise roared like a hurricane as a horde of creatures poured onto the rocky, sunlit ledge from below. The flood of predators swept toward the small cave, a tsunami of leaping, flying, running, buzzing, spinning shapes and colors.

Nell, Geoffrey, and Zero ran toward Andy and squeezed into the uncertain sanctuary of the slashing fissure.

Zero turned and dropped to one knee. He banged the water-rifle's nozzle against the rock, jarring loose the salt clumps, and pumped the trigger. Finally getting a spray, he swept it high and low through the entrance at the advancing swarm.

The wall of wasps retreated in a wave of warning

pheromones, but one wasp slipped through into the cave.

It buzzed above them, bouncing off the walls, and then dropped down before Copepod. The dog grabbed it with a snapping growl, chewed it in his powerful jaws, then spit it out, barking vigorously at the remains.

Watching from the Hummer, Dr. Cato gripped the dashboard, trying to peer into the gloom of the cave on the far curve of the ledge. "They're trapped!" he shouted.

"I knew this would happen," Cane yelled furiously.

Thatcher watched in fascination over Cato's shoulder.

Geoffrey and Nell sprayed their rifles over the crouching Zero's head at the cave entrance, and a sunlit mist of water fell in the opening between them and the swarm.

Outside the spray curtain, a mass of voracious creatures continued to fly and leap over the cliff, gathering in front of the cave. The mass swirled in dizzying, constant motion, the flying bugs whirling in figure-eights and circles as they advanced and retreated. Any creature that paused too long among them was descended upon and torn to pieces. With each blast from the soakers, the swarm retreated and then re-surged.

"OK," Geoffrey said. "I'm ready to concede there are no benign species on this island, so let's get the fuck out of here."

Nell merely gasped, which didn't reassure Geoffrey.

As if coalescing from the light and mist and the jungle behind it, a spidery shape suddenly appeared, hanging in the cave entrance before them. Its thick silvery fur seemed to reflect the colors of the sky and jungle. What seemed to be a face became visible at the bottom of its body, a wide mouth slowly opening above two large oval eyes, staring at face-level at the four humans. Its cello-shaped body dangled by one slender tendril as it unfolded six long limbs to either side of the cave, trapping them inside it.

From inside the Hummer, Cane and Thatcher saw the animal suddenly shimmer into existence, hanging on the cliff face between the advancing swarm of creatures and the cave's opening.

The sergeant cursed and reached for his rifle. "I told them not to go!"

"Wait!" Thatcher peered through the windshield at the strange animal, which seemed to fade in and out of the shadows.

"Oh my God, Nell . . ." Cato muttered.

"It's a trap!" Zero hissed, crouching inside the fissure. "Andy was the bait!"

Nell fought off the fear that threatened to paralyze her as she stared at the grinning face of the creature in the cave entrance. She grabbed the Beretta and raised it.

The monster's head emitted a loud, warbling voice: "It's VEEE-EEE-DAAAAAAY!"

Nell, Geoffrey, and Zero were dumbstruck, uncertain if their captor had spoken or simply made sounds that resembled words.

Zero remembered the animal he had heard echoing his own voice in the jungle. He turned to Nell. "Shoot it!"

Inside the Hummer, Thatcher's fascination turned to alarm at the piercing voice.

"Oh no, no, no . . ." Dr. Cato murmured.

Cane's mouth gaped open in surprise, his grip tightening on his rifle.

The door opened and Cane and Thatcher saw the old scientist jump out of the Hummer.

"Fuck!" said the soldier.

Dr. Cato slammed the door shut and vaulted over the log.

Thatcher watched with amazement as the scientist ran around the bend of the cliff, shouting "Hey! Hey! Hey!" and waving his thin arms.

"What the hell does the old fart think he's doing?" Cane yelled.

Nell ignored Dr. Cato's shouts. She kept her eyes locked on the eyes of the spider-like animal that now imprisoned them in the fissure.

A second wave of beasts leaped shrieking onto the ledge from the jungle below, including two spigers the size of African lions.

Dr. Cato suddenly appeared, shouting near the edge of the cliff.

One of the spigers swung toward the scientist.

"Come on! HEY!" Cato shouted, and in a microsecond the nearest spiger stabbed a two-meter spike straight through his polo shirt and out his back.

"Noooo!" Nell screamed.

A surge of creatures swarmed the old man's body, temporarily distracted from the humans in the cave.

Nell's scream drew them back.

Like a wall of eyes, teeth, and claws, the stampede, led by the spigers, one of which was still swallowing Dr. Cato's right leg, rushed the humans in the cave.

Nell pointed Cane's Beretta with shaking hands at the dangling creature that had trapped them. Closing her eyes, she squeezed the trigger.

"No!" Andy screamed, shoving her hand, but it was too late.

The gun fired as the creature spun on its tail in a blinding motion toward the oncoming rush of animals. With six arms, it flung six dark disks through the air.

The curving disks thudded one after another into the two leaping spigers, which dropped instantly, their hindbrains severed. The dying spigers shrieked like erratic police sirens and convulsed, gouging their spiked forearms into the ground as they struggled to drag themselves forward toward their spiderlike attacker.

The entire mass of rats, badgers, wasps, and

drill-worms swerved back from the cave to tear greedily into the writhing spigers.

The hanging creature dropped to the ground. It rolled from its four spidery arms onto its two multi-jointed legs as its tail coiled into a cavity under its belly. Standing nearly seven feet tall, it flung four more disks: four smaller animals went down.

Then the creature crouched, standing only five feet high as its "knees" bent like muscular grasshopper legs to either side. Walking forward on second calves that extended where a human's ankles would have been, its "legs" ended in flat, furry hand-feet. White fur shimmered with rainbow colors over the entire creature, which Nell thought now resembled a crablike kangaroo crossed with a praying mantis.

Copepod ran to the creature's side.

Nell darted forward to protect the dog.

But then she stopped as the dog wagged its tail.

The creature patted Copey with two left hands, swiveling its eyestalks to observe the humans in the cave. With a cupped hand, it gestured at them, then it trotted toward the Hummer on its two springing legs. Copepod stuck right by its side.

"He wants us to follow." Andy ran forward, then turned to look back at the others. "You need to come with him if you want to live."

Zero looked at the others, his mouth open. Then he ran, following Andy's lead.

Geoffrey hesitated only a second, then followed, pulling along Nell, who seemed to be in a state of shock.

Andy nodded toward the ravenous pile of creatures squirming by the cave entrance as he ran toward the waiting Humvee. "They'll be finished feeding soon. Then they'll multiply. You don't want to be around the babies, believe me." He glanced back at Nell and Geoffrey. "Move it!" he urged.

They glanced over their shoulders at the snarling riot as disk-ants began rolling in white lines over the ledge into the explosion of red and blue gore.

Sergeant Cane froze as the bewildering creature climbed nimbly over the fallen tree, the dog leaping and scrabbling at its heel. It pushed itself up with two hands on the hood of the Hummer and looked through the windshield right at Cane and Thatcher. As he lifted the radio mike, Cane could swear the damn thing smiled at him.

6:52 P.M.

"This is Blue One. We found a survivor. Repeat, we found a survivor. Copy?" Cane's voice quavered. Over the radio, he heard the others cheering at his words.

Andy appeared right behind the creature and opened the passenger door, and the creature, to Cane's amazement, climbed inside the Hummer.

Copepod and Andy jumped in behind it, as the others scrambled into the back, squeezing Thatcher against the window. Cane grabbed his gun from Nell's hand and pointed it at the creature.

"Is the survivor OK, Blue One?" came a voice over the radio.

Sergeant Cane, with the radio mike in one hand and his pistol in the other, could hardly breathe as he looked at the large thing that now sat beside him and folded its multi-jointed arms and legs. Turning its long neck, it studied him with colorful, swiveling eyes and its mouth opened wide, revealing three curving teeth as wide as hatchet-blades on its upper jaw. Cane was too frightened to know whether it was grinning or snarling at him now.

"Blue One, do you copy? Is the survivor all right?"

"I'm all right, tell them!" Andy urged.

"Uh—affirmative! We . . . will uh . . . we'll bring him back to base," Cane managed.

Thatcher peered at the animal from the backseat, a strange chill gripping him and cold sweat breaking out on his forehead.

Rats began thudding like softballs against the sides of the Hummer. Drill-worms landed on the windows, twisting their maws into the bulletproof glass and actually leaving scratches.

"You better turn that faucet on," Geoffrey warned from the backseat.

"That's great news, Blue One! Great news! In that case, I've got a lot of scientists who want to do some specimen-collecting down here. Copy?"

Cane remained frozen as the creature began touching the roof and steering wheel with four hands while its eyes darted rapidly in different directions.

"Uh, copy that, Blue Two," Cane muttered into the radio.

"Come on, Cane, turn the water on!" Nell said.

Confused, the sergeant set down the radio mike and opened the roof-faucet, spraying saltwater over the Hummer, keeping his gun on the creature. After a moment, the bugs scattered and the creature pointed excitedly at a drill-worm the size of a locust stuck to the windshield. The struggling worm's three wings had popped out of the panels under its head and were pressed flat against the glass by the water's surface tension. The writhing arthropod sprayed some kind of oily chemical from its abdomen, creating a rainbow sheen on the glass as the windshield wiper knocked it off.

The creature in the front seat nodded at Cane and made a kind of thumbs-up sign to Andy using both thumbs on four hands. It turned its head on its twisting upper body and widened its mouth at Cane, nodding rapidly. Its bristling, translucent fur flashed with stripes and dots of colored light.

"Blue One? Are you there? Copy?"

"Answer them, Cane!" Geoffrey said.

Cane picked up the radio mike. "Um . . . we might . . . uh . . . uh . . . collect some specimens, too. Blue One out."

"Go where he's pointing!" Andy yelled.

"What in the FUCK is going on!" the soldier hollered.

The creature hummed as its six-fingered hands traced the contours of the dashboard, stroking the words on the controls and gauges.

"I do *not* like this!" Cane continued.

The creature recoiled a little from the sergeant. Then it grasped his wrist with two hands and plucked the gun from his fingers with two other hands with such speed and strength that Cane was disarmed before he could even think of squeezing the trigger. With one protruding eye, the creature peered curiously down the weapon's barrel.

"No, Hender! Here, give me that, OK?" Andy said. "Very bad!"

The creature turned its head to Andy. Then it tossed him the gun, which Andy caught nervously.

"Oh my god," Nell murmured. "He *understands* us?"

"Give me my weapon!" Cane screamed as anger ignited the adrenaline in his bloodstream.

"Don't worry!" Andy assured him, handing him back his gun.

The creature made a zither sound from the small sagittal crest on its head as it stroked the brown, tan, and green pixels of camouflage on Cane's uniform. For an instant the pattern seemed to be projected over the creature's plush coat.

"Come on, you guys, you've got to see where he lives!" Andy told them.

"Does that thing . . . speak *English?*" Thatcher asked in a hoarse whisper. He sat frozen and staring with wide eyes at the beast in the front seat.

"No, he doesn't speak *English!*" Andy rolled his eyes, and smirked at the ruddy scientist. "This isn't a *Star Trek* episode, dude! He saved my life, that's all I know. And he saved Copey. He makes great chili, too."

"No way." Zero laughed, a wide grin fixed on his face as he videoed feverishly from the backseat. "Sir Nigel Holscombe, eat your *heart* out, baby!"

Cane kept his gun on the creature, which made musical noises as it investigated everything around it while continuing to look at Cane with one motionless three-striped eye.

"This animal," Thatcher spoke with slow, quiet urgency, "is more dangerous than anything on this island."

Geoffrey, who was only now shaking off the shock of their close call on the ledge, watched in astonishment as the creature patted the panting bull terrier on the head. "You were just saying what an atrocity it would be to destroy life on this island, Thatcher. Change your mind?"

"This is different."

The Hummer rocked gently as a powerful earth-quake rumbled through the ground.

"Come on, let's go," Zero said. "We shouldn't stay in one place too long!"

The creature put all four hands on its head and its eyes retracted under furry lids.

"You guys feel that?" The voice of Blue Three's driver crackled over the radio.

"Yeah, that was a bad one," the driver of Blue Two answered. *"Whoa, check it out!"*

A piece of the unbroken rock wall on the south side of the island crumbled and crashed down, leaving a fang of blue sky in the island's rim.

"We might have less time than we thought, guys," Blue Two's driver said.

"Keep on task till they call us back to base," Blue Three crackled.

"Roger that," Cane replied. "Out." He turned to the others. "I'm not sure what we're doing driving around with one of the things we're supposed to be nuking, God damn it!"

"What?" Andy looked at Nell, bewildered.

"The President gave the order to sterilize this island, Andy," she explained.

"Great," he said. "But what about the people?"

Sergeant Cane was sweating visibly. "You call *that . . .* a *person?"* He stared warily at the creature that was examining him. "Are you sure it doesn't speak English? I mean I swear we heard it speakin' English back there, God damn it!"

Andy looked at Cane's uniform suspiciously. "So is *he* in charge now? Are you the guy with the nukes, Commander G.I. Joe with the karate grip? How much have I missed here, anyway?"

"It's OK, Andy," Nell soothed. "The President also asked us to see if any life on this island could be saved."

Geoffrey stared at her in surprise. "Change of heart, Nell?"

She looked at him as tears welled in her eyes. "This is different . . ."

"Come on," Zero yelled. "We gotta check this out! This is fricking amazing! Go where he says, man! Go! Go!"

"We need to find out what we have here and then report to the President as soon as possible, Sergeant," Nell said. "Everything depends on it. OK?"

Cane gritted his teeth. The creature's hands ceaselessly tested everything around it, including Cane's helmet. He closed his eyes, breathing hard. "All right. But I'm under strict orders about not allowing anything unauthorized off this island alive!"

"Does that include us?" Andy wanted to know, seething. "Are you going to nuke us, too, Commander BUTTHOLE?"

"Don't push me, sir."

"Yes, don't push him, Andy," Nell agreed.

Geoffrey nodded. "Let's all just get along, now."

Cane backed the Hummer out slowly and then he gunned it up the slope.

"Wheeeeeee!" the creature fluted.

7:03 P.M.

The Hummer's Mattracks rolled to a stop beside a towering baobab-like tree at the north rim of the island. About a dozen of these gargantuan trees clung to the edge of the island. From a distance they'd looked like toadstools, with vast umbrellas of dense green foliage.

"It lives here?" Cane was staring.

"Wait till you see his hobbit hole," Andy said. "Oh, hey, if we're going to transport them off the island before all the nukes go off we better take something to pack their things in!"

"*Them? Pack their* things?" the soldier said.

Andy nodded.

"We can use the specimen cases in the back here." Nell glanced at Geoffrey; he nodded and reached for them.

Copey barked enthusiastically and jumped out first. Up here, near the island's rim, the air was considerably fresher. The sound of the jungle below was a buzzing high-pitched white-noise.

The scientists each carried one of the aluminum specimen cases from the back of the Hummer.

Now that he was outside the vehicle, Cane carried his M-1 assault rifle, glancing warily at the branches overhead. They were far away from the teeming jungle at the island's heart—but what lurked in the giant tree above them was anyone's guess.

"Are you sure we're all right, Andy, next to this thing?" Zero pointed his video camera up into the tangled canopy.

"Yeah, we're fine if we stay close to the tree."

A perimeter of salt seemed to have been excreted into the soil around the tree's trunk. This seemed to hold back the Henders clover from attacking the creamy gray surface of its trunk, which was as wide as a house. Stepping stones led over the salt perimeter like a Japanese rock garden.

Though it had originally appeared to them like a spider with six legs radiating four meters, the creature now seemed compact. Two legs folded up in back like a spider's. Its middle arms apparently acted as forelegs, and its upper arms tucked up against its long neck so that the first joints or "elbows" resembled pointy shoulders from which surprisingly human arms hung down. The hands on all six of its limbs had three fingers and two opposable thumbs. The scientists and the cameraman drank in the details of its anatomy and its elaborate and effortless motion with speechless wonder.

The long elastic tail from which the creature had dangled over the cave was now coiled inside a potbelly. A sheen of color played over its thick fur like the Aurora Borealis. Its head was onion-shaped, with an understated sagittal horn on top. It had a high-browed forehead over a wide and graceful mouth, and no sign of a nose. As it looked at them, its large oval eyes had a sly, feline look, moving independently in different directions. The eyes blinked with furry eyelids whenever their stalks retracted. Slanted triangular lobes projected to either side of the creature's sagittal horn like brow-ridges over its eyes.

The shape of its wide mouth and lips had a duck-like friendliness, with smiling corners and an eager peak on its wide upper lip. Its expression had an elegant confidence that the humans found disconcerting. Reaching out one of its upper hands, the creature touched the barrel of Cane's assault rifle with delicate curiosity.

Cane jerked the barrel back and aimed the weapon at its head.

"No!" Nell shouted.

Copepod barked frantically.

"Chill, dude!" Zero said, lowering his camera.

"You can trust him, Hender," Andy told the creature.

"It has a *name?*" Thatcher sounded bemused.

"It's cool, Cane." Geoffrey spoke with more confidence than he felt. "This thing just saved our lives, remember?"

"It's cool, Cane!" the creature sang, freaking the soldier out. Cane felt cornered. He darted a glance at Thatcher, who nodded at him discreetly, signaling patience. Cane backed down, and nodded back at Thatcher.

All watched in astonishment as the shimmering creature stepped delicately onto the stones, then turned toward them and gestured for them to follow. It opened a round door that was nearly imperceptible in the bulging trunk of the ancient tree.

Inside, engulfed by the flesh of the vast tree, they stepped into another surprise.

"It's the fuselage of a World War II bomber," Zero murmured.

Andy nodded. "Yep!"

Only the nose of the plane poked out of the massive trunk, hanging over the cliff at the far end. Through the twisted frame of the cockpit window, which seemed to have been covered by a stitched patchwork of clear plastic, they saw the sun setting over the sea.

"The house that Hender built," Andy announced.

" 'Hender'?" Nell said.

"That's what I call him. Or her. Or both."

"Hender didn't build this B-29," Zero said. He canvassed the scene in broad pans.

With four hands, "Hender" pantomimed a plane trying to pull out of a steep nose dive and failing. It made a noise that was an uncanny approximation of an explosion.

"Do you suppose he saw it crash?" Geoffrey asked the others.

"That had to have been at least sixty years ago."

"I think Hender's old," Andy told them. *"Really old."*

"I wouldn't be surprised," Geoffrey agreed. "Is he a solitary animal? Does he live by himself?"

"Yeah," Andy said.

"What's that got to do with how old he might be?" asked Nell, intrigued, as she glanced at Geoffrey.

"I'll explain later," Geoffrey said.

"Good."

"It's a radical theory."

"Good."

"Way outside the box."

She gave him an appreciative glance, then smiled.

None of the humans could take their eyes off the remarkable creature for more than a moment as it moved gracefully toward the nose of the plane in which it had made its home. The fur on its body emitted soft fireworks of color as it pointed at the control panel in the cockpit. Like a weird recording, it spoke:

"This concludes the Pacific Ocean Network broadcast, May 7, 1945. Once again, it's VEEE-EEE-DAAAY! Victory in Europe!"

Geoffrey and Nell glanced at each other in speechless astonishment.

"He must have heard that on the plane's radio," Zero whispered.

"Yeah," Andy told them. "And I've heard him do Bob Hope, too."

"I thought you said it didn't speak English," Cane snapped.

"He doesn't. I've taught him a few words. And he repeats things he heard on the radio back then, but he doesn't understand them."

It was pleasantly cool inside Hender's lair, and the air had a faintly sweet and spicy smell, somewhat like Japanese incense, Nell thought. She could see that Hender had collected a variety of wine bottles, bell-jars, fishing floats, a peanut butter jar, a mayonnaise jar—precious glass vessels had somehow miraculously survived their journey from civilization to Henders Island in cargo containers, steamer trunks, crates, and wrecks across great gulfs of time and distance.

With his three free arms, Hender shook some jars which held insect-like creatures, and their agitated glow filled the shadowy room with a flickering light.

"He catches fresh drill-worms and wasps by putting a piece of meat in each jar," Andy explained. "You should see his rat trap."

The glass vessels glowed green as Hender shook them, casting orbs of light. Nell could see scraps of what looked like trash or beach litter tacked to the walls and ceiling.

Hender's guests seated themselves on crates inside the B-29 fuselage, some of which were lined up like a bench against one wall with an old rubber raft draped over it. Stenciled on the raft in faded black letters was a name.

"Electra?" Nell said in excitement. "This couldn't really be Amelia Earhart's raft, could it? That was the name of her plane, wasn't it?"

Geoffrey stroked the cracked rubber, shaking his head as if nothing could surprise him now. "It seems old enough."

Hender brought out a gourd of some sort.

"Andy, how did you survive six whole fucking days here, man?" Zero asked.

"That first day, Hender came down from the tree next to the lake and grabbed me," Andy answered. "I thought I was dead. But I woke up here. I wasn't dead and he had fixed my glasses with something like masking tape. See?" One arm of his glasses was bandaged at the joint.

The creature served them something in cups of cut-off plastic soda bottles and they were stunned by the dexterity of its multiple hands.

"It's tea-time," Andy said.

"Tea-time!" the creature sang.

Thatcher curled a lip as the creature served him a cup.

It handed Nell a cup.

"Thank you," she nodded. "What is this?" she asked Andy.

"It's OK. It's actually pretty good. I call it Henders tea. But it's more like chili, though. And it has meat in it. Rat meat. It tastes like lobster!"

Nell hesitated, crinkling her nose. Then she sipped, and found the "tea" was more like a tangy salsa than chili and, after the initial surprise, it was good. "Tastes like cherry lobster cinnamon gazpacho . . . with a hint of curry!"

"Thank you." Geoffrey accepted a cup as he observed the anatomy of the creature's two-thumbed hands, longing for a sketchpad or a camera to document them.

"Thank you, thank you, thank you," the creature hummed.

Nell and Geoffrey looked at each other, trembling with amazement.

Cane accepted a cup with undisguised dread. It was clear that the soldier would be happier when his mission was over and Henders Island was in ashes.

"Thank you!" the creature said, making Cane jump.

"Thanks, dude," Zero nodded, setting down his camera and taking his cup.

The creature held its head cocked at Zero for a beat. "Thanks, dude," it echoed.

Geoffrey sipped the "tea" and scrunched his face at the strange taste.

"He makes it from eggs that grow on this bonsai plant he feeds rat-meat to," Andy explained.

"Not bad," Zero decided cheerfully, chugging the contents. "Oh hey! I almost forgot!" He unzipped a pocket in his cargo pants. "This is for you!" He presented a still-sealed plastic bottle of Diet Coke to Hender.

"Oh hey," the creature trilled, its arms unfolding in an "X" of delight.

Thatcher sneered as Zero twisted off the top and handed Hender the Coke.

"It's a little warm, but here ya go," Zero told the creature.

They watched as the creature tasted the soft drink. Its coat scintillated as it guzzled the sweet liquid down. Both of its eyes pointed at Zero and Cane's hand tightened on his gun. Then it belched loudly, smiling wide and smacking its lips.

Zero chuckled. "He likes it!"

"Yes," Thatcher said drily. "I can see the ad campaign already. He'll make Coca-Cola a fortune."

Zero gave Hender a thumbs-up. "Cool, dude!"

Hender gave Zero twelve thumbs-up. "Cool, dude!"

"It's extremely good at mimicry," Thatcher observed.

Hender swiveled his head to look at Thatcher. "It's extremely good at mimicry," it said in a perfect imitation.

"Hender's good at everything," Andy declared.

Thatcher cast his eyes around nervously at the oddball collection of recovered objects decorating the walls. The trash seemed crudely grouped by the various alphabets used in the labels—

Mandarin, Japanese, Arabic, Thai, Cyrillic, and Latin. "Not much sign of a culture. Aside from our own garbage," he remarked.

"I think we're his hobby." Andy finished his tea. "I think he's been collecting our junk for a long, long time."

Thatcher pursed his lips dismissively. "Magpies collect human refuse. And mynah birds mimic our speech."

Nell leveled her eyes at Thatcher. "Dr. Redmond, there is obviously profound intelligence in this being."

"Oh, I certainly believe we must consider intelligence as a factor in determining what kind of organism we are dealing with here, Dr. Duckworth," Thatcher retorted. "This creature may prove to be as deadly as we are, though I sincerely hope not."

"Whatever Hender is, it's certainly deadly to your theory, Thatcher," Geoffrey remarked. "Your perfect ecosystem seems to have produced intelligent life, after all. And it managed not to wipe out an environment that's lasted longer than any other on Earth. Hender here is living proof that you're wrong, old boy! Looks like you might not get that Genius Grant, after all."

Thatcher's face turned deep red. "There is absolutely no shred of proof that this organism has intelligence equivalent to human beings! It—"

"Wait, wait!" Zero interrupted. "Look!"

Hender had been scratching the burnt tip of a thorn on the back of what appeared to be a candy bar wrapper.

Hender handed it to Sergeant Cane.

The wrapper trembled in the soldier's hand as he read what appeared to be a scrawled word: "Signal."

When Hender heard Cane read the word out loud, his head bobbed up and down, and his coat flushed with kaleidoscopic patterns of color. Hender grabbed the wrapper from Cane's unresisting hands. With one of his eyes looking at the wrapper and one focused on Cane, the creature said: *"Sig-nuhl?"*

Startled, Cane recoiled.

Hender grabbed the charred thorn and with it, wrote on the inside of a clamshell.

He thrust the shell at Nell.

She looked at it in astonishment, then read the word out loud: " 'Coke.' "

She showed the shell to Geoffrey.

The creature gestured to his mouth and then to her mouth, then to Cane's mouth, and then to the shell, excitedly.

Nell nodded. "Coke," she said again.

Hender's fur burst with colors as he took the shell from Nell and sounded out the syllable. *"COKE!"*

The creature rose on his bottom legs, pressing his back against the roof and making a variety of high-pitched noises. Then, with all four extending hands, he pointed at various items of litter tacked to the walls and ceiling of the fuselage.

Nell laughed in delight at the first item Hender pointed at on his wall.

"Tampax!" she and Geoffrey exclaimed simultaneously.

The creature extended all four arms in an asterisk of excitement over them. "Tampax!" Hender echoed, indicating a foil condom packet.

Nell, Geoffrey, Andy, and Zero yelled, "Trojan!"

"Wonderful." Thatcher rolled his eyes. "I see our garbage has already exposed our most intimate biological details to this creature."

Hender pointed to other items.

The scientists called them out: "Kodak! Yoo-Hoo! Vegemite! Bactine! Fresca! Fanta! Nestlé Quik! Wrigley's! Milk Duds! Milky Way! Purina Cat Chow! Orange Crush! Thera-Flu! Mylanta! Zagnut!"

The creature lifted a hand and squeezed his eyes shut. "Stope," he said.

Hender must have heard, Geoffrey realized, examples of how every letter in the Latin alphabet was pronounced.

Hender opened his eyes. They flicked in different directions as he scanned the downed plane's dusky interior. With two hands he jostled the hanging jars. They immediately lit up to generate some light, then, with a third hand, he pointed at a scrap and gestured silence with his fourth. In a humming voice that warbled like an oboe, he said: *"Fro-zun Myoolet."*

The six humans were shocked into silence for a few heartbeats. The creature was undeniably applying the rules of pronunciation on his own now: he could not be merely copying what he heard them say.

"Frozen Mullet," Geoffrey corrected.

The creature's eyes fluttered and his mouth pinched downward at the corners. "Mullet?" He held one hand up and closed his eyes. "Stope."

Geoffrey corrected him again: "Stop."

The creature's eyes opened and swiveled toward Geoffrey as he placed four hands on his four hips. *"Stop?"* he honked. He sounded irritated.

All but Thatcher and Cane nodded vigorously.

"I really don't see the point of this," Thatcher objected. "When we obviously have to—"

"SHUT UP!" Nell, Geoffrey, Zero, and Andy shouted.

"He's learning to read," Geoffrey said. "So shut up, Thatcher!"

"Shut up, Thatcher," Hender fluted, and his wide mouth seemed to smile at the red-faced zoologist.

Thatcher looked at Hender with dread and then at Cane. The soldier sat rigid, with eyes fixed in an inward stare.

"It doesn't know what it's saying!" Thatcher scoffed.

The creature pointed to a series of sun-bleached aluminum cans lined on a shelf: *"Coo-ers, Bud-wee-izer, Fahn-tah, Hawaye-ee-an Punch!"*

"Yes! Coors, Budweiser, Fanta, Hawaiian Punch!" Nell encouraged.

Cane's eyes squeezed tight and he grasped the gold crucifix on the chain around his neck as he gripped the stock of his assault rifle.

The creature waved four arms at the ceiling, then leaned forward. *"Dane-jer. Cah-ooti-own. Hazar-doo-us mater-ee-als. In case of ee-mergens-ee open escap-ee hatch. Abandun sheep!"*

Geoffrey nodded, thrilled. "Yes! Danger. Caution. Hazardous. Emergency. Escape! Abandon ship!"

Hender nodded at each of Geoffrey's corrections. "Yes, danger caution hazardous! Escape! Hender signal ah-thers. Hender signal."

Geoffrey's mouth fell open.

"He means it!" Zero said.

Nell leaned forward with sudden urgency. "How many others? How many?" With her fingers she counted slowly. "One-two-three-four—"

Hender nodded. "Four others."

Thatcher sank back against the wall of the plane, a grim conclusion visible in his expression. He glanced again at Cane, who was now whispering over his crucifix.

The creature hurried toward them suddenly and they shrank away before they realized he was motioning for them to follow. He stepped through the biggest of several round holes that were cut into the side of the wrinkled B-29 fuselage.

"Time for a tour," Andy said.

"Tooouuur!" the creature grunted, nodding his head on his bobbing neck.

7:10 P.M.

They followed Hender up a spiral stairway that seemed half-natural and half-carved inside the massive tree.

In niches beside the stairway, various man-made glass vessels glowed faintly green. Hender flicked these jars as he passed them, and each brightened as bioluminescent bugs swirled inside, illuminating the passageway and revealing more signs, trash, labels, and artifacts tacked to the walls and hanging from the ceiling.

Hender paused before a chest-high niche and tapped a bug-jar inside it. Inside the niche the humans saw a propped-up coconut. It wore a somewhat askew scarlet cap and bore a crudely carved human face blended with eerie elements of Hender's anatomy. Lying next to it was a pocketknife with an ivory handle, which Hender picked up and handed to Nell.

"It looks like scrimshaw," she said. "A name's carved on it here, see?" She showed it to Geoffrey.

Hender took it from her and read it out loud: *"Hen-ree FERRR-reeeers."*

"No way," she whispered. "Henry Frears?"

"Yes, OK!" Hender warbled.

"What's the matter, Nell?" Geoffrey asked.

"Henry Frears was the name of the man the *Retribution* lost while collecting water on the island," she said.

"Huh?" Geoffrey said.

"Captain Henders recorded it in his log when he discovered the island in 1791."

"Where'd Hender get a coconut?" Zero muttered.

"If this is Frears's hat," Nell said. "Then Hender may have actually seen him. That would make Hender over 220 years old!"

"I told you," Andy said. "I think he's a lot older than that."

Hender whistled and gestured with three hands for them to follow.

They passed another niche displaying another carved coconut. This one wore a WWII American officer's cap. A long gouge in the side of the coconut was smeared with red pigment.

"Maybe the captain of the B-29?" Zero suggested grimly.

They passed more rooms, peering into them with frustrated curiosity, as they hurried behind their tour guide up the winding passageway.

In another niche, an uncarved coconut gazed out

at them. This one was faceless. It had dried red seaweed for hair and wore a Mets baseball cap.

"Hey, my cap!" Nell exclaimed. She reached for it and put it on her head with a half-smile at Hender. "I left it behind on StatLab."

Hender's head swiveled down toward her on his long neck, and he nodded. "Nell, yes!" he croaked, seeming to awkwardly mimic her smile.

She glanced back at Geoffrey with wide eyes. "He said my name!" she whispered.

Strung along the corkscrewing ceiling was a collection of glass fishnet floats and plastic buoys. More random garbage, battered and bleached, seemed pinned to every available square inch of wall space. As they came around a curve they saw, mounted above them and illuminated by a freshly-riled jar of bugs, what appeared to be the faded figurehead of a Spanish galleon, a mermaid carved in wood, half human and half fish.

"Looks like a cargo cult," Thatcher mused as they came around another bend in the stairs and amidst the flotsam saw a life preserver stenciled with faded dark blue letters: R.M.S. LUSITANIA.

"Thank you, God!" Zero laughed as he videoed it with his handheld and head-mounted cameras.

Nell glanced at Geoffrey behind her, not knowing whether to laugh or cry. Geoffrey nodded and impulsively squeezed her hand.

As they came through a level passage they saw

artifacts that were clearly more recently acquired: pieces of ROVs, an Army helmet, even an Incredible Hulk action figure.

Hender opened a door. They emerged on a huge branch under the umbrella of the tree's canopy.

Below, attached to the trunk of the tree, hung an enormous waterwheel-like structure.

From the wheel spooled a thick cable of braided green fiber. The cable ran through a pulley on a branch that reached over the cliff.

A basket the size of the *Trident*'s large Zodiac hung at the end of the cable against the orange glow of the setting sun, swinging slowly in the steady wind that blew seven hundred feet above the sea.

Hender pointed at the basket and then at some of the garbage stacked in piles on the wide branch.

"Hender's got an elevator," Andy told them.

"That must be how he got his collection! The elevator must go down to a beach where he got all this stuff."

"Trash," Thatcher said, glancing back at Cane. "Humanity's calling card."

"Um," Zero looked around nervously, "should we be out here?"

"It's OK, Zero," Andy assured him. "The tree gives off some kind of bug repellent. We're safe here."

Nell laughed. "This is a *plant*," she sighed. "The first actual plant on this island!"

Andy smiled. "Too bad it doesn't have a flower, Nell."

"I wonder if they evolved together." Geoffrey watched Hender climb nimbly to a high branch and extend his arms in a double V. A soulful, lilting call resonated through a chamber in the creature's cranial crest.

A distant chorus of four similar horn-calls answered from across the bowl of the island.

"We've heard that before," Andy said. "Remember, Nell?"

Tears of shame brimmed in her eyes as she remembered the nightmarish voices the outboard mikes had picked up in StatLab echoing across the island. "Yes . . ."

"So there are four more of them," Thatcher said.

"OK," Geoffrey said, decisively. "We need a pow-wow. *Now.*"

7:23 P.M.

Hender led them back down to the B-29 fuselage, where Andy managed to tell him with hand signals that he and his human friends needed some privacy.

Hender nodded. He gestured with four hands toward the nose of the B-29, where the humans proceeded to congregate as Hender stayed near the front door, his back turned discreetly.

"We have to save them," Nell began, standing

before the patchwork window in the cockpit. The way the plane jutted over the ocean, she felt almost as if they were flying.

Cane stood with his eyes closed as if this were a bad dream. Words had come out of the mouth of what looked like a prop in a horror movie—it had called him by his *name,* and now there were more of them coming. He could not piece this together with the world he came from; it seemed like the world was splitting in two beneath him. He did not see the soul of his Creator in this monster. He saw another force, of awesome power, that had acted without any regard for human sensibilities to invest this animal with the appearance of a soul. Cane was convinced he was closer than he had ever been to the presence of the Devil.

"I was about to give up on this island myself," Geoffrey told the others. "But I think we just found the only benign species possible here: *intelligent beings.* Think of it!"

"We have to tell the President," Andy said. "We have to stop them."

"Absolutely," Zero said, recording them with both cameras.

"Let's get to the Humvee and radio the base," Nell decided.

"Hold on." Thatcher raised a hand. "We are under extremely strict orders from the military about transporting any species off this island . . ."

Nell glared at him with a fierce challenge in her

eyes. "Are you suggesting that we destroy these creatures? Is that what you're saying, Thatcher?"

"I'm saying nothing, I'm merely questioning: What is it that makes this species any more valuable than the hundreds of species we are about to incinerate, Dr. Duckworth?"

"I can't believe you're even asking this," Nell said, flushed with anger. "Hender *thinks*. He knows his past and plans his future. He's a *person*—like you and me."

"Surely, that's their *worst* recommendation!" Thatcher shook his head, laughing contemptuously. "It makes Hender's kind more dangerous than a plague of locusts. Don't you see?"

"They don't have to be like a plague of locusts, Thatcher. They have a choice," Nell argued. "Locusts don't have any choice."

"Exactly," Thatcher agreed, mildly. "Which makes us much worse than locusts. It doesn't take many of our choices to add up to global devastation on a scale no other creature could ever match. We didn't have to come to this island, Dr. Duckworth—but we did. And if we hadn't, none of the creatures on this island would have to die now. Would they?"

"Spare us the irony, Thatcher," Geoffrey said. "We're here now, and we have a moral obligation, damn it."

"Before we saw Hender you wanted to save this island," Nell reminded Thatcher.

Thatcher jabbed an angry finger at her. "And you wanted to *nuke* it!" he snarled. He looked at the others, seeking an ally. "Hasn't it occurred to any of you that this creature is far more dangerous than anything else on this island precisely *because* it is intelligent? My God, this planet will be lucky enough to survive *one* intelligent species—but *two?* Are you all mad?"

Geoffrey scoffed. "Intelligent life must have managed to live on this island in harmony with its environment for millions of years to evolve into Hender. Face it, Thatcher, that theory of yours, that intelligent life must destroy its environment, is *wrong*—and these beings are the proof. One of my own theories has already been shot down by this island, if that makes you feel any better. I thought an ecosystem with so little symbiotic cooperation couldn't even exist, let alone outlast every other system on Earth. I was wrong, too. Get over it, Thatcher. Welcome to the wonderful world of science."

"It's funny," Nell mused. "I thought this island would prove my theory that plants pollinated by insects would exhibit extreme genetic drift in isolation. But there were no pollen-bearing plants here. There aren't any plants, except for this tree." She looked at Thatcher sadly. "But what we have found instead—it's like a miracle, Thatcher!"

Thatcher glared back at her, and smiled contemptuously.

"I had a theory," Zero piped up, "that if you could find the most remote island on Earth, you'd find paradise. Guess my theory's shot to hell."

"Henders Island," Andy said. "The place where theories come to die. Right, Thatcher?"

"What we are doing to this island only underscores the danger of making any special exception for this species," Thatcher insisted. The edge in his voice was unmistakable.

"This isn't a chapter in your book, Thatcher," Zero growled. "This isn't about winning some stupid scientific argument. We gotta save these guys, come on!"

"They're *people,* Thatcher!" Andy said.

"No, they're not!" Cane spluttered and then fell silent when he caught Hender watching him from the other end of the fuselage.

"Yes, they are!" Andy yelled.

Cane's grip tightened on the forestock of his rifle.

"Relax, dude," Zero told him.

"Look, Thatcher." Nell leaned forward. "It's no doubt true that without our intelligence this island would never have been found, and none of this would be necessary now. For life's sake, I regret that anything on this island must be destroyed. But it would be murder to knowingly kill other intelligent beings, just as it would be murder if we were to allow other species on this island to reach the mainland. It would be murder because, unlike anything else on this island, Hender and beings like him can choose *not* to be monsters. And so can we. That's why they deserve a chance. Surely you can see that, can't you?"

Thatcher studied her with smoldering contempt. "That choice produces saints and sinners, Dr. Duckworth. Pacifists and terrorists. Angels and devils. And there is no way to predict which. To bring this creature and his ilk to the mainland will expose the rest of the world to a peril it could never withstand."

"OK, so who's for saving them?" Zero asked, giving Thatcher a deadly stare as he raised his hand.

Nell, Geoffrey, and Andy raised their hands. "Yes!"

Cane looked through the window as twilight filled the sky.

All the others looked at Thatcher, waiting for his response.

Behind his eyes, wheels turned, recalculating the odds against him.

Suddenly, the zoologist sighed.

"All right," he nodded in apparent resignation, and raised his hand. "Of course, I will abide by the group's decision, as it seems that everyone's mind is made up. Sergeant, are you all right? I should get you back to the car. Come on." He took Cane by the arm, and turned him toward the door. "We need to radio the base to tell them what we've found."

"We've got twenty-two and a half hours left

411

before we have to evacuate this island," Geoffrey said, glancing at his watch. "You better tell them we have to start making arrangements immediately to transport these creatures."

Andy followed them to the door as Hender stepped aside to let them through.

As soon as Thatcher pushed it open, Cane vomited outside.

"Eew, yuck!" Andy pulled the door shut behind them and went back to the others.

"Yuck!" Hender nodded.

7:29 P.M.

Thatcher patted Cane's heaving back, looking over the twilit fields below as wheels turned in his mind like the gears in a slot machine. He noticed strange shapes were sprouting out of the purpling field below the tree, attracting little clouds of glowing bugs.

"I don't know what's gotten into them," the zoologist said. "This is exactly what the President warned us about, trying to get live species off this island. How are you feeling, Sergeant?"

"Feeling fine, sir!" Cane sounded off, lying.

Thatcher helped Cane over the stepping stones to the Humvee. He climbed in first and reached down to help the soldier, who shrugged off his help as he gripped the doorframe and pulled himself into the driver's seat.

Cane quickly slammed the door behind him. His face was very pale and streaked with sweat. He squeezed the steering wheel, hanging his head between his arms as he took long, shuddering breaths.

Thatcher looked out the windshield over the island. Glowing swarms drifted like ghosts over the fields below. The ring of the jungle had a dim pink glow as a wispy fog filled the basin around the barren core, which stood out like an island in the fog. "Well, this is far worse than anyone could have imagined, Sergeant. It's an *abomination*." He turned to look at Cane. "Against God."

Cane closed his eyes, breathing faster and gripping the steering wheel with one hand, his crucifix in the other.

"These freaks of nature were not meant to coexist with humans on this Earth." Thatcher was an atheist, but this approach seemed like the best bet, he thought, given the circumstances. "Why else would they have been separated from us since the beginning of time, Sergeant? My God, what in heaven's name are we trying to do? The scientists back at the base are going to want to *save* this species—precisely *because* it is intelligent!"

Thatcher glanced at the soldier and then looked back out the window as swarms of bugs moved across the slopes below. "I guess after you win some of the most prestigious awards in science your colleagues just stop listening to you."

"You'd think they'd listen to you more," Cane muttered.

Thatcher snorted laughter and stared thoughtfully at the Army base, a mile in the distance. This discovery would certainly derail the entire thesis of his book just as his career was taking off. The fact that he was here when intelligent life was discovered living in the oldest sustained ecosystem on the planet would cause a sensation. And a professional humiliation after his Redmond Principle had predicted intelligent life must destroy its own environment. His Tetteridge Award would suddenly be worthless. Ridiculed, even. *It could even be revoked.* The other precious awards would never materialize. The markers would come due, the alimony. But there was something else, something irrational pulling him, a primal temptation that he had faced many times, a belief in his *luck*—which placed him in natural opposition to the world. He could never resist betting against the house.

Thatcher sighed. "I wish I hadn't won those awards, Sergeant. Maybe if I had never won them my colleagues would listen to me now. Maybe they would listen."

"*I* hear you, sir." Cane's voice was low and serious.

Thatcher shook his head, not looking at Cane. "Those *things* will become part of our society now, Sergeant, if they leave this island. They'll be

414

sharing our neighborhoods, our jobs, our schools—even our hospitals and cemeteries. How are you going to explain *that* to your children? They're clearly physically and mentally superior. They probably procreate faster than we do. We'll be signing our world over to them. What are your orders, Sergeant? I mean, I don't wish to interfere with military matters, of course. But, what if you were to find someone trying to smuggle live species off the island . . ."

"My orders are to shoot on sight anyone attempting to smuggle live specimens off the island, sir!"

"Ah, yes. That's right. Tell me, Sergeant, just hypothetically—if you found yourself in the extraordinary position, if you were lucky enough to be in the right place at the right time to save life on Earth, even if it meant disobeying your orders—are you the sort of person who would do it? Or are you the sort of person who would obey your orders, no matter what the consequences might be for the human race?"

"Hypothetically *how,* sir?"

"What if you radioed in and told the base we are collecting specimens but don't mention exactly what we found? It's 7:30 now. Could you meet me at 9, down there, out of sight?"

Thatcher indicated a slight rise in the ground about thirty yards down the slope from Hender's home. It was probably one of the moldered wings

415

of the B-29, long ago engulfed and dissolved by clover.

Cane looked hard at Thatcher. "Then what, sir?"

"Then we might be able to just drive away, Sergeant."

"Sir?"

Thatcher shrugged. "They have no other means of transportation. And while you're gone I can make certain that they don't have any way to communicate with the base."

"That would be *murder,* sir."

"Taking those creatures off this island would be *genocide,* Sergeant. Of the entire human race."

After a moment of silence, Cane asked, "Where would I go?"

"Anywhere. Until nine o'clock."

"What would we say?"

"We could say we got attacked while collecting specimens and that the others didn't make it, Sergeant. Our companions foolishly insisted on leaving the vehicle and we wisely stayed inside. That almost happened already today, didn't it? You haven't yet told them what happened to Dr. Cato. We say they all died with him. In less than forty-eight hours, this whole island is going to be nuked. How much more simple could it be?"

Cane stared ahead through the windshield for a long moment. Then he switched on the Hummer's ignition. "Rendezvous at twenty-one hundred hours, sir," he said. But he refused to look at Thatcher.

Thatcher got out and heard the distant din of the jungle below as Cane drove away.

He noticed the faintly glowing swarm on the field below change direction and streak up the slope toward him.

Thatcher turned, tripping, and ran.

7:33 P.M.

Thatcher burst in and slammed the door behind him.

Copepod snarled at him.

"Not good, Thatcher," Hender said, startling him.

"I agree," Nell said. "What did they say, Thatcher?"

"Please call off this dog!" Thatcher scowled.

Hender whistled and Copepod ran to his side. Hender stroked the dog with his two right hands, and Thatcher studied Hender for a moment. He didn't answer Nell's question.

"What did they say, Thatcher?" Geoffrey pressed.

"The seismic activity must be interfering with radio reception," Thatcher answered. "Cane said he had to get closer to transmit a message."

"My God, that guy was scared out of his wits!" Zero said.

"You should have gone with him to make sure the right message gets through to the President,"

Nell said, running a hand back through her hair in frustration.

"I wrote it all out for him," Thatcher snapped. "He said he would be right back!"

A hard earthquake jolted the fuselage.

"Aye-yai-yai-yeesh," Hender trilled.

"This isn't good," Geoffrey said, reaching for handholds and glancing at Nell, who seemed struck by a dawning thought.

They looked around at the curiosities now swaying from Hender's roof.

"The quakes have been getting worse," Andy said. "All the hendros are upset about it."

"Hendros?" asked Thatcher.

"I call them hendros," Andy said. "Short for hendropods."

Nell looked at her watch. "Cane better not take too long, Thatcher. Considering everything that will need to be done to get the hendros safely off the island, we don't have much time."

"We should have enough," Geoffrey reassured her, and he jabbed a look at Thatcher.

7:54 P.M.

Twenty minutes later, Andy asked, "Where's our driver, Thatcher?" for the fifteenth time.

Hender was bouncing a blue plastic ball back and forth with Andy, who sat on the floor in front of him as they all waited for Cane to return.

418

"How should I know?" Thatcher repeated, glancing at his watch again.

"Maybe they're putting a caravan together or something." Geoffrey had been marveling at the creature playing ball with Andy, watching how its arms moved and joints flexed, and observing the psychology and culture in its intelligence, its humor, its playful interaction with Andy.

"This place will probably be crawling with the military any time now," Zero said.

"Can you imagine how this kind of news might be going down back at the base?" Nell asked, her unwelcome thought recurring.

Zero snickered. "Yeah, it must have blown their fragile little eggshell minds."

"We have to think about how to safely transport them. Andy, you should travel with Hender."

"Make sure the Army knows that, Nell," Andy said, batting the ball back to Hender. "People don't listen to me."

"They better come soon," Geoffrey said.

Zero shrugged. "All we can do is wait."

"We can't wait too long," Nell warned.

Despite Andy's clumsy returns and outright misses, Hender used four hands, even his fifth and sixth when necessary, to save the ball every time in a mesmerizing volley. Copepod sprawled between them, panting with excitement.

When stretching out with all limbs extended, Hender had the appearance of a spider. When seated, however, Hender had a paunch between his pelvic-ring and his middle ring and tended to rest his upper forearms on top of his potbelly. Sitting across from Andy with his upper arms folded up like shoulders against his long neck, he seemed like a cross between Buddha and Vishnu, with widening pink and emerald rings of light effusing on his photophoric white fur.

Nell and Geoffrey caught each other watching the ballgame. They laughed, sharing their awe, and climbed down to sit on the floor near Andy.

"You know, something may have made it off Henders Island already," Geoffrey speculated.

"Let me guess," Andy said, volleying the blue ball. "Stomatopods?" He missed the return, and Hender saved it.

"Right. Mantis shrimp! You had the same thought?"

"What do you think attacked the NASA rover? Thirty-five-foot mantises came out of that lake."

"Wow," Geoffrey said. "Angel should be here!"

"Angel?" Nell said.

"My office mate. Angel Echevarria. A stomatopod freak. He spotted the resemblance to mantis shrimp from the *SeaLife* footage. Hender has a vague resemblance to them, too, especially the way he folds his upper arms. And his eyes."

"You think mantis shrimp may have evolved *here*?" Nell asked.

"Stomatopods probably evolved only 200 million years ago," Andy pointed out. "This place has been isolated much longer."

"Right, Andy," Geoffrey said, "but the South Pacific Ocean is considered to be the center of the mantis shrimp's adaptive radiation. Henders Island was right here, passing through the middle of it. The superior attributes of the mantis shrimp could be explained by this hyper-competitive ecosystem—and they're continuing to spread around the world at an amazing rate. They may be the only species that escaped Henders Island."

"Yeah, maybe." Andy missed again and again Hender saved it.

"So are you saying this *creature* evolved from a mantis shrimp?" Thatcher had been silent for a long time, repeatedly checking his watch.

"No, of course not," Geoffrey replied. "No more than we evolved from a spider monkey, but we may have a common ancestor."

"He doesn't look like a crustacean," Thatcher argued.

"But he might, if crustaceans kept evolving in the same direction lizards and mammals eventually went," Geoffrey replied. "If left alone, would they have followed a path similar to mammals? Would their exoskeletons shrink and then submerge under a waterproof keratinized epidermis to ward off dehydration, like reptiles, birds, and us?"

"Cuttlefish once had a nautilus-like shell that

became internalized over millions of years," Andy remarked.

"Maybe the same genes that led to cuttlefish color-displays led to this evolutionary branch, as well."

"I like the way you think, Dr. Binswanger," Nell said. He smiled.

Hender tapped Andy's knee impatiently and Andy fumbled for the ball, offering it to Hender.

"That's absurd." Thatcher shook his head. "Lobsters are more primitive than stomatopods and are thought to be their ancestors. That would mean that *all* arthropods evolved on Henders Island!"

"Ha!" Andy said. "Stomatopods and mantises are in the same class of arthropods, Malacostraca, sure, but they're in totally different subclasses. Only Schram thought they could be descended from the same primitive eumalocostracan ancestor, but most carcinologists rejected that as a needlessly complicated family tree, Dr. Genius Award! And nobody, but *nobody,* would say stomatopods *descended* from lobsters. Jeesh."

"All right, so my classification of crustaceans may be a bit rusty." Thatcher's face flushed nearly as red as his mustache. "The point is, *all* arthropods could not have evolved here!"

"Not only do I think it's unnecessary for all arthropods to have evolved on Henders Island for mantis shrimp to have originated here," Geoffrey replied evenly, "but I also think it's possible that all arthropods *did* evolve here, Dr. Redmond. Back when this fragment was a part of the Pannotia supercontinent."

"Henders Island must have been much larger through most of its history," Nell confirmed. "God, there could have been an entire civilization of Hender's kind back then. Who knows how far back they go?"

"Wow, man," Zero chuckled, sucking it all into his lens. He saw a red indicator light blinking in his handheld camera. "Fuck," he said, and he quickly switched its memory stick.

"Fuck, fuck, fuck!" Hender sang.

"Don't teach him that, Zero," Nell scolded.

"Sorry." Zero aimed the freshly loaded camera.

"I still don't see what you're driving at," Thatcher said, glancing at his watch again.

"The mantis shrimp is by far the most advanced crustacean on Earth. It may have evolved separately on this fragment of Pannotia before escaping from it 200 million years ago. You have to think outside the box, Thatcher." Geoffrey smiled at Nell.

"The curse of man." Thatcher pursed his lips under his thick mustache. "That 'box' we're so good at thinking outside of is the natural order, Dr. Binswanger."

"That box is conventional thinking, Dr. Redmond," Geoffrey shot back.

"What is rational is madness to nature. The innocent attempts of the questioning mind invariably lead to re-orchestrating a symphony that has been tuned and syncopated over millions of years."

"The history of Hender proves you wrong," Geoffrey retorted.

Thatcher's jaw tightened. "There are only a few of these creatures now, presumably. How can you predict what will happen when there are a million?"

"How can *you?*"

"Hold on a minute, I'm troubled by something here," Nell interposed. "Are you saying that my favorite food—lobster—may have evolved here on Henders Island?"

Geoffrey nodded. "Well, yes, from a first wave of migration, when it was Henders Supercontinent."

She smiled. "So how could the fact that they live alone increase their life span? You mentioned that before. Incidentally, I love the way your mind works, Dr. Binswanger." Her mahogany-red hair was tangled and her shirt was still damp after being doused with seawater. Geoffrey's pulse quickened unexpectedly as she leaned forward, her hands planted one after the other in front of her crossed legs, openly admiring something about him that people rarely noticed as she looked in his eyes.

Thatcher checked his watch, nibbling nervously on a few last peanuts that had slipped out of an airline packet into pocket number four.

Andy caught the ball and turned to Geoffrey. "Oh yeah, I almost forgot. Hender has a fossil collection."

"What?" Nell, Geoffrey, and Thatcher realized that fossils from Henders Island would be like fossils from Mars.

Andy grinned. "Yep. And they sure look like pre-Cambrian biota to me. He's got the most primitive *Anomalocaris* I've ever seen."

"They found some fossils when they excavated the hillside for the Army's base, but nothing identifiable," Nell said.

"Since our driver—ahem!—seems to be taking his time getting back here, Thatcher, let's take a look!"

"They must be arranging a rescue party," Thatcher said.

"I hope you're right," Zero said, glaring at him.

"Where are the fossils?" Geoffrey asked. "We need to make sure they come with us!"

"Hender," Andy said. *"Fossils?"*

Hender nodded, turning and reaching under a counter made from the planks of wooden shipping flats lashed together. With all arms he pulled out a stack of four flat hexagonal baskets apparently woven of some tough fiber.

He swiveled like a crane, and with all four arms

425

he carefully lowered the heavy stack onto the floor. Then he opened the flap of the basket on top.

Geoffrey and Nell kneeled on the floor, breathless.

Thatcher could not resist, rising to peer over their shoulders.

"These are *soft-bodied* fossils," Geoffrey whispered.

"My God, the detail is exquisite," Nell murmured as she observed a reddish feather-like worm with snail-stalk eyes profiled as if in a snapshot.

"They look older than Burgess specimens," Geoffrey said. "Even nearer to the beginning of the Cambrian Explosion—"

"Look! There's a primitive version of *Wiwaxia*, and . . . could that be *Hallucigenia*?"

Nell pointed at a red cameo of a half-spherical animal with small spikes on its curving back. A tiny spiked worm was embedded in the silvery olive-colored shale.

"They could just be juveniles," Thatcher said.

Nell lifted the slab to reveal another leaf of stone showing fantastical animals trapped in mid-somersault, mid-glide, and mid-pirouette by a sudden mudslide 600 million years ago.

"Larger," she said. "But still more primitive."

"The others may have been juveniles," Geoffrey told her. "But these adults are still more primitive than any Cambrian fossils I've seen. Look at the radial symmetry in these arthropods!"

"Look at this quilted seaweed—my God, these could be the missing links between Ediacaran and Cambrian life!" she breathed.

"This could be the page that's missing—the moment before the Cambrian explosion before life branched into our world and this one!"

Zero captured it all on video. "I'm sold, kids. Don't worry about me!"

"Fossils," Hender said proudly.

"Yes, Hender," Nell said, extending her hand.

Hender took it carefully in his four gentle hands, his eyes widening, their six "pupils" focusing on her. "It's OK, Nell," Hender hummed.

"Yes," Nell nodded, and laughed. "It's very OK, Hender!"

"We better pack these away to take them with us," Andy said. "He's got more in smaller baskets, too, all around here."

"Hot damn," Zero said and looked heavenward with one eye. "With this footage I can retire to Fiji." He laughed. "Not that I will."

"No? What'll you do, Zero?" Nell took the handheld camera from him, turning it around and pointing it at the photographer.

"Well," Zero smiled, unaccustomed to this side of the lens, his face lighting up. "I'll probably sail around the world and make some documentaries. Maybe even write a book!"

"Great!"

"I guess we can all write a book after this."

Geoffrey laughed as Nell turned the camera on him.

"And probably all get Tetteridge awards," Andy said. "Right, Thatcher?"

Nell zoomed in on Thatcher as the older man smirked.

Geoffrey grinned. "I wonder who'll play me in the movie?"

"Tom Cruise, no doubt," Thatcher muttered.

"Yeah, that's funny. 'Cuz I'm black and Tom Cruise isn't black, and that whole thing. Yeah."

"Imagine the book Hender will write." Nell turned the camera toward Hender.

"Now there's a guaranteed Nobel," Andy said.

Hender suddenly gestured to Andy and moved to the window of the cockpit.

"He wants some privacy," Andy translated.

They watched the alien being look out over the sea, where he had so rarely seen the vehicles of human beings passing in the distance.

Nell handed the camera back to Zero.

Geoffrey noticed a World War II signal handbook on the floor beside his foot. It was opened to a page with Morse code. He picked it up, and Nell noticed it.

"Andy," she asked.

"Yeah?"

"Do you know Morse code?"

"Nope. I was rejected by the Boy Scouts."

"We don't have a way to signal the base from here anyway," Zero reminded them.

Nell took the book from Geoffrey. "Hender must have figured out the word for *distress signal* or *emergency* and matched it to the Morse code for S.O.S.!"

"Wait a minute, are you saying *Hender* signaled us?" Geoffrey exclaimed.

"Impossible," Thatcher said.

"Hender set off that EPIRB, " Nell breathed. Her eyes glowed with excitement.

"Jesus," Zero whispered.

"Oh wow!" Andy said.

"What's an EPIRB?" Geoffrey asked.

"The emergency beacon that first brought *SeaLife* here," Nell told him. "The earthquakes might have been worrying him—he may have thought the island was in danger. He could have seen the word 'emergency' on the EPIRB in the sailboat that washed ashore and figured out how to turn the beacon on!"

"Yeah, baby!" Zero said.

" 'Help,' cried the spider to the fly," Thatcher said.

A shape appeared in one of the dark holes in the fuselage above Nell. She gasped. Another of Hender's kind peered in warily at the astonished humans. Glowing patterns of blue and green fluctuated on its white-furred body and limbs in the shadow before it emerged into the green-lit chamber.

Thatcher sucked in a breath and took an involuntary step backwards.

Behind the first, another appeared, and then another and another, each with a unique pattern and palette of colors. In their hands and on their backs they carried bundles, pouches, and packs containing an odd assortment of objects—customized tools, toys or weapons made of native materials, and man-made materials collected from the beach and put to original uses.

The four newcomers hopped gracefully down on their springing legs and approached the humans, creeping on four or even all six limbs, their heads downcast, as if approaching deities.

Hender went to greet them. He gave Andy the same hand signals they had exchanged earlier, and then the others of his kind followed him to the cockpit at the far end of the fuselage.

The beings huddled for a whispered, musical conference.

It was dark now in the nose of the plane. Only a starlit sky silhouetted the alien creatures against the B-29's cockpit jutting over the ocean. From a distance the new arrivals seemed faintly sinister as they darted glowing eyes back at the humans.

Hender shook some glass jars full of jungle bugs to light up the cockpit. Following Hender's example, all gave friendly waves at the humans, then went back to their discussion.

Nell's heart pounded. To be in the presence of Earthlings who may have preceded human beings by millions of years made her feel oddly alien herself. It was an extraordinary sensation. "An intelligent species," she whispered.

"It sounds like each one is speaking a different language," Geoffrey whispered.

She nodded. "Maybe that's why Hender's so good at languages."

"They're a little smarter than you thought, eh, Thatcher?" Andy taunted.

Thatcher showed no expression. "Oh, yes."

"Why would they have different languages?"

"Maybe they're very, *very* old," Nell suggested.

"You'll have to explain that to me," Geoffrey said.

"Well, maybe each of them is the last of a separate cultural or ethnic group. Their colorings are fairly distinctive."

"Maybe," Geoffrey mused. "But they would have to be incredibly old, Nell, to have that much genetic and cultural variation."

"Like I said, they *are* incredibly old," Andy insisted.

Geoffrey considered his own principle of life span as he watched the alien beings silhouetted against the moonlit window of the seventy-year-old aircraft. Suddenly Fire-Breathing Chats seemed remarkably tame compared to this. "It's possible they don't really have life spans," he blurted even as the thought struck him.

"Huh?" Nell asked. "You'll have to explain that to me."

"I will." He nodded.

"The hendros have tunnels that are probably fossilized root structures connecting these giant trees all around the island's rim," Andy put in.

"How many trees are there?" Geoffrey asked.

"Six or seven, I think, and they all live alone in separate trees. That multi-colored guy is a painter. The black and blue-striped one seems to invent traps and weapons and other things. The orange one's a musician. I think the green-and-blue one is a doctor."

Nell noticed the combinations of colors effervescing on their fur as Andy pointed each of them out. "How do you know what they do, Andy?"

"I went to a dinner party with them at the doctor's tree. After dinner they traded some stuff. Hender traded some things he collected on the beach."

"How cool is *that?*" Zero said.

"I think the *hendros* have made up their minds," Thatcher observed sourly.

The discussion seemed to have been settled and the creatures were now coming back to the humans. Hender approached ahead of the others and spread two arms out. "Henders eat humans now," he said.

Thatcher stiffened.

Hender held up one finger. "Joke," Hender said.

"I taught him that word." Andy laughed. "Don't panic, Thatcher!"

"Joke, Thatcher." Hender nodded in agreement.

"He's got a future on *The Tonight Show*," Geoffrey said.

The other hendros watched the humans laughing and looked at each other in amazement.

8:42 P.M.

Alien as they appeared, Hender's kindred were each strangely beautiful, with graceful limbs that expressed different styles in motion. Able to locomote with two, four, or six limbs, either swinging from the ceiling or walking on the floor, each of the beings moved in ways disconcertingly different from the others. It was as if five antelope had discovered five completely different ways of walking using the standard four legs. Their fur varied widely, too—not so much like different breeds of cat, more like people wearing different clothes. Watching them, one could only conclude that each had a unique style, and, in this respect, were essentially human. Only humans—juggling, walking, crawling, swimming, skydiving humans—displayed so much individual choice simply through movement.

"See others." Hender's woodwind-like voice had a melodious tone. "Thank you thank you thank you. Emergency exit. *Hazar-do-us!*"

"Yes, Hender. Hazardous!" Geoffrey nodded. He gestured to himself, then pointed at the door.

"When others come, emergency exit. OK? Yes?"

Hender smiled, revealing the three wide teeth that wrapped around his upper and lower jaws. He nodded vigorously. "Yes, hazardous! Emergency exit! Thank you, OK, Geoffrey!"

Hender translated for the four other hendropods, whose eyes flicked back and forth between him and the humans.

Under her breath, Nell told Geoffrey, "You speak pretty good Hender."

"Hender uses only imperative verbs and simple nouns—probably from associating the words with pictures on directions and warning labels. They're designed so no one has to be able to read to get the point, but often have a variety of verbal translations."

"I'll be damned," Zero muttered. "And I always hated those things."

Nell smiled, delighted. "Who would have thought warning labels would be the Rosetta Stone?"

Thatcher had been staring off into space, but he abruptly broke his silence. "I still don't see how they could evolve here."

"That's easy," Andy piped up. "They disappear."

Nell looked at Andy, puzzled.

"I think their fur can sense light and somehow reflect it on the opposite side of their bodies. Hey, Hender. Disappear! Don't worry—he likes doing it. He knows it freaks me out!"

Hender nodded at Andy and smiled as his thick fur fluffed out.

Although they were looking right at him, Hender . . . vanished. The background seemed to emanate through him, leaving only his grin and two eyes visible.

"Dear God," Thatcher murmured.

"It's the freakin' Cheshire Cat, man!"

All of the hendropods followed suit, blending into the background except for their colorful eyes and smiling teeth.

"Holy shit." Zero videoed as he laughed.

"That must be how their ancestors managed to slow down long enough to think in this environment," Nell said, thoughtfully.

"And make tools," Geoffrey added.

"They can step outside this crazy food chain."

Geoffrey's eyes lit up as a piece fell into place. "That's it! Death by predation is so common here that none of these species needed a biological clock to enforce a life span. When these guys developed invisibility . . ." He turned toward Nell, excited. "They may have become virtually immortal. Which allowed them to preserve the integrity of their gene pool by minimizing procreation! Intelligent creatures could not reproduce very frequently on such a small island," he murmured. "In a group this small, the risk of compromising the gene pool would be too great. So the longer each generation lasts the less opportunity for genetic corruption. It's a scenario that I never imagined before!"

"So Hender's kind might actually be immortal?" Nell whispered. "My God . . ."

"There are monkey versions of Hender in the jungle that disappear, too," Andy said. "Quentin and I called them shrimpanzees. Hender doesn't like them very much because they steal from his traps."

"Sounds like a much safer species to rescue, if you ask me," remarked Thatcher.

"Hey, Hender saved all of our lives today, asshole!" Andy retorted. "Shrimpanzees would have had you for lunch. And dinner, maybe."

"Dozens of people have died on this island in only a few weeks, Dr. Redmond," Nell said. "We may seem safe right here for the time being, but we wouldn't last more than a few minutes outside this tree."

"By the way!" Andy rose and slid his glasses up his nose, raising his eyebrows at the ruddy zoologist. "Just out of curiosity, Thatcher, where the FUCK is our driver?"

"He should have been back by now," Thatcher snapped back, hotly.

"What have you done with him, Thatcher?"

"What in God's name are you suggesting?" the older man spluttered.

"I'm starting to wonder about you. I mean, just how far would you go to protect the biosphere from intelligent life, anyway? After all, people are the biggest danger on the planet, right?"

"I resent whatever you are trying to imply," Thatcher shot back.

"If he doesn't come back soon, Thatcher, we won't stand a chance trying to cross this island!" Zero said.

"And even if we stay here, we'll go out with a big bang." Geoffrey studied Thatcher thoughtfully.

"Are you absolutely dead nuts positive you got the message across to that kid?" Zero said.

"Or should we start panicking now?" Nell asked.

"What exactly are you accusing me—"

Another quake wrenched the ground, twisting the fuselage around them.

The hendropods reappeared and moved closer to the humans.

"With this kind of seismic activity, the military could already be evacuating the island for all we know," Geoffrey said.

"Maybe the Army doesn't want the hendropods to get off the island, and they're just going to leave us behind!"

"He may have had an accident," Thatcher conceded, realizing it might be true and gambling heavily that it wasn't.

"Maybe he got ambushed by God-knows-what-out-there," Geoffrey said.

"OK," Nell said. "That's too many maybes, guys. Zero, can your camera zoom in on the base so we can see what's going on?"

Zero set his camera up on a tripod outside Hender's door. Switching to night vision, he saw a greenscape with the broken ring of jungle around the bottom of the island lit up like a galaxy. He zoomed in on the Trigon over a mile away and saw helicopters coming and going and Humvees speeding back to the base.

"Hell, it looks like they're packing it in and getting out of here."

Zero panned west. He saw that the crack in the far wall of the island had grown. Seawater had swelled the pool that had saved his life to the size of a lake.

"That crack's opening up. The ocean's coming in."

"Shit!" Nell moved aside so Geoffrey could look.

"When water hits old dry fault lines . . . Bang! Instant earthquake," Geoffrey peered through the viewfinder. "And every quake will just let more water into the island's substratum."

"Terrific," Zero muttered.

"Do we trust Thatcher?" Geoffrey asked abruptly.

Nell frowned. "The answer lies in the question."

"I don't think he has the courage to kill himself along with us," Geoffrey told her.

"You're probably right. So he probably told Cane the right thing to say. But Cane might not have done it. And I'm beginning to wonder if, even if he did, we can count on being rescued. I know it's an awful thing to have to think about, but we have to be realistic. Thatcher might not be the only one who doesn't like the idea of intelligent life getting off this island. Maybe the news didn't go down too well with the powers that be. Or maybe Cane just ditched us."

"I was thinking the same thing. That kid was pretty freaked out," Zero said.

"And we don't have any means of communication or transportation," Geoffrey said.

A swarm of glowing bugs swept over the moonlit purple fields. "Time to go back inside, kids," Zero warned.

8:50 P.M.

Nell, Geoffrey, and Zero entered the B-29 and closed the door tight behind them.

A tense Thatcher sat surrounded by curious hendropods, who were fondling his red beard and peering into the pockets of his clothing. One discovered a peanut straggler that Thatcher had missed and one of its eyes bent down as it examined it closely—then it grabbed the peanut with its lips and crunched it while registering what seemed to be a smile of pleasure with its wide mouth. Between two arching fingers it offered Thatcher what looked like a miniature dried embryo.

Andy had been keeping watch through the cockpit at the far end of the fuselage.

"Hey, you guys," he yelled. "They're leaving *without* us!"

The humans and the hendropods moved forward and looked out through the patchwork windshield of the B-29.

Thatcher stayed, sitting near the door, and checked his watch.

8:51 P.M.

Two Navy ships were leaving glowing green wakes of bioluminescent phytoplankton churned up by their propellers as they shipped out. Rounding the cliff below, a ship appeared, heading north.

"The *Trident*!" Nell shouted.

Geoffrey raised an eyebrow. "Eh?"

"It's the ship from *SeaLife*," Zero explained.

"Oh," Geoffrey said.

"I never thought I'd be so glad to see her!" Nell said.

"Wait a minute!" Zero pulled out a palm-sized short-range video transmitter from one of his pants pockets and unfolded the transmission dish.

He quickly hooked up a jack to the camera and another to a speaker and handed the transmitter to Geoffrey.

"Aim the antenna at the *Trident*," he said. "There

may be just enough juice left! This thing's only got a seven-hundred meter range but we might get a bounce off the water. Come on, Peach!"

8:52 P.M.

Peach was playing Halo 5 with earphones on, listening to "Sabotage" by the Beastie Boys and crunching spicy cinnamon Red Hots between his molars.

He vaporized a gallery of monstrous aliens with furious efficiency and, suddenly, his Spider Sense detected a status message in the upper right corner of the computer screen:

INCOMING TRANSMISSION.

Peach lifted an earphone. "What the—"

He jockeyed the keyboard and swiftly brought up the feed.

Nell, Andy, and Zero waved frantically in a window on the screen. Behind them stood a cluster of creatures that looked like something from his videogame.

He was stunned for a beat, then fumbled for the volume.

"Peach! Peach! Are you there? Help!"

Peach could not unravel his tongue. He fumbled with a microphone jack. "Zero? Is that you, man?"

441

Peach pulled an extra wireless headset mike out of his hair and positioned it in front of his mouth. "Boss! Boss! You better get in here!"

8:54 P.M.

The door of the bridge banged open and Cynthea ran in, startling Captain Sol and First Mate Warburton.

"Stop the ship, Captain," she said breathlessly. "Drop the anchor!"

"Are you insane? Not when the U.S. Navy just told us to reach minimum safe distance from a NUCLEAR BLAST."

"It's Nell and Zero and Andy. They're stranded on the island, Captain! They need help!"

Captain Sol cocked his head at her. "Andy? The poor lad is dead."

"We'll be out of range of their transmission if you go any farther," Cynthea pleaded. "Stop the ship!"

Captain Sol frowned but reluctantly nodded at Warburton to cut the engines, testing the sincerity in Cynthea's eyes with a hard look. "Radio *Enterprise* and tell her we've got a distress call," he ordered Warburton.

"No!" Cynthea shouted. "You better come see this first."

Captain Sol's frown deepened. "Lady, so help me if this is some kind of publicity stunt—"

"What should I tell them, Captain?" Warburton asked.

Captain Sol gritted his teeth. "Tell them . . . we've got engine trouble."

"You are my *god*, Captain Sol!" Cynthea kissed both whiskery cheeks. "My sea god!"

"All right, that's enough of that now!"

Captain Sol shook his head at Warburton, then hurried off the bridge after Cynthea.

The first mate spoke to the *Enterprise* in the smooth voice of a late-night dee-jay: "Hello there, *Enterprise*, we've got a little engine trouble and we're working on it right now. We should have the problem fixed momentarily."

8:55 P.M.

Captain Sol and Cynthea watched the monitor above Peach as he patched in the audio. The picture was frazzled by static.

"Now why the hell shouldn't I tell the Navy to send a rescue crew, damn it, Zero?" the captain demanded.

"Maybe because they don't want to rescue what we found," Zero said.

"They may be deliberately abandoning us, Captain," Andy said.

"Well, what in God's name could you possibly have found?" the captain asked. "Everything on the island's about to be nuked! How much worse can it get, for Chrissakes!"

"Captain Sol, please take a big breath," Andy

443

said. "Did you take one? OK. Now close your eyes and when I tell you, open them . . ."

Captain Sol did no such thing.

"Andy," Nell sighed.

Moving Hender into view, Andy yelled, "OK, open them!"

Hender's fur flushed with fireworks of green and pink light as his eyes darted in different directions.

Peach whispered, "Have you ever seen anything like that?"

Captain Sol swallowed a curse. "I am not allowed to make a decision like this, people. The Navy's orders are to shoot first and ask questions later if anything is smuggled off this island!"

"But these beings are *intelligent,*" Nell insisted.

"Go ahead, Hender," Andy urged, and whispered to Hender.

"Hello, Captain Sol," Hender fluted, and he waved two hands human-style. "Please. Help. Us."

Captain Sol grabbed the back of a chair to keep from keeling over.

Cynthea put an arm around him, looking at the screen. "You're recording this, right, Peach?" she asked.

"Oh yeah, Boss."

8:58 P.M.

"These new tri-engines are temperamental as heck, and I guess they're a bit rusty," Warburton crooned

444

on the radio to the *Enterprise.* "One of them gets out of sync, it sets off a chain reaction, and before you know it, they all just . . . freak out!"

The first mate winced at his own B.S.

"What's the ETA on engine repairs, Trident*?"* came the response from the *Enterprise. "Over?"*

"Uh, not sure, *Enterprise.*"

"OK. Trident*, you are drifting closer to shore, there, copy?"*

"Yes, *Enterprise,* we copy. We'll drop anchor and continue to effect repairs."

"Marcello!" Warburton gestured to the seventeen-year-old crewman, who was kissing his St. Christopher's medal.

Marcello let go of his medal and dropped anchor at the same time.

The steel claw bit into a solid rock holdfast two hundred feet below the surface.

"Copy that, we think that's a good idea, Trident*! Uh, you're going to need to get moving within one hundred nineteen minutes or abandon ship. Is that well understood?"*

The anchor bit rock and the line stretched taut as Warburton started letting it out farther toward the shore.

"Understood, *Enterprise,*" he answered, gritting his teeth. "It takes a lot less time than that to fix these things, usually!"

"OK, Trident*. Keep us informed.* Enterprise *out."*

"So they might not want us to get off the island, Captain Sol," Andy said. "Do you get it now, what we're trying to say?"

"Yes, Andy," the captain said. "I think I get it!"

"Can't we launch the mini-sub?" Cynthea asked.

"With two Sea-Wolf anti-sub attack submarines listening for exactly that? Christ, they can probably hear what we're saying right through the hull of this ship."

"We gotta do something, man," Peach said.

Captain Sol nodded, stroking his beard. "Maybe we can let out the winch on the Zodiac and let the tide carry it in closer. . . . But how the heck can you get down to us?"

Everyone in the B-29 cockpit turned to the right to look at the basket hanging from the branch of Hender's tree.

"Hender," Geoffrey pointed. "Exit?"

"Water hazar-doo-us. Hender no water."

"Of course, they go at low tide!" Nell said.

"Exit OK Hender," Geoffrey said. "Exit safety OK?"

"Dane-jer! Dane-jer!" Hender shouted, pointing down.

"Humans below help," Nell said. "Safety. Raft. Safe!" She pointed down and nodded.

"Rescue, raft!" Geoffrey added. "Safety!"

"Raft." Hender nodded at Nell with what she

could have sworn was skepticism. He closed his eyelids for a moment, then looked at Nell with both eyes. "OK. Safety."

Hender turned and spoke to the other hendropods.

"OK, Captain Sol," Andy said. "We're going to be coming down in a basket sort of elevator thing . . ."

"What?" Captain Sol said.

"Go on deck and look up at the cliff. We'll wave some lights so you can see us."

Geoffrey motioned to the other humans, and they each scooped up some bug-jars.

They waved them in the window of the cockpit.

Thatcher glanced over his shoulder at the others as he slipped out the door.

He checked his Timex Indiglo watch, pressing the crown to light up its face, and peered down the hillside. He heard the engine of the Humvee and saw headlights beaming from behind the B-29's rotting wing farther down the slope. He sighed as a wave of relief washed over him. Then he ran toward the lights.

9:00 P.M.

In the control room aboard the *Trident* the video started to fizzle and fade.

"We're losing you, Zero," Peach said.

They heard the cameraman's voice as the transmission died: *"Look up . . . for us!"*

447

Moments later, they saw the *Trident*'s deck lights flick on and off twice. "They spotted us," Geoffrey said.

"Come on, Andy," Nell said. "Let's pack their stuff in those specimen cases."

Nell and Andy ran to the other end of the fuselage to start packing the hendropods' possessions into the aluminum cases. The other hendros ran past them and climbed into the hole to the spiral stairs that led to Hender's elevator. But Hender paused beside Nell, watching her place his things inside one of the cases.

"Go now, Hender. Exit," Geoffrey said, behind him. "Nell will come with us."

Hender twisted his head around and looked at Geoffrey. "Nell will come with us," Hender repeated, nodding. He turned to Nell and both his eyes bent down and looked into hers. Suddenly, without warning, he embraced her, wrapping four arms around her.

Nell was alarmed as his four hands pressed against her back—but his touch was surprisingly gentle, and as her fingertips reluctantly touched the smooth fur on his belly colors expanded like petals blossoming. Pink and orange blooms of light opened all over his silvery body, along with shifting stripes and dots of green, and without warning she was laughing. Tears spilled over her eyelids as she realized that she had found her flower, after all.

"Thank you, Nell." She felt his voice hum through her like an oboe.

She ran her fingers gently over the thick, glossy coat. "Hender go now," she said. "OK?"

"OK, Nell. Hender go now."

9:01 P.M.

As Thatcher ran down the slope, he dodged weird transparent fern-like growths that sprouted over the clover fields in the gloom.

Down the slope about a hundred feet, the head-lights went dark. Thatcher could hear the idling engine cut off as he finally reached the Hummer.

9:02 P.M.

The alpha spiger launched its two-ton body off its rear legs and catapulting tail, lunging up the hillside in a thirty-foot leap, as it followed the tracks of the Humvee up the slope in the moon-light.

Behind the red beast two smaller spigers the size of polar bears, the two members of its pack, pounced up the hill.

Drool lubricated their vertical jaws and their eyes darted rapidly on stalks, canvassing the hillside around them in vibrant, vivid detail. An army of parasites, from scavenging disk-ants to centipede-like worms, coursed through the giants' fur like sea monsters battling all attacking bugs to a standstill and protecting its wounds so they could heal.

The alpha spiger bore a deep scar on one side of its face where a wolf-sized rival had slashed its head before it had bit the youngster in two. The others in its pack had devoured the spiger's other half.

The alpha spiger spotted the Humvee rolling to a stop on the slope above. It doubled its speed.

9:04 P.M.

Nell and Andy packed the cases to the brim with the haversacks of each hendropod and started stuffing as many fossils as they could squeeze into the rest, even slipping some inside their pockets, reluctant to leave anything behind.

"Nell," Andy said. "Thank you."

"What for?"

"Coming back to get me."

"Oh! No problem, sweetie." She laughed and gave him one of her signature hugs.

"I thought I was dead," he said, tearfully. "I couldn't believe they saved me. But the hendros really took me in, Nell, they really did. Considering what they're going to do to the island . . ." He paused, eyes closed tight. Finally he sighed, and opened his eyes to meet hers. "Anyway," he said, "thanks."

"Thanks for finding them, Andy." Nell let him go and squeezed his shoulder. "Your name will go down in scientific history as the one who saved the hendropods from extinction. Come on—we don't have much time. We need to go." They each carried two stuffed cases up the stairs, leaving the fifth case for a second trip.

9:04 P.M.

The cataract of the Milky Way filtered through the screen of the tree's dome-like canopy. A heavy branch reached out over the cliff from which a row of branches protruded like monkey bars.

They watched as the hendropods turned headstands on the wide branch and, with their four long legs, reached out and grabbed the side branches. The creatures swung across, rotating with one limb after another.

When the hendropods reached a pulley that hung from the bottom of the branch, they jumped down the thick cable into the big basket.

"*Mmm.* I don't know . . ." Andy quavered, assessing their precarious escape route. "Hey! Where's Thatcher?"

The others shot quick glances around.

"I'm not waiting for Thatcher," Zero announced. He jumped out to catch the first rung of the "monkey bars" and then swung over the seven-hundred-foot plunge hand-over-hand on the side branches.

Geoffrey went after him. They both made it look fairly easy.

"Lookin' good, guys," Nell called as they slid down the cable into the basket.

"Uh, how are we going to get these over there?" Andy pointed at the cases.

"Uh-oh," Nell said. "Hend—"

As Nell started to call them, the hendropods sprang back up the cable and swiftly spread out along the "monkey bars," forming a chain back to the main branch. As she handed them off they tossed the cases along the chain to Zero and Geoffrey, who caught them in the basket.

"Your turn, Andy," said Nell.

"I can't do this."

"Come on, Andy!" shouted Zero. "Just don't look down!"

"I didn't know you were afraid of heights," Nell said.

"Who *isn't* afraid of heights?"

"It's not that far, just go!" she said.

Andy jumped with a terrified yell and caught the first branch.

"Hand over hand!" shouted Zero.

Andy glanced down the sheer cliff face and began thrashing his legs wildly.

Hender stood by Nell on the main branch. The

four other hendropods hung from the monkey bars, watching Andy.

"Go Andy!" Hender said.

Andy reached for the next monkey bar and grabbed it, but when he swung for the rung after that his hand missed and he fell.

She heard Andy's scream. Hender jumped from beside Nell and plunged down the cliff as she looked down.

Hender grabbed Andy's ankle with an outstretched hand as two hendropods leaped from the rungs in sequence.

Like the pieces from a Barrel of Monkeys game, one hendro stretched a hand out to grab Hender's tail while hooking tails with the one behind it, who held the tail of a fourth, who clung to the ladder with all six hands.

As Andy plummeted down the face of the cliff, the hendropods' tails stretched to the limit and then sprang back and jerked him upward like a bungee cable.

At the top of the recoil, Hender handed Andy off to the fourth hendropod at the top of the chain, who quickly passed him to a fifth hendro hanging from the pulley.

The fifth hendro dropped Andy, who had been screaming throughout, into the basket.

Zero and Geoffrey patted his back with amazed congratulations as Andy popped his head up, speechless.

9:05 P.M.

Thatcher slid into the shotgun seat of the waiting Hummer, breathing hard from his run. "They have no way to contact the base," he said, slamming the door.

"You sure they don't have one of these?"

"What's that?" Thatcher wheezed.

"A satphone."

"No, no. They would have used it."

"The scientists think the island is sinking," Cane whispered. "They're going to nuke it ahead of schedule, twelve hours from now, they say, if there's anything left to nuke. They're evacuating the lab and deep-freezing the last specimens for transport. We could just leave now, no problem, sir."

"We've got a problem. Those scientists are trying to escape with *four more* of those wretched creatures, Sergeant. They're planning to use that elevator they built. They're getting the ship from that TV show to pick them up."

Cane solemnly reached under the seat and pulled out his rifle and some ammo clips. "You know my orders, sir. My orders are clear."

"You're not . . ." The scientist's eyes widened, "going to *shoot* them?"

Sergeant Cane released the safety on his weapon. "With extreme prejudice, sir."

"I mean—you're not going to shoot the humans?"

454

"The humans were warned of the consequences. They're no better than terrorists smuggling WMDs."

"But—" The gears were jamming in Thatcher's mind. He noticed specimen cases in the back of the Humvee. "What are those, Sergeant?"

"When I was driving around down there I ran into a bunch of panicky eggheads, no offense, sir, who asked me to take some specimens back to the base. They fumigated the canopy and knocked out a bunch of rats."

Thatcher saw the taped labels on the cases that said HENDERS RATS. "So those are live specimens . . ."

"Not for long," the soldier replied darkly. "They'll whack 'em back at base camp. Deep freeze."

"How will we explain that? I mean, if the others don't come with us, how will we explain how we got those specimens?"

"It doesn't matter anymore, sir. We'll just say we caught the others trying to smuggle specimens off the island: in other words, we tell the truth. My orders are clear, regardless of what you may want to do. This mission is now official, and not hypothetical, sir."

"Right . . ." Thatcher said softly. He looked at the cases of live specimens, thinking fast as he reeled forward different scenarios in his mind and, seeing three bars come up down one path, decided to gamble. "Give me a gun, Sergeant. I don't intend to sit out here unarmed."

Cane paused, studying the scientist for a moment. Then he reached down to his holster, unsnapped it, and handed Thatcher his Beretta.

Cane reached for the door. Thatcher's fingers tightened on the weapon as soon as the soldier turned away, but his arm froze when Cane turned back to him. Then, in the window behind Cane, Thatcher saw a giant shape rising like the neon marquee of the Flamingo Hotel.

Thatcher forced himself to remain calm and lowered the gun to his lap. "You're sure you don't want me to come with you? It could be dangerous," he said.

"I'll be fine," replied Cane. "I'll be right back."

When the young soldier opened the door to step out, a black spike ripped the door from its hinges. A second spike pierced Cane from his neck to his pelvis, and lifted him out of the vehicle like a gruesome marionette, dead.

Thatcher reached over from the passenger seat and switched on the ignition. When the Hummer started, he shifted it into gear. It rolled forward as the spiger, joined by another, and then a third, ripped into the soldier's body.

Thatcher scrambled into the driver's seat of the rolling Hummer and gripped the steering wheel. In the rearview mirror he was certain he saw two of the spigers follow him.

He pointed the vehicle down the slope, grabbed the satphone from the seat and one of the specimen cases from the back, then he shifted the Hummer into neutral and jumped out, getting lucky as he hit a relatively bare patch of ground and sprawled flat.

Thatcher raised his head inches from a bloom of fetid purple clover to watch the empty Hummer pick up speed on the darkened slope, chased by the two smaller spigers. The big one, having finished with Cane, lunged down the field to join the hunt.

Thatcher stood up and ran. The creature's bizarre tree house was fifty yards away, and he could barely hug the bulky specimen case under one arm. He had dropped Cane's pistol somewhere, but he wasn't about to stop and look for it.

The alpha spiger's rear eyes and hindbrain spotted the zoologist running behind them up the field. It abandoned the chase of the Hummer, spun instantly on a spike, and launched after Thatcher. The other spigers followed.

Thatcher shifted the case from arm to arm, gasping for air as putrid gases wafted over the purple field.

The spigers ran at full speed, pushing off their powerful middle legs and digging in their cleated tails and hind legs to propel them forward. In mid-leap they curled their spiked tails back under them to take the blow of their landing and drove their

spiked front arms into the ground to pull them forward as their middle legs pushed off and their tail
and hind legs launched them again.

Thatcher huffed and puffed as he jumped over
glistening clovores blooming on the starlit slope.
He stuffed Cane's satphone in the inner pocket of
his vest and didn't look back. He barely registered
the distant concussion of the Hummer plunging
over a cliff into the jungle below. As it exploded,
distracting the spigers for a precious beat, he put
his head down, and ran for his life.

9:08 P.M.

On their monitors inside the Trigon's control
center, three Army Radio Telephone Operators
noticed Blue One on the move in the theater of
operations.

"Blue One just took a nosedive!" one RTO
reported, turning to his CO in the communications
room.

The Commanding Officer on duty opened a
radio channel. "Blue One, what's your status,
damn it!"

"I don't think they'll be answering, sir," the RTO
said, staring at the screen. "They must have fallen
about fifty feet off a cliff before they hit jungle."

"When did they last check in?"

"About twenty-three minutes ago, sir. They were
collecting specimens."

The icon indicating the Hummer's transponder vanished from the map on their screens.

"Fuck it!" the CO snarled. "Send a search-and-rescue chopper, but don't drop anyone in. I'm not leaving one more soldier on this goddamned island, is that understood?"

"Yes, sir! But there were some VIPs on board Blue One, sir. Um . . . Dr. Cato, Dr. Redmond, and Dr. Binswanger . . . and Nell Duckworth. Plus that survivor they picked up."

"Oh, Christ. I'll call General Harris—Jesus Christ!—the shit's going to spray on this one, guys. Fuck! My order still stands, Lieutenant. Do not drop anyone in there, under any circumstances."

"Yes, sir, Colonel! That's affirmative."

9:09 P.M.

Thatcher stumbled the last ten feet to the door as the spigers closed the gap behind him, coming within one leap of their quarry. He shoved the door open as the alpha spiger landed on the doorstep.

Thatcher heard the whistle of its arms slash the air behind his head as he slammed the door to Hender's house, wheezing and gasping for breath. He tore the taped label from the specimen case, and then he pushed himself up the spiral stairs. Reeling and dizzy, Thatcher thought his blood pressure was going to pop his eyes like corks.

9:09 P.M.

The alpha spiger's warning signals triggered as it sensed the tree's pheromones and the warning pheromones of other creatures that had approached it. But the spiger was disoriented; the electromagnetic flux generated by the island's seismic activity interfered with the predator's instincts as a static of confusing impulses fired in its brains.

The spiger drew its tail forward underneath it and dug it into the ground, cocking its giant rear legs as it lowered its head at the front of Hender's house.

Then it slung its mass forward, clawing out with its spiked arms, and smashed the door to pieces with the top of its head.

As it thrust its body into the fuselage, the nostrils on the alpha's forehead sampled the scents in the air and found a strand of Thatcher winding up the stairway.

9:10 P.M.

Nell watched Hender carry Copepod with four hands as he swung to the creaking basket.

"Where's Thatcher?" Andy called from the basket, his voice echoing off the cliff.

"I don't know," Nell said, looking around.

"I'd like to know what that explosion was." Geoffrey stood beside Andy in the basket.

"Screw Thatcher, let's go!" Andy urged.

"I'll go get the last case and see where he is," Nell said.

She turned—and there was Thatcher, flushed and panting for breath, and hugging an aluminum case. She looked him up and down. "Good timing, Thatcher. Come on!"

She grabbed the case out of his hands, and saw his look of surprise.

Without a second thought she handed the case to Hender, who swung across the monkey bars and tossed it to the others in the basket before returning to Nell.

"Our turn," Nell told Thatcher.

Thatcher stood at the edge of the cliff looking at the rungs reaching out over the cliff. "Good God!" he said. "There is no way I can do this."

"Hender!" Nell called.

9:10 P.M.

The spiger extended its spiked front legs two yards in front of it and shimmied rapidly up the spiraling tunnel of stairs.

Since it did not have vertebrae, it stretched forward as the legs attached to its three bony rings grabbed hold and hauled it forward up the stairs like a muscular Slinky.

The other two spigers caterpillared their way furiously through the corkscrewing tunnel behind it.

9:11 P.M.

Pairs of hendropods grabbed Thatcher. He had frozen stiff in panic, making their job far more difficult. They carried him across the hand-ladder bridge and finally dropped him unceremoniously into the basket.

The door from the trunk of the tree exploded into a thousand pieces.

Nell whirled as two six-foot-long spikes reached through the shattered door.

A huge alpha spiger squeezed through onto the branch thirty feet behind her. It folded its spiked legs under it like a mantis shrimp as it scuttled forward, scanning her with swiftly moving multicolored eyes. Waves of orange, yellow, and pink light pulsed over waving stripes around its jaws.

"Nell, *hazar-do-us!*" Hender shouted.

"Come *on,* Nell!" Andy yelled.

The spiger's vertical jaws, three feet tall, opened wide and she could smell its sour breath as it raised its striped haunches up behind it.

"Nell! *Jump!*"

She turned and jumped, grabbing hold of the first rung. Hender was there to meet her, but she swung quite capably hand over hand as Hender backed away rapidly in front of her, using four hands and keeping one eye on the spiger at her back.

The spiger advanced to the edge of the branch where she had jumped, smelling her, the eyes on its head and haunches locking on their target—then it used all six legs and its tail to hurl itself through the air after her.

Hender grabbed Nell with his legs and two arms, pulling her forward just as the spiger's spikes lashed down through the air inches behind her head.

The spiger plummeted past the basket, snapping its jaws a few feet in front of Thatcher's face, and fell with a piercing wail seven hundred feet to the sea below.

Hender dropped Nell into the basket and jumped in behind her.

The thick cable of rope had apparently been woven from some kind of pale green fiber. The basket was made of the same fiber laced through large skeletal plates from some creature, perhaps the mega-mantis. It creaked now and stretched, dangerously overloaded.

"OK!" Hender said.

The other hendropods warbled a musical cacophony as the two remaining spigers peered over the edge of the branch, trying to gauge the distance to the basket that dangled like a feast before them.

"We gotta *go!*" Zero shouted at Hender.

But Hender stood motionless, looking upward. "OK, dudes!" he yelled. Hender reached an arm two meters up and pulled a rope that unlatched the pulley; the basket descended as the huge wheel turned.

The hendropods, normally solitary, clung to each other in the center of the basket, watching the spigers above.

The island that had been their home and world forever disappeared into darkness as they descended.

Geoffrey and Nell found themselves lying next to each other on their stomachs, looking over the edge of the basket at the sea as they sank alongside the ancient cliff. Geoffrey waved a glass jar of glowing bugs over the side.

"Impressive moves back there, Duckworth. I thought we might lose you."

"Thanks. I always was a tomboy."

"In case we don't make it, I just wanted to say . . ." He looked at her urgently, dropping all sarcasm. "There's nothing sexier than a brilliant woman— even if she has a funny last name."

"You mean I'm not beautiful?" she said.

"Maybe that came out wrong . . ."

She laughed and kissed him quickly on the lips as they plunged down toward the swirling sea. "In case we don't make it," she told him.

9:17 P.M.

The crew of the *Trident* spotted the faint light sinking down the cliff and Captain Sol unlatched the winch to let the Zodiac out.

Two crewmen paddled the Zodiac as the winch-line unspooled.

"It could work, Captain," Cynthea said, standing next to him at the stern of the *Trident*.

"Yes, it could work, Cynthea." Captain Sol sighed as the deck heaved and some big swells moved under the ship.

Second mate Samir El-Ashwah and crewman Winger paddled the Zodiac.

"So far so good," Samir said. "Steady, mate."

Winger saw the *Trident* rolling on a swell behind them. "Looks like the Navy's kicking up some wake on the way out."

"Bloody great," Samir said.

Heavy seas rolled toward them, submerging the towline and buffeting the Zodiac.

Samir pointed above. "There! Ya see 'em?"

A small green smudge of light was slowly descending the cliff.

"Yeah!" Winger exclaimed, narrowing his eyes against the saltwater spray of the buffeting waves.

Samir switched on a flashlight and wedged it in the bottom of the boat, lighting up the inside of the Zodiac like a lampshade.

9:19 P.M.

"There they are." Nell pointed at the glowing raft bobbing hundreds of feet below. "See 'em?"

"Yeah!" Zero said.

As they dropped the final hundred feet, it looked as if they were perfectly aligned with the Zodiac. Too perfect: the basket halted directly over the Zodiac so that they couldn't see it just below them.

The swells lifted the Zodiac and slammed it against the bottom of the basket. "Oh, fuck!" Winger yelped.

The wave subsided. Samir and Winger frantically paddled the Zodiac out from under the basket, which was now quivering ominously.

Vibrations rolled down the long cable, which throbbed like a bass string.

Pieces of rock sheared from the cliff and sliced into the sea: a terrific quake was rumbling through the island.

"This island's exploding!" Andy shouted.

"Calm down, Andy," Nell said, reaching out to squeeze his ankle. Copepod yapped frantically.

The basket tipped and swung as the falling rocks tumbled into the water all around them.

The hendropods cringed as seawater from the incoming waves splashed over the basket.

"Jump in the Zodiac when the basket swings that way," Geoffrey instructed.

"Are you kidding?" Andy exclaimed.

The moment arrived and, when Andy didn't move, Geoffrey pushed him out of the basket. He landed, screaming, in the Zodiac. Geoffrey turned to the hendropods, pointing. "Jump, OK?"

9:20 P.M.

"Trident, what's the status on the engines?" demanded the radio transmission from the *Enterprise.*

"Uh," First Mate Warburton answered the hail from the bridge. "We think we've almost got the magnetometers synched up, *Enterprise.*"

He grimaced at Marcello, who was muttering prayers over his St. Christopher's medal.

9:21 P.M.

As the basket swung sickeningly to and fro, Geoffrey and Nell tossed the cases into the Zodiac.

Zero jumped into the raft, and Copepod followed at the urging of Andy. The little dog seemed happy to see the familiar raft. The hendropods, Nell, and Geoffrey were the last ones left in the wobbling basket.

"Here comes another set," Samir said, looking over his shoulder. *"Duck!"*

Everyone in the raft ducked as another giant wave slammed them into the bottom of the swinging basket.

The basket moved to one side as the next wave lifted the Zodiac. One of the stays of the basket snapped.

Everything except for Nell and Geoffrey rolled out of the basket and into the boat.

"*Allahu Akbar*!" Samir exclaimed as all five hendropods tumbled into the raft around him. One of them clung to his legs with three hands.

Nell and Geoffrey clung to the basket as it splashed into the cold black water.

The basket's heavy cable began plunging down around them in giant folds that crashed into the sea.

"We made it," Nell gasped, treading the icy water beside Geoffrey as the basket submerged, disappearing within seconds from view.

"Not yet," Geoffrey warned. "Let's go! Swim, Nell!"

They swam hard for the Zodiac as great elbows of cable smashed into the water behind them.

Suddenly they found themselves on top of a furry mass floating in the water.

"Keep going!" Geoffrey yelled.

Nell saw the mouth of the giant spiger lolling open underneath her like a face in a nightmare. To her horror, her foot grazed its lower jaw, but it moved loosely as she shoved off in panic. The spiger's spiked arms reacted slowly, rising from the water on either side of them, grasping at the two scientists as they swam for the raft.

"Hurry!" Andy yelled.

"Come on, girl!" Zero urged.

Nell swam forward in the chilling water with a renewed burst of adrenaline, passing Geoffrey. She crossed the last ten yards and grabbed the edge rail of the Zodiac, and she reached back to snag Geoffrey's hand.

"Hit it!" Samir shouted at the *Trident* eighty yards away.

Captain Sol engaged the winch to reel in the floundering Zodiac at top speed.

"Look!" yelled Andy.

"Oh noooo!" Hender cried.

A giant branch of Hender's tree plunged down the face of the cliff: two glowing creatures clung to its side.

With one hand towing Geoffrey, Nell was losing her grip on the Zodiac against the dragging force of the winch. Andy reached down to grab her wrist, but too late. The edge rail ripped from her hand and she and Geoffrey slipped behind in the churning water as the Zodiac pulled away.

"Keep swimming," yelled Geoffrey.

Nell turned to see the massive branch crash into the sea behind them. The heaving shockwave lifted Nell and Geoffrey and threw them into the raft, pushing it closer to the *Trident*.

The hendropods shrieked and retreated as the wave crashed over the boat and swept Hender over the side.

Hender screamed a piercing peal of anguish and immediately sank up to his neck, reaching his arms out of the seawater in all directions.

The wave deposited one of the glowing spigers

that had held onto the branch right behind him in the water.

The spiger seemed stunned from the fall, floating on its side.

"Hender!" Andy shouted.

"Andeeeeee!" Hender squealed.

"Cut the winch!" Samir yelled.

The other hendropods emitted a chatter of quick high screams at Hender and watched in terror, unable to help.

To everyone's surprise, Andy dove in.

9:34 P.M.

The hendropods sent up a chorus of shrieking whistles in the distance as Captain Sol disengaged the winch.

"What just happened?" Cynthea asked.

"I don't know, but it wasn't good!" Captain Sol growled.

9:34 P.M.

Andy's glasses flew off when he hit the water, but he could see the sinking glow of Hender through the murk and he dove down to grab his arm and pull him up. Hender gave a whistling gasp as his head emerged from the ocean. Andy spun Hender's body around and began kicking to push him toward the raft, paddling with his size-eleven shoes as hard as he could.

"Reach, Hender, reach!" Andy yelled, and spluttered seawater.

Hender wheezed and shuddered.

"You're close, come on, Hender!" Andy heard Nell shout, and it inspired the marine biologist to kick harder.

Nell saw the floating spiger convulse on the surface of the water behind Andy. "Reach, Hender!" she implored.

The hendropods shrieked and cowered at the bow, retreating from the spiger and the sloshing water in the raft.

The humans reached out over the edge of the raft and Hender stretched out one of his long, trembling upper arms.

Andy pushed Hender forward with one hand pressed against the thick silken fur of his back as he stroked the water with his other.

Nell dove in and grasped Hender's trembling hand, while Geoffrey grabbed her foot and held on—but her Adidas shoe slipped off, so he grabbed her bare foot, and then all the humans grabbed Geoffrey around the waist and pulled to keep him in the raft.

Hender was torn from Andy's grasp as the humans grabbed hold of his various hands. As soon as they hoisted him out of the water his entire trembling body twisted and shook the water from his fur violently. Andy treaded water for a moment, trying to catch his breath, then a wave crashed against the

471

side of his head and he choked, coughing water. He popped his head up, disoriented, and turned to see a fuzzy patch of glowing colors moving toward him with a spreading blackness at its center.

Spasms contorted the stunned spiger as it kicked its legs and raised its head out of the water. "ANDY!" screamed Nell, as she and the hendros comforted Hender. Flexing open all four jaws in a final convulsion, the spiger saw Andy now.

"Turn around, swim, *fast!*"

Confused, Andy swam toward the spiger.

The other hendros all moved from the bow and waded into the water sloshing inside the raft. In the center of the Zodiac, they clung to each other and one reached out a long arm toward Andy like the boom of a crane.

"Turn around, Andy!" Zero hollered. "Damn, it—*turn around!*"

Suddenly, Andy realized the blurry glow was not Hender.

Andy swiveled in the water.

The hendro's hand dangled in front of his face.

He grabbed it.

9:35 P.M.

"Hit it!" Captain Sol heard Samir shout from the aft deck, and he engaged the winch at top speed as he yelled over his shoulder at the bridge, "Weigh anchor, Carl! Half-speed now!"

Warburton exhaled and nodded at Marcello as he picked up the radio, fingering it for a moment before speaking in his most casual airline pilot voice: *"Enterprise, we fixed the problem and are now under way. Over?"*

"Good news, Trident," boomed the response. *"God speed."*

Warburton gave Marcello a low-five. "Thank you, *Enterprise.* God speed to you as well. See you at Pearl!"

9:38 P.M.

The hendropods and humans scrambled from the half-swamped Zodiac onto the aft deck as the *Trident* picked up speed.

Everyone aboard was dumbstruck as their new passengers came aboard.

Cynthea videoed the event with her camcorder, her hand steady as rock as she reeled in the historic moment and came face-to-face with a drenched but determined Zero, who was videoing her.

Geoffrey and Nell were the last ones remaining in the Zodiac. With the rest of the crew's attention on the hendropods, she took a deep breath and said, "There's almost nothing sexier than a man who knows the right thing to say at a very scary moment."

Drenched and weary, he grinned happily, handing the last case up to a waiting Thatcher. As she helped him up to the deck he smiled at her, and then frowned: *"Almost?"*

The shivering hendropods approached the humans repeating "Thank you!" to everyone they met. Copepod barked as he greeted the crew, who were too dazed by the hendros to be amazed by the miracle of his resurrection.

"Madone," Marcello breathed as he stared out the aft window of the bridge at the scene, and he crossed himself hastily.

"They need showers," Nell told the captain. "Saltwater isn't good for them."

"Good, get them below!" the captain said. "Let's get them out of sight, damn it, until we figure out what to do!"

Nell and Geoffrey quickly led the hendropods below.

"I'm going to get Copey something to eat, Captain."

"Good God, Andy, that damn dog made it! Will wonders never cease—yes, carry on, lad, get the little beast something to eat!"

"You are the captain, I presume?" Thatcher asked. He was hugging one of the aluminum cases they had brought aboard to his chest.

"Yes, sir, and you are?"

"Thatcher Redmond. I'm a scientist. Where should we store these cases?"

Captain Sol saw four others laid out on the poop deck. He frowned. "What's inside them?"

"Just artifacts and belongings of the hendropods."

"Hendro—?"

"Our guests." Thatcher smiled.

"Oh, I see, yes! Samir, can you help Mr. Redmond stow these cases? Use one of the empty cabins in the starboard pontoon."

"Right, Captain. This way, Mr. Redmond. I'll take a couple of those," said Samir.

Cynthea clutched Zero's hand. "*Tell* me you have hours and hours of footage, Zero," she crooned.

Zero tapped the NASA headband camera on the temple, turning it off, and placed it on her head like a tiara. Then he dropped a Ziploc bag full of memory sticks from one of his pockets into her hands. "Cynthea, I am your lord, master, and God Almighty, for all eternity. Get used to it, dollface!" With a knife-edged Gary Cooper grin, he hauled off and gave Cynthea a mashing kiss, complete with a dip.

When he let her up for air she seemed ten years younger. "Now, now," she purred, shaking a coy finger at him.

"A deal's a deal," he growled in her ear and she giggled in delight.

9:41 P.M.

Nell told Hender to follow her and he told the others. They sprang on two legs down the stairs

475

inside the central hull of the *Trident*, their heads bobbing and stretching and twisting as their eyes pointed in all directions.

"Where are we going?" Geoffrey asked, bringing up the rear.

"To the gym."

"There's a gym?"

"They wanted us all to have ripped abs. You didn't watch the show?"

"No."

"Thank God. OK, Hender. In here." Nell motioned them into the ship's gymnasium, a wide white room lined with gleaming new exercise equipment. An alcove at the far side contained six shower stalls and a separate locker area with benches.

Nell led them between the shower stalls and opened the last one on the right. She reached in and turned the water on.

"No water!" Hender said.

"OK water. Not salt. See?" She reached in and tasted it. "OK?"

Hender reached out gingerly and touched it. "OK!"

"You can go in—"

Before she could finish, Hender walked into the stall, and then he rippled with a rainbow shiver as he felt the water turn warm. "Oooo."

"OK?"

"Ooohkaaay," Hender sighed ecstatically.

Nell laughed.

The other hendros each opened their own stalls without assistance, turned on the water with only minor fumbling, and stepped in.

"Wow, they catch on fast!" Geoffrey said. He noticed his hands were shaking. Even as a scientist, especially as a scientist, he still felt a religious awe in the hendros' presence. Just seeing their alien heads pop over the shower stalls at each other, tittering and chirping, was a revelation of the humbling power of life that could create fantasies in reality and invest such disparate matter with a divine spark. He realized Nell was watching him. He shrugged, speechless.

"I know," she murmured.

Andy came in with a stack of towels.

"Just in time!" Nell said. "They're actually taking showers!"

"WOOO-WAH!" one of the hendros squealed, and the shower door nearest Geoffrey burst open as the creature leaped out, dancing and dripping. Geoffrey reached in and adjusted the knob to bring the temperature down.

"There, that's better. OK now!" He nodded as the hendro's color slowly turned from fiery red back to soothing greens and blues. The hendro reached into the stall and twisted the knob with one hand back and forth, feeling the water with five symmetrical fingers. Then it warbled a descending scale of strange consonants. Hender answered with a rising scale from his shower stall. The blue hendro then stepped back inside and closed the door with a soft *click*.

"I hope they leave some hot water," Geoffrey said. "I could use a shower, too."

"All I want to do is to get out of these wet clothes," Nell said. "And then sleep for a week. Andy, can you take care of them from here? You can give them each a room in the starboard pontoon."

"Sure, Nell. Where are you going?"

"Shopping," she replied. "Come on, Geoffrey."

He raised his eyebrows but said nothing as he followed her down the corridor to a large room forward of the gym.

It was the largest walk-in closet Geoffrey had ever seen. Rows of clothes arranged by sex and by size hung from long racks stretching the length of the room.

"These should fit." She tossed him some jeans and a T-shirt. "Underwear and socks there." She pointed at a tall stack of shelves near the door.

"Incredible."

"Yeah," she agreed, pulling some khaki slacks off a hanger. She took another T-shirt like Geoffrey's and some panties and socks from a drawer. "That should do it. Now let's take that shower."

Geoffrey snagged some briefs from the shelf and backed away from the door as she turned off the light and closed it behind her.

"There are a few advantages to being on a floating television studio," she told him.

"Is there enough water for so many showers?" Geoffrey said, hurrying behind her.

"Sure. There's a desalinization plant on board. Three thousand gallons a day."

"Amazing. I plan to use two thousand of them right now."

When they returned to the gym, the hendros were out of the showers, each holding a pair of towels in random hands as they uncertainly watched Andy pantomime drying his back. A few tried to copy his motions before dropping the towels and giving a quivering twist up and down their bodies that sent a spray of water in every direction. "OK, that'll work!" Andy said. "Oh, hey, guys."

"Hey, Andy."

Zero came in the door with a fresh camera and memory stick. "Did I miss much?"

"They just took showers," Nell reported.

"Oh wow."

"OK, Hender," Andy said. "Let's take a tour! I'll take them to their rooms, Nell."

"Where are we putting them up?"

"In the starboard pontoon."

"Oh, yeah. I'll come with you," Zero told Andy. "You coming, Nell?"

"We got to get out of these clothes. We'll catch up."

Andy looked at Geoffrey for a moment and back at Nell. "Sure." He smiled and shook Geoffrey's hand. "I never thanked you, Binswanger. So . . . thanks." Andy looked at Nell and grinned, nodding his head as he left. "Follow me, Hender!"

The hendros followed Hender and Andy, and Zero tailed them all down the passageway, camera to eye.

Nell closed the door to the gym.

"Now, I figure the best way to do this is we can take our clothes off in the shower stalls, then I can leave first to get dressed and you can come out after."

"Yeah, that works," nodded Geoffrey, glad to have a game plan.

They put their fresh clothes on the benches in front of the lockers and then pulled their shoes and socks off.

Nell looked at her single old beat up Adidas, the other having fallen into the sea. "My favorite tennies," she mourned.

"Sorry. Keeping your foot from becoming a spiger snack seemed more important. Any shoes on board?"

"*Oh,* yeah. We'll pick some out after we're done."

They walked toward the showers feeling giddy as teenagers for some reason. Both silently reminded themselves that they were mature and trustworthy adults. Level-headed and mature scientists. He took the shower in the far right corner and she took the one next to it.

They turned on the showers and started draping their seawater-soaked clothes over the dividers.

"Is there any shampoo over there?" she asked.

"Uh, yes."

His arm came over the stall with a bottle of red Suave shampoo.

"Thanks."

She touched his hand as she grabbed it and quickly started humming as she started washing her hair.

"You're getting out first, right?"

"Right." She lathered up and then rinsed off, trying to forget that they were both naked. "Need the shampoo?"

"No, I got it."

She stepped out of the stall and grabbed her towel. "OK, I'm going to the locker."

"OK, I'm not looking."

She wrapped the towel around her waist and walked with her back to him. As she quickly turned the corner into the locker area and started drying herself off, she was thinking about Geoffrey and sex and sex with Geoffrey and keeping her eyes resolutely on the photographs taped to the lockers. As she straightened to dry her hair, she noticed the laughing snapshots of the obnoxious Jesse, and beautiful Dawn, and ever-polite Glyn, and bragging Dante and the others, and tears spilled without warning from her eyes. She sank down on the bench and brought a hand to her face as she quietly sobbed.

"Nell." The warbling clarinet-like voice startled her. She looked up to see Hender in the middle of the gym, rubbing his chin with one hand and cocking his head.

She tugged on her towel but was sitting on it and had to stand up to pull it around herself. Hender was creeping forward the whole time, his eyes scanning her up and down and sideways.

"Hello, Hender!"

"Nell," Hender warbled softly, moving gently closer.

She backed away and Hender stopped, turning his head to look at the photos on the locker doors. He reached his hands out to touch Glyn, Dawn, Jesse, and the others who had died when they landed on the island twenty-four days ago. He touched Dante's picture with recognition. He turned his head to her and his eyes withdrew under his furry lids. "Nell thank you."

Hender softly padded out of the room on six feet, his head down.

She sniffled and stared after him. Then she rubbed the tears from her eyes, dropped the towel, and reached for her panties.

"Here I come!" Geoffrey warned, rounding the corner.

"Oh, I'm not dressed yet!" Nell yelped.

"Oh!" Geoffrey lifted his hands in surprise and his towel fell from around his waist.

With a speed that astonished even him, Geoffrey hurtled back around the corner. They doubled over, helpless with laughter.

"OK, get dressed, woman! How long do you take, anyway!" he howled.

"I'm doing it!" she snorted, throwing her towel in his direction. "Put a towel on!"

10:17 P.M.

Nell and Geoffrey, who had managed to get dressed without further incident and choose shoes from the garish collection of sneakers provided by *SeaLife*'s generous sponsors, entered the bridge with Samir and Andy.

Thatcher watched them climbing the stairs to the bridge and he followed, slipping in after them.

Warburton, Captain Sol, and Marcello were already there and in a troubled mood.

"The hendros are all tucked into their own private quarters," Andy reported. "They definitely prefer to be alone. When Samir and I showed them how to use the toilet, I think they fell in love."

"They definitely like peanut butter," Samir said.

"And shrimp," Andy said.

"We've got to check in on them." Nell looked at Geoffrey, who nodded.

"Copey isn't leaving Hender's side. Somehow he found Hender's room."

"Is that where that dog went?" asked Marcello. "He wolfed down the steak Cook gave him and then took off like a shot."

"Where's Cynthea?" Captain Sol asked.

"She's with Zero, I think."

Warburton and the captain shared a look.

"We were just trying to make a plan," Captain Sol told them.

"Any ideas?" Geoffrey asked. He wore an orange *SeaLife* T-shirt.

"That wasn't exactly the answer we were looking for," Warburton said.

"Sorry. By the way, my name is Geoffrey Binswanger."

"Welcome aboard, young man." Captain Sol shook his hand, firmly, glancing from Nell to the handsome scientist curiously. "Hello, Mr. Redmond, you don't have to skulk around back there. Come and join the conversation."

Nell and Geoffrey turned to see Thatcher in the doorway, his face flushing red. He waved weakly at the others.

"As I was saying to Carl," the captain continued, "I don't like keeping secrets from the Navy."

"We're being hailed, Captain," Warburton reported. "This is *Trident*, over?"

"*Trident, we can see that you're at safe distance now. We have been instructed by the President to*

484

let you know that you can proceed to port without further restrictions. Copy?"

"Very well, *Enterprise.* Thanks for the escort."

"No problem, Trident. *Just part of the Navy's job. Please proceed to Pearl Harbor for final inspection and debriefing. Good working with you.* Enterprise *over and out."*

Everyone sighed loudly in relief as Warburton clicked off the radio.

Thatcher cleared his throat. "Now what?"

"We have to phone the President," Captain Sol decided. "He has to know about our guests."

"When the Navy gets a little farther away," Nell pleaded.

"They'll be in this vicinity for a while," the Captain reminded her grimly. "They're nuking an island ten hours from now."

"How can we call the President?" Thatcher asked.

Warburton pointed to a phone charging in its cradle on the wall. "Satellite phone. Just dial zero and the country code."

"What's the country code for the United States?" Thatcher asked.

"One."

"Hmm. That figures."

"Can we trust the President?"

"We have to, I think, Andy," Geoffrey told him.

"It's a risk," Nell warned.

"Either the President or the Army deliberately left us behind on that island!"

Nell's face went pale. "We don't know that, Andy."

"It's less of a risk than not calling him," Captain Sol argued. "We'll get a little breathing room between us and the Pacific Fleet first, and then call in the morning. In ten hours, a nuclear bomb is going off and I intend to be far away."

"Will we be safe?" Nell asked.

"The Navy said nine miles is the minimum safe distance, and we should reach that in another twenty minutes, so we'll be OK, but I'd rather get as much distance between my ship and that island as possible. I suggest everyone grab a little shuteye in the meantime. Tomorrow will be a full day."

"Captain," Thatcher said, "how would one go about getting something to eat on this boat?"

"Ship," Captain Sol corrected. "Nell, could you show Mr. Redmond the galley?"

"It's 'Doctor,'" Thatcher said.

"Eh?"

"Dr. Redmond."

"Oh . . ."

"I'm starving," Nell interjected. "How about you, Geoffrey?"

"Yeah, I'm hungrier than a spiger."

She laughed. "This way, you two."

10:34 P.M.

In the mess, they sat at a table, Nell and Geoffrey eating tuna fish sandwiches and Thatcher nibbling at a veggie burger with pickles.

"So, Thatcher, do you still think we made the wrong decision?" Nell asked.

"The question is moot," Thatcher grunted, wiping his mustache with a napkin.

"But do you?" she persisted.

"As Geoffrey says, everyone's wrong sometimes. Eh, Binswanger? The Redmond Principle is obviously in error. Intelligent life is not destined to destroy its own ecosystem. You win some, you lose some. It's playing the game that counts."

"That's mighty big of you, Thatcher," said Geoffrey.

"Why, thank you, Geoffrey." The zoologist inclined his head.

"Yes, I thought you might still be harboring some resentment." Nell reached for a pickle.

"Never! It is clear that we have just saved a species of life whose intelligence is at least as advanced as our own."

"We're not out of the woods yet. There's no telling what will happen when we let the President know what we saved. Out here in the middle of nowhere, they could make up any cover story they wanted. But if we don't tell them, and they catch us smuggling, we stand even less of a chance."

"Who are 'they'?" Thatcher asked, raising an eyebrow.

"I don't know," Geoffrey admitted. "The President. The Navy. The Trilateral Commission, the Bilderbergers, the Priory of Sion. Does it matter? If this ship were lost at sea, how would anyone be the wiser?"

Thatcher smiled. "A calculated risk." He took the last bite of his burger. "Well, kids, I'm an old man in need of a soft bed. It's been a long day."

"Did they give you a nice cabin?" Nell asked.

"Yes, thank you, my dear." Thatcher rose from his chair.

"Good night," Geoffrey said.

"Good night," Thatcher bowed his head and smiled. Then he left them.

"Well that sandwich hit the spot," Geoffrey remarked, after a moment.

"Nothing but the best," Nell said. "Dolphin-safe."

"Let's check in on the hendros."

"You read my mind, Dr. Binswanger."

11:01 P.M.

Nell led Geoffrey down the corridors below deck to the starboard pontoon, where they spotted Cynthea and Zero outside one of the cabins.

"Where's Hender?" Nell asked.

"In there," Cynthea pointed, sourly.

"Andy just kicked us out," Zero told them.

"Why?" Geoffrey said.

"He says Hender's sleepy."

Nell laughed and tapped on the hatch. "Hi, Andy,

488

it's Nell! Can Geoffrey and I say good night to Hender?"

"Sure, come on in!"

Cynthea frowned.

The door opened a crack. "Just no more filming, OK? Don't let Cynthea in."

Nell smiled at him through the crack. "OK. Sorry, Cynthea."

Andy admitted Nell and Geoffrey into the room.

Hender was hopping on the bed as Copepod jumped up onto the mattress and back down again, barking excitedly. Then Hender stepped down from the bed and reached his upper arms out toward them, nodding happily.

"Hello, Hender," Nell said, taking one of his hands as Geoffrey took another. "OK?"

"OK, Nell! Hello, Geoffrey!"

Geoffrey laughed. "Hello, Hender!"

"Have they eaten anything, Andy?" Nell asked.

"Yeah, the cook boiled three bags of frozen shrimp. They loved them. So did Copepod. They let him eat from the same tray with them."

Nell laughed. "Do they really seem all right? Do they need anything?"

"Yeah, they're OK, Nell."

"That's great," Geoffrey said, watching Copepod chase himself through Hender's legs. "OK, Hender? Yes?"

"Yes, Geoffrey. OK. Thank you thank you thank you!"

Copepod ran to Nell.

"Copey, sweetheart, you OK, too?" She smiled as she kneeled and took his licks, scratching his shoulder blades. The little dog moaned in ecstasy.

"Copey good," Hender piped.

"Copey won't leave Hender's side," Andy confirmed. "Talk about a dog whisperer. He could have his own TV series."

"Maybe he will!" Nell smiled. "What about the others? How are they?"

"They're asleep already. They showered, ate, used the toilets, and conked out as soon as they got to their rooms."

"Wow!" Geoffrey grinned. "OK, good night, Hender. Good-bye. OK?"

Nell reached out and gave Hender a full hug and whispered next to his head. "Safety, Hender. Safety now!" Even as she said it she wondered if she could keep that promise.

"Safety, Nell," Hender echoed softly, his fur effulging warm colors where she touched his back.

Geoffrey watched, gasping at Hender's display, as she pulled back.

"Good-bye, Geoffrey and Nell," Hender nodded. "OK, sleep, right?"

"Yes, sleep! Right!" Nell saluted.

"Good night," Geoffrey waved.

"Good night, good night, good night!" purred Hender, saluting and waving with four hands.

11:14 P.M.

"He catches on awfully quick," Nell whispered after they had shut the hatch of Hender's cabin.

"My God." Geoffrey shook his head. He yawned, and he realized suddenly that thirty-one hours had passed since he'd last had a decent night's sleep. "Uh, where exactly would one go to grab some shuteye on this ship, Nell?"

"Follow me."

Nell led him through a corridor to the port pontoon and turned left down the passageway.

"Here," she said. "My room. Don't worry. I'm tired, too."

"You're full of surprises." Geoffrey smiled wryly. "Aren't there other empty cabins available?"

"Maybe . . ." she answered. "I really don't know."

She switched off the light as she climbed onto her double bed and pulled the pillows out from under the bedspread, tossing one to him.

"It's horizontal . . . I'll take it!" Geoffrey climbed on, too, and rolled over on his side away from her.

The air was chilly in the cabin and Nell turned and spooned against him.

"It's all right," she told him. "Go to sleep. It's just a cuddle instinct, as practiced by the North American wolf."

"Oh really?"

"It's common to all mammals."

He chuckled.

"Go to sleep," she whispered. "It's for *warmth!*"

"Hmmm," Geoffrey wondered, feeling very good with this woman pressed against his back, her breath soft against his neck. Suddenly he felt the need to sleep tug him down hard and he yawned again. "Did you ever notice how many scientists' names match their chosen field of study?" he asked drowsily. "I'm thinking of doing a statistical study and writing a trifling monograph on the subject . . ."

She giggled, yawning too.

"Bob Brain, the famous South African anthropologist who discovered all those big-brained hominids."

"Steve Salmon, the ichthyologist."

"Mitchell Byrd, the famous ornithologist."

"I had a dentist named Bud Bitwell."

"No."

"Yeah."

"Did he change it to that?"

"I don't think so, but knowing him, he actually might have. That would have to be a statistical factor."

"Then, of course, there's Alexander Graham Bell."

"Silly, but it qualifies."

"That one always got me as a kid. Hey, and our own geologist, Dr. Livingstone."

"I had a geology professor named Mike Mountain."

"I had a botany professor named Mike Green."

"Yeah, that qualifies."

"Then there's Charles Darwin."

"Uh . . . ?"

"A Darwinian biologist?"

"Yeah, almost *too* obvious. And Isaac Newton, the Newtonian physicist."

"Let's not even mention Freud."

"Not even mentioning Freud is like mentioning Freud."

She snuggled closer and sighed sleepily. "Exactly."

"You are so outside the box."

"Well, names do appear to be a common factor, Dr. Binswanger. You may be onto something," she said against his neck, too tired to move her head. "Let's see now. By your theory, I should be . . ."

"By my theory, if you were subject to being influenced by your name, Duckworth, which I believe derives from 'duckworthy,' or someone who tends ducks, today you might well be studying duck-billed dinosaurs."

"I did go through a duck-billed dinosaur phase." She chuckled.

"Aha! I rest my case."

"You're a genius. So what does Binswanger mean?"

"Well," he said.

"I know: sometimes a Binswanger is just a Binswanger."

"Ho, ho."

Suddenly, for the first time in a long time, she felt safe, and she knew he was safe, and that the hendros were safe. She needed to feel safe again, she thought with a pang. In less than nine hours, life on Henders Island would be no more.

"You have to explain to me sometime why you think hendropods might be immortal . . ." she muttered.

"I will, I will," he said. "Sweet dreams, darling." The word came, astonishingly, naturally.

"*Hmm,* yes, thank you, you, too." She smiled, and they both fell instantly asleep.

SEPTEMBER 17

2:29 A.M.

Thatcher pressed the crown to light his Indiglo wristwatch in the dimly lit passageway and used the glowing watch face to illuminate the hatch handle.

He pulled the handle and crept into the storage room where he had helped stow the aluminum cases. He removed his watch. Using its glowing blue face, he inspected the cases until he found the one with label streaks on the side.

He took the case, then slipped quietly down the passageway to the *Trident*'s broadcast control room in the starboard hull.

He tapped first on the door, to make sure no one was there. Hearing no response, he slipped inside.

The room was dark. The troll that inhabited it had finally gone to his quarters directly across the hall to sleep, and had left his banks of machines in sleep mode. Their red status lights flickered in the shadows like eyes.

Thatcher unlatched the aluminum case and poured out the contents of Pandora's box.

Six dead-looking Henders rats tumbled onto the floor. Their legs immediately started twitching and clawing.

"Welcome aboard the S.S. *Plague Ship*, you little bastards," Thatcher whispered. "Go forth and multiply."

He closed the door quietly behind him. The passageway was empty and silent except for the *thrum* of the ship's engines. He ran toward the stern.

A minute later, he was jumping into the large Zodiac that still trailed the *Trident* between the port and central pontoons. He took out a Leatherman tool from pocket number eleven and used its serrated knife to slice through the nylon towline.

The Zodiac slipped away on the *Trident*'s wake into the spring night.

"Survival of the fittest, Dr. Binswanger," he murmured triumphantly at the ship as it motored forward into the gloom.

He pulled out the satphone he had taken from the Hummer, then fished out a GPS locator from another pocket in his vest. Gazing at the shrinking *Trident* on the dark sea, he punched a number into the satphone.

A grouchy voice answered after a few rings.

"Stapleton! I just knew you'd be up, old friend! What's that? Well you're up now. It's Thatcher. Yes! I need help, *mon frère*! I had to abandon ship and I am currently on a *raft* in the *South Pacific*. Yes, I'm serious! You can't imagine *how* serious! It's a long story. Take down my GPS coordinates before I lose you: Latitude 46.09, 33.18 degrees south,

Longitude 135.44, 44.59 degrees west. Send the Navy! I'll fill you in on the details later! I need your help, my friend! OK, you have a pen? Latitude . . ."

7:09 A.M.

The spring sun of the southern hemisphere warmed the cheeks of the sleeping Thatcher Redmond as it rose.

The satphone in his vest pocket rang, waking him up from a strange dream in which he was floating in a raft on the open ocean . . .

He sat upright at the stern of the big Zodiac and was astonished to see the vast broadside of the guided missile frigate U.S.S. *Nicholas* cutting into the sea beside him. Stapleton had come through! He had to think fast.

"Yes, hello!" Thatcher said into the phone. "I am Dr. Thatcher Redmond. I must have hit my head and fallen overboard last night into this raft," he improvised, breathlessly. "Unless someone else struck me!"

"Is that the ship, sir?" came the voice, apparently from the giant ship.

Thatcher turned and saw the *Trident* on the horizon. He had expected the damn ship to be miles away by now.

"Yes, that's it!" he said, thinking fast as probabilities shifted in his mind. "That ship is infested with dangerous animals illegally smuggled off Henders

Island. I am an award-winning scientist, and I'm simply appalled that this sort of thing can go on and no one is doing anything about it!"

"Did you say animals are being smuggled on that vessel, sir?"

"Yes, yes! Dangerous animals! From Henders Island!"

There was a long silence as the raft rolled up and down on the ship's wake.

Over the ship's loudspeakers came an answer: "A RESCUE HELICOPTER FROM THE U.S.S. *STOUT* WILL COME FOR YOU WITHIN THE HOUR, SIR! JUST HANG TIGHT!"

The Navy frigate sliced through the water toward the *Trident* with alarms sounding.

As he propped himself against the stern to watch the U.S.S. *Nicholas* close in on the *Trident*, Thatcher sat back and repressed a smile. He reached into his pockets to see if he still had anything to snack on squirreled away.

7:15 A.M.

The ship's klaxon sounded, and all hands emerged groggily on the *Trident*'s foredeck. Three Navy ships bore down on the *Trident* from three points on the horizon.

Captain Sol's voice reverberated over the intercom: "All hands on deck! The Navy is ordering us to abandon ship!"

Geoffrey and Nell ran to join Peach, Cynthea, Zero, Andy, Warburton, and Captain Sol on the bridge.

They heard the stern voice of a Navy officer on the radio now: *"All passengers are ordered to abandon ship with nothing but their persons! The* Trident *will be scuttled. All passengers are ordered on deck* now!*"*

The voice did not wait for an answer but continued to repeat its implacable demands.

"Tell him we need to speak to the President!" Nell cried.

Captain Sol cut in. "This is *Trident.* We have a special request and would like to appeal directly to the President—"

"Trident, you will comply with our demands immediately. Is that understood?"

"We're screwed," Zero muttered.

"Hey, wait a minute," Geoffrey said. "We're on a floating television studio!"

Cynthea looked tortured as she shook her head. "The Navy took away all our satellite transmission equipment after we lost Dante—"

"I still have a videophone," Peach interrupted.

"Peach!" Cynthea gripped his shoulders.

Peach handed her a spare wireless headset from around his neck.

"You're my hero!" Cynthea yelled.

"I know, boss."

"Go get it, go set it up!" Cynthea shouted after

him as Peach and Zero ran out the hatchway down the stairs.

Cynthea put on the headset and adjusted the mike.

"Set it up on the bow, Peach! Make sure to get the battleships in the frame," she commanded through the headset. "We'll make a human shield!"

She grabbed the satellite phone in the bridge and punched in a number. She winked at Nell as she said, "Hi, Judy, this is Cynthea Leeds. Put me through to Barry, sweetie!"

Captain Sol grimaced as the Navy ships grew rapidly on the horizon in the wide window of the bridge.

7:16 A.M.

Peach and Zero tore down the passageway. Zero opened the hatch of the control room—only to see five Henders rats leaping straight at him.

Zero's reflexes were barely fast enough to slam the hatch in time. A cold sweat washed over him. "Fuck, fuck, fuck!" He looked at Peach with wide eyes.

Hender popped out of a hatch farther down the companionway and Copepod jumped out behind him. Hender yawned, scratching his head and belly with four hands, and saw the two humans. Suddenly, he heard or smelled something that made him leap down the passageway on four legs

500

toward them. Copepod stayed at his heel, snarling.

"Ooooooh," Hender said, and he made a staccato call like a rising clarinet scale.

The other hendropods burst from their rooms and ran down the hall to join him, shooing the humans away.

The five hendros huddled around the hatch to the control room and then they rushed in one after another, banging the hatch closed behind them.

"Come on, Peach," Cynthea urged over Peach's headset.

"Um, there's a delay, boss," Peach said.

"There's no time for delays!" she snarled.

Zero shook his head at Peach.

Peach winced. Then, ignoring Zero's objections, he opened the control room hatch and ran in, slamming it shut behind him.

He grabbed the videophone, camera, laptop, and microphones while the hendropods, appearing and disappearing around him, fought off the rats launching viciously at him. One scratched Peach's forehead with a raking claw arm but another hendro shot the rat through its arching center with a whirring obsidian disk. A few severed locks of hair revealed Peach's brow, where a thin cut started bleeding. But Peach didn't shout. He focused instead on the equipment he needed.

Peach lurched out the hatch with gear under his arms. Still inside, the hendropods slammed the hatch behind him, the bottom of his pant leg caught with two rat arms pierced through the jeans. He yelled and jerked his foot to rip free and the hatch opened for an instant as the rat was pulled back in before the hendros slammed the hatch shut again, freeing his leg.

"Come on!" Zero yelled.

"What about them?" Peach gestured at the hatch.

Copepod barked at the hatch, his body rigid as he jumped and clawed frantically at the door.

Andy came running in. "Where's Hender?"

"In there," Zero answered.

Andy reached for the hatch. But Zero stopped him.

"No," he shouted, then turned and ran after Peach. "Get the hendros up here as fast as you can but don't open that goddamned door, Andy!"

7:18 A.M.

Thatcher munched trail-mix as he watched artillery shells prick white plumes off the *Trident*'s bow.

The Zodiac drifted into the wide foamy plain of the *Nicholas*'s wake. The salt was thick in the air as the billions of bubbles churned by the frigate's propellers fizzed on the surface of the sea around him.

He squinted with grim satisfaction at each delayed concussion that rolled over the waves. He was betting that after the chaos subsided, anyone on the *Trident* would be lucky to be alive. Certainly none of them would be able to exonerate themselves even if they were. It was also extremely likely that the hendropods would be killed along with the rats when the ship was finally boarded by the Navy and they were discovered.

Thatcher knew his story was rock solid, that his reputation would win the battle of credibility, and that history would forever cast the others in shades of doubt, no matter the outcome. The odds were that he would gain even more stature before all was said and done simply by opposing them, even if by some miracle they did survive. He had, after all, witnessed them smuggling live, extremely dangerous specimens off Henders Island, in direct violation of a Presidential order, a crime tantamount to global terrorism. And the scene of the crime was about to be vaporized forever by a nuclear weapon.

He had been hoping that he would not have to call any attention to the *Trident*—the long shot he had pictured was the voracious rats taking over the ship, which would have eventually run aground or been boarded so that the rats would then start spreading at some port of call or random landing point. And the seeds of mankind's destruction would have been planted, though too slowly to ever reach him in Costa Rica. What a show it would be to watch the

Earth's man-centric ecosystem collapsing across whole continents during the last twenty years of his life.

But he could settle for the crew and passengers of the *Trident* discredited as terrorists and quite possibly killed in a confrontation with the Navy; there was really no downside.

"Free will, Dr. Binswanger," Thatcher goaded the younger scientist from afar, reciting the Redmond Principle, "can and will do *anything*." He bit his lower lip as he realized that he wasn't a fraud, after all, and the notion seized him with a paroxysm of laughter. After doing away with his own son, and now possibly an entire intelligent species, if not his own, he had categorically proven the Redmond Principle, *all by himself.*

7:20 A.M.

The Navy ships continued to close on the *Trident* as another warning shot erupted off her starboard side.

"Hurry it up, Cynthea," Captain Sol urged. Then, on the radio, he said, "We are complying! We are complying!"

"All hands on deck now, Captain!" came the response.

Cynthea still clung to the phone. "Barry, this is television history! No—it's BIGGER THAN TELEVISION, sweetie! Come on! Say yes!"

7:21 A.M.

As the crew gathered at the prow of the *Trident*, Zero and Peach set up the videophone equipment, looking over their shoulders at the two huge Navy ships bearing down port and starboard.

7:21 A.M.

"Hender," Andy shouted through the door of the control room. "We have to go!"

7:21 A.M.

The Zodiac rolled over a series of high swells, as Thatcher watched the Navy ships closing in on the *Trident.*

He recognized the bottom of a jar of Planters cashews buried under some rubber fins and scuba gear. He dug it out and was disappointed when he twisted off the lid to see that there were only three left.

7:21 A.M.

Cynthea furiously negotiated with the *SeaLife* producers on the phone and finally played her trump card: "We could all get KILLED, Barry—on LIVE television!"

7:22 A.M.

Cynthea ran down the stairs from the bridge toward the bow, screaming, "OK, set it up! Set it up! We're going live right now! Don't ask! Where are they?"

The crew of the *Trident* was clustered on the prow, with the two ships looming in the background, perfectly framed. But no hendropods.

Running to the prow at full tilt, Cynthea stepped in front of the camera and played reporter. "What remains of the crew of the *Trident* is now being threatened by the United States Navy. Abandon ship or go down with the ship is their order. Why?" She looked in vain toward the companionway but saw no sign of the hendros as she vamped. "Because today we have saved a *remarkable* species from *total* destruction!"

Another shot exploded directly off the bow.

7:23 A.M.

"We have to exit, Hender," Andy shouted. "Go now! Now, now, *now!*"

Andy reached for the door handle and the hatch opened inward.

Hender looked out. "OK," Hender said. "Hi Andy!"

Copepod barked in response.

Cynthea saw Andy run out on the foredeck. The five hendropods glided behind him.

The nearest Navy ship was now on top of them, slicing past their port side, its loudspeakers blaring out over the decks.

"YOU ARE ORDERED BY THE UNITED STATES NAVY TO ABANDON SHIP NOW. CARRY NOTHING WITH YOU OR YOU WILL BE FIRED ON."

When the hendropods saw an arcing waterspout fired from a water canon on the deck of the destroyer, they whirled and ran in the other direction.

Andy caught Hender. "No, it's OK, Hender! Come on!"

The hendropods turned around slowly at Hender's humming and clicking calls. Then, reluctantly, they continued behind him and Andy toward the bow.

Behind them, one last Henders rat crouched in the hatchway through which they had come, rubbing its spikes together as it chose a target.

It bolted across the deck toward the hendropods just as they entered the frame of the videophone.

As the rat launched itself through the air, Copepod growled inches from Hender's ankle.

Hender glanced at the ocean with one eye before casually batting the rat overboard with a deft block by its rear foot.

The rat thrashed in the water before sinking into the sea.

Nell, Geoffrey, Andy, Captain Sol, Warburton, Cynthea, Samir, Marcello, and the rest of the *Trident*'s crew gathered the hendropods between them on the foredeck, creating a human shield as Cynthea had commanded.

With the combined stress of the moment and the sight of the gigantic ships moving through the sea around them, all of the hendros vanished.

11:24 A.M. Eastern Daylight Time

All the major networks and cable news channels displayed on plasma screens in the White House Situation Room were muted.

The President and his advisors stared in astonishment at only one screen—the one that carried the live feed from the guided missile destroyer, U.S.S. *Stout*.

"Captain Bobrow, can you hear me?" the President asked the captain of the *Stout*.

"Yes, sir."

"Get me a closer view of the folks on deck, if you can, Captain."

"Yes, sir. We're getting you a closer view now."

The image zoomed in as a camera on the decks of the *Stout* showed the *Trident*'s crew clustered at the bow.

"Isn't that Nell?" the President said. "That's Nell

508

Duckworth, I believe, isn't it, Trudy? I was told she died in an accident on the island. And there's Dr. Binswanger."

The others were impressed once more by the President's Rolodex memory for names and faces.

"What's going on here, Wallace? Lay off the shells, Captain Bobrow, damn it. I want you to stop firing, is that understood?"

"Yes, sir, Mr. President, those are from the other guys."

"Well, hey, you other guys, stop firing," said the President.

"Yes, sir!"

"What is that . . . some kind of distortion?" the Defense Secretary asked.

"We need a closer look there, Captain Bobrow."

"Yes, sir. We're coming around."

The Press Secretary suddenly cracked the door of the Situation Room and stuck his head in. "Mr. President! Turn to the Discovery Channel, sir!"

"What?"

7:25 A.M.

The bullhorns sounded again from the nearest ship:

"ABANDON SHIP TRIDENT! CARRY NOTHING WITH YOU OR YOU WILL BE FIRED ON!"

"These are the amazing people of Henders

Island," Cynthea declaimed triumphantly into Peach's microphone.

Marcello kissed his St. Christopher's medal.

Cynthea gestured at the hendropods, but stopped, bewildered. They were gone. "What happened? Where are they?"

4:25 P.M. Greenwich Mean Time

Sixty million people worldwide were watching TV when the live-feed from the *Trident* cut into their regularly scheduled programming.

Within two minutes, that number had leaped to over 200 million. The number continued to rise as the media feeding-frenzy accelerated through the swarm of satellites encircling the Earth in real-time.

11:26 A.M. Eastern Daylight Time

The President listened to Cynthea Leeds speaking from the bow of the ship on the television. Whatever species of Henders organism the TV producer was referring to was nowhere to be seen.

"The President of the United States and the Navy are about to destroy not only us, but a new and intelligent species of people who have as much right to exist on this planet as we do! More, even!"

The loudspeakers of the *Stout* echoed over the deck in the background, "TRIDENT, YOU ARE IN DIRECT VIOLATION OF UNITED STATES NAVY DIRECTIVES. BEGIN ABANDONING SHIP IN THIRTY SECONDS, OR YOU WILL BE FIRED ON."

"I don't like it, Mr. President," the Secretary of Defense insisted. "Why are they not complying? Are they crazy?"

7:27 A.M.

The Navy ship's bullhorn rang out in the background.

"ABANDON SHIP NOW! COMPLY NOW!"

"And so the United States Navy continues its countdown to its sentence of execution," Cynthea narrated.

There was an unbearable silence. The *Trident* crew looked at their watches and winced as the seconds ticked down. The Navy had stopped firing warning shots, but no one was sure if this was a good or bad thing.

Andy whispered in what he hoped was Hender's ear. "Go on, Hender."

Hender suddenly appeared in brilliant, rippling colors. "Hello, people!" he said in a fluting voice. "Thank you for saving us!"

All the hendropods blushed into vivid color beside him then and waved at the camera in

511

Peach's hand as they fluted together, "Thank you! Thank you! Thank you!"

11:27 A.M. Eastern Daylight Time

"Well . . . what the . . . ?" The President's mouth hung open.

The astonished Commander-in-Chief glanced at his defense secretary and then back to the frightened people who stood defiantly on the bow of the *Trident*.

Half a billion people were watching the hendropods as the omnivorous eyes of humanity opened across the face of the Earth.

Some laughed at what they saw and thought it was a joke. Others scoffed and thought it was a fraud. Some recoiled and thought it was a horror, and others wept in awe and called it a miracle. Still others trembled with rage and believed it was the Apocalypse.

People watched in real time as their world was instantly turned upside-down. All who watched knew the human race had arrived at a moment of judgment that would mark its destiny and its character, and its world, forever, and the war over the meaning of that moment had already begun in living rooms, cafes, bars, and dormitories across five continents.

"Sweet Jesus H. fucking Christ," the President said.

Behind the backs of the *Trident*'s crew, the camera showed the Navy bearing down as the second ship circled across their starboard bow, and a third ship appeared on the horizon.

Nell grabbed the mike from Cynthea. "Mr. President, if you are watching, you must spare these special beings!"

Admiring Nell's chutzpah, Cynthea reclaimed the mike from her, whispering *"Finally,* a little drama, Nell. Good work, girl." Then she shouted into the microphone, "So now we wait with the rest of the world to see what their fate and ours will be!"

Marcello watched the second hand of his watch as it crossed the 30-second mark, and he placed his hand on Hender's arm as he closed his eyes.

Hender patted Marcello's hand and Andy's shoulder reassuringly as his eyes moved in separate directions.

Nell squeezed Geoffrey's hand hard.

The destroyer's bullhorns crackled, and a voice boomed over the decks: "THE PRESIDENT HAS ORDERED US TO STAND DOWN. WE ASK PERMISSION TO COME ABOARD."

"Drama!" Cynthea exalted.

Then they all cheered, hugging each other across species as the U.S. Navy stood down.

7:29 A.M.

Thatcher recognized the blue lid of a glass jar wedged between the bottom and the pontoon of the Zodiac. Another nut jar. Thank God, he was starving.

He tugged it, planted his feet on the pontoon. He pulled it out and twisted it open as he brought it close to peer inside.

Henders wasps and drill-worms spilled out of the jar onto his face and eyes. It was seconds before he realized it was one of Hender's bug-jars that they had waved hours earlier to get the *Trident*'s attention.

Thatcher screamed and knocked the satphone overboard as the drill-worms punctured his eyelids and one of the raft's air chambers simultaneously.

He writhed, tangled in lines and scuba gear, shrieking as the Zodiac partially deflated and one side folded around him. His panic slowly turned to shocked disbelief. Thatcher saw a burst of light as the worms corkscrewed into his optic nerves, and then there was darkness, and a while later there was no more.

8:12 A.M.

All the way from Whiteman Air Force Base, Missouri, the dull black B-2 stealth bomber cruised at Mach 2 at an altitude of twelve hundred feet over the South Pacific ocean.

"Look at that, Zack! The thing's already breaking apart," said the copilot.

As they approached the island they could see one of its walls collapsing into the ocean as they approached.

"Damn! OK, let's lay this egg," said the pilot.

Before the aircraft cleared the cliffs of Henders Island, the bomb bay doors opened and a B83 gravity bomb fell forward. A parachute deployed and like a two thousand pound lawn dart, the warhead plunged five thousand feet.

As the aircraft pulled up, the bomb's hardened nose penetrated forty feet into the rocky core of the island. The reverberating clap of the missile's impact with the stone heart of Henders Island drew rats, spigers, and swarms, which converged around the neat hole punched into the island's bull's eye. A 120-second delay began ticking down inside the bomb so that the pilots could achieve safe distance before its one-megaton nuclear warhead detonated.

"That's gotta be the most expensive can of Raid in history," the pilot remarked as they left the island at twenty miles a minute, covering nine miles in about thirty seconds. The boomerang-shaped B-2 banked in a wide circle as they gained altitude.

"Check it out, Zack," the copilot said.

The two men looked over the expanse of the carbon-graphite composite wing as a brilliant light popped like a giant flashbulb in the bowl of the island.

A 250-foot deep crater a thousand feet wide was instantaneously excavated at the island's center from the initial blast.

Within four seconds every living thing on the surface of the island was vaporized and the ashes blasted over the rim in a cone of smoke. Sand turned to glass. Rock flowed red-hot as a sun-like inferno filled the bowl.

The bomber pilots watched the eruption of light bloom on the island like a yellow rose.

"Don't look at it too long," the pilot warned. "Burns the retinas."

"We're past the nine-mile range . . ." the copilot said. "God, you can feel the heat of that thing from here!"

The intense light faded as a giant funnel of dense smoke rose out of the bowl three miles into the sky.

"We better stay ahead of the shockwave," the pilot said, and he throttled up to just under the speed of sound.

"Target confirmed killed, Base. Copy?"

"Copy that. Mission accomplished. Come on home, boys."

SEPTEMBER 18

6:34 A.M.

Nell and Geoffrey gazed from the prow of the *Trident* at the crimson dawn.

Geoffrey cocked his head and studied her wryly for a moment. "So, I've been meaning to ask: What's sexier than a man who knows the right thing to say?"

"A man who knows when not to say anything."

Geoffrey lifted her chin to meet her smiling lips with his.

6:35 A.M.

Hiding inside a hatchway, Zero videoed them kissing, and Cynthea whispered restlessly in his ear: "Are you getting that?"

Zero popped his left eye open at Cynthea. *Yup,* his eye said.

6:36 A.M.

Hender's grin and eyes appeared first as he seemed to materialize behind the two young scientists on the prow.

They laughed to see him.

517

6:36 A.M.

"Oh wow . . ." Cynthea whispered. "Get that, get that, *get that, baby!*"

6:37 A.M.

Hender moved between them and hugged Geoffrey and Nell with four arms, and together they faced the uncertain dawn.

ILLUSTRATIONS
AND MAP

Phylum *Parathropoda*	Subphylum *Pentapoda*	Class *Syminsectaformes*
Subclass	Order *Henderhymenoptera*	Family *Rotaformicidae*

Disk-Ant
Rotaformica hendersi

The "disk-ant" was the first animal life encountered on Henders Island. With a ring-shaped brain, this rolling pack hunter no bigger than a half-dollar carries three generations of offspring on its back.

Are they related to Starfish? No, disk-ants are distant relatives of insects!

> HENDER NOTE: *These were the most feared of all the animals on our island. We traveled high in the trees to avoid coming into contact with them, since they tended to stay closer to the ground.*

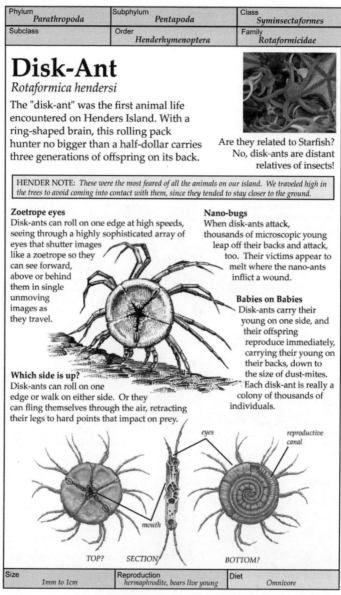

Zoetrope eyes
Disk-ants can roll on one edge at high speeds, seeing through a highly sophisticated array of eyes that shutter images like a zoetrope so they can see forward, above or behind them in single unmoving images as they travel.

Nano-bugs
When disk-ants attack, thousands of microscopic young leap off their backs and attack, too. Their victims appear to melt where the nano-ants inflict a wound.

Babies on Babies
Disk-ants carry their young on one side, and their offspring reproduce immediately, carrying their young on their backs, down to the size of dust-mites. Each disk-ant is really a colony of thousands of individuals.

Which side is up?
Disk-ants can roll on one edge or walk on either side. Or they can fling themselves through the air, retracting their legs to hard points that impact on prey.

eyes

reproductive canal

mouth

TOP?   SECTION?   BOTTOM?

Size *1mm to 1cm*	Reproduction *hermaphrodite, bears live young*	Diet *Omnivore*

A Field Guide to Henders Island

Page 27 of *A Field Guide to Henders Island* by Geoffrey Binswanger-Duckworth, Nell Duckworth-Binswanger, and Andrew Beasley, 1st edition.

Phylum	Subphylum	Class
Arthropoda	*Crustacea*	*Malacostraca*

Subclass	Order	Family
Hoplocarida	*Horridocarida*	*Rodentocarididae*

Henders Rat
Rodentocaris hendersi

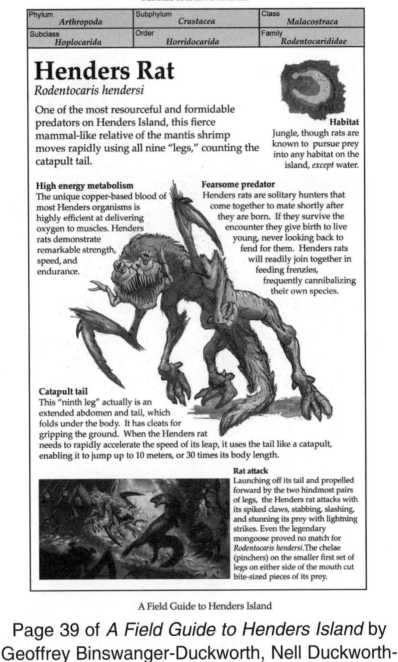

One of the most resourceful and formidable predators on Henders Island, this fierce mammal-like relative of the mantis shrimp moves rapidly using all nine "legs," counting the catapult tail.

Habitat
Jungle, though rats are known to pursue prey into any habitat on the island, *except* water.

High energy metabolism
The unique copper-based blood of most Henders organisms is highly efficient at delivering oxygen to muscles. Henders rats demonstrate remarkable strength, speed, and endurance.

Fearsome predator
Henders rats are solitary hunters that come together to mate shortly after they are born. If they survive the encounter they give birth to live young, never looking back to fend for them. Henders rats will readily join together in feeding frenzies, frequently cannibalizing their own species.

Catapult tail
This "ninth leg" actually is an extended abdomen and tail, which folds under the body. It has cleats for gripping the ground. When the Henders rat needs to rapidly accelerate the speed of its leap, it uses the tail like a catapult, enabling it to jump up to 10 meters, or 30 times its body length.

Rat attack
Launching off its tail and propelled forward by the two hindmost pairs of legs, the Henders rat attacks with its spiked claws, stabbing, slashing, and stunning its prey with lightning strikes. Even the legendary mongoose proved no match for *Rodentocaris hendersi*. The chelae (pinchers) on the smaller first set of legs on either side of the mouth cut bite-sized pieces of its prey.

A Field Guide to Henders Island

Page 39 of *A Field Guide to Henders Island* by Geoffrey Binswanger-Duckworth, Nell Duckworth-Binswanger, and Andrew Beasley, 1st edition.

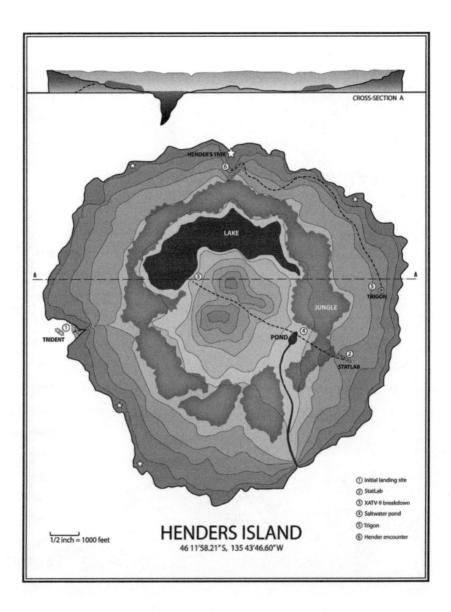

Map of Henders Island

Preliminary sketches of a spiger by Nell Duckworth
on board *Trident*, August 26 — "motion studies."

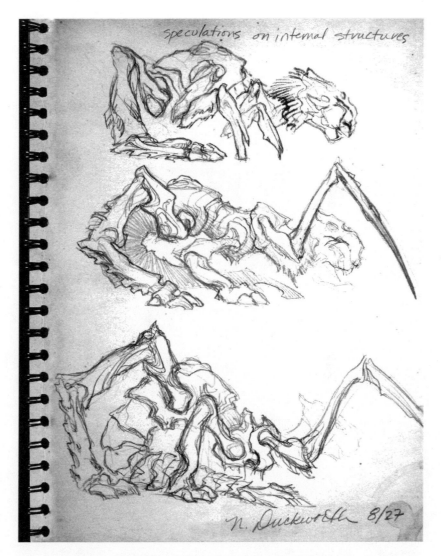

Preliminary sketches of a spiger by Nell Duckworth
on board *Trident*, August 27 —
"speculations on internal structures."

ACKNOWLEDGMENTS

Thanks to Dr. Donald Lovett, one of the foremost authorities on osmo-regulation in crustaceans, for his enthusiasm, patience, and courage, no matter how frightening the ride became.

Jennifer Limber, Mike Fahy, Daren Bader, Phil Steele, Kate Jones, and so many others were the autotrophs of the Henders ecosystem. And especially Michael Limber.

Stephen Jay Gould for his fantastic journey through evolution, *Wonderful Life*.

Dr. Michael E. Dawson of the Associates of Cape Cod lab for giving me the same tour Geoffrey took. Dr. Mark McMenamin, years ago, for letting me know that the fossil I found at the Marble Mountain in California was just a ball of algae and a trilobite leg that washed ashore on an ancient beach. Good enough for me—wow.

My beautiful editors, Kate Miciak and Sarah Hodgson, who felt it, too; Loren Noveck and Glen Edelstein, for helping to make this dream a reality; Peter McGuigan, Stephanie Abou, Hannah Gordon, and the rest at Foundry, the best.

Verne, Wells, Conan Doyle, Boulez—*and Crichton*. And a happy 200th to you, Charles Darwin.